WHERE THE RIVER MEETS THE SOUL

S. NICOLE

TO ALL THE BLACK GIRLS WHO DESERVE
LOVE AND DESIRE MAGIC

MAP

Scan the QR code to view the map of Vyelan!

TABLE OF CONTENTS

Map	v
Pronunciation Guide	ix
Heriath's Plant Journal	xii
Chapter 1	1
Chapter 2	13
Chapter 3	23
Chapter 4	29
Chapter 5	36
Chapter 6	43
Chapter 7	57
Chapter 8	63
Chapter 9	67
Chapter 10	80
Chapter 11	88
Chapter 12	95
Chapter 13	104
Chapter 14	120
Chapter 15	129
Chapter 16	142
Chapter 17	154
Chapter 18	164
Chapter 19	172
Chapter 20	182
Chapter 21	190
Chapter 22	201
Chapter 23	214

Chapter 24   222
Chapter 25   242
Chapter 26   247
Chapter 27   266
Chapter 28   277
Chapter 29   284
Chapter 30   293
Chapter 31   298
Chapter 32   311
Chapter 33   315
Chapter 34   324
Chapter 35   329
Chapter 36   335
Chapter 37   340
Chapter 38   350
Chapter 39   356
Chapter 40   366
Chapter 41   372
Chapter 42   379
Chapter 43   387
Chapter 44   393
Epilogue   399
Acknowledgments   405

PRONUNCIATION GUIDE

<u>*PLACES AND LANDMARKS:*</u>

Vyelan [VEE - eh - lih - n]

Nafsi [NAH - f - see]

Duskwick [D - uh - sk - wih - k]

Amberwich [AM - ber - wih - k]

Mysticane City [MIH - st - ih - cane]

Whitburn [wh - IH - t - burn]

Kaelora City [KAY - l - or - uh]

Vauxworth Canyon [VOX - were - th]

Elderheim [EL - d - er - hi - m]

Pine Valley [p - eye - n]

Lake Irridover [EAR - ih - doe - ver]

Trosthek Mountains [TRAH - st - eh - k]

FIRST NAMES:

Kofir [KOH - fee - r]

Elysi [eh - LEE - see]

Heriath [her - EYE - ih - th]

Merilla [m - uh - RIH - la]

Yamala [yuh - MAH - luh]

Evreux [EH - vh - row]

Zyl [ZIH - l]

Lindel [LIH - in - duh - l]

Tansae [TAN - say]

Aurora [uh - ROAR - uh]

Endel [en - DEH - l]

Xilleria [zih - LAIR - ee - uh]

Lytea [lih - TAY - uh]

Wynira [wih - NEE - ruh]

Loraine [lor - AY -n]

Fedarius [feh - DAIR - ee - us]

Cloveris [cloh - VEH - rih - s]

Nasir [n - ah - SEE - r]

Natiq [n - ah - TOK]

Tandall [TAN - dah - l]

Kelvin [KEHL - vih - n]

Mitchel [MIH - ch - uhl]

Orion [oh - REYE - uhn]

Ardin [AR - dih - n]

Ardale [AR - day - l]

LAST NAMES:

Valurae [vuh - LORE - ay]

Balastina [ba - LUH - stee - nuh]

Morelli [mor - EH - lee]

Devaris [deh - VAR - ihs]

HERIATH'S PLANT JOURNAL

A COMPREHENSIVE GUIDE TO VYELAN'S BEAUTIES AND DANGERS.

<u>HEALING PLANTS:</u>

Elysir

<u>Description</u>: A winter bloom with glowing blue petals. This flower was the work of the late mystic Kofir in an attempt to save his wife Elysi from the illness that resulted in her death.

<u>Attributes</u>: This plant is the main antibiotic in Vyelan with a strength above all others. It is the base of all medicines across Vyelan and can be combined with any healing herb to enhance its properties.

Severia Cane
[seh - VEH - ree - uh]

<u>Description</u>: A dark green leaf with a strong earthy taste and smell.

<u>Attributes</u>: This herb is commonly used as a tea base. Due to its strong taste, it can also cover the bitterness of most medicines. It can be combined with other herbs and gives a sense of vitality to the body. It is also a good aromatic for aroma therapy or a simmer pot.

Twilight Nox

Description: An orange and purple flower that blooms at night.

Attributes: This plant is a stimulant and can be used in emergency medications for severe allergy attacks. In moderation, it can be used for stomach issues and mild pain relief.

Gilliflower
[GIH - lih - fl - ow - ur]

Description: A wildflower with tall green stalks and tiny white blooms that grow in bunches at the end.

Attributes: It is often used as an aromatic or suppressant to calm the mind.

Darkened Lilac

Description: A tall green stalk with flowers that resemble lavender. The blooms are dark purple instead of light.

Attributes: A mild stimulant used to treat shock.

Water Hemlock

Description: A green leafy plant found growing out of or submerged in water.

Attributes: Contains protein and is used in food dishes as well as medicine.

Windroot

Description: The blanched roots of **Water Hemlock.** Their name comes from their unique spiraled shape.

Attributes: Strengthens the immune system.

Jester Mint

Description: Green leaves with a distinct and pleasant mint smell. They are named after their ability to grow in odd places. They can often be found growing from the trunks of trees, on high branches, underwater, and even on the stems of other flowers.

Attributes: A popular aromatic and tea flavor. It can also be used in dishes for a delicious garnish or palate cleanser. Also a good anti-inflammatory

Iverian Periculum
[eye - VEH - ree - ihn / peh - RIH - cue - luh - m]

Description: More commonly known as ***Dragonleaf***. This plant is very similar to Water Hemlock but can be differentiated by the red veins on the underside.

Attributes: Is often used in small amounts for heart health. Heavily regulated and can only be sold by a certified herbalist.

**Cinnamon*

Description: The brownish-red inner bark of a ***Cinnamon Tree.***

Attributes: This plant is a spice that is often used in food but also comes with a number of healing properties. It is an anti-inflammatory as well as good for the heart.

**Ginger*

Description: The root of a flowering plant. It gives off a strong and distinct scent.

Attributes: A spice often used in food that also helps with digestion and immunity.

Cofenia Seed
[co - FEH - nee - uh]

Description: A brown seed from the pod of a Cofenia Tree.

Attributes: A temporary mood and energy booster. Is often served roasted, in desserts, or ground into a drink.

Hervinia
[er - VEH - nee - uh]

Description: The sap from **Hervine Trees.**

Attributes: Often made into syrup, it is used in emergency situations to induce vomiting and settle the stomach in case of poison.

Forox Wintercress
[FOR - ox]

Description: More commonly known as ***Bloodroot***, this small black berry can easily be mistaken for common edible berries so it's identified by the shape of the leaves. It is a flowering plant whose flowers appear white with a pink center and purple tips.

Attributes: This plant is a dangerous neurotoxin that can kill within days or minutes depending on the concentration of berries one may come across. Most die via nervous system failure once they come in contact.

Treatment(s): Elysir (only to extend life expectancy)

Cure(s): None

Estrosse
[EH - strah - s]

Description: A yellow bloom with four points and green filament

Attributes: Used to dye clothing, but dangerous upon consumption.

Treatment(s): Hervinia and Windroot

Cure(s): Windroot and Water Hemlock

Sativa Divinorum
[suh - TEE - vuh / dih - vih - NOR - uhm]

<u>Description</u>: Also known as the ***Shrieking Void.*** An orange flower with dark blue spots in the center.

<u>Attributes</u>: A dangerous hallucinogenic that shoots purple spores when the stem is broken. The spores can cause visions of smoky black specters and force the victim to hear a loud shrieking for an extended amount of time. Effects can only be waited out. No physical damage occurs to the body, but most victims experience psychological damage.

<u>Treatment(s)</u>: Shock - such as pouring cold water over the patient. Distraction - drown out the noise if possible. Connection - have a loved one try to reach their mind over the effects of the spores.

<u>Cure(s)</u>: None

Violetta Thorn

<u>Description</u>: Thick vines with large red thorns.

<u>Attributes</u>: An invasive species that grows just as unpredictably as Jester Mint. It uproots other plants and steals nutrients and resources. The thorns cause a nasty rash where they come in contact with skin. If left untreated, the rash can easily become infected.

<u>Treatment(s)</u>: Balsam made with Jester Mint applied twice daily.

<u>Cure(s)</u>: Jester Mint

The Violet Meadow

Description: A three-headed, bell-shaped purple flower with yellow filament

Attributes: This plant grows in a new spot each sunrise and acted as a game for Kofir and Elysi.

Sugar Pine Trees

Description: A tall tree with green needles for leaves.

Attributes: The pinecones act as fertilizer and the sap is used for food dishes. These trees are also believed to house the souls of those who have passed on. They act as an anchor for loved ones to visit their deceased family members.

Starberries

Description: Small blue berries that grow at the crown of its bush near the Nafsi.

Attributes: This plant is bioluminescent. When crushed and mixed with river water, they glow a soft purple light.

*Rainbow Eucalyptus

Description: A tall thick tree that grows in Kaelora City. The bark of the tree has swatches of various colors.

Attributes: A gift from Kofir to Elysi on the day they were married. They make a good home for birds and bring beauty to the city.

*Moonflower

Description: A trumpet-shaped purple flower with tiny white dots on the surface of the petals

Attributes: They only open at the first touch of moonlight and are the main food source for Luna Moths. The white dots mimic the stars in the sky.

Crimson Shadebush

Description: A small red berry that grows in groups of three

Attributes: Often used for food garnish or for its red color in drinks

Solar Holly

Description: Small yellow flowers

Attributes: A common wildflower that grows in fields during the warmer months.

Gooseberry

Description: A small berry that comes in green, red, or purple

Attributes: They are delicious as a snack, juice, or in dessert. Their ripeness determines their flavor. Green ones tend to be more sour while red or purple is often sweet.

Oregano

Description: A green stalk with tiny leaves at the ends

Attributes: They are often used to flavor or garnish food dishes.

Oranges

Description: An spherical orange fruit that grows from a tree

Attributes: They can be eaten raw or cooked into a variety of dishes. Often consumed as a juice.

Priscilla Vine

Description: Thin green vines with heart-shaped leaves

Attributes: A common and rapidly growing house plant that's used for decoration. They are often found growing on the outside of buildings as well.

*Water Lily

Description: An aquatic flower that grows from the bottom of Lake Irridover.

Attributes: They protect fish from predatory birds and provide shade to keep the water cool. They also prevent algae growth and keep their environment clean by absorbing excess nutrients.

*Wheat

Description: A tall beige stalk grown in crops

Attributes: A crop used for bread as well as other kinds of food and drinks.

*Daisy

Description: A small white wildflower with a yellow center

Attributes: They are a good source of vitamin C, as well as indigestion relief, soothing coughs, and slowing bleeding.

CHAPTER I

The rains of Vyelan had run dry and the devastating drought laid
the Nafsi River a barren ditch. The waters brought life to the land for
centuries, its strength reflecting that of Vyelan's people. The elders
of the land, to ensure the health of their people, ventured out for a
solution. After years of searching, they came upon a mystic of nature by
the name of Kofir.

Kofir was a kind man and, though only in his twentieth year, offered
to help the elders of Vyelan. He traveled with them to the Trosthek
Mountains and conjured an infinite snowstorm atop them, the melting
snow creating a steady source of water for the river. Overjoyed, they
offered the nomadic mystic a place in their land and Kofir agreed,
enchanted by the bountiful greenery the land possessed.

Each year, the land grew stronger and so did Kofir. He traveled
from one end of the Nafsi to the other, spreading his knowledge and
blessing the plants and herbs with unique and wondrous magic.
The people loved him dearly as his knowledge brought them new
understanding of the nature around them.

In his thirtieth year, he came upon a woman collecting water and
began a conversation with her as he would with anyone else. Though he

had come to be revered by the people, he was merely a man. While most had forgotten, she hadn't. She treated him with kindness as if he was no more than a passerby on the street. The sun shone brighter that day and something about the way she spoke enraptured him. He found himself returning to the river bank in hopes of finding her again. Days later, she returned and again they spoke. The peace he felt in her company was nothing like he'd ever experienced before.

When he departed from her village, they continued to speak through letters she would send to the villages he would stop in during his journey. Each letter would bring him unspeakable joy, the sound of her name a melody on his lips: Elysi.

After a year, he finally returned to her village and found her at the bank of the Nafsi once more. This time, however, he could not bear to leave. Their love was unbreakable. They were soon wed and settled in a valley to live out the rest of their days. They lived twelve long and happy years together until one day, she suddenly fell ill from *Bloodroot*. A vicious berry disguised under innocent blooms. Kofir spent the day caring for his wife and the night creating a plant with strong enough healing properties to save her. After endless toil, he had finally done it. He grew the flower in the dead of winter and revealed his work to Elysi, but it was too late. The bloodroot had found its way to her heart and the flower he'd created could only slow its effects. He was grateful that the bloom allowed him a few more weeks with his beloved before she passed.

Kofir was heartbroken. A month flew by, but his heart could not be healed. He spent that time traveling the land and eradicating bloodroot from Vyelan's soil so no one would ever suffer the same fate as Elysi. Though he loved the people, each day without her was torture. Suffering he could not bear for a lifetime. With nothing left, he returned home.

He took the seeds from his creation and planted them atop her grave, affectionately naming them *Elysir*. After paying his respects, he traveled to the head of the river in the Trosthek Mountains.

In that cave, under the light of the moon, he stepped into the waters and spoke a vow:

"Surely as our love is unending, so shall this river be. May the souls united here be reborn and reunite. My eyes shall be opened by a mark in the valley where life begins and ends."

With that, he summoned all the power he could muster and bound both his and Elysi's souls to the Nafsi. The tears from his eyes formed a magical gem known as the Water Stone, connecting their souls to the river and providing strength to the land. With his life force physically bound, he went on to join his lover in the afterlife.

The flower bloomed each year and the seeds spread across the land, growing along the bank of the Nafsi from one end to the other. It is said that to this day their souls continue to reincarnate and find each other, providing magic to the land.

Their love a steady and ever-flowing stream.

I shut the book with a blissful sigh as I stare up at the ceiling of my home. Years and years of being read this tale and it never gets old. My head rolls to the side and I catch a glimpse of the clock on the bedroom wall. *Just in time.*

I hop out of bed and change into my work attire before bouncing over to the bathroom. I tie my shoulder-length locs up into two messy ponytails and pick at the ends until they shoot out like a firework. The white seashells woven into them complement my large white birthmark. Its irregular borders mimic any natural land mass and act as a unique feature I've come to love. The lack of color starts at the center of my hairline and slopes down the side of my nose, wrapping around to the back left side of my jaw. I trace over it gently, a grin tugging at my lips. Blowing myself a kiss in the mirror, I exit the house and follow the beaten path.

The sun is rising over Duskwick village and the streets are busy as usual. The sounds and smells bring me joy as I walk to the Herbal Clinic. People move between vine and moss-covered buildings to take care of business. Those running stalls on the main road shout today's prices and the freshness of the produce for sale. I wave hello to many of the stall owners as I pass by, receiving smiles in return.

Arriving at the clinic, I find Miss Merilla, the head herbalist, already taking inventory. Her gray hair sits in a bun atop her head, the bells on her sleeve jingling as she adjusts her glasses.

"Good Morning, Miss Merilla."

"Good Morning, Heriath. You're right on time. I assume that's what I asked for?" she asks, pointing to the basket on my arm.

"You can add these to your count," I nod, setting my basket on the counter. "This is everything from the list you gave me. I even waited until this morning to pick the windroot so the healing properties would be at their peak for use."

"Very good, Heriath. You've always been a fast learner. I'll take these down," she says as she observes the basket's contents. "You can help me take count of the herbs on the bottom shelf before we get busy."

I nod, "Sure."

I survey the containers on the shelves. Each one holds an herb or an herbal mixture that makes it faster to make simple medicines. I jot down how many we have of each one and finish in a few minutes. Checking over my work, I frown at the results. "Hey, Miss Merilla? When does our next shipment from Mysticane City come in?"

"In a few days. Why?"

I bring her the clipboard to point out the issue, "We are low on gilliflower. I need it to make the next batch of medicine for at least three patients today."

"Oh my, that is a problem, isn't it? Do you think you'll have enough to fill those three orders?"

"Maybe. I can try," I say, unsure. "I hate that we have to rely on shipments."

Miss Merilla places a hand on my shoulder as I stare down at the clipboard, "I know dear, but the land can only keep up with demands for so long." I sigh in frustration. The way things are going, we'll soon be forced to choose who to give medicine to.

"Can't I use some of the-"

"No, Heriath," she says sternly.

"Just a little, Miss Merilla?"

"You know we can't use it unless it's an emergency."

"That flower, even a tiny bit, can help people. It can *cure* people."

"And that is why we save it. We are lucky to have any at all, you know that."

I take in a deep breath as I set down the clipboard. She's right. Even with the shipments, less and less has been coming in, which means even the big cities are running low.

"I'm sorry," I apologize. "I didn't mean to fight you on it."

She gives me a warm smile, "It's alright. I know it's hard, but our job is to do our best with what we've got." I nod and return her smile as the bell over the front door chimes.

"Well, let's get to work."

"That should do it, hun," I say as I finish.

The little boy smiles brightly as I grab a berry lollipop from a cup by the examination table. He reaches eagerly for it with his freshly wrapped arm.

"Thank you again, Heriath. I seem to come home to a new bruise every day," his father chuckles, ushering the boy off the table. He pats his son's head as the boy licks away at the lollipop.

"No problem. I used to be the same way." I grab a small bag and place some balsam and extra gauze inside, "Put this on his arm and re-wrap it for the next two nights. There's some extra in there for the next time you come home to a scrape." He takes it with a smile and hands me his payment. I lead them to the door, wishing them a good day as they leave the clinic.

"That's the third time this month," Miss Merilla says, grabbing the materials I used to take to the storage room. "That boy is very lively."

I grab a cloth to clean the exam table, "True, but he's always well-behaved when I wrap him up."

"Between you and me, I think he visits so often just for those lollipops," she laughs. Her voice is dampened by the wall between us as she moves into the next room. I toss the dirty cloth into a bucket with a few others, making a mental note to wash them later. The bell over the door chimes and I look up to see a couple in the doorway.

The woman smiles at me as she enters, "Hey there, pipsquirt." I roll my eyes with a grin. Quite the ironic nickname for someone who's five inches taller than her. Despite our height difference, we look about the same. Brown eyes, mine a shade or two darker than hers. Dark skin and black hair. Mom said if we weren't born four years apart we could be twins.

"What are you doing here?" I ask, stepping around the exam table to hug her. Her arms wrap around me tight. She's the definition of small but mighty. I place my hand on the top of her head, feeling the short thick hair underneath my fingers. "You did another big chop?"

"Yeah," she says, letting go. I draw air into my lungs dramatically and she rolls her eyes with a laugh.

"Evreux, your wife is trying to kill me," I groan, looking up at the man beside her.

"Oh please, I didn't hug you that hard," Yamala says.

"You do have an iron grip, my love," he smiles. He places a gentle kiss on her temple that brings a goofy grin to her lips. They've been married for three years and still behave like lovesick puppies. She always claimed that fate brought them together. I'm not one to believe in fate taking charge, but sometimes things do happen in a way that can't be explained otherwise. Fate or not, his soft gaze is proof that his love for her is undeniable.

"You know you don't have to come here for your medication anymore. I can bring it over," I remind her. She gives me a pointed look and I raise my hands in defense.

"Well, hello Yamala," Miss Merilla greets as she enters the room. "Punctual as always."

I step back and look between them, "So you *aren't* here to see me?"

"Sorry, baby sis," she pouts. Evreux helps her take a seat on the exam table as the wall clock chimes. Well, chime is putting it nicely. That thing is about 50 years old and every time it goes off I swear I can hear it cough.

"Well, it's my lunchtime," I state, looking over to Miss Merilla.

The bells on her sleeves jingle as she waves her hand, "Go on, dear."

"Will I get an update this time at least?"

"That's up to your sister," she replies. I look to Yamala before giving her a slight nod. With that, I grab my lunch bag from a cabinet under the counter before leaving out the front door. A familiar anxiousness wells up in my stomach as I approach the town square.

Even though her medication is working, her state is getting worse. I settle on the ledge of the fountain that sits in the center of the town square, listening to the music that pours out of every window. The melody takes my mind away from the conversation going on in the clinic right now. A couple laughs together as they dance on the front porch, spinning each other around. Their hands clasp together, sunshine glinting off their golden wedding bands. I feel a smile creep onto my face. Their happiness is palpable. Something in my heart longs for that kind of feeling.

I'm nearly done with my lunch when I see Miss Merilla exit the clinic and wave in my direction. I stuff the last bite of my sandwich in my mouth and hastily make my way over. I swallow as I approach the doorway. *Something's wrong.*

A dark shadow hangs over the sunlit room. Yamala is still on the exam table, Evreux standing beside her. His arms are wrapped around her shoulders while her face is buried in his chest. I send a questioning glance to Miss Merilla as she steps inside and shuts the door.

"Heriath, we have a bit of news for you," she says, placing a hand on my shoulder. She looks over to Evreux who gives her a nod. His hair flows over his orange shirt as he opens his mouth and shuts it again. My concern grows at the silence and I'm practically begging him to speak.

"There's no easy way to say this, but she's gotten worse," he says softly.

My brows knit together, "Worse how? I thought it was a simple bug?"

"It *was* a little bug at first, but once she recovered, it left her immune system very weak," he explains. "A bit of what she had, or maybe something new, evolved and took advantage of her weak immune to grow."

"It's attacking her muscles," Miss Merilla cuts in with a somber look to Yamala. "And it will most likely reach her heart." I glance between the two of them, Yamala's face still buried in her husband's chest.

"Isn't there something that can slow it?" I ask, wracking my brain for solutions.

"Her immune system took too long to recover and the muscle decay is already too far ahead," Evreux adds.

"Something can always be done," I state.

"Heriath-"

"Water hemlock is great for muscle growth with all its proteins. Or maybe windroot for immune boosting if that's what she needs," I suggest somewhat frantically.

Evreux sighs dejectedly, "We've been coming to Miss Merilla for help and regular check-ins. We accepted a while ago that all we can do is slow its effects."

"No, that can't be it. You can't give up yet," I plead, turning to Miss Merilla. "What about the Elysir we have left?"

"Again, my dear, it's only for emergencies."

"*This* doesn't count as an emergency?" I shout.

"It would take a series of doses to get ahead of the decay. We simply don't have enough," she explains. I understand that as an herbalist, but as a sister my selfishness takes over.

"So that's it? You call me in here to tell me that my sister is dying and there's nothing I can do about it?"

"Heriath," Yamala finally speaks. She lifts her head from Evreux's chest and faces me with somber eyes. "I know you want to help, but even your abilities are limited. I just wanted you to know."

I stare at her for a moment, "How long have you known?"

Her eyes fall to her lap, "A month." I nod and bite the inside of my cheek.

I look over to Miss Merilla, "And you knew too?" She doesn't meet my eyes and I nod again. I get patient confidentiality and all, but that doesn't stop the claws of betrayal from sinking into my chest.

"Please don't be upset with her. I told her not to tell you," Yamala says softly as she stands from the exam table. I stare at the ground as she makes her way towards me. She reaches out to me, but I dodge her hand. Her hand withdraws and she stands frozen for a few seconds before it drops to her side.

"I'm sorry," she murmurs.

I sigh, "It's not your fault. I just...I need some time."

"Okay," she mumbles.

The bell over the door chimes and an elderly man enters, freezing with the door half-open. I'm sure the atmosphere is pretty heavy. "Oh, are you busy?" he asks.

I swallow the lump in my throat and put on a small smile, "No, I can take you in the back room. I'll be there in a moment."

"We'll get going," Evreux says. He approaches Yamala from behind, placing a hand on the small of her back. A small smile on his face acts as a poor attempt to shield the sorrow in his eyes, the look a love of its own. I nod as he leads her to the door.

"Heriath?" she calls. I turn to face her with raised eyebrows. "Could you come over for dinner tonight?" I look away when her gaze forces a lump in my throat again.

"I don't think I'll be hungry," I reply.

"Please?" Even without seeing it, I know she's pulling her classic pout. The one that can get anything from Dad to this day. "Breakfast tomorrow then? I'll make my blueberry pancakes." I guess she knows how to get me too. I hesitantly agree and she thanks me as she leaves the clinic. Taking a deep breath, I force a smile and make my way to the back room.

After I check over the old man, I stand and put my medical tools down on the table, "Everything looks good, sir. You're in perfect health." He steps down from the table with a smile.

"Sixty-seven years old and still livin' large," he says happily, pumping a fist in the air. I can't help but laugh. Despite what I can't do, this is what makes my job worth it. He pays and I wave goodbye as the door closes behind him.

Bringing the supplies to the storage room, I see Miss Merilla sitting with a jar in her hands. Her head hangs, causing her glasses to slide to the tip of her nose. I set my things down and draw closer, kneeling in front of her chair. I push her glasses up and tilt my head to meet her eyes, "Miss Merilla, what's wrong?" She holds up the jar so I can see its contents. Five dried blue flower petals sit at the bottom of the jar.

"This is all that's left. In our last shipment we didn't receive a single petal," she says softly. "Five years without it blooming and we've finally run dry."

I rarely see Miss Merilla anything other than happy. Losing our most valuable resource is frustrating, especially after spending so many years with it. I've only been working here for five years, so the lack of Elysir was a given when I started. Miss Merilla has been here for over

30 years. She's seen miracle recoveries, small injuries, large injuries, and even people die on her watch. Something I hope to never encounter. We've been able to balance our knowledge, but nothing can replace what we've lost. I carefully remove the jar from her hands and place it back on the shelf. "I'm really sorry about your sister. I tried to help as best I could."

"I know," I respond, my voice stale.

"I would have told you, you know that."

"I know," I repeat, meeting her gaze. I give her a reassuring grin or, at least, the best one I can muster. "Let's focus on getting through the rest of today, huh?"

She gives me a crooked smile and nods. I pick up my clipboard and move to the front room.

What a wonderful morning.

CHAPTER 2

I lay at the bank of the Nafsi River, wind rustling the orange and brown leaves above. The smell of the earth and the feeling of the tall grass between my fingers relax me. The sunlight on my skin brings me warmth and soothes my mind after an awful night's sleep.

I reach into the pocket of my skirt and grab the small watch from inside. I click it open and sigh at the time. Need to cut my sunbathing short if I'm going to make it to Yamala's before work. I grip the handle of the wicker basket beside me, lifting it as I stand. I follow the desire path I've created from a year of coming to this same spot and pass through the small garden behind my home. It started out as a few of my favorite flowers, but since the land in Duskwick is starting to run low on general plants we use at the clinic, I started planting those too. Basics, such as severia cane, are easy to grow. Plus, I'll never complain about the butterfly friends I've made along the way.

I push through the gate and slip into my house through the back door. The inside has about as much greenery as the outside. I've mounted a few strings of ivy to the walls that grow up and across my ceiling. Fresh flowers from my garden sit on the island in the center of my kitchen. I set the basket down and quickly arrange the herbs I've collected into bundles before grabbing my satchel to leave.

Once I reach Yamala's house I knock on the door and step back, shifting my weight from side to side in a steady bounce. I hear the lock click and it swings open to reveal Evreux in an apron. His mouth spreads into a grin, "You made it." I nod as he reaches to hug me. I accept his embrace with a smile of my own, his body heat contrasting the coolness of his turquoise necklace. "Come on in," he says.

Embroidery hoops hang on the walls with cheesy sayings on them such as *'Life sucks, Eat cake'* and *'Today's Menu: Eat it or Starve'*. Yamala has always enjoyed silly things like that. The home combines both their personalities wonderfully. The two are like earth and sky and it is reflected in their home. Yamala is lucky she married someone who has an artistic touch. The earthy tones Evreux picked out complement the star charts that hang around. Of course, he isn't the biggest fan of the silly embroidered quotes when it comes to aesthetics, but he loves that they were made by his wife and likes to be supportive.

Evreux's dark hair swings behind him, brushing the back of his thighs as he leads me down a hallway decorated with their wedding pictures. We reach their bedroom and he slips inside for a moment before the door pulls open. I lean around his frame to see my sister laying on the bed, a book in hand.

"Hey big sis," I wave. "Good Morning."

"Morning," she waves back. She pushes off the bed and Evreux places a hand on her shoulder with a look of concern. She brushes it off with a smile, "I'll be fine, honey."

Reaching beside the bed, he pulls out a cane and hands it to her. I eye the cane with concern but leave it alone as she leads me out of the bedroom.

"Did you finish the batter?" she asks Evreux.

"Yes ma'am. Though it's missing whatever secret ingredient you refuse to tell me," he responds with narrowed eyes.

"I told you already. The secret ingredient is love."

"Well, I put a lot of love into that burnt toast the other morning and you still spit it out," he says pointedly. I stifle a giggle as we reach the kitchen and she leans her cane against the ice chest.

"I promise I'll tell you one day," she muses. She gives him a quick peck on the lips and he groans as she shoos us to the living room. We idly chat while she works her magic. My stomach growls in anticipation at the wonderful smell that wafts by.

"Order up!" she calls. Evreux hops up to help her with the plates, returning with heaven in his hands.

"Finally," I grin as he sets the plates on the large coffee table.

"Can't rush perfection," she says, bopping me on the head. I laugh softly as I shove a forkful into my mouth. *Perfection indeed.*

The conversation grows as we eat. It feels like forever since I've gotten to talk to her. With work piling up and how distant she's been, it's as if I haven't seen her in a month outside of me delivering her medicine. I missed her expressiveness, the way she moves her hands as she talks as if to paint a picture. She goes on and on about how she was recently put in charge of the charting team. She loves her job as a celestial cartographer. She even makes each new chart twice so she can bring one home to hang up.

After a while, all the plates are empty. Her voice is cheerful, but her hands have now settled in her lap. Evreux takes our plates to the kitchen and shortly returns with a glass in hand.

He extends it to her, "Here, my love." I grin as I read *'It's my turn to wine'* on its side. She takes a sip before a spark of realization lights in her eyes.

"Oh, we finished setting up my new study," she says.

"Can I see it?" I ask.

"Sure!" She places the glass on the table and hops up, only to wobble and grip the wooden surface. Evreux rushes to her side to brace her. "I'm fine," she says softly. My cheery mood is dampened by reality as he guides her to sit again, returning to the kitchen to grab her cane.

"Sweetheart, you have to take it slow," he reminds her as he returns. He rubs her back and lifts the glass from the table again, "Here. Finish your medicine first." She stares at the glass before hesitantly taking it.

I tap the coffee table, "I should get going, actually." I feel her gaze on me as I stand from my seat.

"So soon?" she asks.

"I need to get to work. Thank you for breakfast."

"Heriath," she calls and I turn to face her. "I know I invited you for breakfast, but I also had a request." I nod for her to continue. "Would you mind not telling Mom and Dad about my condition?"

"You haven't told them?" I ask in disbelief.

"No."

My brows furrow. "But why? And why didn't you tell *me*?" I ask, finally releasing the question I've been holding since yesterday. "You expect me to hide the fact that my sister is dying?" A lump forms in my throat. "That's not fair, Yamala. How long do you plan on hiding this? Was I not supposed to know until your funeral?" My voice quivers despite my attempt to remain calm.

"They'll know in time. I know it's not the best option, but I need them to hear it from me," she explains. Her voice is calm, but the eyes never lie. She's scared. My brave older sister is scared. The same girl that used to climb tall trees with ease, hunt for trolls in the forest, and catch lizards for fun. The one who moved all the way to Kaelora City alone to follow her dreams. My eyes soften as I realize death is creeping up on her, approaching while she watches. She's staring it in the face and being forced to wait until it's at her doorstep.

"I'm sorry," I whisper. The base of her cane taps against the ground as she stands. Her arms wrap around me and I hear the cane clatter against the floor, the weight shifting from it to my waist as she holds me.

"You're my little sister. I love you, and I just wanted to protect you," she says, her voice shaking slightly. The concept isn't unfamiliar. I've seen child patients where I had to tell them one thing and their parents another. During a visit, no matter the age, the goal is to ensure physical and mental well-being. If the patient is panicking, they can't be effectively treated. I don't hold it against her for wanting to protect us. She's always been headstrong. Even when sick at home, she hated being treated like a piece of glass, and I'm sure she's trying to avoid a similar situation. For once, I put aside the herbalist in me. My arms encircle her shoulders to pull her close and my chin rests atop her head. Right now, she needs a sister.

"I know. I'll always be here for you, and I'll try my best not to worry," I say. She pulls back enough to look up at me. "And, at your request, I won't tell Mom and Dad. Medical confidentiality and all that, even if you're not *my* patient."

She smiles, "Thank you. I know it seems like we are ignoring the issue, but we aren't giving up. There are just some things you can't change," she says. She steps back and into Evreux's arms, "I can promise you that, despite the circumstances, I'm perfectly happy."

I nod and hold out two fingers, a tear trailing down my cheek. She grins and does the same, touching her fingertips to mine. Our middle fingers shift downward while our pointers curl together until our fingers form a heart shape between us. She'd thought the action silly years ago when I excitedly asked her to try it, but it soon became a silent way of showing our love when emotions flared and the words were too hard to say.

No matter what the future may hold, she's here with me now and despite what she may think I can still do something about it.

"I need to go to Mysticane City," I blurt. Miss Merilla pauses, a small crate in her hands. Mostly likely full of contents from our latest delivery.

"Good morning to you too, dear," she with a pointed look.

"Oh, yes. Good morning," I laugh awkwardly. I may be determined, but not enough to get under the skin of a sixty-two-year-old woman. Her stern expression relaxes and she nods.

"Now what's this blather about going to Mysticane?" she asks, moving to the back room.

"I want to see if Iron Brimstone has any Elysir reserves," I state as I follow behind her. She sets down the crate with a huff.

"Heriath-"

"I know, I know, but I refuse to believe that it's all gone."

She slides the crate in my direction and I reach in to unpack it, pulling out rolls of gauze.

"I admire your ambition, but what exactly do you plan to do, my dear?" she asks. "That company is as stubborn as clinging priscilla vine. If they don't care about the river itself, what makes you think they'll bend the rules for us?"

I bend down to place the gauze in a lower cabinet, "I don't know, but I can't sit around doing nothing." I stand and turn to face her, "I'd rather do something and fail than have not tried at all." She observes me for a moment before relenting with a soft smile.

"I'm not going to stop you, am I?"

"No ma'am," I grin.

"Alright. You can take the spare steam wagon we have in the back and leave tomorrow."

"Thank you," I say, stepping forward to give her a hug. She gives me a squeeze before pulling back, her hands on my shoulders.

"It's good to be hopeful, but I want you to keep reality in mind. If you don't find what you're looking for, I need you to be there for your sister."

I nod firmly as the bell over the front door chimes. The day moves at a snail's pace. Patient after patient, the same tools and welcoming smiles. Luckily, we had no emergencies. The time I did get in between patients, I spent checking the steam wagon to make sure it was ready to make the trip. The confidence I had when I first arrived slowly fizzles throughout the day, replaced by a building anxiousness. By the time we close up shop, I've checked the wagon a hundred times and have gone over a mental checklist twice that.

I bid Miss Merilla a good night and walk down the path to my parent's house. Sure, I'm twenty-one years old with my own place, but I'll always take advantage of having my family right down the road.

"You have everything you need for a trip?" Dad asks as he stabs the last of his food with his fork. I nod in response as I push the food around on my plate, struggling to find my appetite.

"Then why do you hesitate?" Mom asks.

"Farthest I've been is Amberwich Village and even then we all went together. The whole idea of going so far from home makes me anxious," I admit. As much as it would be nice to travel, to see the land Miss Merilla speaks so highly of, I don't know if I'm ready. My dad pushes his chair back, standing to clean the table. He reaches for my plate but pauses as he notices most of my dinner remains. His hand moves to sit on my head, something he often does to comfort me when he's not sure what to say. I smile at the weight of his hand before he removes it to take my plate.

"Maybe I just need to sleep on it," I sigh, pushing back my chair.

"Why don't you stay here for the night?" Mom suggests. "You could sleep in your old room?" I agree and her smile almost brightens my mood. *Almost.* "Great, I'll get what you need."

Hours pass as every possibility of what could happen runs through my mind. I groan as I crumple another sheet of parchment and toss it into the waste bin next to the small desk. I pull out a blank sheet and begin again. I'm unsure how long I've been attempting to scribble a decent list of travel items and destinations, but the growing pile of parchment in the waste bin is a testament to my frustration.

I stand and grab the map of Mysticane City beside me. My feet thud against the floor as I walk in a figure-eight pattern, the movement helping me think. My fingers pull at the soft fabric of my nightgown when a knock sounds at my bedroom door.

The door cracks open to reveal my mom, an oil lantern hanging from her forearm. The light accents her yellow nightgown and matching bonnet. "Hey, honey. You alright?" she asks. "Sounds like you're going to wear a groove in the floor."

"Sorry," I mumble. She steps inside and closes the door. She places the lantern on my bedside table and takes a seat, patting the empty space beside her. I sigh and move onto the bed.

"Still worrying about your trip?" she asks. I nod, laying my head on her shoulder.

"So many things could go wrong. What if-"

"Ah ah ah, don't. You know that once you start your what-ifs, it only makes things worse," she interrupts.

I sigh, "Sorry, you're right." She wraps her arm around me, pulling my head to her chest. Her warmth and heartbeat soothe my nerves.

"You know, I remember when you were younger. Your father would take you into the woods when he went to chop down trees. You would always return with scrapes and bruises and he would stutter about how he was watching you the whole time," she laughs.

I couldn't help but laugh as well, "I did run off a lot."

"You always loved finding new things and making your own little adventures in the forest. No matter what injury you came home with, you always got up and went back out there. Nothing could stop you." Her voice is gentle as she recounts the past. I remember always having fun in the forest. I would hop on tall rocks, pick flowers, and play in the river without a care in the world. I'd bring Dad shiny stones and he would always pocket them with a smile before going back to work. I do miss it.

"I was lucky to have someone there to bandage me up," I said, nudging her.

"That's right, but now you can bandage yourself," she says, her smile evident in her voice.

I sit up to look her in the eye. "Mom, what do you think about all this?" Her hand takes mine, gently lifting it into her lap.

"It doesn't matter what I think; it's what you want that matters."

"That's what I was afraid you'd say," I huff. "I just don't know if *I'm* the right person to do it."

"Well, if your fear is stronger than your desire to make a difference, then maybe you aren't the right person. I believe in you, but whether you believe in yourself or not is a choice *you* have to make."

I hum softly. "Fear only has as much power as you give it, right?" I recite the words she'd repeated to me countless times in my youth.

"That's right," she says, kissing my forehead. "I know you'll find what you're looking for, but for now I think you should rest."

"Thanks, Mom," I say as she stands from the bed. She grabs her lantern and heads for the door. "Hey, mom?"

"Yes?" she asks, turning back to face me.

"I love you."

She chuckles lightly as she closes the door, "I love you more."

CHAPTER 3

I lift my hand from the steering wheel to scratch at my palm for the hundredth time. I have been driving for eight hours now, and the vibration of the wheel is irritating my skin. My dad gave me a quick rundown on the ins and outs of the wagon's functions, including that this might happen so I packed a soothing balm. I yelp in surprise as I hit a bump. My hands fly to the wheel, trying to steady myself on the, now, cobblestone pathway. I push the engine lever forward, slowing it down.

A pathway splits a row of large buildings. I pass under a large iron archway that reads *'Mysticane City'*. The buildings are a combination of houses, stores, stalls, and inns. Steam wagons roll down the path while dozens of people walk around and dodge between them. The setting sun illuminates the large building in the center of the city. The middle tower has an enormous clock that acts as an eye over the bustling crowd. I'm in awe of the sheer size of everything. So much so, that I nearly run a woman over. I swerve, apologizing profusely as she shouts at me. Duskwick Village is nothing compared to this.

Soon, I come to a stop in front of the three towers. The two on the side match in height while the middle tower trumps them both. Next to me are rustic double doors made of wood, with metal bolts adorning the frame in a pattern to resemble a mine entrance. The letters carved above the door read *'Iron Brimstone Mining Company'.*

I park on a side street and grab my satchel before locking the wagon to secure my items inside. Citizens and workers flow in and out of the building through entrances, one on each side of the large double doors in the center. I take a deep breath and a step forward.

Here goes nothing.

"I just want to speak to one of the herbalists," I repeat to the scowling man behind the counter. One of the miners pointed me in the right direction once I entered. I have only managed to receive the expected response of 'there isn't any Elysir left'. Sadly, my follow-up questions haven't gotten me anywhere.

"I already told you, medical assistance here is reserved for employees. Any other matters will require an appointment with one of the executives," he deadpans, not sparing me a glance. He could at least look at me instead of scribbling on his clipboard.

"It would only take a minute. It's a very pressing matter and-"

"Look miss," he groans, finally meeting my gaze with an arched eyebrow. "You think I don't have other *pressing* matters to deal with?"

"I understand that, but-"

"If you understand then you'll come back with a scheduled appointment. Now are you going to leave or will I have to call a guard?" I square my shoulders with a huff and turn to leave the building.

My grip on my bag tightens as I walk down the main pathway I rode in on. Swarms of people quickly travel to their destinations. I find myself apologizing repeatedly as I bump into people, trying to find something familiar. Most don't respond or shoot me a glare until I run face-first into the chest of a tall man.

"Hey, watch it," he growls.

"I'm sorry," I murmur. He pushes past me, grumbling about tourists. I'm so out of my comfort zone I'm unsure if the feet I'm walking with are my own. I can navigate a forest day or night, but a city? I'd have better luck growing a water lily out of a rock.

I reach into my satchel, pulling out a short list that consists of a few clinics and an extra address Miss Merilla gave me. Logically, I assumed my trip to Iron Brimstone wouldn't result in much so I planned a few other places to hopefully gather some more information. However, my focus is severely blurred by the intensity of my new environment.

The clamor of steam engines, conversations, and entrance bells that hang in front of shops is something I'm certainly not used to. The smell of food and factories combine with the sound to form an overwhelming experience. My heartbeat thrums in my ears. I take in a deep breath to steady my nerves, but instead, I feel my chest tighten.

I shove the list back into my bag as my breathing quickens and I realize I've stopped walking. *Maybe I should go back?* The noise turns into a steady high-pitched ringing. My gaze is fixed on the ground, my heart beating harder with every person that bumps past me. I force myself forward with one heavy step at a time. I take random turns as my steps grow faster, trying to find any place to escape the noise. My eyes begin to well up with tears when I notice a safe haven. A gold and bronze revolving door stands in front of me with the word *'Library'* engraved at the top.

I push my way inside, feeling the cool air brush against my cheeks.

Quickly walking deeper into the building, I lean against a bookshelf in a far corner and slide to the floor. *I'm alone.* I bury my head in my arms as I hold my knees to my chest. *So many people and yet, I'm alone.* My body shakes. Why did I do this? I have no idea what I'm doing here. I lift my head slightly, tears blurring my vision. The ringing has stopped and I can hear myself sobbing. My fingers dig slightly into my arm, a slight sting cutting through my numbness.

I hate this.

I hate this.

I hate this.

"Excuse me?"

I jump as I feel a hand on my shoulder. My head swivels to see a blurry figure standing above me. I wipe my eyes and a strangely familiar face comes into view. Two beaded braids frame his gentle features while the rest of his curls are up in a frohawk. Dark freckles dot his light brown skin. He retracts his hand, a clacking sound coming from his many bracelets.

"Are you okay?" he asks. My throat locks up and I look back down at my lap. He kneels next to me, "Can you not speak?" I look back at him, noticing concern eminent in his expression. "It's okay, if not," he says softly. "But, would you at least like to get off the floor? My office is a lot quieter than this."

I notice the historian's badge that hangs around his neck. *So he works here.* My mind is too fuzzy to properly weigh my options, but quiet is something I desperately need right now.

After a moment, I hesitantly nod. "Wonderful, let's go," he says, standing to extend a hand toward me. I try to reach, but my muscles seem to be frozen in place. Frustration builds in my chest. I feel a sting in my eyes and bury my face in my arms again. A minute passes and I hear his clothes rustle as he settles next to me. "I can stay here until you are ready. Is that alright?"

I awoke this morning with an open mind and a pocket full of optimism. I wanted to see and experience new things, and here I am, paralyzed for that exact reason. Now I have a stranger watching me struggle. We don't even know each other. I mean, would I have to pay him? Did he follow me here? I take a deep breath, my sobs growing quieter. He wants to help me. I don't know why he's insistent on helping, but it would be nice to not be alone. I look up at him and nod, accepting his offer.

I use the next few minutes to breathe, letting each deep breath slowly unwind my tight muscles. I stretch my fingers, then my arms as I lift my head from my lap. Wiping my face, I slowly push my legs out to straighten them. *Finally.* My body still feels a bit heavy but I can at least move around. I slowly begin to stand and use the bookshelf to steady myself. The man was sitting with his legs folded and eyes closed. His hands rest in his lap. Is he meditating? I hesitantly tap on his shoulder and his eyes pop open.

"Ready?" he asks. I nod and follow behind him as he leads me through the lobby, which I now notice is built to resemble a tree. Large roots run up the walls and gather at the center point of the ceiling. Multicolor stained glass shards hang from thread to form a beautiful light show on the upper walls. Each floor has railings with branches wrapped around the banister. It's absolutely amazing. The warm glow of the bronze lamps provide a welcoming environment and enough light to read and study at the tables. The man turns down a corridor that leads to a series of rooms. Each door has a gold plate above its frame with a number on it.

"These are studies and classrooms," he said, noticing my intrigue. "My office is down this way." I follow him through two more hallways before reaching a door with a nameplate on the wall beside the frame.

'Zyl Devaris'

Devaris. That name. Why do I know that name?

The office is typical. A desk littered with papers and some bookshelves with a few trinkets here and there. "Make yourself at home," he says, gesturing to a chair in the corner. I take a seat as he walks to a bookshelf in the corner. "Would you like some tea?" I nod and he smiles. He presses a button next to the bookshelf and swings it around to reveal a rack with jars of herbs. He mumbles to himself as he looks over them before pulling one down. "I'll be right back."

He rushes out the door and I go back to focusing on my breathing. I feel better now that there is less noise. The only noticeable sound is the wind chime that hangs outside of his window, which is cracked open to let in some fresh air. A breeze comes through, rustling some papers on his desk. It knocks some smaller papers off of the bookshelf where the jars of herbs sit. I move to pick them up, neatly stacking them when I realize they are letters. I glance at the name on the envelope and my eyes widen.

What are the odds?

CHAPTER 4

'Merilla Devaris'

Miss Merilla.

She mentioned her son worked in the library here in Mysticane before I left.

"I've got your tea," I hear from behind. I turn to see Zyl standing in the doorway.

"You're Miss Merilla's son," I say, my voice a bit hoarse from crying. He moves to set the tea down on his desk.

"Oh, you *can* speak. That's good. Umm, do you know my mom?" he asks, a hand moving to tug at one of his braids. He slides the beads up and down nervously and it hits me that this is the first thing I've said to him.

"Sorry, I didn't get to introduce myself," I start as I set down the letters on the edge of his desk. I pick up the tea and saucer carefully, "I'm Heriath Balastina, I work in the clinic with your mom back in Duskwick Village. She's mentioned you to me before."

He breathes a sigh of relief, a hand flying dramatically to his chest.

"Oh! I thought for a moment that you were stalking me or something. Or that I did something wrong. I mean, I don't remember breaking the law recently, but knowing my luck, I probably did it by accident. I do, however, remember my mom mentioning you in a few of our letters." He grabs the letters from his desk and returns them to the shelf.

"Oh, speaking of letters," I mention. I reach into my satchel and pull out an envelope Miss Merilla gave me before I left. "She told me to find your house and give this to you, but seeing as I'm here already..." I shrug.

He takes it from my hands and carefully opens it while I take a sip of tea. The taste of jester mint fills my mouth along with the familiar sweetness of honey. I commend his choice of herbs. I assume he knows of its relaxation properties because of Miss Merilla. He finishes reading the letter and slides it back into the envelope, "How's the tea?"

I give him a smile and a nod, "It's wonderful, thank you."

"Of course. It's lucky that we ran into each other. Judging by how I found you, you seem to be a bit out of your element," he says.

I grimace, "Yeah. Something like that." I return to my seat as he organizes the papers on his desk into neat piles. I watch as he whirls around the office. His white shirt and brown flowy pants fit his slim figure nicely. The colorful cloak draped over his left shoulder adds a flair to his otherwise simple outfit. The beads on his two braids match his beaded bracelets and necklace. His attire is oddly colorful for someone who grew up downstream, but it suits him well. He arranges his pens, documents, and other items until everything is perfectly in place. With a deep breath, he sits at his desk, pulling a pair of glasses from the collar of his shirt and sliding them on.

"So, what brings you to this maze of a city? I can't see anyone from a small village coming here without a reason," he asks. I set my teacup onto its saucer, resting it in my lap. I thought it would have been detailed in the letter.

"I'm trying to find out if the Elysir has truly run out here in Mysticane. We haven't been getting any shipments of it for a while."

"Interesting. Why here?" He lifts a mug from his desk and to his lips while I speak.

I take another sip of my tea, its warmth soothing my throat. "Westbrook receives shipments from here. So I foolishly thought I'd stop by and ask," I explain. My gaze falls to my lap to observe the small waft of steam rising off of the liquid in my cup. My index finger rubs against the side of it, causing a steady ripple.

"Why do you consider it foolish? Seems like a logical next step to solving a significant issue." His question is followed by a small clunk as he returns his mug to his desk.

"Because I was kicked out like a stray cat," I deadpan, looking up at him. His lips twist as he tries to suppress a smile. "Oh, you find that amusing?"

"No," he coughs, clearing his throat. "I simply find your choice of words amusing. However, I'm not surprised they kicked you out. They're very strict on appointments and if you're an outsider you're usually out of luck on the first go around."

"Good to know," I roll my eyes.

"Don't feel too bad. That company doesn't care about maintaining any resources other than its own. I mean that old crook of an owner promised to heal the river for years and now look where we are. If only the dead could take accountability," he grumbles with a shake of his head. The same disdain Miss Merilla has whenever the company is mentioned swirls in his matching brown eyes. He really is the spitting image of his mother, in joy and rage.

"Honestly, the new owner isn't much help either," I mention. "I thought with his death we would at least get information on what he did to the Nafsi in the first place."

"If only it stopped there," he groans.

"What do you mean?"

He reaches and grabs a book off the shelf next to him and drops it on the desk, "Take a gander at that." I slide it closer to me, examining the cover. *'Vyelan: The Waters of Time'*.

"A history textbook?"

"This one was published a long time ago. It was the textbook my mom learned from. The one she used to teach me about our land." He reaches further down on the shelf and grabs another one. This one is noticeably thinner and more modern. "This," he says, angrily slamming the book onto the desk. "Is the recent textbook that they wanted me to teach from when I first arrived here."

I take a closer look at this new one. *'The Waters of Time'*. My eyes fall to the bottom where the words *'Funded by Iron Brimstone Mining Company'* are in bold letters. I open it and find the Nafsi chapter in the table of contents while Zyl flips to the same section in the other textbook. The chapters both start at the drought and Kofir coming to conjure the snowstorm, but the newer textbook has omitted Elysi and Kofir's love story.

"They erased it," I say softly.

"All of it," he responds.

"I didn't realize it was ever in textbooks. My mom read that story to me from a book of legend."

"The soulmate story is a part of history. My parents and grandparents grew up with this story as fact. Once Iron Brimstone got large enough, the city jumped at their offer to fund new, modern textbooks and didn't even care when they removed the story."

"But you teach magical history, don't you?" I ask.

"Here at the library I do. I wanted to teach it in schools, but every place I went told me this textbook was outdated. Apparently, Iron Brimstone argued that without proof of the Water Stone's existence, the story shouldn't be treated as fact."

"Well, why hasn't anyone searched for it? It should be in the Trosthek Mountains."

"Since the company developed their mines there, no one can go digging around without their permission. Trust me, I asked," he sighs. He runs his fingers over the aged pages of the old textbook, "It only took one generation's worth of time for the story to be altered completely in the minds of most people."

"I had no idea," I breathe.

He sighs and returns to his seat, "I try the best I can to keep the story alive. The *real* history. I wish I could do more." His feet kick back up on the desk as he adjusts his cloak. "Anyway, enough of that. Tell me about you."

"Me?" I ask. "There's not much to tell."

"Well, you could tell me if you're feeling better," he shrugs, taking another sip from his mug.

"Yes, I am," I smile.

"I don't mean to pry, but does that happen often?" he asks, nodding towards the door. I start to pick at my fingers.

"Not in a while. It used to happen more often when I was younger. I usually have my family around."

"But there was no one to help you here," he says softly, piecing my thought together. I nod silently. He hums as his eyes shift around in thought.

"Well, you're welcome to stay here for a while, but you will need to get back out there," he says, reaching for a drawer behind his desk. I can hear some items shuffling around before he pulls out a pair of earmuffs. "The city can be overwhelming. These should help. Plus, you won't get weird looks since it's approaching Midwinter."

I take the earmuffs with a soft smile, "Are you sure?"

"Positive. Besides, you can return them to me at home. Mom said in the letter she gave you my address already and that you'd be staying with me in the meantime," he shrugs.

"You're okay with that?" I ask, surprised.

"I trust my mom's judgment. Unless you're telling me I shouldn't?" he smirks with a raised eyebrow.

"I promise not to rob you," I say, crossing my heart.

"Good," he nods. His eyes shift behind me and I turn to see a clock. It's been almost an hour. "Shit, I'm late!" he exclaims. He falls backward as he tries to get up from his chair. I hear a loud thud as he hits the ground, the bookcase rattling at the force. I stand to peer over the desk, stifling a giggle.

"Are you okay?" His body twists as he kicks the chair to the side and pulls himself off the ground. He rubs the side of his head, which I assume was the cause of the thud.

"I'll live. I'm late for a tutoring session with a student," he explains as he grabs a few things from his drawers and shoves them into a satchel. "Sorry I have to leave so abruptly. It was great to meet you."

I move to grab my bag, "It was wonderful to meet you too. Your mom speaks highly of you."

He blushes slightly, "I'm only a historian."

The clock chimes with a sound clear as day. That rust bucket at the clinic back home certainly reflects Miss Merilla's age. "Gotta go! Bye,

Heriath," he waves as he rushes out the door. I laugh at his chaotic exit, waving back as though he can see it. My gaze falls to the earmuffs in my hand, running my thumbs over the soft fur.

At least I have one point of familiarity in this daunting city.

CHAPTER 5

This city is beginning to be an endless source of frustration. Even after finding the clinics I wanted to visit, I still wound up at a dead end when they failed to provide any useful information. Luckily, my stress is no longer heightened by the noise.

I glance down at the last clinic address on my list and come to a halt in front of a small building. I slide it into my satchel and take a deep breath as I push the door open. A small bell rings as I step inside an empty lobby. I pull the earmuffs off and place them in my satchel.

"Hello?" I call. I make my way to the front counter and crane my neck towards the back room. A crash comes from behind the door and I hesitantly take a step around the counter. I reach out for the door handle, but just before I can grab it, the door flies open.

A boy a few years younger than me pushes past, stumbling towards the counter. He falls to his knees and yanks open the cabinet behind it. Bottles and jars knock against one another as he searches for something. He hops up with a few items in his hands and a frantic look in his eye.

"Sorry, I'll be with you in a few minutes," he rushes out. He's nearly hyperventilating as he returns to the back room. I succumb to my curiosity and pull the door open to find a small hallway with three exam rooms. The first door on the left is wide open. A woman riddled with bruises lays on the exam table. The boy sets his armful of jars on a small counter only for one of them to roll to the floor and shatter. He curses, bending down to pick up the glass.

"Hey, don't do that," I shout. He jumps and turns to face me, brown eyes sheening with tears. He's way too young to be the head herbalist here. My eyes fall to the small silver medallion that sits around his neck. *So he's only an apprentice.* I approach him and twist my satchel to show the bronze medallion that hangs from a short chain on the side. An image of Elysir is etched into the center. He stares at it for a moment before looking back up at me.

"You're an herbalist?" he asks.

I nod in response, "Where is the head herbalist?"

"I don't know. He left me here and then she showed up hurt and I've never had to deal with an emergency before, especially not on my own and-"

"Okay, okay," I say calmly. I gently grab his shoulders and hold his gaze. I take a deep breath and he mirrors my action, his eyes coming more into focus. I can feel him shaking underneath my hands. "You got a name?"

"Lindel."

"Okay, Lindel. What do you know?"

"Um, she has a bad cut on her shoulder and said she got hit in the head pretty hard. She was dizzy when she arrived, but I was more concerned about the blood," he says.

I nod and remove my satchel, "Okay, let's check her out. Can you get a cannula set up?" He nods firmly and rushes to the other side of the room to start. I approach the table and tap the woman carefully. Her eyes pop open to reveal bright green irises. "Good, you're awake. Can you speak?"

"Yes," she replies softly. I give her a small smile as my fingers dig carefully into her blonde hair. *No bleeding from her head.*

"I'm Heriath. Do you know your name?"

"Tansae." *The wrapping on her shoulder is done well.*

"Perfect. I'm going to take a look at you, okay? I need you to keep your eyes open for me."

"I'm tired," she breathes.

"I know, but we need you awake to get a proper assessment. Just a few minutes," I explain. I move to stand over her and lift one finger above her face. "Follow my finger with your eyes, please?"

She hums in response, but her eyes squeeze shut and her arm jerks slightly, "Shit." I look over to Lindel who's inserted the cannula. He gives me an apologetic look while I repeat my instructions. Tansae opens her eyes again and follows my finger. The smooth movement of her irises eases my nerves.

"Okay, you're doing good."

"She's cold," Lindel remarks, his hand on her arm.

"Do you know what that means?" I ask him.

"Shock?"

I nod, "Get a blanket."

"Yes ma'am." He bolts to the front room while I make my way to the counter opposite her table.

"Can I sleep now?" Tansae groans.

"Not quite yet." I sort through the jars Lindel brought along with other inventory until I find the two herbs I need. I grab a mortar and pestle to make a simple mixture. Lindel comes back with a blanket and drapes it over Tansae. I measure the proper amount of darkened lilac and windroot before turning to Lindel.

"Think you can handle finishing this for me?" I ask, extending the mortar to him. He takes it from my hands with a more confident grin.

"Yes ma'am."

I wave dismissively, "No need for formality." I lean against the counter and watch as he grinds the herbs into a powder. Once it's done, he adds a bit to a cup of water and brings it to Tansae.

"Here. Drink this and you can rest," he says. She thanks him and downs the mixture. Her face twists at the sour taste as she hands the cup back to him. We clean the room in silence to allow her to sleep before returning to the front room. I shut the door with a heavy sigh.

"Do you think she'll be alright?" Lindel asks, tying the bag full of the broken glass we picked up.

"She'll be fine. Your wrapping on her arm was perfect," I reply.

His gaze falls to his hands as a shy smile spreads on his face, "Thank you."

"As for her head, it seems she was just knocked around a little. No serious damage."

"That's good." He pauses his movements as he meets my eyes again," I don't know what I would've done without you. Any longer and she might have-"

"Hey," I interrupt. "You did nothing wrong, Lindel."

"But I panicked and you were so calm and collected," he says. He plops onto a stool, shoulders slumping as he stares at the floor. I move behind the front counter and crouch beside him. He peers over at me through the short braids that frame his face.

"That's only because I have more experience," I reassure him. "Nobody should have to face an emergency situation alone. My head herbalist back home has been practicing for over thirty years and she always needs extra hands."

He raises an eyebrow, "Really?"

"Really. Why did your head herbalist leave you here anyway?" I question.

He scoffs, "I don't know. He's always running out for one reason or another, but I could always handle it. I don't know what happened to me today. I saw her arm covered in blood and she nearly collapsed." He digs the heels of his hands into his eyes as if trying to wipe away the memory. I can't imagine what was going through his head when she crashed in here. I adjust myself to sit on the floor.

"You know," I start. He drags his hands down and peeks at me through his fingers. "I was a disaster the first time I saw a serious wound. He came in with a broken leg. Bone jutting out of his shin, covered in blood, and he would not stop screaming. Now, I don't blame him, the guy was in pain, but his screams sent me into a panic. I completely lost my mind and was no help whatsoever," I laugh softly.

"Were you alone?" he asks.

"No, Miss Merilla was there. She took care of him while I stood frozen in my spot. Once I finally managed to move, I was put in charge of helping him recover during his stay."

"At least you had her to help."

"My point is," I say, pulling a hand from his face. "Look at what you managed to accomplish. You got her into the room, cleaned her up, and bandaged her to perfection. You even managed to keep her awake and calm."

A small grin lights his face, "I guess I did."

"Though, that's all I could really expect from an apprentice," I shrug.

He sits back a bit, "What's that supposed to mean?"

"What?" I muse, standing from my spot. "You think you have some kind of skill just because you've got that badge?" He glances at the medallion on his chest before glaring up at me.

"Hey, I earned this. I studied and practiced and-" He cuts himself short when he notices the sly smile spreading across my face. His expression softens and an airy laugh escapes his lips. I give him a nod and grab my satchel to pull it over my head.

"Thanks for your help," he grins.

"It was nothing," I reply, turning to leave.

"Speaking of help, what did you come in for?" he asks. Realization hits me like a steam engine. I nearly forgot myself. I lean my elbows against the smooth wood.

"Do any of the clinics here in Mysticane have Elysir in stock? At least, more than the few petals they've stopped providing recently."

He hums and stares up at the ceiling, "Not here. We're most likely as lacking as your clinic back home."

"And that makes you the fifth and final clinic to give me that answer," I sigh.

"There is one thing though," he mentions. "I've heard that Iron Brimstone keeps a stash just for their herbalists. Since they only treat their workers, it stays within company circulation."

"What?" I spout. "How do they still have enough?"

"I don't know. They seem to have plenty, even enough for some herbalists to take home a few petals for personal use."

"How do you know all of this?"

His eyes roam before landing in his lap, "My mom works there."

"Do you think I could speak to her?"

"I don't know. She tends to work late, but sometimes she has lunch with me if I pull the 'I'm your only son' card," he chuckles. "I'll talk to her tonight and see if she can spare some time. Maybe noon tomorrow?"

"Sounds good," I grin. He waves me goodbye as I leave the clinic with a new sense of hope.

The southern edge of the city is vastly different from the cacophony behind me. It's an open area with lush green grass that flows into the valley where Lake Irridover resides. The houses are made of more traditional materials and have no issue allowing nature to take its course. Vines peek through the stones and climb up the walls of each cottage. The Nafsi flows to the right of the small buildings and continues downstream, heading for the mountains that rise up from behind the rooftops. The wagon is jostled around on the dirt path, but I manage to find Zyl's house, a quaint wood and stone cottage that is complimented by its natural surroundings.

Zyl welcomes me in and shows me to the room where I'll be staying before returning to his office. I set my items in the far corner, much too tired from the day's events to unpack. I toss my clothes aside and slip on my nightgown as a cool breeze blows through the window. I take a seat on the bed and reach forward to close them, noticing a three-headed blue flower growing right outside. The beauty of it brings a soft smile to my face as its petals sway in the cool breeze. I lean over to blow out the lantern on my nightstand, allowing the room and my mind to fall into darkness.

CHAPTER 6

The clinic's bell rings as I swing the door open. Excitement adds a pep to my step and a swish in the long green skirt that clings to my waist. Faint voices grow louder as the door to the back hallway opens.

"You know I can't rely on anyone but you, Lindel," an elderly woman says. Lindel appears from behind and hands her a pouch with a grin.

"I'll be here as long as you need me, ma'am. Tell your granddaughter I said hello. I put an extra lollipop in the pouch for her," he winks. The woman pats his head and thanks him. I give her a nod as she walks towards the door, the bell ringing again as she leaves. Lindel heaves a sigh and takes a seat behind the front counter.

"Regular of yours?" I ask.

He nods, "She comes in for regular check-ups but lately she's had this increased fear of death. Freaking out whenever a new mole appears. I give her a bit of grace due to her age."

"We had someone like that back home, except he was only twenty-four," I laugh softly.

"It's things like that that make you stare at your medallion for an hour once you get home," he replies. He points to a chair near the entrance and I pull it up to the counter to take a seat.

"So, did you manage to get your mom to come visit?"

"In fact, I did," he says. "Though you are a little early."

I glance over at the clock placed on the wall above his head, "Oh."

"It's actually a good time. Tansae was asking about you earlier this morning. Said she wanted to meet the other herbalist who helped her."

"She's awake?"

"Mhm, I moved her to the second room on the right since that one has a bed. You can go talk to her if you like," he says, gesturing to the hallway door. "I have to organize a few things up here."

"Thanks. Come get me when your mom gets here?"

"Of course," he nods. With a smile, I slip into the back hallway and knock carefully on her door. A faint voice tells me to come in and I find Tansae lying back on the bed holding a dagger above her face. She twists the blade, watching the sunlight glint off of it.

"Afternoon," I greet. Her head rolls to the side, eyes widening slightly.

"Hey, you're-"

"Heriath. I was here yesterday."

"Yes. I'm glad you came back. I've been meaning to thank you for your help," she says, placing the dagger beside her on the bed.

I take a seat in a small chair next to the bed, "Oh, it's nothing. You look a lot better. How's your head?"

"I had a headache when I woke up," she shrugs. "Lindel did a check-up and said I was fine, but advised I rest another day to be sure."

"Good. It's nice to know he's feeling more confident in himself today."

"Yeah, he flew into a panic when I got here, but I'm glad you could straighten him out."

"Well, don't be too harsh. He may be an apprentice but he shows promise." She hums in response. "Speaking of your head, what happened? If you don't mind me asking."

"Oh, that," she groans, rolling her eyes. "I was on my way back from Kaelora City when-" A knock at the door interrupts her before Lindel pops his head into the room.

"Sorry to interrupt, but my mom is here, Heriath. She's in a hurry so you might want to come out front."

"Oh okay," I reply. "Sorry Tansae, this should be quick." She shrugs and gestures to the door. I follow Lindel to the lobby to find a woman unpacking a small bag onto the front counter. Her afro is pulled up into a puff atop her head with a red scarf wrapped around it. It stands out from her otherwise green and brown attire that's common in our practice. Colorful variations of quartz and limestone make up her necklace and bracelets. She's put together despite her frazzled demeanor as she arranges things on the counter.

"Oh, there you are honey. Here's your lunch," she says, pointing to the food before us.

"Thanks, Mom," Lindel says, walking behind the counter. He takes a seat and extends a hand in my direction. "This is Heriath. The woman who helped me out yesterday."

His mom turns to me with a tired smile, "It's a pleasure to meet you. I'm Aurora." Her accent is thick and has the twang of people from Eastbrook. There's a comfort in that sound that reminds me of my grandfather before he passed.

"You as well," I reply, extending my hand. She takes it and before I could shake, she pulls me in for a hug.

"I can't thank you enough for helping my boy. He has it hard here, ya know. With that owner running in and out and whatnot." She pulls back from the embrace, crows feet on full display. "Though it wouldn't have happened had the boy signed on as my apprentice."

"Ma, I told you I didn't want any favoritism," Lindel groans.

She turns to face Lindel, hands on her hips, "And look where it landed ya, son."

"Just doing my job, ma'am," I intervene.

"Oh nonsense," she waves dismissively. "Call me Aurora. Besides, I'm sure that woman you helped is grateful. Is she doing any better?" she asks.

"Tansae? She's doing fine. I was talking to her before you arrived and her fields are plowed straight."

Aurora's face drops and her eyebrows jump up, "Did you say Tansae?" I glance over at Lindel curiously.

"Yes."

"Where is she?" Aurora spouts.

"Second door on the right," I say, jutting my thumb to the door behind me. Aurora steps past me and pushes through the threshold, rushing down the hall. She flings the door open and Tansae jumps.

"Shit," Tansae swears, a hand grasping her chest. Her eyes narrow at us as I appear behind Aurora in the doorway. "Aurora? What are you doing here?"

"I could ask you the same thing. What happened?" Aurora demands.

"Well," Tansae scoffs. "I was attacked on my way back from Kaelora City. They tried to rob my steam wagon which reminds me that we should start putting the branding on the inside of the wagon to avoid that problem."

"Why didn't you come to the company herbalists?" Aurora asks, taking a step forward.

"Let's see," she starts, sarcasm dripping from her tone. "I was bleeding and they managed to knock me in the head bad enough that I could hardly drive into the city. I stopped at the closest clinic I could find. Would you rather I bleed to death trying to drive deeper into town? Would you rather me run somebody over?"

"Okay, okay. I'm sorry," Aurora says softly. "It's been quite the day. I've got three injured miners I had to put on bedrest just this morning."

"You work for Iron Brimstone?" I ask Tansae.

"Yes I do," she answers, not sparring me a glance. "However, Aurora, that doesn't answer why you're here."

"Well, I came to thank this young lady for helping Lindel, but I guess I owe her double for saving your skin. I told you not to go it alone," she says pointedly.

I raise my hands in protest, "You don't owe me anything, Aurora."

"Look, I didn't ask to be accosted by those people or by you. So, if you don't mind, I'd like to relax while I heal," Tansae retorts. Aurora takes a deep breath and backs into the doorway again.

"I'll leave you to it, I guess. Don't you cause these folks any of the trouble you've caused me," she says.

"Of course not, Aurora. You know you need me," Tansae says with a grin. Aurora simply turns away to retreat to the lobby. I glance between them before following after her, closing Tansae's door behind me.

"What was that about?" I ask.

She sighs deeply, "That young woman is the daughter of Cloveris Morelli and a royal pain in my ass." I freeze at her words.

"Wait, hold on. She's the *daughter* of the owner of Iron Brimstone?" I gape.

"Which is why she shouldn't have been traveling alone, but you'd have better luck finding a whale in the Nafsi than getting her to change her plans," she groans. She pushes up the circular wire-framed glasses that sit on the bridge of her broad nose. Her eyes wander to the clock on the wall again.

"Umm, Heriath? Didn't you have something to ask my mom?" Lindel speaks up.

"Oh right." Aurora gives me a curious look. "Lindel told me you may know if Iron Brimstone has any Elysir they can spare?"

"Oh, I'm sorry dear. We ran out of supplies a few months ago."

My brows furrow slightly, "Really? He said you had reserves specifically for company herbalists."

"We did for a while, but even our luck has run out," she says. I turn to Lindel who is scraping the bottom of the container to get the last of his lunch onto his fork. The smell of which has left me with a craving.

"Lindel?" I call. He looks up, eyes shifting between us. "Didn't you tell me they had an abundance of reserves left?"

"You told her what?" Aurora asks. A simmering tension grows as we both stare at him. The boy swallows, eyes shifting to the floor as he lowers the container to his lap.

"I've seen you bring some home and I assumed that meant the reserves were full, or at least had enough to afford to give you extra," he explains. I look to Aurora who gently pulls off her glasses with an awkward laugh. She pulls at the edge of her shirt, using the material to clean her lenses.

"I doubt it was Elysir you saw me bring home. There are many blue flowers we use in our practice," she says.

"But they don't all glow like-"

"That's enough, sweetheart," she deadpans. Lindel shuts his mouth and continues scrapping at the bottom of the container. Aurora looks at me as she returns her glasses to her face. "I'm sorry, but as I said before

the reserves are bone dry. I can let you know if anything comes up."
There's a strain in her smile that piques my curiosity, but I fight the urge
to push.

I nod, "I understand. Company rules and confidentiality."

"We know it best," she says, patting the bronze medallion that
hangs from a short chain on her leather belt. She glances at the clock for
a third time and slides her hands into her pockets. "I'd better get going.
The clinic will fall apart without me." She gives Lindel a peck on the
cheek and waves goodbye as she leaves.

"Hey Aurora, could you-" Tansae appears from the hallway, pausing
as she notices her absence. "Is she gone?"

"Just left," I reply.

"You should be in bed," Lindel scolds through a mouth full of food.

Tansae groans, "I know. I was going to ask her to bring me clothes
from home."

"Are the clothes I gave you not okay?" Lindel asks after swallowing.
"I know they're a bit big, but-"

"Big is not the problem," she responds. She grips the edge of her
shirt and pulls it away from her, glaring at it as if the fabric were made
of ants. "This beige is horrendous. I'm already injured. Do I have to look
like an Eastbrook fielder too?"

"Hey, what's wrong with Eastbrook?" Lindel says defensively.

"You guys already work in the dirt all day. You don't have to blend
in with the wheat."

"Alright, that's enough," I interrupt. "Come on, Tansae, let's go
lie down." She sighs defeatedly and follows me back to her room,
grumbling along the way. "It's only one more day, hun," I reassure her.
She lifts her dagger from the bed with a roll of her eyes as she plops
down in its place.

"So, Tansae. Where are you from?" I ask, trying to change the subject.

She looks at me for a second before turning back to her dagger, "Mysticane City. I grew up here."

"What was it like growing up in a big city?"

"Well, it was loud," she scoffs. "The streets are always busy, as are the people, but somehow the chaos feels like home." I return to the chair I sat in earlier as a small smile rises on her face.

She turns to me, "What's your story?"

"My story?"

"Yeah. Are you a troll? The daughter of an ancient goddess? A tree that turned human?" I laugh at her dramatic hand gestures as she lists off ridiculous things.

"I can assure you, I'm only human," I respond.

"How'd you get into herbalism?" she asks, finally landing on a more realistic question.

"My mom taught me," I answer. "I used to get banged up quite a bit when I was younger. She would take care of me, and after a while I became interested. It always looked like so much fun to make medicine in the mortar. She got me some herbalism books for my tenth birthday and I've been in love with it ever since."

"Found your passion early in life. That's good," she says with an approving nod. "You must be close to your mom."

I smile fondly, remembering my mother's smile that night when she came to talk to me. I've always been her little girl. "Yeah, I am. What about your family?"

"It's complicated," she sighs. "My father passed away a few years ago and my mother..." she trails off. I almost regret asking now.

"I'm sorry. You don't have to talk about it if you don't want to."

"No. No, it's alright. My parent's marriage was more of a business partnership, honestly. My mother and I have never really been close, and my father...he taught me everything I know."

"It must have been hard growing up under a large figure like your father." She gives me a curious look before realization washes over her features.

"Aurora told you?" I nod.

"I'm sure you miss him," I say softly. She nods. A beat passes. The atmosphere grows heavy and I start to pick at my fingers. "Um, why were you traveling to Kaelora City?" I ask, cutting through the silence.

"I wanted to see what their reserves look like. If they were better off than we are downstream."

"And?"

"Dry as the great drought. They ran out a month or two after we did."

I hum and sit back in my chair, the sour taste of defeat forcing my lips to press into a flat line. "Guess we're both out of luck," I murmur.

If both cities are out, I don't know what we're going to do. With Westbrook being the main resource of medicinal herbs, Vyelan heavily relies on us to provide them. The land, however is becoming more barren over time due to our failing attempt to recreate the kind of healing ability the Elysir possesses. We may have taken advantage of the Elysir. Using it as the base of all balsams and other medications was practical. It was a great immune booster and the strongest antibiotic we had. The ideal healing herb that failed its first mission and was left as a gift to all of us.

"You alright?" she asks, shaking me from my thoughts.

"Hmm? Yeah, I'm okay."

She lays back on the bed and stares up at the ceiling, "I'm sure the

Elysir means a lot more to you Westbrook villagers."

You have no idea.

I stand from my seat, "I should be going. You need your rest." She nods and I reach for the door when I'm stopped by her calling my name. I turn back with raised eyebrows and she rolls her head to the side to face me.

"Think you could come back tomorrow? I'll go nuts if I'm here alone for another day," she asks.

A small smile tugs at the corners of my mouth, "Sure."

"Another dead end, huh?" Zyl asks as I plop onto the couch. His home is a nice space and larger on the inside than one would imagine. An open floor plan where the kitchen and living room meet and a hallway past it with two bedrooms and an office. The second bedroom typically being reserved for his mother's visits.

He walks over from the kitchen and leans down to gently hand me a cup of gooseberry juice. I take the saucer from his hands with a sigh.

"I don't understand what's going on. The Nafsi has provided for Vyelan for so long and then it suddenly stops? There's got to be a reason," I huff. Zyl takes a seat in a plush chair across from the couch.

"I think we all know the reason," he mumbles into his teacup.

"You really think Iron Brimstone contaminated the Nafsi?"

"It's a reasonable explanation. Most of downstream Vyelan thinks so," he shrugs. With the company being the closest to the river any number of mistakes can happen. He takes a sip of his tea or tries to. His face contorts as he jerks the cup away with a hiss, "Too hot."

I set my own cup on the coffee table between us, my craving for juice dissipated by my mood, "Something's missing."

"Missing?"

"This whole situation is like a book with ripped-out pages. The magic infused into the soil of Vyelan hasn't been impacted since the regions are perfectly fine."

Zyl's eyebrows knit together, "Could you elaborate?"

I adjust myself in my seat, "As most people know, plants require certain conditions to grow properly. During Kofir's travels, he blessed different areas with specific plants. Herbalists separate these areas into regions to better understand where to find what when foraging. To put it simply, Eastbrook has the majority of Vyelan's food and crops, Westbrook covers medicinal herbs, upstream has our aromatic and colorful plants, and downstream has our minerals and winter plants since they are closer to the mountains." He nods and I continue.

"He also enhanced the conditions of each region so that the land may be bountiful each year. Kofir infused magic into the soil of each region to maintain the right balance of nutrients for the health of the specific plants that grow there."

He hums, "So there are two sources of magic. Soil and Water."

"Right. That's why the Elysir not growing proves the issue is with the Nafsi alone. Sadly, we can't heal it without the mystic's abilities." My thumb and middle finger massage my temples as the past few days of failure begin to form a headache. I shut my eyes. I've tried not to let it weigh on my heart. Zyl's voice travels to my ears as he mutters under his breath.

I open my eyes, "What is it?" He snaps out of his thoughts and meets my gaze.

"Oh, I was theorizing. The soulmate's story. It's the only portion of our history that's tied directly to the Nafsi's magical energy. The new explanation in the textbooks claims that Kofir infused the river with magic when he initially healed it, but if that's the case then the magic wouldn't be changing every few years."

"The magic changes?"

"Of course. The river has been studied before. The energy required to grow Elysir slowly fades over the years before it's revitalized." He lifts his teacup to his lips and takes a sip before continuing. "When I was studying in Kaelora City, there were these colorful trees whose vibrance was dictated by the amount of magic in the river. It's the only other plant ever known to be affected by the river's magical energy. A scientist friend of mine noticed how the color would fade over time and become vibrant again at some point."

"But don't leaves change color with seasons?" I point out.

"That's just it," he grins. "These trees have color in their bark. Not the leaves."

"They sound beautiful."

"They are. I got to see them fade and grow in vibrance. It was something magical." His eyes shift to the side but appear distant, as if he's watching a memory play out before him. I clear my throat and he shakes his head to disrupt his thoughts. "Right, my theory. Those trees don't follow the same kind of pattern explained in text. If the river's magic were consistent, the color would never fade. However, it seems to occur each generational cycle according to studies in the Kaelora Archives. Now, if we assume the soulmate's story is in fact real, it would line up with this timeline since each generation has a reincarnation of Kofir and Elysi's souls. If the magic has faded enough that the Elysir can't grow anymore, then it means either the soulmates of our generation haven't met yet or the ones in the past generation never did."

"So what exactly are you proposing? That we try and find the soulmates of our generation?" I laugh. "A bit far-fetched."

"Not as far-fetched as you might think. The mystic should have left clues behind, something he could use to find his partner. The spell Kofir cast could lead us right to them if we figure it out."

"Okay, okay," I say, crossing my arms. My head falls back to stare at the ceiling as I process this new information. "Assuming we *are* correct and we figure out the clues, this would only be plausible if the Water Stone is real."

"I believe it is." I give him a look and he leans forward, "Think about it. Why would Iron Brimstone try to bury a story everyone knows in books of legend if there wasn't a possibility it could be true?"

"No one thought to question the river's magic until the Elysir stopped growing and the textbooks were changed years before that," I add. "They must have found the Water Stone and changed the information to hide the truth, but that doesn't seem like enough reason."

"Why not?"

"Well, why would they hide it unless they could predict the magic running dry? If everyone knew the Nafsi has its own separate magic and had proof-"

"The company would have been ruined when the Elysir stopped growing."

"Exactly."

"But that means something must have happened to the previous soulmates," he points out.

"True, but that's not our current problem. We need proof of the Water Stone's existence."

He hums and sits back in his chair again, "Right. We'd have to find a way into the mountains to see for ourselves.”

My eyes widen, “Or maybe we don’t. We would just need someone who’s already seen it.” I jump up from my seat and rush to the front door, snatching my cloak off the rack next to it.

“Wait, where-”

“Get started on figuring out those clues, Zyl. If we’re right about this, we’re going to need them.” Before he can ask another question, I’m out the front door and running down the path to the clinic.

This is my last chance to take a step forward and I can’t afford to waste it.

CHAPTER 7

It takes me a while to find my way back to the clinic in the lantern-lit streets. I was proud of myself for convincing Lindel to let me inside, but that pride has since shriveled now that I've explained Zyl's theory to a confused Tansae.

"That's a bit far-fetched," she says, rolling over to face away from me.

"I know, but it could be true. If it is, we stand a chance of healing our land before any significant damage is done. We just need to know if the Water Stone is real. You're the closest person to the top of that company."

"So?"

"You've been in the Trosthek Mountains."

"That doesn't mean I've seen it," she says hesitantly.

"Well, even if you didn't couldn't you go find out? Isn't it worth the search?" I ask. She groans and sits up, turning to face me.

"This is what you woke me up for?" she grumbles.

"Isn't it?" I press further. She stares at me for a moment before running her hand through her hair. She pulls it all to sit over one shoulder and mindlessly plays with the ends.

"I can understand why this is important, but nobody is that selfless."

I sit back in my seat, blinking wildly, "What's that supposed to mean?"

"You told me you came to Mysticane to look for Elysir. The one thing you haven't told me is why."

"Does that matter?"

She crosses her arms and leans back against the bed, "You're asking for well-protected information. I want to know what you'll gain from this venture." I sigh and pull my cloak tighter around my shoulders. *Fair enough.*

"To put it simply, my sister is dying," I explain. "It's the only plant strong enough to push her healing past her illness."

"So she asked you to come find Elysir for her?" she questions.

"No, she didn't. I came on my own without her knowledge. That's the selfish part." I clasp my hands together and lean forward so my elbows rest on my knees. "I'm not some kind of savior. I want to heal my sister and if it happens to save more people then even better. This could be the way." Her gaze shifts to her lap, her bottom lip tucked between her teeth. I lean closer, my voice calm, "Tansae, you have the information we need and it doesn't just benefit me. Iron Brimstone could wipe clean its reputation."

She stares at her lap and I hold my breath as I await her answer. She soon sighs and looks back to me. "Do you guys have a plan?" she asks.

"Zyl's working on it as we speak, but you have yet to answer my question. Does the stone exist?"

A soft grin tugs at her lips, "It glows the most beautiful blue you've ever seen."

"Ah, the sleeping giant has awoken," Zyl jokes. His hair is pulled up into a high ponytail with a few curly strands left out to frame his face. A different colorful cloak covers his shoulders with bracelets to match. He has quite the collection of jewelry.

I close his office door behind me and roll my eyes, "Don't pretend you're up bright and early on the days you don't have to work."

"Actually, I am and a simple thank you for the eggs and toast would suffice," he says with a playful glare.

"Thank you." I approach his desk to see an array of maps splayed out before him along with the pages of notes and ideas we stayed up working on. "What are these?"

"Well, with my free time this morning, I've been searching the maps charted during the years Kofir was alive. The archives here have some of the maps he charted himself to keep track of where new plants he created were placed."

"Okay, so how will that help us?" Another knock sounds on the door and Zyl nods for me to answer it. I open the door to find Tansae with a slip of paper in her hand. Her blonde hair is tied back in a low ponytail by a blue ribbon. A matching blue cloak is wrapped around her shoulders, the small opening of it revealing her white blouse and black pants.

"Oh great, I'm in the right place," she says, pushing past me.

"Good morning to you too," I greet, closing the door once again.

"You must be Zyl," she says, extending a hand to him. "Nice to meet you."

He shakes it with a nod, "Likewise."

"As you were saying," I prompt.

"Yes," he clears his throat. He pulls up one map and a copy of the story from beneath a few other pages. A few papers fall off his desk, but he waves it off. "Heriath and I discussed Kofir's spell last night. The part that stood out was the last line: *My eyes shall be opened by a mark in the valley where life begins and ends.* Now, where life begins and ends most likely means either the soul itself or the Nafsi, the life of our land. The mark on the other hand could be anything, maybe even some magical thing we don't understand, but the realistic idea is location. This was a map from the archives that Kofir made himself. He even marked where his first home was which was located in a valley right here."

Tansae squints at the area Zyl points to, "This map is ancient. Does that area even exist anymore?" Zyl smiles knowingly and pulls out a second map, this one more recognizable.

"Based on geography," he drags his index finger across the map before landing in a single spot. "This is the same place as the original map. I cross-referenced it with the many cartographs of Vyelan until I got to our most recent one." I lean forward and read the words beside his finger: *Pine Valley.*

"Well, it's a valley," I mention.

"It was a valley in Kofir's day too. I'd say that's our best bet," Zyl replies.

"Think we can get an exact location?" Tansae asks, lifting the map into her own hands.

"I was working on it when you got here," he replies, taking it back from her. "While I can't figure out exact coordinates, there is another clue in some journals he left behind." He pulls out a leather-bound book held closed by a hook and eye clasp from his desk drawer and my eyes widen at the sight.

"Is that really one of Kofir's journals?" I ask.

"Oh no," Zyl waves, flipping through the pages. "This is a copy of his personal one. The originals are under lock, key, and glass. Luckily, he cared enough to leave us with so much information. Here we go. The Violet Meadow."

"What's that?" Tansae asks.

"It's an herbalist legend of sorts," I answer. "A rare plant that no one is able to grow but Kofir. There's only one and its existence is mostly passed by word of mouth."

"Well, its existence is proven true by this passage here," Zyl continues. "The violet meadow is a three-headed purple flower that Kofir created for Elysi. It changes location each day but never strays far from the house. It acted as a sort of game for them."

Tansae plops into Zyl's desk chair, "So, once we get to Pine Valley we need to find the house with this flower growing by it?"

"Yes. Though we do have to hope the person living there is around our age since we are looking for our generation's soulmates."

"That sounds easy enough," I comment, extending my hand to Zyl. "Do you mind?" He shakes his head and hands me the journal so I can take a look.

"That's all I have for the first location," he sighs.

"The first?" Tansae questions.

"Yes. Mystic Kofir had two homes, one upstream and one downstream," he explains, bending down to pick up the few pages that fell from his desk. Tansae lifts her feet to make room for him.

"Can't you figure it out on the maps like you did the first one?"

"I could, except the maps and journals I need are in Kaelora City Archives," he says. A small thump draws my attention from the journal and Tansae stifles a giggle. Zyl pops up from behind the desk, papers in his left hand as his right rubs the back of his head.

"You okay?" I ask.

"Fine. I should tape some pillows under this desk with how often that happens," he chuckles. I set the journal down on the surface of the desk, a buzz of energy rushing through me. This could work. This could *really* work. There's only one question left.

"When do we leave?"

CHAPTER 8

TANSAE'S POV

He had told me the story a hundred times at least. He said one day I would understand what I had to do, but I hadn't known then what he meant. It confused me at the time. He was a man always on the straight and narrow, never taking time to indulge in legends and childish wonders. Especially something like Kofir and Elysi's story. It wasn't until I was shown the Water Stone that I finally understood the implications of what the soulmate's tale could mean for Vyelan. What it could mean for the company.

Father was right. The soulmates are the key, but I didn't even know where to start looking. Until now. Heriath has a plan and I have an opportunity. One that I can't afford to waste. Despite the river's condition being beneficial to us over the past few years, the tables are starting to turn. Healing it will prove useful, but I have to tread carefully.

I push my way inside Iron Brimstone Headquarters, staring up at the large staircase that leads up to the main work area for the logistics and business teams. Many gears and tools are fashioned into railings that gleam in the light. Two doors stand on either side of the staircase that leads to the courtyard where two more towers stand tall. I take the left door and follow the path toward the medical center. Trees shade the walkway and the center of the diamond-shaped courtyard where a few workers are eating lunch. Some pass by with pickaxes leaning against their shoulders, chatting away about something or other.

The bold lettering above the clinic's arched doorway brings a grin to my face as I enter. A few herbalists roam the space, some appearing more battered than others. It's always easy to tell who was on the day shift versus the night shift. I give a nod to those who bid me a good afternoon as they rush past. I approach the counter and ring a small bell that sits in the corner. My fingertips tap the wooden surface as I wait, my patience growing thinner by the second when I seem to be ignored. I grab the bell to ring a second time when a hand covers my own.

"Looking for me, right?" Her clothes are wrinkled and small bags are forming under her eyes. I take a small step back when I notice soot smudges on her arms and hands. I return the bell to the counter and wipe my hand against my pants.

"What happened to you?"

She sighs, "Just come with me." I follow her as we weave our way through the busy lobby and down a hallway to her office. Once inside, I shut the door behind us and she turns to me with her arms crossed.

"What do you want," she asks coldly.

"Now Aurora," I tsk, leaning against the door. "Is that any way to greet a friend?" She scoffs as she moves to sit in her office chair. Pulling a folder from her desk, she begins to leaf through the file.

"You're right, it isn't. Now what do you want?" she repeats. My amused grin falters at her snide comment. I cross my arms, eyes wandering up to the ceiling.

"You know, after all I've done for you over the years, I think I deserve a bit more respect. What do you think?" I ask. She shuts the folder and tosses it haphazardly onto her desk before turning to me with a disingenuous smile.

"What can I do for you today, Tansae?"

"Better," I grin, pushing myself off the door. "I need some dragonleaf from you." She eyes me carefully as I slowly walk around her, lifting things from her desk to busy my hands.

"What for?" she asks.

"Oh, I don't think that matters."

"It does, actually."

"It hasn't before," I answer, turning to look her in the eye. "Are you questioning me?"

I lean forward, hands resting on the arms of her seat as I stare her down. She holds my gaze with a fire behind her eyes. Nothing I haven't seen before. She's always been a tough woman, my personal nurse throughout my childhood. Her age and motherhood have rendered her fearless. To most things at least. Intimidation has never been an effective tactic when she's concerned, but I always get a kick out of trying.

"Questioning you is not against our agreement," she says.

"Amendments can always be made."

"Why do you need that herb?"

"I believe that's my business," I respond, standing straight. "Yours is to know where it is and retrieve it. That's your job, isn't it? The job I so graciously allowed you to keep." Her jaw clenches and my smile returns.

"This isn't like the windroot I gave you last time. This one is-"

"Four doses should do," I interrupt. I step around her and walk toward the door. Her chair scrapes against the floor as she stands.

"I need to know this is for a good reason," she states firmly. "One that will help someone." I pause, my hand on the doorknob as I stare at the floor for a moment. *Poor sweet Aurora.* I lift my head and face her as I pull the door open.

"You know, I'm glad your husband made it through the last month despite your mistake with my previous request," I coo, a smirk tugging at my lips. "I'd hate to push his luck."

Just like that, the fire was gone. I could almost see the ashes fall to the ground as they had so many times before.

Her stance remains firm, but her eyes shift down, "Four doses."

"That's why you're my best friend," I wave, stepping through the doorway. Now to get the rest of my things ready for our departure at dawn.

CHAPTER 9

HERIATH'S POV

Logistics, logistics, logistics.

Preparation for a sudden trip zapped most of our energy. Buying clothes, packing medical supplies, and convincing Zyl that he didn't need to bring every book in existence was nearly impossible to complete in one afternoon. Luckily, we managed to get the bulk of our items loaded before nightfall.

I attempt to wipe the sleep from my eyes as I walk through Iron Brimstone's headquarters. A few workers point me in the right direction to the loading bay where I find Zyl crouched and digging through a large sack.

"Good to know someone is awake enough to drive," I joke, nudging his shoulder with my knee.

He glances up at me, "There you are. You know you could've left with me this morning."

"I know, but I had to make a stop by the post office," I say.

"Sending the good news to your sister?"

"I have no good news to send," I answer. "I did feel my parents and your mom should know I'll be gone for a while longer."

He pauses for a moment before shrugging with a nod, "I suppose that's true."

Tansae's head pops out from the trailer, "Alright, we are fueled up and checked out. Should be a smooth ride with this baby." Her hand slaps against the wood twice before she hops over the two small steps on the side of the wagon, landing in front of me.

"You got all the supplies I need?" I ask.

"Yup. Aurora gave me the last of it this morning. Would've been sooner if she wasn't so slow about it," she grumbles. I glance at Zyl who shrugs.

"Alright, well thank you."

"And don't worry, it won't be coming out of your pay. I intend to pay you fairly for your services," she says. I nod and she gestures toward the wagon for me to board. I hop up the steps and enter the trailer to set my bags down.

Despite being a large wooden box, the trailer is quite nice. There is a rug laid out on the floor to make it more comfortable with enough space for two people to lay down. Small curtains cover the window on the back door. It feels like a tiny home. Sadly, I doubt I'll be able to catch up on the last few hours of my new sleep schedule.

I take a seat and toss my bags atop my clothes trunk. Zyl climbs in and places his sack on the other side of the trailer with a thud.

"I thought I told you not to bring all those books," I scold playfully. He chuckles as he plays with the beads of his necklace.

"It's a twelve-hour trip to Whitburn and seven more to Kaelora, I need to be entertained," he defends.

I laugh softly, "Fair enough. How many did you pack?"

"Only one or two more than the amount you approved of. Plus, I got you this." He reaches into the sack, knocking a few objects around as he sifts through it. His hand emerges with a leather-bound book, my name etched in gold lettering on the front. My eyes widen as he hands it to me.

"Oh, Zyl. When did you make this?" I ask, opening it to find empty pages.

"I figured you could use it as a plant journal. You've learned about the regions and their contents, but seeing them in person is something new entirely. You could take notes or draw. If you draw. Do you draw? If you do, I'd love to see some of your work. If not, I'm sure you could figure it out. Maybe you could use it to practice or-" He cuts himself off as I stand and wrap my arms around him.

"Thank you, Zyl," I murmur.

He returns my embrace, "You're welcome."

"Touching," Tansae groans. I roll my eyes at her and return to my seat. "Are we ready to go now?"

Zyl looks over to her, excitement glimmering in his eyes, "You've been a wilting daisy all morning. Come on, aren't you excited? There's so much to explore and information to gather." She sighs at the ground before meeting his eyes again with a grin.

"I suppose this will be fun."

A third streak of ink stretches across the page of my notebook as we run over another bump in the road. Logically, I knew it would be hard to write in a moving vehicle, but geez. I tear the page out of my journal, shooting a glare at Tansae in the front seat.

"Hey, take it easy," I all but shout.

"Hey, I can't control every pebble we come across," she shouts back. Tossing it next to the other three pages I've torn out, I shut my journal deciding I'll write later. My eyes fall to Zyl who has had his nose buried in several books for the past few hours.

"Looking for something?" I question. His head remains tilted down, gaze never leaving the pages. He shuts his current book and picks up another one to leaf through. I clear my throat and he blinks, finally looking up at me.

"Oh, sorry, did you say something?" he asks with a sheepish grin.

"What are you doing?"

"I'm just making sure I didn't miss anything the first time I looked for information," he answers.

I lean back against my trunk, "You sure are diligent."

"Have to be in this line of work," he shrugs. I observe as his fingers gently run over the pages, eyebrows drawn together as he reads. His intense focus brings a slight wrinkle to the bridge of his nose. I place a hand over the page he's reading and he looks up at me.

"I admire your persistence, but it's been hours now. Take a break?" I offer.

He scans the books surrounding him before relenting with a sigh, "It would be nice." He closes the book in his lap and begins to pick up and stack the others.

"You know," I start. "You're different than she described you."

"She?"

"Your mom. Every time she received a letter from you she'd be happy for days. For a while, I assumed you were a little boy."

He shakes his head as he laughs, "She tends to embellish."

"Well, she seems awfully proud of you."

"She loves to brag about the little things. Everything is worth celebrating to her, but I'm mostly a homebody when I'm not at work."

"Yet you jumped at the chance to go across Vyelan," I point out.

"Can you blame me?" He leans back against his own trunk, tucking a few of his curls behind his ear. "This is a once-in-a-lifetime chance. To have a hand in something so meaningful is a dream come true for someone like me."

"A historian?" I question.

"A screw-up," he chuckles, sitting forward.

My eyebrows knit together and I tilt my head, "That seems harsh. I know you're clumsy but-"

"No," he sighs. "It's not just that. I haven't had the best track record for getting things right. I owe everything to my mom, especially after the things I've done."

"What do you mean?"

His hand lifts to run through his curls, tension gripping his shoulders, "When I was seven and my mom started the clinic, I was left home with my father most days. I wasn't his pride and joy, but he didn't seem to hate me. I drove him crazy, though. I've always been clumsy. Broke and spilled things. I hurt myself constantly. One day he couldn't take it anymore and he left."

My eyes widen, "Zyl, you can't possibly think it was your fault."

"He said so himself. At least, in the letter he left for my mom to find. I came across it years later while I was cleaning up. He told her he couldn't handle her screw-up of a child. That I wouldn't be worth much." He places his hand atop the stack of books beside him. "I've always wanted to prove him wrong, you know? But every time I tried something new I messed it up. So, now I just stick to what I know. Use what I have to help others who can do it better."

"But doesn't it get tiring? Being in the background all the time?" I ask.

He shakes his head, "Not at all. The past is...safe. Facts can't let you down. I study and I teach history because it's something I know I'll get right. Plus, the past goes on forever. There's always something new to find."

"Right and wrong isn't always factual, you know," I reply.

He shrugs, "I know. Sometimes what's right takes a risk, but I've never been at the forefront enough for *my* right and wrong to have any weight."

"And you like it that way?"

"Well, I don't have anyone's life in my hands like you do," he points out. "I may have the blood of a healer running through my veins, but there's a special kind of strength that you herbalists have. The ability to push through fear in a way I doubt I ever could."

"Not exactly," I say, shaking my head. "It's not so much pushing past the fear, but that others come first." He raises his eyebrows along with a smirk as understanding dawns on me. *Others come first.* He's not taking the coward's way out, just using knowledge to push others forward. The same thing Kofir did for Vyelan all that time ago. "I suppose without the past the future would be scarier, wouldn't it?" I laugh softly.

He nods, "Now you've got it."

"But you do know your father leaving wasn't your fault right?" I ask.

He laughs, "I'm not fourteen anymore."

"Hey, I'm just checking. Those kinds of things can get to a person," I huff, crossing my arms. His brown eyes sparkle as he pulls a book back into his lap. He seems to have it all figured out. The past can be helpful and I'm sure history is a solid thing to cling to, but the future is always unpredictable. Despite it all, he seems at peace and I'm sure he knows the only constant is change.

"I wish I could say I found my passion through love like you did, but either way, I found my place and I'm happy to be here," he grins.

"And you're good at it too," I add. "I could never sort through dusty old books all day."

He sits back, "Excuse you, but these dusty old books are what taught you about herbalism. I think you ought to show a bit more respect." He playfully sticks his nose in the air with a huff, forcing a laugh from me. The steam wagon comes to a stop and we both look towards Tansae as she enters the trailer.

"Why'd we stop?" I ask.

"I need a break," Tansae groans, stretching her arms in the air. "We're at a small village so I'm going to stretch my legs and find a snack."

"That sounds good."

"We'll come with you," Zyl adds, standing from his spot. I move to stand but the way my body shifts causes a sharp pain at my waistline. *Oh no.* I groan, feeling the sharp pain become a dull continuous one. I turn and open the trunk behind me, digging through it to find the bag of herbs we brought. *Shit.* I can't believe I forgot to bring it.

"I'll hang back here, actually," I say.

Tansae narrows her eyes at me, "What's wrong?"

"I started my period," I answer.

"Now?"

"Now." I feel another sharp pain and grab my stomach. Why didn't I check before we left to come on this trip? Oh right! I was too worried about the trip itself to think about when I would start my period. "Think you can grab me something to help with the pain?"

"I'm not too handy with herbs," Tansae admits.

"I can get it," Zyl chimes in. I open my journal and scribble what I need on the page before handing it to him.

"Twilight nox. Oh, and also some oranges if he can find some," I instruct.

He takes it with a nod, "Got it." I thank him as he leaves and Tansae follows behind him. Once I have my privacy, I grab my sanitary belt from my trunk and slip it on, the straps holding tightly onto my hips. Luckily, I had the mind to pack one. I clip a thick cloth to the center and adjust it, groaning through the pain. Why does putting this on require so much damn movement? Though mild right now, I know the pain will be getting worse.

I sort through my bag to see what I do have and find cinnamon and ginger root. Thank goodness. I take out my mortar and pestle, using them to grind the spices together until they form a thick paste. Using my finger, I place some on my tongue. The bitter flavor causes my face to twist. I pull some of my bedding out of my trunk and curl up in the corner. Hopefully, rest will postpone the full effects for now.

A half-hour later, Tansae returns with a small bag in hand. I slowly lift my head from under the blanket and give her a curious look when Zyl is nowhere to be found.

"Don't worry, he got the right stuff," she says, holding it towards me. I reach for the bag with another expression of gratitude. I wrap the blanket around me as I slide the mortar and pestle back by my side. Tansae sits across from me as I get to work, her eyes fixed on my movements. I remove a small jar from the bag, orange and purple petals resting on the glass bottom. Pulling out a few, I carefully place them in the mortar. I grind the twilight nox in with the cinnamon and ginger before adding a bit of orange juice and honey. I feel myself relax as my arm continues its repetitive motion.

"What are you making exactly?" she asks.

"It's an herbal remedy my mom taught me," I say, my gaze remaining on the task at hand.

"I don't think I asked, but is your mom an herbalist too?"

"No, but she is a mom of two, so she's gotta know how to patch a few scrapes. Plus, everyone in Westbrook knows the basics. This is my grandma's recipe."

"So you learned it from her?"

"No. I never knew my grandma, but my mom would tell us stories. Grandma was the worst cook, so she focused on other things like this. She actually made this mortar and pestle herself."

She hums, "Think you got your gift from her?"

"That's what Mom says," I laugh softly. "Along with her healing hugs and dazzling smile. Hearing Mom's stories made it feel as if I knew her for a thousand lifetimes. Whenever I make this remedy, somehow, I feel her with me."

The wagon rocks slightly as Zyl hops on board causing my ingredients to shift in the mortar. I give him a look and he smiles shyly, "Sorry, I'll be gentle."

"You know," I say, turning back to my work. "You never really told me about your mom. Is there anything you learned from her?" I can't see Tansae's expression, but I'm met with silence. I feel a pressure rise in my chest along with a pang of regret. Maybe it's too soon. "You don't have to-"

"It's fine," she interjects. I hear her suck in a breath, slowly releasing it between her teeth. "My mom is different from my father and I. She isn't a bad person, she's just...she doesn't understand."

"Doesn't understand what?" I ask. I grab a jar from the trunk and place a cheesecloth on the rim. Smoothing the paste onto the cloth, I pour water in and start to strain. The water runs through the paste, creating a smooth yellowish-orange liquid.

"My father was a businessman. He taught me everything I needed to know before he died, but my mom didn't get it. Business is tough. It's a cutthroat world out there and you need to be cutthroat in order to succeed. My mom is nice, but it's never gotten her anywhere."

"I'm sure she's taught you something. Right?" I finally look up to see her holding her dagger, gently flipping it in her palm. Stray hairs cover her face just enough so I can't fully gauge her expression.

"Basket weaving," she scoffs. "We had enough money where she didn't have to work, but she insisted on doing something. I don't blame her. She tried to teach me how to make them..." she trailed off.

"That sounds like fun," I say, cautiously.

Her eyes are trained on her dagger. The light reflects onto her face as she turns to the side, her jaw clenched. "Sewing and cooking I get. Those are life skills, but basket weaving? I mean, she even tried to teach me to crochet blankets and suggested I try collecting things like rocks," she laughs. Her tone drips with patronization as if it was the most ridiculous thing in the world. My brows knit in confusion. She doesn't seem to hate her mother, but there is a disdain. Almost jealousy, like when someone gets a larger slice of cake at a party. She slides the dagger back into her sheath, hand gripping the hilt, "It was a waste of time."

I am lucky to have a good relationship with my mother, it's something that not many people can say. I'm sure there are things I don't know about her and it's not exactly my business, but I can't help wondering why she feels this way.

"Did you ever learn to weave baskets?" Her features soften slightly and her eyes light up for a moment, but only a moment. Like a fragment of a positive memory entered her mind before it was snatched away again by something stronger. I notice the grip on her dagger loosen slightly before her hand falls to her side. She turns away, answering so softly I almost miss it.

"Yeah. I did."

The engine roars to life as Zyl settles in the front and the wagon begins to roll forward. I take a few sips of my remedy, relishing the sweet taste. Once done, I screw the lid onto the jar and place it snuggly between the clothes in my trunk before reaching for a medium-sized pouch. My dad insisted I take some money from him and, though I initially had no intention to use it, I'll admit it will come in handy. I reach inside to count the cost of the items, pausing when I find a piece of paper atop the coins. I pull out a note with a small chain wrapped around it. I untie the note and unfold it carefully. The handwriting is awful, but I soon recognize it as my dad's.

Dear Heriath,

I know you're worried about your journey, but I trust all will be well. You're a wonderful young woman with wit beyond my understanding. I trust that you can handle yourself and return to us safely. I hope this money can carry you as you travel. You'll find that I added a little something extra. This will keep you from getting lost when you wander into the forest. My dad taught me with it before he taught you. Keep it safe and it will guide you. You'll do wonderful things, starshine. We love you and will be here when you return to congratulate you on a job well done.

Your dad,
Cendil Balastina

Setting the note beside me, I carefully pull the chain out of the bag. The sunlight glistens off of the circular object attached to the end of it. I examine it, memories flooding to me as I realize what it is. I press the button on the front and it clicks open. A thin plate of glass covers a small, hand-painted star chart with a curved needle in the center that swings gently between the N and E. The small weight in my hand sends a smile across my face as I close the compass and turn it over. My fingers trail over the constellations engraved onto the back. Yamala showed me where those same constellations were in the sky. The grass was itchy against my back, but I was so absorbed in her teaching that soon enough, I didn't notice it anymore.

"What's this?" Tansae asks, scooting closer to me. My eyes lift to meet hers and I hold out the compass so she can see.

"I um…I got this from my father." The reflection of light off the compass creates a sparkle in her eye as she observes its details.

"Wow," she whispers. I hold it between us and click the button so it pops open. She stares down at the star chart inside, "Is this accurate?"

"I think so. My sister told me it is," I respond.

"She studies stars?"

I nod, "Charts them too. We used to camp on our back lawn when we were younger. She begged my dad to cut a hole in our tent so she could see them."

Tansae shivers at the thought, "Lying on the dirt for fun seems rather brave to me."

"Not a fan of the outdoors?" I laugh.

"Not unless there's a shower nearby," she answers. "I'm guessing you use this for foraging?"

"Yeah. My grandpa used this to teach me how to navigate before he passed. Especially after I showed an interest in herbalism." She hums softly, a gentle smile tugging at her lips. "What about yours? Your dagger, I mean."

"Oh, I got it from my father. Why?"

"Nothing. It's beautiful," I say softly.

The handle has a curved rain guard with a diamond on each end. The hilt is wrapped in dark leather with a golden 'M' carved into it. Hanging from it is a red string with green and gold beads. The kris blade is half black, half silver, and leads to a golden tip. It's a beautiful work of craftsmanship. Her fingers gently run under the blade as mine ran over my compass moments ago. "Yeah, it is. He wanted me to be safe. He always carried this thing with him and I never quite knew why. When he died, he left it to me."

"Both our fathers are paranoid, huh?" I joke as my eyes meet hers again.

"I guess so," she laughs softly. Gold flecks swim in a pool of green as her expression mirrors mine. A few moments of silence pass between us before she clears her throat, "I um...I should let you rest." She sheathes her dagger and moves to the front seat.

The silence holds something new. Memories of the past and emotions from the present. The fondness we both share for our family is contained within what we carry with us. Both items hold a promise of a future that contains risk and the unexpected. The warmth of the past burns into a flame of passion, no matter how similar or different our lives may be.

My thumb rubs over the constellations on the compass in my pocket.

Maybe we have more in common than I thought.

CHAPTER 10

After stopping in Whitburn for the night, we quickly grab breakfast and are up and moving again. As we ride, I look up from my journal to take in my surroundings. The trees grow taller and the flowers grow brighter in hue as we travel. The smell changes from earthy to sweet with the growing amount of aromatic plants around us. After seven hours, we reach Kaelora City.

It's a wondrous sight to behold. Similar to Mysticane in size but doesn't feel nearly as cold. Color runs the streets. Bright outfits and brighter jewelry glitter and shine in the midday sun. The noise from the busy streets consists of vendors, music, and idle chatter. The wagons that roll by are smaller and the buildings are less daunting, allowing me to more easily adjust to my surroundings. My nerves are a bit high, but I try my best to stay calm to avoid a repeat of what happened in Mysticane.

We come to a stop at an inn and work together to unload Zyl's belongings. He's decided to stay in the city to research while Tansae and I go ahead. His trunk thuds against the floor and I stand straight, arms reaching up to stretch my back. Tansae tosses his other bags on the bed in the center of the room.

"That's the last of it," she says, rolling her shoulders. "Think you can take over driving until we get to Elderheim?"

"Yeah, I got it," I respond. "I'll meet you down in a second." She nods and leaves the room as I turn to Zyl. "You sure you'll be okay?"

"For the hundredth time, Heriath, I'll be fine on my own. I'm a grown man," he laughs.

"I know, I just-"

"Hey," he cuts me off. He gently places a hand on my shoulder, "Don't worry about me and focus on the journey ahead, okay?"

A small smile spreads across my face, "Okay."

He returns my smile and envelops me in a hug, "Use my earmuffs if you need them."

"I will." I squeeze him in return before leaving the room with a wave. Tansae has the wagon fired up when I return and I plop on the driver's bench beside her.

"Ready?" I ask, grabbing the wheel.

She nods, "Let's go."

The Nafsi drifts away from us and takes a detour. For the past few hours we've been surrounded by forest, but the terrain is starting to change. Flowers turn to pebbles and trees turn to boulders. The green lush is soon replaced by orange and reddish stone walls that stretch far above us. The layering in the rock is magnificent. I've never seen anything like this before.

"Hey, Tansae, where are we?" I ask. She blinks wildly, coming too from what looked like a few minutes of zoning out.

She looks around, "Dammit."

"What?"

"We're in Vauxworth Canyon," she answers, leaning down quickly to fiddle with the engine.

"So this is the canyon. It's beautiful." I look down as pebbles run underneath the wagon. The array of shades of red, orange, and gray turn what would otherwise be dull rocks into a river of fire. The engine releases a puff of steam as Tansae pushes the lever forward.

"Why are we slowing down?" I ask. She shushes me with a finger to my face and I jerk back in surprise, fighting the urge to smack her hand away. She removes the dagger from her hip.

"What is wrong with-"

"This is bandit territory," she whispers. "We need to get through as quietly as possible."

She sits at the edge of the seat, dagger in a vice grip. Her eyes cast a wide net over her surroundings. She is vigilant and poised, a whole new side of her. I look around too, trying to keep an eye out for anything strange.

There are no obvious signs of people living here, at least not that I can see. They must live up at the top of the canyon. The sound of the rocks under the wheels of the wagon seems to grow louder as the ride drags on. My breaths grow shallow. I feel like I'm breathing too loud. I glance over at Tansae. How in the world is she so relaxed? It feels like an hour has passed by the time we exit the canyon and I can finally breathe.

A rustling sound from the bushes catches our attention and my muscles tense up again. Tansae's head snaps towards it as she unsheathes her dagger, standing quickly. I grab onto the seat, ready to run to the back of the wagon if necessary. Call me a coward, but I'm no fighter. In the corner of my eye, I see something charge towards us. I hold back a scream as Tansae jumps off. Her shoulders slump as it comes into view. A gray fox runs past the front of the wagon with a tiny one following behind. Tansae releases a huff as she slides her blade back into its sheath.

She hops back onto the wagon and quickly pulls the lever so that we are at full speed again. "Well, that's over. You alright?" she asks. I give her a *the fuck do you think* look that makes her laugh.

"I'm glad my mental exhaustion is amusing to you," I say flatly.

"Sorry, sorry," she says, calming her laughter. "You looked like you were gonna pass out."

"Wait, don't tell me you lied to freak me out," I say accusingly.

"Oh no, the canyon *is* bandit territory. It's just obvious you aren't used to tense situations."

"Hey, that's not true. I've dealt with plenty of tense situations," I say defensively.

She scoffs, "Yeah? Like what?"

"I work with medicine. You think I haven't dealt with a tense situation when everyone who walks in the clinic door has an illness or injury of some sort? Not to mention the dwindling amount of herbs and supplies we've been dealing with-"

"Okay, okay I get it. Sheesh," she interrupts. My jaw twitches as a bubble of irritation forms in my chest, rising to my throat before a swallow it down again. It's not wise to fight with a travel partner, but from the finger in my face to her cutting me off, I really want to come 'cross her forehead. Not to mention the dull pain at my waist thinning my patience. I take a strained deep breath and force my jaw to relax.

Only a few more hours.

We finally reached Elderheim and I gladly handed the reins over to Tansae for the last leg of the trip to Pine Valley. I lift my hand to shield my eyes from the bright rays of the setting sun. Once they adjust, I am met by the colorful array of flowers and plants dotting the field of the valley below us. The main road leads down a hill and into Pine Valley where the earthy tones of the village seamlessly tie in the nature around it. Resting left of the houses is a forest with tall grass and towering sugar pine trees. The Nafsi flows at the far right edge of the field which has a small pathway cut to access it. My exhaustion is nearly forgotten at the sight. It's breathtaking.

"Wow," I whisper in awe.

"You might want to sit unless you plan on rolling down this hill," Tansae says playfully. I realize I'm standing and take a seat, my eyes fixed on the picturesque view in front of me. I wonder how many plants I use are natural to this area. Our shipments come from all over Vyelan since each herb has its native areas, but there are so many colors in that field. I feel an itch to explore, to caress every soft petal and examine each leaf with care. To have pure herbs in their truest form is a dream come true. I wonder how the field would look if Elysir was still growing here. I imagine the blue would draw out the purple of the twilight nox, complementing the abundance of reds, yellows, pinks, and oranges.

The tall trees look down at us with watchful eyes, energy like a protective embrace. Nature has spoken to me from a young age, but this feels different. Special. My feet touch the soil once we find the inn and I stretch. Finally, after days of travel, we've made it and with a bit of sunlight left.

I clap my hands together, "Alright, let's get started."

"The sun is setting, Heriath. I think we should turn in for the night," Tansae suggests. "We've already been driving all day."

"But we're so close, I can feel it," I exclaim, a burst of energy rushing through me.

"I understand that, but we can't search at night."

I huff as she slings her bag over her shoulder. It's reasonable I suppose. "Fine, we'll search in the morning."

Tansae showers first and flops onto one of the beds in our shared room. I bathe and clean my blood cloths, replacing the one I have on before settling into bed.

I toss, I turn, I stare at the clock, and, finally, I give up. Sitting up in bed, I rub my eyes with a sigh. I guess sleeping through half the day doesn't bode well for your sleep schedule. I look over at Tansae who is splayed out on the other bed snoring softly. I approach her and carefully shimmy the blanket from under her, unfolding it to place over her figure. I silently approach the window of our room. The ground floor view showcases the field of flowers. Even at night, the colors remain vibrant. The window frames the sight, turning the small room into a gallery exhibit. I glance back at Tansae for a moment. Well, I'm not getting to sleep anytime soon.

I quietly pull on a jacket and boots, grabbing my journal and a small knife from my bag in case I'm not alone out there. I leave a short note for Tansae and slip out the door.

Cool air welcomes me with a brush against my cheek as I exit the inn. The crunch of gravel under my boots provides ambient noise that keeps the silence from overwhelming me. Fireflies illuminate the path as they bounce from flower to flower, allowing the vibrant hues to shine in the darkness. Despite my curiosity, I refrain from entering the field for fear of disrespecting such a beautiful place. It feels almost sacred. The way the sun blesses each leaf with life and the moon allows its beauty to be appreciated through the night. I opt to study the plants that grow near the path. twilight nox, a few estrosse, and a red one I don't quite recognize in the darkness. I can get a better look at that one in the morning.

I reach the end of the pathway and stand at the bank of the river. I place my bag on the ground, removing my boots so my feet can rest in the water. The coolness shocks me at first, but I soon grow accustomed to the low temperature and allow my legs to relax. The breeze that blows by is warm in comparison to the water.

My palms meet the gravel and I lean back, allowing my arms to hold my weight. The moonlight caresses my face as I take in the night sky. If I remember what Yamala taught me, the moon is in its waxing gibbous phase. Man, the way it took her weeks to teach me waxing versus waning. Those nights camping on our back lawn were some of the best nights with her. My eyes grow misty as I remember us dancing together at her wedding, the silver hair clips and embellishments glittering as bright as her smile. That magical night under the stars she loved to teach me about. The same stars I sit under every evening. When she left home to start her life in Kaelora City, she left me with knowledge of the murky blue above me so we'd always be connected. I wipe my eyes, feeling the tears begin to fall.

I've ventured to the far end of Vyelan and somehow, the feeling of the river against my skin takes me back home. My eyes fall to the water as a few leaves flow past my feet. I follow them until they escape my view. Leaning forward, I rest one arm on my knee while the other reaches out. My fingertips dip into the water and the liquid rushing through my fingers brings a smile to my face.

There is reassurance in the Nafsi. It connects us all. Every city, every life.

As long as I can see it, I know I'm okay.

As long as I can feel the coolness against my hand, the memories it holds will come back to me.

As long as it flows, I know the current leads home.

CHAPTER II

I groan, pulling the covers over my head as my brain registers the light pouring in through the window. The door to our room slams shut and my eyes shoot open. I sit up, ripping the covers off me to see Tansae whirling around the room. My shoulders relax as I wipe the sleep from my eyes.

"Where's the fire?" I ask, my voice thick with exhaustion. She continues digging through her things, not responding. "Um, hello," I say, waving my hands. "Wanna tell me what the rush is? Do I need to be running?" She finally pauses when she pulls out a sheet of paper from her bag, reading it over. I flop back onto my pillow and pull the covers over my head with a sigh. I get a few seconds of peace before the covers are ripped off again. "Hey-"

"I found it," Tansae says.

"Found what?" I ask, not bothering to hide my annoyance.

"The first soulmate," she says excitedly. "I walked around this morning and I think I found the violet willow."

"Violet meadow," I correct her. I slide off the bed and make my way to the bathroom to brush my teeth. Her boots thud against the ground as she follows me.

"Whatever. It's at an old house at the far end of the valley," she chirps. I hum in response, spitting my toothpaste into the basin.

"That's great. It's kinda early though, how long have you been out?"

"Early? You're kidding, Heriath, it's noon. I've been up since eight." My head shoots up and I turn to her with wide eyes. Noon? I know I stayed up late, but did I really sleep till noon? She dismisses my shock with a wave of her hand, "No worries. We still have plenty of hours in the day and this time we can walk to our destination."

I quickly finish up and get ready for the day, slipping on a long skirt and top. The warmer upstream weather embraces me as we make our way to the far end of the valley. Tansae details her morning adventures while we walk, words crashing into each other. The mention of cofenia seed explains the rush of energy that puts a bounce in her step. I focus on finding the violet meadow when the houses become more sparse. A spot of purple catches my eye from a front porch and I raise a hand to cut off her rapid complaints about the stall owner who sold her a disgusting breakfast.

"Is that the house?" I ask.

"Huh? Oh, yeah. That sign wasn't there before though." We step closer and I crouch to observe the beautiful three-headed bloom that grows from between the cracks in the wood. "Out for work, signed Endel," Tansae says. I stand and meet her side to read the sign that hangs on the door. I point to the logo underneath the short message.

"We just passed this place on the way here," I mention.

She groans, throwing her head back, "Oh come on." I laugh softly and hop off the porch, her following two steps behind as we return to the front end of the valley. We soon stand in front of a small shop with a hand-carved wooden sign hanging from the doorframe.

'The Whistling Wind Chime'

It's a small place, no larger than a typical wooden shed, and riddled with trinkets. Tiny wooden statues, silver and bronze wire figures, wrapped stones, necklaces, earrings, and so on. I duck under a few lanterns as I step inside, the windows of them made with thin plates of colorful glass. I'm careful to not bump into the two customers who are perusing the jewelry boxes and hairpins. Light floods in through the windows and I find myself staring at the many wind chimes that hang from the higher part of the ceiling.

Tansae approaches the counter at the back of the shed and peaks around it for any workers. I spot a sign on the desk that sits below a smaller wind chime with pipes lined up in a row. *Ring for service.* I carefully swipe a finger across the pipes, the light tinkling sound bringing a smile to my face.

"One second," someone shouts from behind a door on the other side of the counter labeled *'Office'*. The door is pulled open to reveal a tall individual about our age.

They are dressed in colorful clothing typical for upstream folk, but their style is unique. Their asymmetrical shirt pairs nicely with their loose flowy pants. Crystal bracelets encircle their wrists along with three distinct ones that are handwoven. The most interesting part of their appearance, however, is their hair. Locs brush against their umber skin. Some are twisted in pairs and others woven into braids, but all are decorated with various hair pins, shells, and beads.

"Good morning ladies," they greet us with a playful bow. "Looking for something special?"

"Indeed we are," Tansae replies.

"Well, you've come to the right place. I've got about everything you can imagine here, all made by yours truly," they grin, gesturing to the room behind us. "Though I doubt I have anything as beautiful as the two of you."

I hum with a smirk, "Bit of a flirt, aren't you?"

"Maybe so, but I'm not a liar," they answer. Their eyes meet mine and their smile falls slightly as they study my face. A moment passes and I can feel heat creeping into my cheeks.

"What?" I ask.

They blink, "Sorry, I- Have we met before?"

"I don't think so," I shrug. "I would say I have one of those faces, but it's kind of hard to miss this," I laugh awkwardly as run my fingers over the birthmark on my left cheek.

They chuckle, "I guess it would be." They step from behind the counter as they clear their throat, "Anyways, what can I help you with? Looking for jewelry, knick-knacks, something to hold 'em?"

"Actually, we're looking for a person," Tansae chimes in. "Does anyone here go by the name Endel?"

They groan, a hand raising to pinch the bridge of their nose, "For your information, my sales registration is in order and I'm tired of being hounded about it."

"We weren't sent by anyone," she reassures them. "Could we maybe talk somewhere private?"

Their eyes narrow at her, "Why can't we talk here?"

"It will sound a bit crazy."

"Well, you aren't off to a great start," they laugh awkwardly. Their eyes glance behind us as another customer walks in. "Look, I have a shop to run here so could you make it quick?" Tansae opens her mouth to speak, pausing when I place a hand on her shoulder.

"Do you understand the Nafsi's current condition?" I ask. They nod in response. "Okay, I'll cut to the chase, but only if you promise to hear us out when you have time."

Their hands slip into the pockets of their pants, "Alright."

"We have reason to believe you can help fix it."

"And why is that?" they question, eyes alight with amusement.

"Because, if we're right, you're one of the reincarnated soulmates." I brace myself for laughter, for them to shoo us away, but instead, they remain silent. Their expression falls flat as they study us, searching for something in my eyes before shifting to Tansae. They don't seem to find what they're looking for before the customer calls them for help.

"Could you two please wait in my office?" they ask. I glance over to Tansae who nods firmly.

"Sure," I answer. We head to their office and take a seat as they finish out front. They return just as I'm trying to get Tansae to sit in any chair other than the main one behind the desk. Endel glances at her curiously and takes a seat in a wooden chair that matches my own.

It takes a while to fully explain the way we got to Pine Valley and by the end Endel's expression is hard to read.

"This is um...unprecedented," they state plainly. They sit back in their seat as they absorb the information. Multiple emotions pass through their eyes, ones I'm all too familiar with. Confusion, fear, and bewilderment to name a few. "So, lemme get this straight. You've traveled all the way here from Mysticane City to tell me that I am one of the reincarnations of the mystic and his wife?"

Tansae nods and I shrug, "Pretty much."

"So who's the other one? Will I get to meet them?"

"We don't know yet," Tansae says.

"Our friend is working on it in Kaelora City right now," I add. The silence thickens as they continue to process. I play with the fabric of my shirt, "You know, I wouldn't blame you if you didn't believe us right away. It's a lot to think about, so if you need time-"

"No, I believe you," they interject.

Tansae sits forward, dropping the pen she was twirling between her fingers, "You do?"

"I do," they respond, looking up at me. I've managed to get a good read on them up until now, but this look is something I can't place. The intensity of it forces my eyes to the ground. They sit forward, elbows on their knees. "I need a bit to think about this though. Are y'all on a strict timetable or," they trail off.

"Sometime within the next five years is ideal," I joke, bringing a faint smile to their face.

"Three days tops," they respond, standing. "In the meantime, I'd like to get to know you guys. Why don't you come over for dinner?"

"That sounds nice," Tansae replies.

"Are you sure?" I ask.

"Of course. My momma loves visitors so I'll give her a heads up," they grin. Endel approaches the desk and lifts a pen to scrawl something on the nearest sheet of parchment. The pen hits the desk with a clack as they fold the page and extend it to Tansae.

She takes it with a smirk, "Sweet, free food."

"I think she means thank you," I say, rolling my eyes. Endel laughs softly and guides us to the front door, waving us goodbye.

"That was easy," Tansae says as she hands the paper to me. I open it to find an address and a small note reading *See you at 7.* I hum in response. There was something behind their eyes. A question? A memory? Was it hopeful belief? Anyone would be honored to know they possess the soul of the man who is renowned throughout Vyelan.

I shake away the thought as we approach the inn.

Just focus on the next step forward.

CHAPTER 12

HERIATH'S POV

"Are you sure we're in the right place?" Tansae whispers as I knock on the red wood of the Valurae's.

"Yes, I'm sure," I answer. I'm surprised we even made it on time. She nearly tore apart the room getting ready. Each outfit she tried on was more presentable than the last and yet she would rip it off despite my approval. This is after asking for my thoughts and then dismissing them with the statement that I had no sense of style. Personally, I think my simple dress is fitting for dinner at a stranger's house. I may not have the brightly colored clothing she owns, but I'm put together. I guess you can take the girl out of the city, but you can't take the city out of the girl.

I reach up to fiddle with my two ponytails, but Tansae smacks my hand.

"Hey, what was that for?" I ask, cradling my hand with a pout.

"You redid your hair about a hundred times before we left. You look fine," she says matter-of-factly.

I shake my hand, letting it fall back to my side as the door opens to reveal a little girl. Her wide eyes stare up at us for a moment before she closes the door. I hear her yell something before it's opened again by a grown woman. A bright smile illuminates her face as she pulls the door all the way back.

"You must be the company we're expecting. You're right on time, come on in," she greets, moving so we can enter. The house is very open with most of the entrance being the kitchen with the exception of a dining table. There are carvings in the wood all around the place. Table legs, chair frames, cabinets, and the stairs even had a branch banister for a more abstract look.

"You have a wonderful home," I compliment.

"Thank you," the woman says over her shoulder while she faces the stove. "Endel does most of the carvings around here. Took months to convince Xilleria to allow him to add his creative touch to the house. Make yourself comfortable." Tansae and I take seats at the table.

"So, Endel is your son?" I ask, trying to create some small talk.

"Today he is," she says cheerfully. Her voice adds to her bubbly attitude as she bounces around the kitchen. Her beaded braids clack and sway with her movements. "Oh, I never introduced myself, did I?"

I shake my head, "No ma'am."

"Oh, no need for formalities. Just call me Lytea," she says with a playful curtsey. She pulls out her apron to mimic a dress, adding to the drama of her pose. I giggle and return her bow with one of my own, "I'm Heriath and this is Tansae."

"A pleasure," Lytea says, wiping her hands on a towel. The side door opens with a slight creak and Lytea launches the towel in its direction. It lands in a clenched fist with a small whump.

"Whoa there, I come in peace," the woman jokes as she enters the room. She lifts a pair of goggles from her eyes to her forehead before wiping her face with a rag. She pulls off her green apron and hangs it on a rack by the door. Placing the kitchen towel on the island, she pulls Lytea into a hug from behind. "What if it was Winnie instead of me, huh?"

"Oh please, you're always two steps behind her. Besides, your reflexes are fast enough to catch it. Now can I have my arms back? You don't want a burnt dinner do you?" Lytea responds. The woman gives her one more squeeze causing Lytea to giggle before letting her go. "Our guests are here," Lytea gestures to us. The woman turns to us with wide eyes and a hint of embarrassment.

"Oh, I didn't realize," she says, clearing her throat. "Hi, I'm Xilleria."

"Drop the tough girl act, sweetheart," Lytea teases with a poke.

Xilleria rolls her eyes and leans over to kiss Lytea on the cheek before moving towards the stairs, "I'm gonna shower so I don't smell like outside. That order took the last of my energy."

Pots clang as Lytea pours the contents of one into another before mixing it with her wooden spoon. A soft hum comes from her throat as she focuses on the food. She reaches into a cabinet to pull out a tiny spice jar, carefully sprinkling some of it into the pot. Her movements are rehearsed and fluid. "Do you enjoy cooking?" Tansae asks.

Lytea nods, "I love it. In fact, I run the kitchen in the tavern right down the road." She stirs the pot's contents again and starts to fill our bowls. "Baby, food's ready!" she calls up the stairs.

Lytea sets our food in front of us, the aroma of it mouth-watering. The sound of footsteps catches my attention as a small girl runs toward the table. Lytea scoops her up in her arms, "Careful there, speed demon." This must be Wynira. Lytea sits her at the table before going to grab a few more chairs and the rest of the bowls.

"I love your hair," I say to the little girl. She shakes her twists to make her beads clack against each other, causing me to laugh.

"What do you say, Winnie?" Xilleria prompts.

"Thank you!" the young girl pipes. I can't help the huge grin on my face.

"Endel," Lytea calls up the stairs. "Boy, you gon' miss dinner. Ima feed it to the dogs."

"Momma, we don't have dogs," he laughs, light footsteps echoing down the stairs. He plops into a chair as Lytea places a bowl in front of him. "This looks great, momma. What is it?"

"Something new I'm trying out. It's a roasted mushroom and codfish stew that I want to add to the menu at the tavern," Lytea explains. "Oh, sorry I didn't ask if you all had any dietary restrictions. I hope this is alright."

"Oh no, it's fine," I try to ease her worries.

"It smells amazing," Tansae adds eagerly.

Lytea wipes her brow with an exaggerated sigh of relief, "Phew! Well, I hope you enjoy it." The table was quiet as we ate with the occasional moan of satisfaction and compliment towards Lytea who accepted with her signature giggle.

After a few moments, they begin to talk about their day and Xilleria joins us. She asks Lytea about work and listens intently to her complaints about the old men who find time to hit on her even when she's in the kitchen. Endel watches Wynira, wiping the drips of broth from her chin only to be fussed at that she can do it herself. I smile at the scene as I place the last spoonful in my mouth. I didn't realize I had finished already. I glance over at Tansae. Her bowl is empty, but she idly scrapes at the bottom with a sullen expression.

"You alright?" I ask.

She jumps a bit as I tap her but quickly recovers, "Yeah. I'm fine."

Her eyes fall back to her empty bowl. "I've never sat at a dining table this small. I'm just a bit cramped is all." I nod, accepting her answer. I'm not sure that prodding for a more honest one will end well right now.

"How's the food?" Lytea asks, eyes meeting mine.

"It's great," I respond with a smile.

"Sure is. My honey is the best chef this end of the Nafsi," Xilleria brags, throwing an arm over Lytea's shoulders. Lytea brushes her off, the tips of her ears turning red under her light brown skin as she turns back to her food.

The conversation takes a turn as Endel explains what occurred in his shop a few hours ago. His parents, of course, have a thousand questions which we try our best to answer. Lytea listens intently while Xilleria's expression is harder to read.

"Wait, slow down," Xilleria interjects, turning to Endel. "I know this sounds good and all, but you can't just be on board right away?"

"I don't know, honey. This is a great opportunity for him," Lytea adds. "Besides, he doesn't get out that often anymore since Winnie came along."

"Hey, I get out," Endel defends.

"Since when?"

"Well, I went to Elderheim a few weeks ago."

"You went with your grandpa for a day and he told us you basically did nothing there," Lytea smirks. "Come on, this could be fun. See some things, make some friends, and if these two women are right you'll find your soulmate." Endel's eyes fall to the floor, his head bowing to hide his face. "Aww, you're blushing," Lytea teases, pulling the tip of his left ear.

He swats her hand away, "Stop it."

"Come on, lovebird. I've seen the stories you write," Lytea continues.

"Hey, those are private," he stresses with a worried glance at us. Lytea laughs and looks up at Xilleria who is still mulling over the presented case. She takes her bottom lip between her teeth and her hand raises to pinch the bridge of her nose.

"Okay, I need the travel plan and some time to think this over," she says.

"It should be fine. Our journey here was safe enough. You're making a bigger deal out of it than Heriath did," Tansae jokes.

"Well, forgive me if I'm a bit indecisive about two strangers taking my child to the far end of Vyelan," Xilleria snaps, causing Tansae to flinch. Lytea places a hand on her wife's shoulder and she takes a breath. Endel stands and the chair scrapes against the floor catching our attention. He goes around the table picking up each of our empty bowls. We watch in silence as he places them in the sink before turning to face us.

"Mom, Momma, I'm not a child anymore," he says calmly. He returns and sits a hand on each of their shoulders, "I know I'll always be your baby, but I have my own life now. I chose to stay here because I love being with my family. In the end, it's my decision to make whether I want to go or not. I understand your concern, but I can handle myself. I promise." He gives them a soft smile which allows Xilleria to fully relax.

"You're right. I'm sorry. You know I worry."

"You wouldn't be my Mom if you didn't," he says, giving her a hug. His lips meet her cheek and she pats his back.

We spend the rest of the night together discussing the details of the trip. Tansae hovers around Endel while I remain at the table. Lytea is all smiles while Xilleria is enigmatic. Her tone never wavers from serious unless she is addressing Lytea. It's adorable the way she's so sweet with her wife, but her frigid demeanor toward me makes it hard to stay focused.

Eventually, Winnie becomes restless at the table and Xilleria takes her to get ready for bed. She gives Lytea a kiss before scooping Winnie in her arms. The girl laughs as her mom tosses her in the air playfully. I feel a hand over mine and turn back to Lytea.

"I know that my wife may seem a bit cold, but she's listening," she reassures me.

"I know it's a big ask, but this is a chance to help everyone," I sigh. "I know what it's like to be worried about a family member. When my big sister moved out I was worried about everything. Every 'what if' loomed over my head like a thundercloud."

"Well, he is twenty-one now and has proven he can handle himself," she grins, looking over at the sink where he stands. "Though it doesn't stop a mother's love."

"I understand."

"It's getting late," Tansae says. "We should head back to the inn." I glance out the window of the side door to see moonlight dusting the top of the shed out back.

"I suppose so," I agree as I stand.

"Already?" Lytea whines. "We were just getting to know each other. I know, why don't you come back tomorrow for breakfast? Endel makes a mean pancake." I look over to Tansae who shrugs.

"Sure," I accept.

"Great," she says. "See you then. I'm gonna head to bed."

"I'm gonna walk them back," Endel offers.

"You don't have to, we know our way," I reassure. He approaches and I take a step back as he reaches past my right ear. My muscles tense a bit as I take in his height. I'm already pretty tall standing at five foot ten, but he's still looking down at me. He pulls back with a jacket in hand that I come to realize was on the coat rack behind me.

"I know, but my parents raised me to be a gentleman. Well, on the days that I am one," he says, slipping the jacket on. "Let's go."

We wave goodbye to Lytea as we leave the house. I breathe in the cool air, my arms lifting as I stretch and a yawn slips through my lips. "Looks like we'll be getting back right on time," Endel laughs.

"Ha ha," I respond dryly, a small smile present.

"I didn't really get the chance to talk to you tonight."

"Tansae kinda stole you away," I remark, gesturing towards her figure that's a good ten feet ahead of us. "I did enjoy talking to your parents. They seem to balance each other out well."

He nods, "They love each other to death. I've always hoped to have a love like that someday."

"Speaking of love, what were the stories that Lytea mentioned?" I ask with a smirk.

He lets out an awkward laugh as his hand moves up to the back of his neck, "Ah, nothin'."

"Oh come on, it can't be nothing. Spill," I prod playfully.

"Nope. No way," he retorts.

I roll my eyes, "Fine." We reach the inn and Tansae slips inside leaving Endel and I alone.

"Are you sure we haven't met before?" he asks.

"Positive. I would remember someone with your sense of style," I grin, gesturing to his attire. "Why?"

A moment passes, "Nothing, it's just...your eyes." The last part leaves his lips in a soft whisper. I find it hard to hold his gaze and choose to stare at the ground. His feet shift as he adjusts his stance, "I'm sorry, I didn't mean to make you uncomfortable."

"Oh no, it's okay. I'm just a little tired," I laugh awkwardly.

He gives me a gentle smile and steps forward to pull open the door to the inn, "Well, I'll let you get some sleep."

I step inside, my hands gripping my upper arms as he bids me goodnight. As I reach our room, I find Tansae passed out already. I guess running around all morning hits you later in the day. I take a seat on my bed and stare out at the field I'd roamed the night before, those two words echoing in my mind.

Your eyes.

CHAPTER 13

"Day drinking? Spunky," Endel remarks as he opens the door.

I look down at the small jar in my hand and roll my eyes, "It's an herbal remedy." I step inside and he closes the door behind me.

"Hey, I'm not judging. Just tell me how you like your eggs with your beer," he jokes. I laugh as I sit at the table. "Where's your friend?"

"Couldn't get her up. She'll be around," I explain, taking another sip from the jar. I had to make another batch this morning since my cramps are back. Not nearly as bad as the first day, but the ideal amount is none. "So, where is everyone?"

He grabs a spatula, flipping a pancake before turning to me, "Mom is asleep. Since she finished the order for that table she's been knocked out for a while. Momma is probably getting ready to come down now. She's working the dinner shift, but likes to keep a steady sleep schedule." He looks at the small clock on the counter by the stove. "Actually, if I'm correct, she should be down in-"

"Good Morning!" a cheery voice enters the room. Lytea descends the stairs in a blue robe that fits beautifully around her large figure. The front of her braids are tied up neatly into a bun while the back flows down over her shoulders. I give her a small wave, "Good Morning, Lytea."

"Here already? You're an early riser."

"Comes with the job," I remark with a tip of my jar. I tilt it back to my lips, taking the last swig of it before setting it on the table with a clack. "Oh, I bought these for you and Xilleria." I reach into my bag and pull out a small assortment of flowers wrapped neatly into a decorative bundle.

Lytea lets out a gasp as they come into view, "Oh, you didn't have to do that."

"I know, but it's the least I could do with you allowing me into your home. Plus, it was nice to meet some of the other herbalists who live here. I hope you like them." She awes at the flowers as I hand them to her.

"Thank you, Heriath. They're stunning."

Endel sets a plate of pancakes and eggs in front of me. A few berries are cut and arranged nicely and a sprig of oregano sits atop the eggs. A fork, napkin, and bottle of syrup are set down by his other hand.

"This looks delicious," I compliment. "Thank you."

"No problem. I make this most mornings," he says, grabbing two more plates. He sets them down on the table before going back to pack the rest of the food into a small container. Lytea sits next to me and digs in with a joyful moan. Endel joins us and laughs, "Enjoying the food, Momma?" She nods eagerly, swallowing her mouthful. I begin eating and let out a hum of satisfaction at the flavors. Simple yet wonderful, but nowhere near Yamala's.

"So," Lytea says between bites. "Do we have a wonderful son, a wonderful daughter, or just an amazing child today?" I look to Endel curiously.

He looks down at his wrist, "Oh, I forgot to put them on. Um, I'm not sure yet. I've kinda been focused on getting breakfast ready, especially since we have guests."

"So, what's the move?"

"I guess, child."

"Excuse me?" she says placing a finger behind her ear. She tilts her head dramatically, waiting for a response.

Endel shakes his head as he lets out a light laugh, "An *amazing* child."

"Great," she says, standing from the table. She moves to give him a kiss on the cheek, thanking him for breakfast again. Putting her plate in the sink, she hums a tune as she goes back upstairs.

"If it's okay to ask, what exactly did she mean by that?" I ask.

"Oh," he says, taking his last bite of food. "That question is Momma's silly way of asking my pronouns. I'm- well, it's easier if I show you." I take my last bite of food and stand, following him to the sink. We put our plates down and he leads me upstairs to his bedroom door. He steps inside and returns with three bracelets in hand. He slides a green bracelet on his wrist, followed by a gold one and a blue one.

"I'm genderfluid and these bracelets indicate what gender I'm feeling for the day. It helps my family know which pronouns to use," he explains. He adjusts them so the gold bracelet sits closest to his hand and holds out his wrist so I can get a better look.

"Macrame?" I ask.

"Yup, you macrame?"

"Oh no, I just remember seeing it in your shop. Did you make these yourself?"

"My family made these for me actually," he laughs. "It was hilarious.

I tried so hard to be encouraging, but it took an hour just to get Mom to understand the pattern. Her stubbornness is probably the only reason she finished it at all.”

“Which one did she make?” I ask.

“The blue one. I helped Winnie make the green one and Momma made the gold.” The strings used to make them have glitter woven in giving them a subtle shimmer. The adjustable ends have beads that match the color of the thread.

“They’re so cute. Which one represents which gender?”

“The blue is for man, green for woman, and gold for neither or both,” he states proudly. “The bracelet closest to my hand are the pronouns for the day.”

“Cool,” I nod, letting go of Endel’s hand. “So today is gold which means neither?”

“Yup, they/them pronouns for the day. If you ever aren’t sure, just take a peek at my wrist. Well, if I remember to wear them,” they say with an awkward laugh.

“Got it. Thank you for telling me and these bracelets are awesome. It’s sweet that your family is so close,” I remark, meeting their eyes. They snap their fingers as a light bulb goes off in their head.

“Speaking of family, I need to make lunch and bring it to Grandpa. You want to join me?”

“Of course.” We head back downstairs and Endel gets to work pulling ingredients from the fridge. I stand near the sink and twist the faucet handle causing them to give me a curious look.

“What? You made breakfast, I can help you clean up before you cook again,” I defend. They hum with a shrug and I go back to focusing on the plates in front of me.

A few minutes later, Xilleria comes downstairs wiping her eyes. We both bid her good morning as she steps into the kitchen. Endel points her to the container with her portion of breakfast while I hand her a clean plate.

"Endel, why do you have our guest washing dishes?" she asks, voice hoarse from sleep.

"Would you turn down an offer to have dishes washed while you cook?" they ask before I can respond. Xilleria looks between us before taking the plate from my hands with a shrug.

"As long as she's sure." I nod, reassuring her that I'm fine. The repetitive task isn't super annoying, and it feels nice to help. Endel finishes up lunch as Xilleria finishes her breakfast, and Endel joins me at the sink to wash the new dirty dishes. I steal a few glances at them as we work.

Their locs pulled back in a low ponytail expose their array of piercings from their lobe to the helix. The tiny stones add color to their face. One short loc hangs free from the ponytail and swings near their face as they scrub the pan. It has a gray color that stands apart from the rest of their hair. I catch myself staring and tear my eyes away, looking back to the sudsy water.

"Hello? Earth to Heriath," they wave. I snap out of my thoughts and force a smile as I grab the pan from them to rinse. "You alright?"

"Yeah, sorry I was just distracted," I choke.

"Well, that's the last of it. You ready to go?" they ask, drying their hands on a towel. I nod as they tie the bag with the food in it and carefully adjust it in their grip. I squint as I step outside and shield my eyes from the sun. Endel leads the way to Mr. Valurae's house with a cheerful pep in their step.

"Do you make lunch for your grandpa often," I question, meeting their pace.

"Yeah, I try to when I get free time. I'm nowhere near as good as Momma, but I'm getting better," they respond. They reach behind their head to pull their hair tie, freeing the remainder of their locs. Their hair falls behind their shoulders as they shake their head. "Do you mind if I ask a question?"

"Go ahead," I permit. They look over at me, twisting their lips as if trying to find the right words.

"I don't want to sound rude, I promise. I was just wondering about your skin?" they ask carefully. I raise my hand to touch the white space on the left side of my face.

"Oh, this? My mom threw a pot of acid on my face as a child," I deadpan. Their jaw drops, eyes bulging out of their head.

"I'm so sorry. I didn't mean to- I mean-"

I burst into laughter as they stutter, trying to find a response. Their embarrassment changes to confusion. I look up to see them staring at me with a playful glare.

"You're playing, aren't you?" they ask flatly as we stop. I bend forward, holding up a finger while I catch my breath. "Yeah, you're playing."

I take a deep breath as I stand up straight, noticing they've turned to walk off without me. "I'm sorry, I'm sorry," I laugh as I catch up. "That look on your face was priceless." A hint of a smile reaches their face as they shake their head.

"So, are you going to tell me the truth?"

"It's a birthmark," I admit.

"Oh, so you were born with it? Lucky."

"Why do you say that?"

"You didn't need some traumatic battle or backstory to have a cool mark."

"That's true. What about yours?"

"My what?"

"Your hair? I noticed you have one gray loc, is that a birthmark?"

"Either you're very observant or you've been staring at me," they accuse playfully. They lean their face close to mine with a smirk. I roll my eyes, pushing their face away with a finger to their forehead.

"Don't get fresh. It was the only one hanging loose from your ponytail," I retort. They let out a small laugh, pulling the loc in front of their face. It's about half the length of the rest of them.

"It tends to do that. Actually, this one isn't mine."

"What do you mean?"

"When my grandma locked her hair, I suggested we each switch one since we are the only ones in our family with our hair like this. I showed her how to do it and I've had it ever since. She passed about two years ago." They smile as they gaze lovingly at the gray hairs entwined with their black ones.

"I'm sorry for your loss."

They release the hair, allowing it to fall back near their face, "It's alright. It hurt like a bitch, but I have a piece of her with me. Plus, I still get to visit her in the forest."

"The pine forest? Is that where you bury your dead?"

"Oh right, you're a tourist. We can go there after I drop off lunch to Grandpa and I'll show you," they offer. I agree as we reach Mr. Valurae's front porch. "Here we are." They knock on the door and a moment later it swings open to reveal an older man. He has the same brown eyes as Endel but lacks the hair. His grin sparkles as he greets us.

"Ah, there's my favorite," he trails off, waiting for a response.

"Grandchild today, and don't play for appearances. We both know Winnie is your favorite," Endel jokes as we step inside.

"Hey, I love you both the same."

"Then how come I don't get candy whenever I come over?" they question. Their eyebrow raises along with a knowing smirk.

"Chile, you're grown. You don't need candy."

"Says the grown man with a stash in his kitchen cabinet."

"If you know where it is, then you can get some yourself. Now, did you come over for a reason or to give an old man a hard time?" Mr. Valurae asks as he sits at the dining table. Endel rolls their eyes playfully as they sit down the bag in front of him. He opens it, peering into the container with a smile. The old man is quite the chatterbox and keeps us entertained between bites. His liveliness is infectious and we stay for another hour or so just talking about any and every thing.

Eventually, we say our goodbyes and make our way back to Endel's house where we find Tansae discussing the possibility of Endel joining us with their parents. Apparently, she'd been there for a while and loved the breakfast Endel made, complimenting their skills. Xilleria has shown her how to carve wood and Tansae shows us her progress on a small figure she's making. She insists it's a dog, but it looks like a misshapen cow to me. We socialize for a while until Endel tells me we need to get going to the forest if we want to make it before nightfall. They pack a few things and grab Winnie before we leave the house once again.

"Oh, you need to take your shoes off," they instruct, looking down at my boots. I stop to pull them off, setting them in a pile of shoes at the edge of the forest. The grass brushes against my bare ankles as we make our way into the brush.

I watch my step as we move through the tall grass, glancing up at Endel to make sure I don't get lost. Their locs are tied up into a bun now, allowing the coppery skin of their neck to shine under the sunlight. Their muscular arms peak out from the pauldron that adorns one of their broad shoulders. A brown vest hugs their sides, leading down to black pants that disappear into the grass.

"What is this place exactly?" I ask, my gaze moving upwards to take in the height of the trees. The sunlight peeks through the pine needles, streaking the grass with fading light.

"This is the Sugar Pine Forest of Pine Valley," they state, gesturing to the greenery around us. "We honor this place since it takes care of the village. The trees give us pinecones to fertilize the flower field, sap for our food, and most importantly," they explain, stopping at a tree. "It cares for us after we die." They place their hand on the trunk with a fond smile, "Hi, Grandma." They sling a small bag off of their shoulder and place it at the base of the pine. Their large hand releases Winnie's tiny one, allowing the little girl to move freely. They reach into their bag and pull out a couple of long purple ribbons.

"You ready?" Endel asks Winnie. One of their hands extends towards her with the ends of the ribbon. She nods happily, grabbing it from them in a fist. "You might wanna take a step back," they say to me. I oblige as they walk one time around the tree and stop facing one direction. Winnie turns to face the same way, giggling excitedly. Endel bends their knees into a running position, "Three, two one...go!"

The two siblings run around the tree laughing giddily as the ribbon winds around the trunk. Their combined effort encases a small portion of the trunk in a light purple hue. They meet in one spot with about a foot left of ribbon. Endel pats Winnie's head, "Good job. Look at how pretty it is."

"Is grandma happy with it?" she asks as Endel takes her end of the ribbon. They lean their ear to the tree before nodding.

"She loves it. She thinks you did a wonderful job," they confirm. Winnie hugs Endel's legs with a giggle. I step closer to observe as they work the ribbon between their fingers, smoothing it out and making sure the ends are even. Their hands are gentle as they handle the ribbon with care. The concentration on their face causes their nostrils to flare slightly. They clasp the ribbon between their palms, "Alright, Winnie, it's time."

She releases their leg and faces the tree, clasping her hands together as well.

"Could we have a moment please?" they ask me.

"Oh right, of course," I stumble as I back away again.

They bow for a moment of silence, holding for ten seconds before they stand tall again. Endel thanks Winnie as they begin to tie the ribbon into a bow, tightening it against the tree. Bending down, they reach into their bag and pull out a small vial of water. They pull out the cork and begin to pour when Winnie lets out a whine.

"You want to do it?" Endel asks. She nods in response, reaching to grab the vial. They chuckle and bring it down to her level so she can help them pour a few drops onto the roots. "Okay, all done," they say, putting the vial away. They wave me over as the two take a seat at the base of the tree.

"You know, I could feel that this place was special when I first arrived here. Is this place where you bury your loved ones?" I ask as I sit next to Endel.

"Not exactly. Our gravesite is farther down the valley, but this is where the souls of our elders come to rest."

"Their souls?"

They nod again, placing their hand against the trunk. "This tree is where my grandma's soul came to rest. Purple was her favorite color so we wrap a purple ribbon around it. When she first passed, the ribbon helped guide her to the tree we chose for her."

"And the water?"

"From the Nafsi, for health and vitality. The people in this valley follow the circle of life and death. Nature takes care of us, we take care of each other, and give back to nature along the way. Since life begins and ends with the soul, we try to preserve it for as long as we can by returning it to where it came from." I absorb their words as I notice more families entering the forest. A father and daughter with an orange ribbon, an older woman with a yellow ribbon, and two men holding a red ribbon.

"So, the forest *was* watching us when we arrived," I smile.

They release a small laugh, "Yeah, you could say that."

I reach toward the tree, stopping an inch short of the bark. "May I?" They give me a nod and I place my hand against it. My eyes shut as a warmth runs through me and the tips of my fingers tingle at the feeling of the rough bark. The energy was the same gentle touch used to check a child's temperature. The same soothing pressure of my dad's hand atop my head. I pull my hand away, holding it to my chest. "I can feel her." I open my eyes to find Endel's hand on the tree next to mine.

"She was a wonderful person," they say softly. "I miss her." I can't help the small part of me that feels jealous. They got to know their grandmother in a way I never had the chance to. Of course, it did save me from the pain of loss, but what is loss if not love with nowhere to go?

Eventually, the sun begins to disappear behind the forest, bringing our time to an end. Before we leave, Winnie pulls a small painting from her bag and shows it to the tree. Endel remarks how Loraine would be glad that Winnie is painting and suggests she leave it there for her grandma to admire.

Wynira quickly runs to Xilleria once we return to tell her about our time in the forest. Lytea rolls her eyes. "I give birth to the girl and she gets attached to Xilleria," she says playfully. I laugh as Endel sets their bag down on the table.

"Don't worry momma, you're *my* favorite," they whisper before placing a kiss on her cheek.

"I heard that," Xilleria says. Endel hides behind Lytea, effectively dodging a towel that Xilleria launches across the island. She's got a strong throw for someone carrying a six-year-old.

"Where is Tansae? Did she turn in?" I ask.

"Yeah, she left a while ago. She followed me around the tavern for a bit. Said that watching me run the kitchen was enough to tire her out," Lytea explains.

"Momma, I don't think you realize how crazy your job is," Endel remarks.

"I think I'm gonna turn in as well," I yawn. I lace my fingers together, pushing my arms behind my back to stretch. I hear a satisfying pop from my mid back and shake my hands out.

Endel nods, "I'll walk you back."

I watch my feet as we walk under the dark blue sky, taking out my compass to click it open. My eyes travel up to the sky, trying to see if any of the constellations inside the compass match the ones above me.

"So," I start. "Did you give any more thought to joining us?"

They shrug, "I've been weighing the pros and cons."

"How do our chances look?" I ask, slipping the compass back into my pocket. *None from here I guess.*

"Let's see. The cons are that I'd be away from my family for who knows how long, and the obvious danger of traveling across Vyelan. The pros are that I'd get to see new things, meet new people, and meet my soulmate at the end of the road."

"And essentially save Vyelan," I add.

"Right, that too," they agree. "So I'd say your chances are pretty good."

"That's good," I respond, looking at the ground. "There's something that still confuses me though."

"What's that?"

"You said you believed us when we first met."

They skip a step ahead and turn to face me while walking backward, "And you want to know why?" I nod. They take a breath, eyes wandering as they try to gather their thoughts. "It's hard to explain."

"Try me," I nudge. We make our way down the small path in the field behind the inn. Our footsteps fall silent as we meet the river's edge and I take a seat, patting the space beside me for them to sit.

They draw in a deep breath, adjusting themselves so their arms wrap around their knees, "I've always had this feeling. These stories in my head. When I was younger, I had a dream of this person. They didn't have a face or a name, but I remember how they made me feel. Safe and warm." Their gaze follows a few stray flower petals and leaves as they float down the current. "I had that same dream for years. It felt as if someone was reaching out to me. Calling me to come home. At some point, it started to happen during the day. Visions that didn't feel like the future or a past I knew."

"Did you ever talk to anyone about it?" I ask.

They nod, "I told momma, but I'm sure she dismissed it due to my young age. After some time, even I began to attribute it to a vivid imagination. That was until more started to appear."

I lean forward, pulling my knees to my chest, "More what?"

"Memories. At least, I think they're memories. I'm always looking through my own eyes so there are only bits and pieces. It's hard to explain," they huff.

"That's alright."

"It's just- I feel it. Whether I know how to explain it or not, it's there. It drives me to search. I've never known what to search for so I tried everything. Pottery, knitting, macrame, jewelry, whittling, sculpting, the list goes on. But no matter how many trades I learn, I still feel like I'm searching for something. I know my purpose, but my soul knows something is missing from my life." They face me with a soft smile, "Then you showed up."

"You think this is what you've been searching for? That you could possibly have a soulmate?" I ask.

"Well, everyone has a soulmate. Whether or not I'm the descendant of the ancient mystic or his wife is what I'm not sure of." They reach up to pull their hair loose from its bun. The moonlight reflects off the silver hair charms that are woven into their locs. I follow the light to the water as they paint white highlights against the surface.

"Hey, Endel?" They hum in response. "I just wanted to say thank you. For today, I mean."

"Why?"

"It was nice to learn new things and a privilege to get to know your family. You have a good life here. I almost feel guilty asking you to leave with us," I admit. I hear them release a deep breath as they move to stand. I follow suit, watching their hands slip into their pockets. A moment slips by and I almost gather the courage to look at them, but that moment wasn't long enough.

"When you left Duskwick, did you plan to leave forever?" they ask, bending down a bit to try and meet my eyes. My gaze falls to the side, avoiding them.

"Of course not," I respond.

Their locs come into view as their head dips down. A small smile plasters itself on their face as they catch my eyes with their own. "Then why do you feel like that's what you're asking *me* to do?"

I don't know. I've always been bad at asking for things. I have a hard time separating a big ask from a small one, but whether we are right or wrong, things should be okay. As my eyes fall to the ground again, I notice that they are bent at the waist in an exaggerated stance.

"I'm not *that* much shorter than you, you know," I comment.

They laugh and stand tall again, "Took you long enough to notice." I roll my eyes, feeling my anxiousness wash away smooth as the water running past our feet. It's nice to be reassured that they aren't upset with us for coming out of the blue. The sound of gravel beneath our feet takes the place of the rushing water as we walk back to the inn entrance.

"I'm glad to see you're amused. Take the time you need to think about it, but I'm warning you that Tansae doesn't share my patience."

"Is she always so...unpredictable?"

"Goal-oriented is a better way to put it. I haven't known her long, but she's all in on the cause." They nod, pushing some of their locs behind their ear. The gray one pops out again, dangling near their face. "You should get back," I mention.

"Right. See you tomorrow? I'd like you for breakfast again." I cock an eyebrow at the wording and watch, amused, as panic sets into their features. "I meant to have you for breakfast, or have you over- I mean- ugh, you know what I mean," they groan with a defeated sigh.

My smirk turns into a smile as I feel a giggle escape my throat, "See you tomorrow, Endel."

CHAPTER 14

HERIATH'S POV

"For the last time, I didn't say anything," I remark in disbelief. Tansae has been grilling me since I stepped back into our room, only taking breaks to indulge in the food I brought. "Why is that so hard to believe?"

"I just find it strange that after all the work I did to convince them on night one, you got them to agree to join us after a day of just 'hanging out'," she says pointedly.

"It's the truth," I defend. "They have their reasons, but they're joining us and that's what matters, right?"

She releases a heavy sigh as she takes another bite of food, "I guess." I sit on my bed, falling back so my head hits the feathery pillow.

"I thought you'd be happier about this," I admit.

"I am. I'm glad they're joining us."

"It's kinda hard to tell," I mutter.

"I am glad they are joining us," she repeats firmly. She puts the empty container down on the bedside table. There is that look again. The one she had when talking about her mom. My mouth opens, but my apology gets stuck in my throat. I chose to spend the day with them. It's not my fault that she wasn't there with us. I don't know if I helped influence Endel's decision, but the important part is taken care of. My mouth falls shut and a nod takes the place of my words.

I sling an arm over my eyes and relax in the darkness it brings. Just a few more hours or so and we'll be back on the road.

I release a grunt as Tansae and I set down the new addition to the wagon trailer. I meet Endel by the front door of the house where they're saying their goodbyes. Xilleria warns them to be careful and come back in one piece. Lytea gives them a few containers of food while Wynira clings to their legs. She's been there since Endel told her they were leaving on a trip.

Endel leans down and carefully removes the little girl, lifting her into their arms. A pout rests on her face, disappearing into laughter when Endel rapidly pokes her sides. "It's okay, Winnie. I won't be gone forever," they say, handing her to Lytea.

"Are you absolutely sure you want to do this?" Xilleria asks.

"Yes, Mom, for the hundredth time," they say, rolling their eyes. They approach her, pulling her into a hug. She returns it, taking in a deep breath. They pull apart and press their foreheads together for a moment before letting go. Endel shifts to hug Lytea in the same manner.

"Let's get a move on," Tansae shouts from the wagon. Adjusting the bag on their shoulder, Endel takes a step back from their family with a smile.

"I'll be back before you know it," they say. We load up the wagon and I settle in the back while Tansae and Endel sit up front. The steam from the engine puffs in little clouds as we start moving toward the entrance of Pine Valley.

I peer out of the window, watching the forest grow smaller as we leave the valley. I sit back against my trunk and close my eyes, allowing myself to adjust to the rocking of the wagon. Being stationary for a few days took more of a toll than I anticipated.

"Eww, what?" Tansae exclaims from the front seat. My eyes pop open and I scoot closer to get within earshot of their conversation.

"What happened?" I ask.

"They like tomatoes and eggs for breakfast," Tansae says, face twisting in disgust.

I look over at Endel who turns to me with a shrug, "It's good." My nose crinkles as I imagine the dish.

"So, not like a breakfast bowl or anything added? No toast or anything? Just tomatoes and eggs?" I question, trying to give them the benefit of the doubt.

"Yep, just tomatoes and eggs," they say plainly.

"See, it's gross," Tansae remarks. I hold up my index finger as another question comes to mind.

"Wait. How are the eggs prepared?" I ask.

"Does it matter?" Tansae asks.

"It does a little."

"Sauteed tomatoes and sunny-side-up eggs," Endel says.

"Nope. Jail." I say, moving my hand to point my index finger at them. Their expression falls to disbelief as we continue to playfully argue about food-related opinions. Apparently, Endel and Tansae hate pickles, but Tansae does like pickled onions, which Endel and I cringe at.

"How do you hate pickled cucumbers, but like pickled onions?" I ask.

"They're good!" she defends. Endel and I exchange a glance before shaking our heads.

The conversation goes on and shifts to other topics. Favorite animals, books, and flowers. Once past the basic stuff, we get to know each other a bit better. I share about my compass, Tansae her dagger, and Endel their bracelets. Having Endel with us adds energy that my first day traveling severely lacked. Before we know it, we reach Elderheim Village and take a moment to stretch our legs.

Endel and I decide to take a look around while Tansae goes to refuel. The sun shines down, warming my skin as the autumn breeze tries to cool me off.

"So, did you have somewhere in mind?" I ask.

"Actually, yes," they say, gesturing to the side with one hand. I follow their movement to see the village's blacksmith shop. I give them a curious look as we step inside. The workers greet us as we enter, their welcome drowned out by the sound of metal clanging. A larger woman approaches us, her muscular arms folding across her chest. "What can I do ya for?" she asks with a smile.

"I'm looking to get a weapon. Something strong, but travel size," Endel says.

"Follow me," she says, turning to lead us further into the shop. I watch the other workers with curiosity. A man pounds into a block of searing hot metal with a mallet, a loud hiss coming from the sweat that drips onto it. Another man pulls molten glass into a star shape with various tools, working quickly but with staggering accuracy. My attention darts back to Endel when I accidentally run into them. I give them a sheepish smile and take a step back.

"These are some of the weapons we currently have in stock," the woman explains, gesturing to a wall of daggers, swords, axes, and other things. She pulls a dagger off the wall and hands it to Endel, "If you want something travel size, this could be a good one for you."

Endel examines it carefully, "This is nice, but do you have a larger one that can still be carried easily?"

"Well, I do have a few cutlasses. Maybe you can find one you like."

"That'd be great," Endel remarks. The woman tells us to wait here while she goes in the back to grab a few.

"What's with the sudden interest in weapons?" I ask Endel. They flip the dagger over in their palm, admiring the blade.

"I did promise my parents I'd come back in one piece. Figured I should have something to defend myself with," they answer.

"You handy with a sword?"

"When I was younger, my grandpa taught me the basics. Wood carving and whittling improved my skills with my fingers and helped me gain strength over the years. I can handle one, but I will admit I'm a bit out of practice."

"Practice? Like sparring with your grandpa?"

"Pretty much," they nod.

"Don't you think it's a bit unfair fighting an old man for practice?"

"Fedarius Anthony Valurae is no regular old man," they say with an insulted look. "He's beat my ass more times than I can count." He *was* quite animated when I met him. A large box slams onto the counter beside us.

"Here we are," the woman says. We peer inside to see an array of cutlasses, each with a meticulous design. "Daggers are a bit more convenient, so we don't sell many of these to locals. However, for travelers, they can be quite handy." Endel reaches into the box, picking one up and twirling it in their hand. They step back and take a few slices at the air.

"Be careful with that thing," I warn, backing up. They release a small laugh as they watch the blade, eyes sparkling with a rush of excitement.

"This size is perfect," they say to the woman.

She smiles, tapping the box, "Great, dig through until you find something ya like." I reach in and grab one, surprised at how light it is. I smirk at my reflection in the blade before noticing Endel approaching behind me.

"This is a cool one," I point out.

They hum, taking a closer look at it, "The blade is nice, but it's dull. The hilt is a bit boring too." I take another look at the gold and black hilt and shrug. I put it back and lean against the counter while Endel sorts through the box. They seem to have a taste for bright colors. "Woah, look at this one," they exclaim. They flip the cutlass so the hilt is facing me. The blade is slightly curved with two sharp hook-like points closer to the hilt and one sharp point at the end. An abstract black design trails from hilt to tip and makes it look more badass. What stands out the most is the handguard on the cutlass.

"It's incredible," I say astonished.

"Do you know how crazy of a project this is?" they ask excitedly. "This blade is a cross between a cutlass and a machete. The black design is gorgeous and the hilt, oh my gosh. This kind of guard is nuts." They point to the straight bar at the top of the hilt. "This standard crossguard is easy to make, but this loop around it is beautifully crafted. It's usually found on rapiers. I can't believe someone had the patience to make something this cool," they rant. I place my hand on the hilt, running my fingers over the leather wrap that encases it. A small purple, diamond-cut stone sits in the center, embedded into the leather. Both edges of the blade are sharp enough to cut well which adds to the beautifully dangerous feel.

Their eyes are alight with wonder and their knowledge of the details makes me smile as they take a few swings with it. They twirl it around their index and middle finger before gripping tightly onto the hilt again. "Oh yeah, this is fucking cool."

"That's the one?" I ask.

"Yes ma'am. No way I can leave this baby behind," they say enthusiastically. "Do you have a weapon?"

"Me?" I have the tools to cut plants and stuff, but no real weapons. I glance at the wall. "I should probably have something," I mumble to myself.

"It's advisable," they say, rolling their eyes. I playfully shove their shoulder and move over to the wall. There are a lot of options as far as design, but given that I'm not familiar with how to wield one I pick up a simple dagger. The hilt is wrapped in black leather for better grip and the blade is a shiny silver. Its lightweight feel and sharp point make it easy to swing and cut. It's good enough to get a good stab in and run.

"This looks good."

Their head tilts, eyes narrowing at the blade, "It's so simple. You sure?"

"I don't think I can handle anything more complicated than this," I admit.

"A lover, not a fighter, huh?"

"Pretty much."

"Hey, maybe Tansae can teach you some basic moves. That dagger she carries around looks pretty serious," they mention.

"Maybe." The woman takes our weapons to another area to sharpen them. She returns with each of them in a sheath and we pay for our things before departing with a wave.

Regrouping with Tansae, Endel rushes to show her the cutlass and giddily rambles about the design. "You're pretty crafty, aren't you?" Tansae says playfully. Endel's hand moves to the back of their neck.

"Yeah, tricks of the trade," they laugh awkwardly.

"Like your shop back home?" I ask.

"Yup, you learn about all kinds of things with a business like that. Though I mostly enjoy making waist beads and hair clips for braids and locs."

"I assume you made these?" Tansae asks, tugging slightly on Endel's ponytail. They quickly grab their hair from her and both of us shoot her an astonished look.

"Yes," Endel answers slowly, eyeing her for a moment. They check their hair before twisting it to show me the golden decorations embedded in it. They must change them out each day. Some were simple clip charms while others were spiral charms with crystals hanging at the end.

"They're beautiful," I say as I admire them.

"Thank you," they smile. "Come on, let's get moving."

I join Endel on the wagon and take a seat up front. Tansae gives me a puzzled look when I reach for the steering wheel.

"I'll drive. You can relax for a bit," I tell her. She shrugs and moves to the back, allowing me full access to the engine and controls. I pull the straps of my new thigh sheath to tighten it around my leg. Despite the extra weight it adds, it is pretty comfortable. Endel went with a baldric holster that easily clips onto the shoulder pauldron they wear. It gives them the ability to have the cutlass rest at their hip or against their back. Leaning forward to start up the engine and we're off again. I can hear Tansae and Endel talking behind me while I remain alone with my thoughts and the road.

I hum a song to myself as we reach the far side of the village. I feel a weight on the bench next to me and turn to find Endel with something in their hands.

"What's up?"

"Oh, nothing. I just have a little present for ya," they say with a cheeky smile.

I knit my brow, "What is it?" They open their hands to show me a golden swirl of wire with a moss agate charm at the end. "You made that just now?"

"Yeah, it's a fairly simple design. Do you mind?" they ask, looking at my hair. I nod and they reach up to my head. "Hold still." I follow their command, feeling their fingers gently tug a bit at my locs and pull one loose from my pigtails. After a few seconds, I can feel the tiny weight and I pull the hair in front of me to admire it with a smile.

"You're fast. We've only been on the road for about ten minutes or so, and where did you get the materials?"

"I may have brought some supplies to keep myself busy on the road," they explain with a hint of embarrassment.

I look over to them happily, "Thank you, Endel."

"No problem, I'm glad you like it."

Pulling my hair once again, I take in the details of the stone. The dark green color reminds me of the forests near my home. I let it fall near my face again, realizing it's on the same side as the gray loc that hangs near Endel's face. I turn towards them, but before I can ask about it, they've returned to the back.

CHAPTER 15

HERIATH'S POV

The Nafsi grows farther from us as we travel along and veer away from the path. The sky is fading to a pink hue, white clouds streaking across it. The warm breeze that has comforted me for the past few hours is getting cooler by the minute. The forest has been slowly disappearing for a few minutes now, the terrain turning to rocks and clay.

To avoid Vauxworth Canyon, and the possibility of an attack at night, we decide to stop in a small village. Because of its size, it lacks a proper inn so Endel and I opt for camping outside while Tansae sets up inside the wagon trailer. I guide us to a spot and examine the ground, picking up sticks and pebbles to clear the area while Endel lays their sleeping bag on the grass. They shimmy into it before quickly sitting up.

"Geez, what was that?" they ask, rubbing their back.

I place the lantern between us and move over to their side. They stand and I move their sleeping bag to find a large rock underneath. I bend down, picking it up to hold in front of them with a smug expression. "You have to clear the area before you just settle in."

"Oh...right."

I bend forward to brush away a few stray twigs, "Have you never been camping before?"

"No."

"Why not?"

"Uh, reasons. Kind of childish, honestly," they laugh awkwardly. Once I'm satisfied, I slide into my sleeping bag and look up at the trees. The breeze pushes and pulls on the leaves above us like the Nafsi's current on a windy day. I trace the stars in my mind to map out the few constellations I can make out through the swaying branches.

"Not an outdoor person?"

"I love the outdoors during the day. All the green and beautiful colors that sprout from the ground, the earthy smell of it all," they grin.

"It's wonderful, isn't it? Maybe next time we'll build a fire."

"Next time?" they ask.

"Oh yeah, you gotta have the full experience. Fire, tent, catching fireflies, the whole shebang," I say as I turn to face them.

"Awesome, I'll be holding you to that," they say as they fall back against their pillow.

"I'll try my best," I sigh, reaching for the lantern. "We should get some sleep." I reach for the lantern to blow out the fire when Endel sits up.

"Oh, could we maybe leave it on?" they request.

"Sorry, do you still need it?"

They rub the back of their neck, "No, I just don't sleep well in total darkness. It's no big deal though."

My bottom lip tucks between my teeth, "Well, it isn't wise to leave the fire lit. Though around here there could be..." I pull myself up and click open my compass, lifting the lantern to read the direction. "Come with me." They follow close behind as I keep my eye on the needle.

I pause and turn to the left to adjust my direction before continuing deeper into the forest. Strange clicks and snaps around us join the sound of crickets and other small woodland creatures. Endel remains quiet, but they tense with each unidentified noise, stepping closer to me for some semblance of comfort. Soon, the smooth current of the Nafsi meets my ears and I know I'm going the right way. *What was that rhyme again? Oh, right.*

"What's that?" Endel asks.

"Huh?"

"You were saying something."

Was that out loud? I feel heat rise to my cheeks, "I was reciting a rhyme to help me find- Oh, there it is!" I crouch by a bush and run my hands against the base of the crown. I pick a few starberries and set the lantern down to remove the glass covering. I scoop a bit of water into the glass container and squish the berries in my hands before dropping them in. "Wanna see something cool?" I ask.

Endel kneels beside me and I flick my wrist, swirling the container. The berries mix with the water and begin to glow a soft purple. Their eyes widen and they take the container from my hands.

"What are they?"

"These are starberries. The Nafsi activates a compound within them to make them glow. The elders of Kofir's day believed they soaked in the starlight, hence the name." They sit in stunned silence as they admire the way the swirling water glows.

The purple hue is reflected in their softening eyes, "I... I never knew something like this was out here. How'd you find them?"

"It's fairly simple. A short rhyme Miss Merilla taught me back home. *By the river, up the stream, under bushels, they shall gleam. Northern west your feet will go, shake them up and watch them glow,*"

I recite.

They smirk with a light laugh, "Catchy. Who's Miss Merilla?"

"My head herbalist. She's the one who took a chance on me when I first showed interest in herbalism."

They set the glowing container to the side, "What do you mean?"

"I was young. Only fourteen when I showed up at the clinic asking to learn from her. Starters are usually sixteen, but I kept coming back in hopes she would teach me something. Herbalists are usually taught by someone certified and have to officially be signed on as an apprentice to start earning their certification. On my fifteenth birthday, she agreed to take me on and two years later she was the one to put the medallion around my neck." I gesture to the starberries, "This, however, was one of the fun experiments we did together. She always found time for fun things like this that weren't on any of my exams. It used to annoy me when she dragged me away from my studies, but I soon figured out what she was trying to teach me."

"And what was that?"

I gently grip the container and hold it to my chest, allowing the purple light to wash over me. "Every plant has a purpose, medicinal or not. The beauty in each living thing is something to be treasured and shared. There's a magic in it that can't be found in books."

"She sounds like a wonderful teacher," they say softly.

"She's always been like a grandmother to me and shared wisdom in the hardest of times."

They look around, locs swaying in the soft breeze that whistles through the forest. Their soft expression lit with fondness as the sounds around us change from potential threats into a symphony of life. For the first time since we entered the forest, they seem to relax.

A soft hum leaves their throat as they take in our surroundings,

"Maybe the forest isn't so bad at night."

I return their soft smile and clear my throat. I reach for the bush again and pick a few more berries to add to the mix before standing.

"This light should last a few hours. Think that'll be enough?" I ask.

They nod, "I should be asleep by then. Thank you."

"Of course."

I guide us back to our small campsite and we snuggle into our sleeping bags. The starberries illuminate our space with a gentle glow. Their hand raises to trace the night sky, connecting the dots that hang in the milky twilight. The shadows bring out their veins hidden under the dark cover of skin. Their strong arm like a trunk with fingers like branches reaching for the moonlight. Their head falls sideways to look at me and I quickly avert my eyes. I try to ignore the small laugh that escapes their throat. It's one thing to stare, it's another to be caught doing it.

"See something you like?" they tease.

"You're very pretty, I was just admiring," I answer honestly, meeting their eyes again.

Their eyes widen in shock, "What?"

"You're pretty," I repeat.

"I heard you, I just- you can't just say that," they stammer. Their hand moves to cover their mouth, but the apples of their cheeks rise to indicate a smile. Their head turns back to face the sky while an arm moves to drape across their eyes. It's my turn to laugh.

"Why not? You started it," I say playfully.

"Whatever," they groan.

After a while, I feel my eyes getting heavy. I yawn and stretch before tucking my arms into my sleeping bag. The smell of nature and the sound of the leaves gently rustling above lull me to sleep.

"Keep your head low, we're going to sneak through slowly," Tansae says as she pulls the wagon's lever. I nod, putting my sleeping bag back into my trunk.

The orange sky mirrors the clay below us as we make our way toward Vauxworth Canyon. The sound of the wheels against the ground fills what would otherwise be peaceful silence. A simmering tension sits on all our shoulders. I tuck just behind the doorway so as to not be seen while Endel keeps watch through the back window, tightening the green bracelet around her wrist. I can't help but be painfully aware of my breathing as my back lays flush against the wooden frame. My hand grips tightly around the hilt of my dagger. I lean slightly to see outside, eyes scanning the canyon walls for any movement. Finding nothing, I turn my attention to Tansae who looks as if she's just driving through the city on a normal day. I half expect her to start humming a tune. Her index finger taps her dagger in a steady rhythm. Her muscles are relaxed and yet I can feel how alert she is, completely aware of her surroundings. I try to mimic her poise but my muscles remain locked in anticipation.

Endel moves against the wall to the left of the window, positioning herself at an angle where she can still observe the path behind us. Her focus is just as palpable, but nowhere near as calm as Tansae. I can tell her shoulders are taut even through her attempt to hide it with crossed arms. Her eyes move to me for a moment and I give her an uneasy smile which she returns. She raises her hand in front of her chest with the palm up before flipping it and lowering it again, telling me to take a deep breath. *Do I really look that stressed?* I follow her advice and she shoots me a thumbs up before turning her attention back to the window. I glance outside again, feeling my shoulders relax a bit as the end of the canyon comes into view.

Almost there.

"Alright, I think we're clear," Tansae says. I jump at her voice, the sound seeming ten times as loud in my anxious mind. I move to sit next to her, my hand at my chest trying to soothe the tightness. She reaches forward to pull the lever when the bushes rustle again.

"Wait," I whisper. Her hand pauses just before the silver handle. Her eyes follow mine as we both stare at the bushes ahead. Tansae grips the handle of the lever, "It's probably just the fox again."

"I...don't know. I think we should-" I'm cut off as Tansae pulls the lever, speeding up the wagon. A huge puff of smoke comes from the engine, covering the view in front of me. I wave it away to see an arrow barreling toward us.

Time slows to a crawl as I dodge just in time so that it flies past my ear with a whoosh. The head of the arrow lodges into the wood behind me while I bite back a scream. I look up to see a man standing on the branch of a tree ahead of us, hidden amongst the leaves. Two more men jump out from the bushes before we can pass them.

Tansae is at the ready, "Shit. Get in the back."

I stand as one of the two men runs towards the back of the wagon, the other lunges for Tansae. She unsheathes her dagger, blocking his with a swift motion. I feel a hand on my arm and rip it away before realizing it's just Endel.

"What are you doing?" she says, pulling me into the back. Endel takes my place in front. The man fighting Tansae kicks the lever forward causing the wagon to stop abruptly. Endel falls to the side, catching herself against the engine. She pushes back onto her feet with a hiss, the skin of her palm now red from the scalding heat. I struggle to steady myself before running to the back window, noticing two women behind us while the other man is out of sight.

I turn back to the front, unsheathing my dagger. No, I don't have the slightest clue what I'm doing but I can't be useless. My eyes dart around before landing on the lever. I grip the hilt tighter. I don't have to fight, we just need to get out of here.

I resume my position in the doorway and peek out just enough to see Endel fighting one of the women that have reached us. She gives the bandit a swift kick, forcing her off the wagon and onto her back. "Endel," I yell. "Can you run?" She glances towards me, twirling the cutlass before bending her knees in a fighting stance.

"Yeah, why?" she yells back.

"Good. Tansae?"

"Kind of busy here," she yells. I open my mouth to speak but I'm cut off by another arrow flying through the doorway. I dodge and peek my head back out, this time being careful of the archer in the tree.

"I need you to force everyone off the wagon," I shout back.

"Why?" Tansae asks. She delivers a punch to the temple of the man attacking her and he stumbles back, tripping on the stairs.

"We don't exactly have time for questions," I respond.

She glances towards me and nods. "Okay, but whatever you're doing make it quick," she says as the missing man charges for her. Tansae and Endel hop off the wagon and lead the bandits away from it.

I place my dagger back in my sheath and take a step through the doorway. Once I'm sure it's clear, I hastily move to the front seat and pull the lever to begin our escape, but it doesn't budge. The engine is nearly at full power. *Something's wrong.* I assess the engine to no avail. Leaning to the side, I check the wheels on the right. The wagon rocks as

Tansae slams into the side, throwing off my balance. I grab the wooden frame to avoid falling off. "Hurry up, Heriath!" she shouts in frustration.

"Something is blocking us from moving," I say as she ducks under the bandit's blade. I continue to tug at the lever, wary of the man as he slips past her to barrel toward me.

She knees him in the stomach and he lurches, hand slipping off his weapon. The blows to his face are strong as she takes him on. Sweat drips from her shoulders as her ponytail bounces with each swing of her arm. She faces this grown man with confidence as if telling herself that no matter what, they're equally matched. She raises her dagger as he stumbles backward. There's a look in her eyes that's new to me. It's frightening, to say the least, but just as assured as always. My eyes widen as her hand shoots down. My eyes are trained on the dagger as she flips it so the blade is parallel to her forearm. The hilt of the dagger strikes the man's temple and he falls to the ground unconscious with a harsh thud. My breathing is heavy as she turns to me, her chest heaving in the same manner.

"Look out!" she shouts.

Pain shoots down my arm and I release a scream as I grab my shoulder, an arrow lodged into my upper tricep. A deep red stains my fingertips. My vision blurs as I stare at my hand, my breathing becoming labored. *Fuck, I wasn't paying attention.*

A loud bang snaps me out of shock. My head snaps backward to see an unsettling gold-plated grin above me. A bandit stands on the roof of the wagon, eyes full of greed. I fleetly leap off the wagon and he follows closely behind, stopping only to kick the lever back into the down position. The bar bends under the force of his boot and I cringe slightly, only relaxing again when it doesn't snap in half. I back up slowly, feeling small under the man's gaze. I'm soon behind the wagon, glancing over at

Endel who is trying her best to fend off the two women at once. My eyes widen as I notice the side of her shirt is sliced, red staining the fabric. I turn back to face the man, his smile sending a shiver of fear up my spine. He's not too big, but I doubt I can take him, especially injured. *I don't have time for this.*

In the corner of my eye I catch a wooden spear that's lodged between the spokes of the back left wheel of the wagon. *That's it.* I shoot a look to Tansae who responds silently with a curt nod. The man follows my eyes and turns to look at her right as she approaches him. She grabs his collar and uses a leg to kick the back of his knees. I take advantage of the time she gives me to move over toward the spear. I grit my teeth and take the arrow in my arm by the shaft. I can't pull it out yet, but keeping it long would only be a disadvantage. My breathing halts as I prepare myself, pulling down swiftly to snap it at the crest. A guttural scream escapes my throat as the arrowhead shifts in my arm.

"Fuck," I growl, throwing the shaft to the ground.

I grab the end of the spear to shift my focus from my arm, but each pull sends a sharp pain up my shoulder that I can't ignore. I take deep heavy breaths as I put my foot on the back of the wagon for more leverage. Adjusting my grip, I pull with all my might and feel it loosen in the clay below the wheel. *Come on, I'm not that fucking weak.*

"One more time," I say to myself. I wipe my hands on my pants and grip the spear tightly. With one final pull, I am able to dislodge it and pull it from between the spokes.

"I got it," I yell. I toss it to the side and rush toward the front when my body smacks against the side of the wagon. Deep brown eyes of a woman pierce into my own as I attempt to recover from getting the wind knocked out of me. I can't tell if she's baring her teeth or grinning.

"Where do you think you're going?" she sneers.

She must have taken a break from fighting Endel. She lifts her dagger, stabbing into the wood as I shift my head to the side. I reach up to grab her hair, ripping her head to the side so I can duck under her arm. Once free from under her, I beeline for the front, but I'm stopped short by an arm around my throat. I struggle against her, falling to my knees as she kicks the back of them. I try my hardest to pry her off, my hands desperately scratching at her arm as panic floods my body. Her grip tightens and my vision blurs as I gasp for air. My head is getting lighter by the second. We fall forward, crushing my fingers under her forearm. Dirt smears against my face as she now lies on top of me, a small pressure against my thigh reminding me of my weapon. The thought of using it makes me nauseous, but I can't feel anything if I'm dead.

One of my hands wiggles free from under her arm and reaches for it. I feel my body getting weaker as my fingers tap against the hilt. I lift my knee and manage to get a grip on it. I pull my dagger from its sheath and squeeze my eyes shut before swinging it down into her leg and ripping it out harshly. A gut-wrenching scream meets my left ear and her arm loosens enough for me to roll out from under her. I drop the dagger and my hands fly to my throat as I cough and hack, trying to catch my breath as quickly as I can. I feel a foot slam against my side, forcing out the air I just managed to gain in those few seconds of freedom. My head knocks against the ground as she climbs on top of me again, this time straddling my waist. Strands of black hair stick to her forehead, her eyes ablaze. I reach for my dagger, but she kicks it away with her uninjured leg. She releases a terrifying, rage-filled scream as she raises her own in a two-hand grip, blade pointing down at me. I manage to catch her wrists as she slams her hands downward, keeping the blade a mere two inches above my throat.

I feel tears well up in my eyes as I use the last of my strength to keep myself alive. I groan, the hoarse sound helping me push through the pain in my left arm. My head swivels to the side and I catch a glimpse of Endel who has succeeded at knocking the other woman unconscious.

"Endel," I call weakly. The use of my lungs causes some of my strength to slip away. The sharp tip of the dagger draws closer to my throat. I try to push harder, but she's still stronger than me. My mind is overtaken by one thought as I draw in a breath to shout again. *I now rest an inch away from death.*

"Endel!" I scream with my remaining strength. My hands shake, the sweat causing them to slip further down the woman's arms. *Half an inch.* I squeeze my eyes shut and the weight disappears. The dagger scrapes against my neck just enough to sting. Her body thuds against the ground next to me yet my arms remain in the air, frozen in the position that nearly failed to save my life. Endel's shadow crosses my face as she jumps over me, her body a wall between me and the woman.

"Go."

"What?" I slur, doing my best to gain my bearings.

"Go, Heriath," Endel repeats. "I'll buy you some more time." My eyes turn towards the wagon before falling back on her. I scramble to grab and sheath my dagger.

I book it for the front seat and climb aboard, finding Tansae at the wheel. She shoots me a smirk, "Beat ya." She starts the engine and pulls the lever to full speed. Endel is right behind me and I extend a hand to help her up when she slips. The woman from before has Endel by the ankle and I quickly grip Endel's wrist to pull her up as she attempts to kick the woman off.

A pain-laced cry meets my ears as the woman sinks her blade into the side of Endel's leg, pulling out with a downward slash to extend the cut. My blood boils at the sound and I step forward. My foot meets the woman's face with a satisfying crack and she releases Endel, allowing me to pull her up onto the wagon.

She makes it just as the wagon begins its acceleration down the pathway. I look up to the trees for the archer. If he's still there, he's hidden well. I scan the leaves carefully when I notice a small shift just as we pass underneath one. The gleam of an arrowhead alerts me as he releases it. I give Tansae's shoulder a rough shove, just in time for the arrow to miss her and bury itself into the back of the driver's bench. The wagon passes under the tree and the steady rhythm of the engine steam is once again the only sound.

A few minutes later, we finally let down our guard and breathe easy. I take a moment to stare at the sky, the fiery orange now settling into a calming blue. The breeze caresses my sweat-covered skin and cools my aching muscles.

I move to the back and take a look at Endel who is now sitting up against my trunk. A trail of blood stains the floor from where she pulled herself up to sit. I meet her eyes and she gives me a small laugh, "Sorry about the mess."

I exhale a deep sigh.

This is above my pay grade.

CHAPTER 16

HERIATH'S POV

"How far until Kaelora?" I ask Tansae.

"It should be another half hour at least," she responds. I groan, turning my attention back to stitching Endel's leg wound. The needle sinks into her skin and she jumps for the twentieth time. The first ten were before I even started.

"Please try to stay still, hun. I could hurt you worse if you keep squirming," I all but plead.

"Sorry," she apologizes for the millionth time. I will say, despite her more painful injuries, she's had a pretty good attitude compared to some patients I've dealt with.

She places a shirt into her mouth with her bandaged hand, hissing into it as I pull the needle through her skin. Cleaning the wound wasn't nearly this difficult, but now that her adrenaline has worn off, helping her has felt more like trying to wrangle a cat into a bath. I'm only a third of the way down the laceration and the uneven path we're riding on isn't doing me any favors.

She takes the shirt out of her mouth, still gritting her teeth from the pain of the needle. I pull it through and her shoulders relax.

"My head hurts like a bitch," she says, resting her forehead in her palm.

"Maybe loosen your bun, it could be a tension headache," I suggest. Endel lifts her hand to set her locs free and runs her fingers through them. I continue my stitching when I notice the wagon slow down a bit and footsteps halt at my side.

"Think you can get to me anytime soon?"

"As I said before, as soon as I'm done with her I'll get to you, I promise," I sigh. Tansae crouches next to me and I create another stitch. She hisses as her eyes run over the stitches I've managed to complete.

"Yeesh, that looks awful," she says. I pause briefly, shooting her an annoyed side eye before continuing.

"You know, I could use a bit of space," I say. The constant movement and pain in my arm are worsening my mood by the minute. My remaining mental stamina is focused on stitching correctly and keeping up my bedside manner to minimize Endel's twitching. Tansae stands again, moving a foot away with her hands up in defense.

"It is pretty bad," Endel says, reaching down. I use my free hand to smack hers and she pulls it back to her chest with a pout. "Hey," she whines.

"Hands off, I gotta keep it somewhat clean."

"Well, there is one good thing coming out of this."

"What's that?"

"I get a cool mark like you," she says with a smile. I stare at her for a moment before exhaling a light laugh, shaking my head. The gray cloud that has hung over my head for the past half hour begins to disperse.

"That's a pretty grim silver lining," I respond.

She turns to Tansae, a light of curiosity in her eyes, "Do you have any cool scars?”

“I do actually,” she says, turning around and lifting the bottom of her shirt. Four jagged pale lines extend about five inches across her lower back. My eyes widen at the sight, but Endel beats me to the question.

“What happened?” she asks in surprise.

Tansae faces us again with a shrug, “I was attacked by a wildcat when I was younger. It got a good hit in, but my dad managed to take it down. In fact, it was this dagger that finished it off.” She pats the sheath at her hip with a proud grin. Endel leans forward intrigued but quickly sits back with a groan, holding her side.

“Careful,” I say, leaning over to check the bandages wrapped around her side.

“Sorry,” she says with a pained smile. *One million and one.* Her unwrapped hand runs over the back of her head, rustling a few locs. “Your dad sounds pretty badass,” she starts, turning back to Tansae. “What kind of cat was it?”

“I’m not sure, I was too busy crying to see what kind it was. I was carried off while he dealt with it, but he came back with a bloody blade,” Tansae explains.

“That’s- Uh oh,” Endel says. I look up to see her staring at her hand, doused in a dark red.

“Where did that come from?” I ask hurriedly, setting down the needle on a piece of cloth next to me.

“The back of my head I think,” she says. I crawl up to sit behind her, leaning against the trunk to hold her head in my hands. Now that her locs are down I can see a half-inch long gash between two of them, the area being covered in dried blood and making the wound out to be a lot worse than it is. By the color of the blood on her hand and the large amount surrounding the wound, it's been sitting here for a while.

"Shit," I whisper. It must've been covered by her locs when they were in a bun.

"Woah," Tansae says, now standing next to me.

"Is it bad?" Endel asks, her voice wobbling.

"No, it's-"

"It's grotesque," Tansae exclaims, eyes wide. I turn to her with a mixture of confusion and shock.

"Why would you say that?" I whisper shout.

"Look at all that blood. You were going to lie to her?" she says, pointing at the wound.

"It's not a lie, and even if I was, it would obviously be to keep the patient calm," I explain.

She shrugs, "Whatever you say doc, but if I had a serious injury I'd want honesty."

"Serious injury?" Endel asks, snapping her head to face us. Her body sways a bit at the sudden movement, "What's wrong? How bad is it?"

I gently place my hands on her face, "Everything is going to be fine. Try to relax." Her eyes focus on mine for a moment and I do my best to give her a reassuring smile. My upper left arm throbs as she relaxes against me, forcing me to hold her up. Damn, she's pretty solid.

Tansae scoffs, "We'll see about that."

I face her with gritted teeth, "Can you just- just-" I pause to breathe. "Let me do my job, please? These things take time and I still have my own wounds to dress. Not all of us can fight well enough to come out nearly unscathed."

Her lips quirk up into a smirk, "That's true enough."

"Drive, woman," I say pointedly. She rolls her eyes with a small *'whatever'* and returns to the front. I lay Endel's head in my lap while I grab some gauze and other materials to clean and disinfect it. I wet a cloth with water when I catch Endel's gaze. Her brown eyes stare up at me, a bit dizzy from the blood loss.

"Am I gonna die?" she asks with a pout. A hint of mischief rests in her pout and I roll my eyes, failing to fight the smile that reaches my face.

"No, idiot, you're not gonna die. You just need a few days of rest."

"Is it bleeding a lot?" This time the question is more genuine.

"Yes, but no matter how small the cut, the head will bleed a lot. It's going to be fine, hun." The term of endearment slips through my lips for the second time, but her eyes widen a bit telling me she just now noticed it. It's more of a habit when I'm doing healing work since people tend to be more calm when I use them. Her eyes cast downwards and I can sense she wants to question it, but she says nothing. I pull her head up so I can begin cleaning the small cut. I am careful to move slowly to avoid worsening her dizziness. Once cleaned and disinfected, I place her head back into my lap so my hands are free to unroll the gauze.

"What?" I ask, catching her eyes trained on me again.

"Nothing," she hums. "You know you knit your eyebrows together when you're focused?" My hands freeze, now fully aware of the rigid tension in my forehead. A strange feeling between embarrassed and flustered flutters in my chest. Endel's bandaged hand reaches up and she places two fingers between my eyebrows.

"You said yourself that I'm gonna be fine. I trust you, trust yourself and relax," she starts, smoothing the space on my forehead with her thumb. "Hun," she finishes with a wink.

My train of thought is completely derailed, but I push past the shock to continue unwrapping the gauze. She giggles and lowers her hand. A slight tingle remains where her fingers were, "All work and no play, huh?"

"You're dizzy," I remark, words finally reaching my brain.

"I'm not that dizzy," she retorts.

I place a hand over her mouth for a second, leaning forward, "Save your strength." I can hear her muffled giggle beneath my palm before she nods, agreeing to keep quiet. I remove my hand and bandage her head before moving back down to her leg and finishing the stitches. Honoring her word, she remained quiet.

Once done, I heave myself to sit against Tansae's trunk, grabbing the things necessary to take care of my own injury. Luckily, the arrowhead is fashioned into a needle point and should cause no extra damage upon removal. Though it's not lodged deeply, I'd rather wait for someone else to remove it. I re-wrap and use a wet cloth to wipe the dirt from my face, wincing at the sore spot on my jaw that I'm sure will bruise.

The cloth meets my throat and discomfort sets in my chest, my hand clenching into a fist. *You're fine.* My fingers reach up to gently touch my neck. I can still feel the pressure of the woman's forearm against my windpipe, the tightness restricting the airflow. I raise the cloth again, but my hands shake, forcing out an annoyed grunt. My heart thrums in my chest, the vibration echoing through my veins. My hands run over my exposed shoulders to soothe the tension. I stare down at my lap in silence. *You're alive. That's enough.*

The minute we arrive in Kaelora City, Tansae rushes to find an inn so she can shower. According to her, the muscle tension and small scrapes come second to the fact that she is covered in dirt and sweat. I gently wake Endel and guide her to the nearest herbalist for a checkup. I'm relieved to find out that my suture skills are adequate and that her injuries will heal nicely. The gauze wrapped around her head is replaced with a smaller bandage and she is advised to take at least two days to recover the pint of blood she lost.

The herbalist takes a look at my arm, this time with less positive reviews. He removes the arrow and stitches me up well. He attempts to treat the abrasion on my neck, but I assure him I can handle it and he thankfully understands.

"How's your leg?" I ask as we walk through the city.

"It certainly feels a bit better. I just need some sleep," Endel responds, her voice bouncing a bit as she figures out the crutches she was given. A yawn interrupts me as I try to respond and I hear a small laugh come from her. "Looks like you're a bit sleepy too."

"What, me? Never," I say through another yawn.

She rolls her eyes with a smile as we arrive at the inn. We make our way inside and decide on a shared room so I can assist with the healing process.

It takes a couple trips to get the trunks into the inn. Endel insists I let her help, but she's only able to carry a few bags once I cave. We take our time setting up and I excuse myself to shower, enjoying the feeling of hot water on my skin. The water runs red from the clay residue that's stuck to my body and I scrub until it becomes clear. The tackiness from my sweat dissolves, running off with the soap as I rinse. I raise the cloth to my neck but that tightness returns and I yank it away. My hands shake and I slam the cloth onto the soap rack in front of me. My head shoots up as I hear a knock at the bathroom door.

"Everything okay, Heriath? I heard a bang," I hear Endel's muffled voice through the door.

"I'm fine," I yell, unable to mask the frustration in my voice. My eyes cast down as guilt creeps over me. I hope she didn't take it personally. I set down the cloth and rub soap onto my hands, cleaning my neck gently with my fingers instead.

A small cloud of steam grazes the ceiling as I leave the bathroom. I pull off my shower cap and my locs brush the top of my shoulders. It's odd feeling them against my ears and face after having them up for so long. I take a seat at the edge of my bed and stare out at the clouds that roll between the tall buildings outside our window. The sun shines bright, lighting up the room with a warm glow and reminding me that it's only morning.

I jump as something touches my elbow and I snatch my arm away. Endel pulls her hand back, alarmed at my sudden movement, "Sorry." I can feel her eyes on me even as I turn back to stare ahead, "Hey, you alright?"

"I'm fine," I mutter.

She reaches toward my neck, "You have somethi-"

"Don't-" I stop short, realizing how loud I am. "Sorry," I whisper.

"My bad," she apologizes. "You just have a scratch on your neck. Her eyes fall to my medical supplies, "Wait, isn't that what the herbalist tried to help you with?" I nod silently. She examines my things, glancing up at me a few times.

"Okay, what's wrong?" she asks.

"I'm fine," I repeat, grabbing a fresh cloth and taking it to the sink. To my dismay, she follows me and watches as the water runs over it.

"I asked what's wrong. *'I'm fine'* is not an answer. You seem frustrated, I just want to help if I can."

"It's nothing, I'm just being dramatic," I state plainly.

"Bullshit."

"Excuse me?" I snort.

"I said, that's bullshit," she says, turning off the tap. "You can't just tell me nothing's wrong when we both are trying to recover from the ordeal we barely made it through just a few hours ago." Her tone is stern but riddled with care and concern. I tear my eyes away and face the sink to wring out the cloth. *This is stupid.*

I raise it to my neck for the third time, trying to ignore the tightness restricting my breath. I start to wipe off the area and the tremor in my hands returns. I keep my gaze on the mirror in front of me, staring into my own eyes and finding nothing but fear. My pulse is nearly visible under my skin.

"Stop," Endel says, gently wrapping her fingers around my trembling hand. She lowers the cloth and steps closer to me. I face away from her and try to pull my hand away, but she refuses to release it. "Stop trying to run and let me help you. Please, Heriath."

"Why do you care?" I snap, immediately regretting my tone.

"You spent time patching me up and keeping me calm the whole ride here and you're asking why I care that you're upset?" she asks. "Why won't you let me help?"

"Because I'm strong enough to handle it," I huff.

"I know that."

"Then why do you keep insisting?"

"Because you don't have to be."

The cold rim of the sink meets my wrist as I allow my hand to relax into hers and she takes the cloth from me. She moves to take a seat on her bed and I follow suit, sitting next to her. I open my mouth to instruct her, but she places a hand over my own that are wringing in my lap.

"I've been watching," she reassures, grabbing the balsam from next to me. "Disinfect and apply this, right?" I nod. "Okay, I need you to follow me. Deep breath in and out, like this," she instructs, demonstrating it for me. My eyes shut and I relax my body. I feel her release one of my hands, the remaining one lacing her fingers with mine and touching the pads of our thumbs together. "That's it, keep breathing," she soothes. Her free hand tucks my locs behind my ear and I draw in a breath at the soft touch. A fluttering feeling enters my stomach that's quickly chased away when the texture of the rag meets my neck.

My eyes shoot open and try to move away, but I'm stopped by a hand on my cheek. "It's okay. I'll be gentle." The soft look in her eyes coaxes me to squeeze mine shut and allow her to continue. Her hand squeezes my own and my heart beats harder, this time not completely a result of fear. The pulse in her thumb is now in sync with mine and I fall into their steady rhythm. Her hand is warm, rough fingers enveloping my delicate ones. My deep breaths reassure me that air can easily flow into and out of my lungs, keeping the tightness of my throat from overwhelming me. "All done," she says and I open my eyes.

I'm met by her warm smile as she lets go of my hand to grab the balsam, scooping a small amount onto her finger. Her eyes fall to my neck as two fingers meet the bottom of my chin to tilt my head up. Her fingers softly rub the ointment onto my neck in soothing circles.

"You're...oddly good at this," I acknowledge.

"When you live with a little girl who's afraid of checkups, you learn how to soothe anxiety enough to get things done," she laughs. Her fingers lift my chin up again to keep my head in place and heat floods my face. I really hope my pulse isn't still visible.

"That should do it." Her hand lowers and yet the warmth of her fingers remains.

"Thanks," I say softly.

"Oh, that was nothing. I mean, you patched up much worse in a moving vehicle," she replies.

"Well, yes, but I couldn't even patch up myself properly," I admit, frustration coating my words. "I'm better than this. I've been hurt before."

Her eyes soften as mine fall to trace the dark lines of my palm. She places a hand in mine again and I look up to meet her gaze. "Hey, don't be too hard on yourself. That situation was new to all of us. Well, Tansae seemed fine, but we both got banged up pretty bad."

"But-"

"Nope, no buts. Mental scars are just as impactful as physical ones, trust me. You fought for your life just a few hours ago, of course your hands still shake. Give yourself some grace, Heriath," she says softly. I can't help but smile at her words as her other hand lifts to readjust my hair charm.

"Wise words," I remark.

She shrugs with an awkward smile, "I try." I can feel her body heat contrasting with the coolness of the ointment on my neck. Her eyes are dark and yet full of the light of her smile. We're close, almost too close. The room falls silent for a moment, maybe several moments but I lose count. Has she always had that beauty mark on her ear? I blink as her one gray loc falls into her face, snapping me out of my trance.

I clear my throat, "Thank you. Again."

Her head hangs, a hand at the back of her neck, "Yeah, no problem." Her locs hang over her ears.

"We should get some rest," I say. She hums in response as I make my way to my bed. I close the curtain and lay on my side, facing the window. I pull one of the extra pillows to my chest. My eyes squeeze shut while Endel shuffles around behind me.

My mind falls back to her words. *Mental scars are just as impactful as physical ones.* What could've happened? This morning left us all with mental scars, some hide it better than others. Despite my stubbornness, part of me is glad she noticed mine.

My fingers touch the spot on my neck. Such a small abrasion, a scratch, yet it made my hands shake. Hers were steady and gentle. I've been treating injuries all my life, but it seems I still have much to learn.

CHAPTER 17

HERIATH'S POV

"Okay, you're all done," I remark, putting away my supplies. Tansae thanks me, standing to slide her clothes over her bruise-littered skin. I set my bottle of balsam to the side, making a mental note to pick up more later. The cycle truly never ends. I knew when I took this job that helping people is a full-time gig, but I can't help but miss when I had set hours. What I wouldn't give to have that rusty old clock cough at me to go home. Tansae releases a sigh as she finishes getting dressed.

"A good night's rest and I'll be good to get back on the road," she says, stretching her back. "I'm beat."

"Tell me about it," I agree. My two hour nap was nice, but my muscles still feel like rocks. "Luckily, we still have this afternoon and tomorrow to rest."

"Tomorrow?" she questions.

"I took Endel to the nearest herbalist and he suggested at least two days rest to recover from blood loss."

"Oh," she says, taking a seat on the bed. "But we can get back on the road after that, right?"

"Probably, but it depends on how she's healing," I respond, laying back. "Stitches like that take longer to heal."

"Does she really need that much time?" she asks.

"Well, I'm sure she could get back on the road after four days or so. She needs to be in a good condition to travel," I state.

"I know we're all tired, but can't she just lay in the back of the wagon?"

"As we saw this morning, anything can happen on this trip. It's safer if she stays here and recuperates enough to handle a challenge," I explain calmly. She's silent at my answer. I glance over to see her arms crossed and eyes shut. "Is there a problem?"

"No, not at all. I just feel we should get back on the road sooner. We can't afford to waste much time," she says. I understand being efficient, but there really is no set time limit for our trip.

"Homesick?" I tease, trying to lighten the mood. "Miss your comfy silk sheets?"

She scoffs, rolling her eyes with the slightest hint of a smile, "Very funny. Honestly, though, I just want to keep moving. We shouldn't get too comfortable."

"And we won't. It's just until Endel is healed," I reiterate. Her bottom lip catches between her teeth, conflict evident in the wrinkle between her eyebrows.

"Fine, but we should get a move on soon." Part of me wants to persist, but that would require more mental effort than I'm willing to spare right now.

"We'll see."

The next morning is pretty busy with me running to get both of us breakfast. Tansae is off to find Zyl at the library so Endel and I are stuck in the room. Multiple charms and bracelets rest on the bed all around her. A desperate attempt to keep herself busy. Eventually, she threatened to place wood chips under my blankets tonight if she didn't go outside soon. Wanting to get good sleep, I caved and suggest an activity. I re-wrap her leg and so far she's been careful to move slowly so as to not pop the stitches. An action that resulted from my own threat to keep her locked up if anything happened to stunt the recovery.

"Where are we going?" she asks.

"Be patient," I laugh.

Endel groans as we keep walking toward the east end of the city. The sun beats down atop our heads while a breeze cools our skin. Endel opted for a green skirt today that the breeze brings to life. A few green butterfly charms adorn the large braid she wove her hair into this morning, matching the woven green bracelet on her wrist. I keep an eye out for signs that lead us to the preserve as we walk, catching the sight of a gate ahead with an archway that reads *Kaelora City Sky and Earth Preservation.*

"Where are we?" Endel asks, looking up to read the sign.

"Well," I start with a grin. "I saw when we were looking for weapons that you were drawn to the ones with bright colors. So, I thought you might enjoy this too." I lift the latch on the side and push it open to enter, feeling my eyes nearly pop out of my head. The trees shoot straight up to the sky. Bright hues adorn the bark from bottom to top in streaks. The dirt path leads down through the thicket, weaving back and forth before branching off into different directions. I feel excitement bubble up in my chest.

"Woah," I hear Endel exclaim, meeting my side. "Are these natural?"

"Yes, apparently they grow like this. Zyl told me about them," I confirm.

"Zyl?"

"My friend I mentioned when we first met. You should meet him later." I walk a bit down the path and place a hand against the bark. It's oddly smooth, the only rough parts being where the tree is delaminating.

"Rainbow eucalyptus. The bright hues of the bark were a gift given by Vyelan's Mystic of Nature to his wife on the day of their marriage, as this is the place they first met." I turn to find Endel reading a sign placed at the edge of the pathway. She gives me a smile before she continues, "We honor this forest as their love keeps the colors bright. It says the preservation status was applied just a few years ago."

We travel down the path for a while, taking in all the sights and sounds. Birds fly over our heads and a squirrel scares the shit out of me when it skitters past my feet, which Endel finds to be comedy gold. I glare at her to hide my embarrassment and pick myself up from the ground. I take out my herbalism journal to record my findings, sketching the shape of the trees and jotting down the colors I see.

After many twists and turns, we reach the river which runs around the eastern side of the city. The trees nearest the river are blanched, nowhere near as rich in color as the trees by the entrance. I drag my fingers over the trunk with a frown.

"I guess the fading magic affects the color," Endel voices my thoughts. I nod silently and approach the river, running my fingers through it. It's getting weaker, all of Vyelan knows that, but seeing the effects in such a physical way makes it more real. "Come on. We still have a lot to explore," Endel urges, a hand gently placed on my shoulder. I stand and we turn away, my gaze lingering on the river for a moment before pressing on.

"Shit," Endel exclaims, jumping back and swatting. It's my turn to laugh as she dodges a bug that whizzes past her face. I follow the bug, watching its wings spread to reveal a green color on the inside as it lands on a tree nearby.

"It's just a luna moth," I say, taking a closer look. Its wings flap as it takes off again, flashing a dark blue on the underside of its wings. "I've never gotten to see one up close before."

"So? It's a bug," she grumbles.

"It means there are moonflowers nearby," I say excitedly, darting my eyes around the underbrush. "Come on, we gotta find 'em!"

I start jogging down the path, ignoring the pain in my arm and her calls for me to slow down. I follow the moth down a few pathways until I reach an opening in the trees that's shaped like a circle. I assume it's a place for people to sit and birdwatch. Lining the area are short stalks of flowers, the purple buds tight at the ends. The moth lands on one of the leaves, stretching its wings open. I hold up a hand behind me to halt Endel's footsteps as she catches up. Taking a seat, I open my journal and quietly begin sketching the moth. Endel plops next to me, whispering a question about my interest.

"Luna moths have green tops of their wings to hide during the day and dark blue undersides to disguise themselves at night since they close their wings while eating," I explain, keeping my voice low. My pen makes short strokes against the paper as I finish the sketch of the wings open. I start my sketch with the wings closed as Endel watches over my shoulder.

The rustling of the leaves and bird song float on the breeze that blows by. I can almost hear a hum of energy in the wind. The nature around me gives me a sense of peace and makes me feel at home. This journey has had its pitfalls, but moments like this make up for it. Being attacked and injured led to us having the time to appreciate things like this moth and the trees. Something so small can bring so much joy to those who know where to look.

"Oh," Endel whines as the moth flies away. "It's gone."

"It's alright. I'm almost done anyways," I reassure. I finish the last strokes on the antennae and lift my pen with a smile.

"Very nice," she says, admiring my work.

"Thanks. I just wish the flowers were open so I could see them, but as their name suggests, they only open at the first touch of moonlight. You know, they have white dots all over the petals that resemble the starry sky? I've only ever seen it in books though," I finish disappointed.

"They sound beautiful," she says softly.

I shut my journal and look over to her, "Thank you for coming out here with me. It's nice to share my interests with a friend."

"Of course. Thank you for bringing me. It's actually pretty nice, despite the bugs," she says with a shudder.

I laugh, "You're like my sister in that way."

"You have a sister?" she asks, tilting her head to the side.

"Mhm," I hum. "Her name is Yamala."

"At least I'm not alone," she laughs. A small smile tugs at my lips and I face the sky. I shut my eyes to let the breeze wash my worries away. She stands slowly and extends a hand toward me. I take it, allowing her to pull me up.

We run into Tansae on the way back and we all go to a tavern. She mentions that Zyl went ahead to lie down. Once we finished eating, we make our way back as well. Workers move about the street, lighting the lanterns that line the walkway. Business owners come outside to light their own as the sun goes down. The cool breeze turns cold, causing a shiver to run up my spine.

"So is everything healing up alright?" Tansae asks Endel.

"I feel a bit stronger than yesterday, so I'd say so," she responds, tapping the hip of her injured leg. I'll need to re-wrap it when we get back to our room.

"Great. So you'll be ready to get back moving tomorrow?"

"Tansae," I start. "You know she needs more time to heal. You can't rush things."

"You said she only needed two days to recover."

"No. She needs two days to recover from the blood loss, but her stitches need more healing time."

"She walked around just fine today from what I heard," she huffs.

"We were going slowly. If anything else happens those stitches could pop right open," I explain.

"Excuse me," Endel interjects. "I'm right here, you know." We both stare at her for a moment and I back off, mumbling an apology. She turns to Tansae, "I know you're eager to get back home and I'm sorry that I'm holding us back, but Heriath is right. I need more time."

Tansae's jaw ticks at her words and she crosses her arms. She says nothing as she pushes her way through the entrance to the inn. I follow after her, suggesting Endel return to our room to get the weight off her leg and assure her I can handle the situation.

I enter Tansae's room cautiously with a knock, "Tansae?" She doesn't respond as I approach her, sitting on her bed while she leans against the wall. "Look, I know it's frustrating, but could we try to make the best of the time we have here?" I ask, trying to get a response. Still nothing. I continue, "We knew this journey wouldn't have a set schedule and we still have time. Is there a reason you want to get back so soon?" My hands wring in my lap as the ongoing silence begins to cause pressure in my chest. Her head finally tilts up so she can look at me, my eyes fall to her lips as she parts them for a second and pulls them shut again. The look in her eyes changes from empty to somber.

"You were right earlier when you asked if I was homesick," she says, looking out the window next to me. The softness in her voice tugs at my emotions. I bite my inner cheek, feeling guilty for being so curt before. If how she's feeling is anything like my night by the river in Pine Valley, I can't blame her for wanting to get home.

"I'm sorry. I know what it's like to miss your family," I say softly. She tucks a stray hair behind her ear, still facing the window.

"Why can't Endel just join us on the road? She wouldn't have to do anything," she persists.

"I've already answered that question," I groan.

"Well, what about you?"

"Me?"

"Yeah. You joined this mission to help everyone, to restore the river's magic so people like Endel can heal faster and better. To help the whole land. Now you're saying that's not important?"

"Woah, I never said that," I defend, standing from the bed. "Endel's well-being is essential to this whole journey. If that wound gets infected or doesn't heal properly, her sickness would add more time restraints."

She scoffs, "The magic is fading daily and you're wasting our time."

"Me?" I say astonished. "This is nowhere near my fault. We were attacked, Tansae."

"Excuse me, but whose sorry ass did she have to save that resulted in these injuries?" she poked, leaning her ear toward me. "Oh that's right, yours. Someone who shouldn't have even been in the fight," she snaps.

My eyes widen at her words and I try to push them aside, but they manage to get under my skin. "Look, you hired me to take care of you. Both of you. I'm doing my job."

"Yeah, and a piss poor one at that," she remarks. "You're only helping so much because you feel guilty that you caused the damn cut in the first place." I grit my teeth, guilt and anger flooding through me at the dismissive wave of her hand.

"At least I'm doing something," I snap. "You kept jumping to be taken care of first even when it was obvious she was much worse off. You don't give a fuck about her."

She turns to me with shock, "Of course I do. I just trusted she could handle herself like an adult and didn't need to be babied by you. Right now you're just proving you don't give a fuck about *me.*"

"That's the entire reason I'm here," I shout. "It's called caring for others, Tansae. If you can't understand that, then this whole conversation is for nothing. You miss your family? Fine, but she's *my* priority and she should be yours too." She stares at me with disbelief, a wet sheen over her green eyes. I squint, confused at her sudden tears.

"She is my priority," she defends. I feel a crack in my own resolve, but I've made my point and I'm going to stick by it.

"Then it shouldn't be hard to understand. She needs to be healthy and we don't know how long it will take to find her soulmate once we get there."

Her jaw tightens, "You know what? You won't have to wait as long as you think." She doesn't wait for a response as she turns to leave the room. I call after her as I follow her down the hallway, stopping when she bangs on Zyl's room door. A few seconds pass and he opens it, eyes widening at the sight before him.

"I said I wouldn't say anything so *you* tell her," Tansae grits. Zyl gives me a worried look as Tansae turns to me with a shrug, "Now we both get what we want, and if you're lucky your sister will still be alive by the time we get back."

I step back from the weight of her words and she pushes past me. Any retort I may have had gets caught in my throat as I watch her return to her room. The door slams shut, shaking the lantern that hangs on the opposite wall. Zyl remains frozen in the doorway.

"What was that about?" he asks.

"You should know," I say pointedly. He avoids my gaze as a hand moves up to run through his loose curls.

"I- well..."

"Zyl, I have no patience left after dealing with her," I deadpan. He gives me a cautious look and sighs. My eyes widen at the next few words that escape his lips.

"I'm the second soulmate."

CHAPTER 18

HERIATH'S POV

I push the door closed behind me as I step forward, "*You* are the second soulmate?"

"That's what I said."

"But- why-" I sigh as I try to organize the slew of questions in my mind. "How do you know?" He releases a sigh of his own as he plops onto the bed. He reaches up to bury his fingers in his hair.

"The violet meadow," he says. I move closer, leaning against the wall across from his slumped figure. "Turns out, there was one at Kofir's second home near the Trosthek Mountains. It grows outside my house."

"I never noticed it."

He leans over to grab his satchel and slips a hand inside, pulling it out to reveal a piece of parchment. I recognize the letters as his handwriting, but the words were not his own.

I grow anxious with the sunrise. My beloved. The reason I continue to walk this plane. Her eyes, the amber of dreams, are fading over time. Aging is not unfamiliar, for that is the circle of life. However, my darling's health has always been a concern. Her heavy coughing in the winter is the sound of nightmares. Her muscles grow weak. The bloom that has brought us so much joy over the years now a constant reminder of her inabilities.

I can only provide so much comfort with my gift. Rooting it in a single spot so she may gaze upon its beauty with ease. Beauty that pales in comparison to the smile that lights her face as she watches the petals sway in the frigid winter breeze. The new hue stands out against the snow so she can always find it. Blue always was her favorite color.

I toil on this final night in hopes of my new creation becoming her saving grace. I pray the stars guide me, for if I fail, the dust upon the ground shall be my brethren.

Realization hits me as I recall the three-headed blossom I saw my first night at Zyl's house. It was the same shape and height as the violet meadow. I hadn't thought twice about it at the time since it was a different color.

Zyl stares down at his lap, "I found that in Kofir's journal. The flower grows in that same spot every year."

"When did you figure this out?" I ask hesitantly.

"Today," he mumbles. I read over the words again before extending the paper to him.

"Why didn't you say something?"

"I was going to."

"When?"

"I don't know," he huffs, standing from the bed. His hands rest on top of his head as he starts pacing the room. "I didn't expect this and I definitely didn't expect you and Tansae to come back so soon. I mean she was so excited to tell me about Enzo-"

"Endel."

"Whatever." His hands slide down to cup the back of his neck as he faces away from me.

"And you told Tansae about this?"

"She burst into the room while I was still processing the new information and wouldn't leave me alone until I told her."

"Okay, but I don't understand why you're upset. Isn't this a great thing?" I ask.

"No," he groans, facing me. "Yes? I don't know. The point is, I'm the researcher. I'm not meant to be this important. I came along to help, not have the pressure of everything on me. The only thing I do know is that two rooms down I have a person who I'm destined to be with and I'm not ready for any of this."

"Alright, slow down." I move to sit on the bed, patting the space beside me. He sighs and sits next to me, face in his hands.

"What do I say to them? What do I do?" he asks, voice slightly muffled by his palms. I rub small circles on his back.

"Truthfully, I don't know. But Zyl, this isn't the same as Kofir and Elysi's story. You and Endel are your own people with your own personalities," I answer. "Things are going to be different and it doesn't have to be some whirlwind romance."

He looks up at me, worry etching lines across his forehead, "But where do you start when you know the ending of your own story?"

I give him a reassuring smile, "I'd start with hello."

This morning has been pretty uneventful, which is good since I spent the night tossing and turning. I couldn't seem to shake off Tansae's words, the guilt keeping me awake as I replayed the attack in my head. Not to mention the promise I made to Zyl to not mention the soulmate thing until he met Endel. The bags under my eyes could carry ten pounds of wheat.

A knock on the door pulls me from the bathroom, but Endel has already answered it. The blue bracelet shifts on his wrist as he pulls the door open.

"What's wrong?" I hear him say, his height blocking the person in the doorway. He steps to the side to reveal Tansae who holds a bag in her hand. She silently approaches me, slipping her hand into it and pulling out a brown cotton pouch. I tilt my head, eyeing it with apprehension.

"What is-"

"Things got a bit...out of hand last night," she says, looking towards Endel as he comes to her side. She glances down at his wrist before looking back at me. "But you were right about Endel coming first." Endel gives me a curious look while my gaze remains on Tansae's hand, the bag bobbing as she offers it to me. I take it, setting it in my lap and pulling the top open to find an assortment of herbs mixed inside. "It's tea for Endel. I made it myself as an apology."

"You made it yourself?" I ask.

"I hope you don't mind, but I took some notes from your journal. I also got some help from the herbalist guy down the road. It should be nourishing, and pretty tasty too," she explains.

"Wow, that's really sweet," I say.

Endel thanks her for the gesture while eyeing her other bag. "So what's that?" She holds the larger bag towards me, her smile turning from proud to awkward.

"This is a goodbye, actually."

I look back up at her, even more confused.

"Goodbye?" Endel asks, voicing my thoughts. "You're leaving?"

"Not leaving per se, just traveling ahead. It's a two-day trip. Besides, you have everything you need right here," she says, nudging him with her elbow.

"Why go ahead of us, though?"

"I really miss my family and I figured it wouldn't hurt to make my way back. You guys can meet me there when, and only when, it's safe for you to make the trip," she says, patting his shoulder. I take the bag from her hand and look inside, slowly removing the items one by one. A tea press, medical supplies, and a sack of money.

"What's this for?" I ask, holding up the money.

"Well, since I'm taking the one we have, I'm leaving you with enough money to rent a steam wagon of the same size. There's also some extra for when you have to stop overnight in a village, plus what I owe you so far for your work."

I look between her and the bag, the weight pulling at my hand. "No, I couldn't- I can't, this is too much," I say, my old friend guilt weighing on my shoulders once again. "We both were a bit dramatic last night, but all this money?"

"Oh, it's not all mine. This trip is financed, you know," she says.

"If you're sure," I respond, setting the money down with the other items. The spread of gifts is slightly overwhelming. I know she means well, but something feels off. "This is quite the apology, Tansae."

She places her hands on her hips with a sigh, "Well, I feel bad about last night and I didn't want to leave on a bad note."

"When are you leaving?" Endel asks.

"Now actually, I'm all packed up. I just wanted to say goodbye," she responds. "You can handle navigating back, right?"

"I think we've got it," Endel says.

"Good," she says, turning to me. "If you get in trouble again, try not to risk your neck."

"I'll...do my best," I say, my discomfort worsening at her tone. It's like she's trying to be playful, but it's coming off weird. "You be careful yourself."

"Will do," she pipes, a smile rising on her face. She claps her hands together, "I'd better be going. Hope you feel better, Endel, and make sure to let Zyl try some. I know he likes tea."

He waves as she opens the door, "I'm in good hands." She gives a two-finger salute before closing the door behind her. There was a moment of silence as Endel and I came to terms with what just happened. He sits next to me, sorting through the items on the bed, "That seemed a bit sudden. What happened last night?"

I twist my lips, opening them with a small pop, "We had an argument. She kept pressing for us to leave, but I didn't think she'd go on her own."

"An argument about what?"

"Well, you." He raises his eyebrows at me in surprise and I continue my explanation, running through the events of the night before. By the end, his head is hanging slightly, eyes falling to his lap.

"I didn't realize I was causing so much trouble. If we needed to leave today, I could've-"

"No," I interrupt. "Don't blame yourself. Both the herbalist at the clinic and myself recommended you rest. Despite our momentum, if you fall ill, it ruins the whole purpose of you being here."

"I guess," he says. His fingers tug on his gray loc that hangs free from the half-up half-down look he's arranged his hair in today. It's not anyone's fault but the person who hurt him, yet Tansae's words were stuck in my head all night. Sure, he had to save me, but if I didn't help he might not have gotten away at all. My eyes fall to Endel's leg, wrapped neatly in new gauze that he must have changed while I was in the shower earlier. "Well, since we have time, we better not waste it," he says, standing. "How many more days before we can get back moving?"

"We can leave the day after tomorrow," I say.

"So, we'll start traveling back around the same time Tansae gets home."

"Sounds about right."

"Good. I'd like to meet my soulmate soon. I wonder what they're like."

I bite my tongue choosing to nod in reply. *You promised.* I open the bag of tea leaves again and observe its contents.

"How's it look?" Endel asks.

"With a pinch of sugar, it'll be perfect."

"Could we maybe grab honey instead? My grandma always made her tea with honey, and I never have tea without it," he says. I nod with a smile as I place the tea bag on the table next to the press. He moves a wooden carving off his bed, a recent project, and sits to put his shoes on while trying to hide a grimace.

"What have you been working on all day?" I ask, putting my shoes on as well. He gives me a smirk, opening the door as we begin to leave.

"You'll see soon enough."

I take a step forward only for my nose to meet his back. I rub my aching nose and step to the side, "What is-" I pause when I notice Zyl standing in the doorway, a fist raised and ready to knock. He lowers his hand and grips the strap of the satchel slung across his body while clearing his throat. His gaze is fixed on Endel's tall figure when he finally manages to speak.

"Hello."

CHAPTER 19

ENDEL'S POV

Up or down.

I stare at my reflection in the mirror as I try to decide what to do with my hair. I've been conflicted all morning. My many attempts to find an outfit left our room a wreck. The sight of the clothes flung over the chair and on the floor isn't doing anything for my current mental state, so I focus on the locs that hang loosely around my face.

My fingers run over my scalp as I attempt an updo. I huff, biting the inside of my cheek as I focus on gathering all of my locs between my palms. A few slip out and I fumble a bit reaching for the hair tie on the far side of the vanity and slipping it between my lips while gathering everything back in place again. A sharp knock at the door pulls my eyes away from my reflection.

"Come in," I say, forgetting about the hair tie in my mouth. It falls to the floor and I lean down to pick it up, not realizing how close I am to the vanity. I groan as my forehead smacks the edge and quickly stand up. My hand raises to my forehead to soothe the dull ache that's rapidly spreading through my nervous system.

"Ooh, are you alright?" I hear from the sudden visitor. When I open my eyes, I see Heriath back from running a few errands.

"I'll be okay, I think," I reply. Her hand pulls mine away from my head before the warm pads of her fingers run over the spot where I'd hit it.

"Well, you look okay," she says, examining my face. "The room however says otherwise." My face heats up slightly as she takes a look around. It looks as if a tornado blew through here, taking my sanity with it. I tug at the gray loc that hangs in front of my face, the tension providing some relief from my embarrassment.

"I uh, had some trouble getting ready," I admit.

"Nervous?" she asks, a hint of amusement present in her eyes.

"You don't have to rub it in," I sigh, shoulders slumping.

Her hands raise in defense, "I'm not. I didn't mean to startle you." Her eyes travel down my figure as she takes in my overall appearance. A frilly white blouse covers my chest and torso, leading down to a brown waist corset with golden clasps that match the gold bracelet that encircles my wrist. I struggled to properly press my black pants and I haven't even put on my shoes, yet Heriath gives me an approving smile. "I think your outfit was worth the mess, however."

"Thank you," I mumble. "But it won't be complete if I can't get my hair situated." I lean down to grab my hair tie and make a second attempt at my hairstyle while Heriath steps around me. My gaze drifts from my movements to hers in the mirror, watching her long skirt flow around her as she begins to pick up spare clothes that have been strewn about. Her hair is up in a small bun in the back, the hair charm I gave her placed in the center of it. I smile softly at the sight. "You don't have to do that you know," I comment, twisting the hair tie around to increase the tension.

"I know, but having a clean space helps you have a clean mind. That's what my mom always told me. Besides, I gotta sleep here too," she replies.

"I guess you're right. Shit!" The hair tie snaps, the elastic stinging my fingers. I shake my hand and my locs fall against my shoulders again. "Great," I huff, taking in my appearance with a frown. I walk over to my bed and flop onto my back. I grab a pillow and press my face into it, half hoping to smother myself. It's been nearly two years since I've been on a proper date and I'm already worried about all the possibilities that could happen while I'm with Zyl. The one thing I can fully control is my appearance and I can't even get that right.

I push a loud groan of frustration into the soft plush, feeling slightly better once the energy is released. A stifled giggle comes from next to me along rustling of fabric as Heriath sets my clothes onto the edge of my bed. I remove the pillow from my face to glare at her.

"I'm glad you find my torment amusing," I grumble.

"I'm sorry," she says. The frame creaks slightly as she sits, her eyes meeting mine. "I've been there. Hair loves to fail you on important days. What do you want to do with it?"

"Cut it all off," I grumble, plopping the pillow back over my face.

She releases a small laugh, "Well, we aren't doing that." The bed frame creaks again and her feet hit the ground. Faintly, I can hear her fumbling around with something before her hand taps my leg. I remove the pillow once again to see her holding a gold ribbon that could only have come from my bag of craft supplies. "May I try?" she asks with a shy smile.

I nod silently and her smile grows brighter. Sitting up, I place the pillow on my lap and she climbs onto the bed, positioning herself behind me. Her fingers feel nice against my scalp as she adjusts my locs to move them where she wants. I can feel her body heat against my neck and settle for counting the floorboards to keep from focusing on her pleasant warmth. She's been so caring, careful of her words and actions even when she's upset. It's admirable. At times, I wonder if I'm just another patient in her mind, but feeling her gently tug at my hair as she arranges it somehow eases those worries.

"Hello?"

"What?" I ask, turning my head slightly.

"I was asking what's on your mind," she says. Her palms meet either side of my head and turn it to face forward again so she can resume working.

"Oh," I respond, trying to organize my thoughts. "I don't know. There's just so much pressure around today going well. I need him to like me. I just don't want to mess things up." She hums in response as I feel the weight of my locs on my left shoulder.

"What is your expectation of today?" she asks simply. "To fall in love?"

"No," I snort. "It's one day."

"Exactly," she says, a lightness in her voice that tells me she's smiling. She moves around me again, scooting off of the bed to stand and extend a hand. I take it, allowing her to lead me to the vanity. My eyes widen as I take in her work. My locs are woven into a four-strand braid that cascades over my shoulder elegantly. The gold ribbon is woven into it, peeking out in places. "It's just one day. All you have to do is get to know him. Think of it as making a new friend."

My gaze falls to the side, "You make it sound so easy."

"You made friends with me, didn't you?" she asks, nudging my shoulder with her own. "Don't worry so much, you're starting to sound like me."

I laugh softly, feeling myself relax as I turn to face her, "Thank you."

"Of course," she smiles. "Is your hair okay? You can take it out if you don't like it."

"No," I respond, shaking my head. I turn back to the mirror to look over it again, running my fingers over the coarse texture. "It's beautiful."

We both turn to the doorway as someone knocks. I stumble as I pull on my boots, bracing myself against the vanity. I stand tall and smooth out the wrinkles in my pants before taking a deep breath.

A date with my soulmate. What could go wrong?

The streets are busy as usual, people weaving in and out of shops and wagons puffing steam into the crowds. It's a brisk day with a small breeze that is just chilly enough that I'm grateful for my long sleeves. Things have been okay so far. Zyl bought flowers and handed them to me with his head down. He informed me that fresh flowers were better for the season since the weather is growing colder by the day and I thanked him.

Lunch is quiet since the tavern isn't busy this time of day. Without the normal commotion, we are required to fill the space with our own voices. Small talk isn't my strong suit, but I enjoy discussing our jobs and families back home. Though, once the basics are covered, the space between us falls silent again. Forks clinking against plates and ceramic mugs thunking against the wooden table replace the little conversation we had. It isn't until we are leaving that I finally speak again.

"Where to next?" I ask as I push open the tavern door. He slips past me, holding his brightly colored shawl tightly around his shoulders to shield him from the breeze.

"There is a street fair on the far side of the city. Plenty of stalls and some places to trade your own goods for others. I used to frequent it when I studied here. We could go there if you like," he suggests his voice low.

"Sure," I nod. I won't lie, it has been awkward between us. I glance over at him as we walk, his messy brown curls brushing against his cheeks with each step. His jaw is clenched as he runs his hand through his curls for the twentieth time today. He's much different now than in our previous interaction. Meeting him was an experience. The way he rambled and stumbled over his own words helped ease me into everything. Yet, the knowledge that we are soulmates is weighing on us, whether we acknowledge it or not.

"Hey, Zyl?" I speak, my voice softer than I intended yet he still tenses.

"Yes?" he responds hesitantly. I stop and he does the same, his features contorting into a look of confusion. His dark brown eyes stare up at me while I gather my thoughts. After running a few different scenarios in my mind, I take a deep breath.

"I'm going to be honest. I am wildly uncomfortable," I admit, biting my bottom lip as I await his response. His eyes widen for a moment and I fully expect him to turn and walk away. To my surprise, a grin lights his face before laughter escapes through his lips. The sound invokes my own laughter, though I don't quite understand his response. He bends slightly forward, a hand covering his face as his shoulders shake. His hand slides up through his hair as he stands straight again.

"I'm sorry, I'm just relieved," he says with rose-tinted cheeks.

"You are?" I ask, eyebrows raising.

"Yeah, I mean this whole date so far has been stressful. I felt like the elephant in the room was riding on my back. I'm really glad you said something first."

"I'm glad I had the courage to say something," I say, a hand moving to rub the nape of my neck. "I haven't been on a date in a while, and never one this important."

"Tell me about it," he sighs. A small grin rests on both our faces from the released tension. For the first time since this date began, it feels like we're just two people. More than strangers, but less than friends.

"How about we just…try being friends," I say. "Forget this whole soulmate business and try to have fun today."

His smile brightens at my suggestion, "That sounds nice." I extend my hand to him and he glances down at it before meeting my eyes again.

"Truce?" I ask. He nods and reaches out to clasp my hand with his own.

"Truce."

"Painting is more my little sister's thing," I defend as Zyl struggles to stifle his laughter. I turn my easel to face me again and he whines as I unclip my canvas material from the wooden slab.

"Wait, I wasn't done appreciating it," he says. I roll my eyes, ignoring the heat on my face. Trying to paint portraits of each other in two hours seemed like a fun challenge two hours ago when I expected that we'd both be average at it. Now, as I admire Zyl's masterful brush strokes of primary colors, I almost regret this decision. My portrait of him looks as if I threw facial features at the canvas blindfolded. The details he was able to include in such a short amount of time truly display his skill and make my poor attempt at art worse by the second.

"Aww, come on. It's not that bad, I swear," Zyl tries to reassure me.

"You don't have to lie," I reply, a smile playing on my own lips. "Your portrait is amazing and it looks just like me. You're a whiz with a brush." I see a tinge of red spread across the freckled skin of his cheeks. *Now who's embarrassed?*

He turns his easel to face himself and removes his own canvas material, "Thank you."

"You could've told me you had painting experience, though." I untie my apron strings behind me to pull it over my head and he follows suit.

"What's the fun in that?" he muses. "Maybe I like maintaining the illusion of the simple historian."

"Those with extensive knowledge are nothing to sneeze at," I respond. "I just didn't know that your knowledge of art was applied. How long have you been painting?"

He shrugs, rolling up his artwork, "A few years. It really picked up once I moved away from home." He hands me a ribbon to tie my rolled canvas with and I accept it with a hum. "What about you? I thought you were the artistic one being that you run a shop."

"While true, paintings are nowhere in the list of items I create," I admit. We approach the stall owner and thank him, paying him his due and using a pen to sign our canvases. Well, Zyl signs his anyway.

It feels nice to openly laugh and talk about things without the pressure of the world on our shoulders. I'd completely forgotten about it while painting and the growing sound of music from further down the path drowns the thought again as we walk to an open area of grassy field.

Four musicians stomp their feet against a makeshift wooden stage. The upbeat tempo drives the movements of a few people that are whirling around with cups of beer in their hands. The stall owners closest to the band sway back and forth to the rhythm, smiling and clapping along. I feel the passion in the fiddler's playing pulling me to the stage.

"You dance?"

"Not really," Zyl says, wincing. "I have two left feet screwed on backwards."

"That explains why you've tripped four times on the way here and spilled your water on me earlier," I tease.

"Hey, I said I was sorry," he pouts, crossing his arms indignantly. He glances up at me, noticing my gaze locked onto the stage. "If you'd like to dance you can go ahead. I don't mind." I pull my eyes from the commotion and shake my head.

"No, I wouldn't want to leave you alone," I tell him, pointing to a small field where others have gathered to watch the dancers. "Why don't we just watch?"

"Okay," he chirps. I gaze up at the purple sky, cracks of pink and orange peeking through and lighting the field. In the dwindling light, I can see an array of flowers dotting the grass with spots of color.

Zyl takes a seat and I settle right next to him as we watch the sun begin to disappear. He pulls his shawl tight around his shoulders, using one hand to hold the two sides together in front of his chest. I lean back onto my palms and feel my body relax.

"You're good company, Endel," he says softly, eyes fixed on the beauty of the horizon.

"So are you," I respond.

"You know, I've studied the soulmate's tale for years, but I never thought *I'd* have one," he admits.

"Why not?" I ask.

He tucks his hair behind his ears, "I don't know. It's easier to believe in miracles happening to others, I guess. Logically, the odds of me having a partner at all are pretty low. I'm not an enthusiastically social person. Plus, I can't dance like you can so the taverns are ruled out. Besides, there's only one pair of soulmates that has ever been confirmed and the chance that it would be me out of the entire population of Vyelan-" he trails off as he meets my soft gaze. "Sorry, I'm rambling."

"No, it's okay," I smile. "I'm glad you feel safe enough with me to do so." He turns to face forward again, placing his chin on his knees and pulling them closer.

"Thanks," he whispers.

"So, what do you think?" I ask, bumping our shoulders. "Am I everything you'd want in a soulmate and more?" He laughs as I playfully flex my muscles. My feigned bravado is broken by my own laughter and he meets my eyes once again.

"I don't know about all that, but I will say today was a pretty good start," he replies. The last of the sun's light shines in his eyes, the breeze blowing a few of his curls across his freckled face. Shadow soon replaces the orange glow, yet the warmth remains.

A soft grin spreads across my face, "Yeah, it was."

CHAPTER 20

TANSAE'S POV

I push forward the silver lever, slowing the wagon as I approach the cobblestone roads of Mysticane City. The hustle and bustle of the busy streets is music to my ears. Finally rolling to a stop in front of Iron Brimstone, I step off the wagon and breathe in the air. It's been two days since I left Heriath and Endel behind, meaning I have one more day before they start traveling again. Of course, that's only if four days is enough rest for Endel.

It's been exhausting for sure. It's one thing to gain someone's trust, but another to spend so much time with them. Truthfully, I needed a break.

I push my way inside and drag my feet as I make my way to the far right tower and slip inside. I set down my bag by the door and pull my shoes off.

"You're home," I hear from beside me. I look up as my second shoe hits the floor and see my mother standing in the doorway of the living room. She's dressed in a simple green slip covered by an elaborate robe with furry trim. Her curled blonde hair cascades over her shoulders with a tilt of her head, brown eyes wide in surprise. Her hands are folded in front of her as her eyes roam over my figure in concern. Matching green house shoes tap against the ground as she walks over to me, immediately reaching for my arm. She lifts it, examining the bruises and scrapes that litter my skin. "Did something happen?"

"I'm fine, Mom," I tell her, pulling my arm out of her grip. She's so fussy.

"I didn't expect you to be home so soon," she says.

"I know, but I've completed my goal," I reply.

"Well, why don't you come tell me all about it? Nasir and I were just having a little afternoon snack," she offers, her voice a bit too cheery for my current state.

"No thanks," I say, pulling my bag back onto my shoulder. "And for the last time, Mom, our personal guards are not here for tea parties."

"It's not a tea party," she defends. "They work hard for us. Is it wrong to offer them a break from time to time?"

I roll my eyes and walk up the spiral staircase that leads to our rooms, "Whatever, just make sure they unload my wagon for me. It's out front."

I don't wait for a response and continue up to my bedroom. I swing the door open and toss my bag into the far corner. The creak of the metal bedframe welcomes me home as I nuzzle my face into my satin sheets. I take a moment to breathe, my muscles sinking into the mattress as I look to my bedside table. A smile lights on my face as I kiss two fingers and place them against the picture that sits there.

"I'm home, Dad," I whisper, staring into his eyes. He stands tall and proud. His three-piece suit, something I rarely saw him without, is snug against his frame in the picture. His short brown hair is coiffed and a hint of a smile is on his face. Mom always joked about how he never smiled with his teeth and how for years she wasn't sure he had any.

A loud thud shakes me from my thoughts as I roll over to face the noise, my dagger unsheathed in a second and pointing at the source.

"Woah, it's just me," Natiq says, hands up in the air. My trunk lays at his feet and I let my guard down.

"What did I tell you about sneaking up on me?"

"It's not my fault you didn't hear me bumble up the stairs with this thing," he remarks, his voice straining at the weight in his arms as he lifts it again. He sets it down near my wardrobe and slides his palms together to dust them off. "How come you're back so early? Did you miss me?" he asks, placing a hand on his chest dramatically.

I roll my eyes, "Can it, Natiq. I'm just here to rest for the day."

"It doesn't exactly make sense for you to come all the way home to rest for a *day* when you've been running around Vyelan," he points out, taking a seat on the trunk. "Spill. Did something happen?"

"No," I groan. Can I just have some peace without having to explain myself to everyone? "I have some time to kill before getting back to work." His hands run over his shaved head, the tone of my explanation being enough for him to quit pestering me.

He pushes off his knees to stand, "Alright if you're sure that's all."

"Natiq?" I call, stopping him before he can walk through the doorway. "Put up my clothes?"

He waves his hand dismissively and continues his way out the door," I'm your guard, not your maid, cupcake." I huff, hearing his footsteps go down the stairs.

I stand and move to grab the doorknob. "You could've at least closed the door," I mumble to myself before shutting it. I land back on my bed, removing my belt from around my waist and setting it down on my bedside table. The hilt of my dagger clacks against the wood. I turn over and close my eyes, letting my exhaustion take over and pull me to sleep.

"You were attacked?" Mom shrieks.

"Mom, I'm okay," I insist, fingers rubbing my temples. This is the millionth time she's interrupted me after she begged me to tell her all about my trip so far. Luckily, I got a good nap in before Natiq convinced me to come downstairs and join everyone. I lift another mini baked potato and place it in my mouth, savoring the flavor of it. I'd never admit it, but I've missed Nasir's treats since I ran out of the few he initially sent me on the road with.

"Come on, Ma, don't spike your blood pressure," Natiq says jokingly, popping a potato into his mouth. Nasir rolls his eyes at his brother's attempt to lighten the mood. She takes a deep breath, giving me the silence to continue.

"Like I was saying, I hired an herbalist to travel with me for situations like this," I explain. "She patched me up pretty good. Of course, I only got a few scratches, so I didn't need that much attention."

She sits back against the couch and tosses her hair over her shoulder, eyeing me with suspicion, "And where is this so-called herbalist now?"

"Heriath had to stay behind to care for one of the soulmates. They got injured pretty badly when we were attacked," I explain. She hums in response and raises her eyebrows with a look that said she was satisfied with the information I'd given her. For now. Her robe flows around her arms as she reaches for her teacup filled with juice.

She's always been one to romanticize her life. Drinking gooseberry juice out of fancy teacups and eating crackers and cheese off our best china. Living luxuriously as always, just mooching off the money Dad left behind. She's gotten more lavish since Dad passed, and for a while, I wasn't sure if it was because she was filling a hole or that she's happy he's gone.

"So, what's the plan?" Nasir asks. He leans over to pick up another bunch of grapes from the lopsided, three-tier cupcake stand. A result of another new hobby my mom picked up recently. I quirked a brow at Nasir, hinting at him to elaborate. "To heal the river?"

"How do they recharge the river, exactly?" Natiq adds. My eyes fall to the floor as I wrack my brain for the answer. The souls reuniting should be enough. I shrug to silently answer their questions, making a mental note to go back through my plan and do some research.

"Well, in the meantime, we could have some fun together," Mom suggests in her usually cheery tone. "I have to deliver some baskets and blankets to the children's home tomorrow. You could come with me?"

"Mom, after all these years you should know my answer is always the same," I groan. Her authentic smile turns awkward. I almost miss the way her shoulders hunch slightly.

"I know you're busy, but now that you're in charge of the company I figured it could help your image," she says softly.

"I don't exactly have time for my image when I'm focused on the upkeep of the company as a whole. Sorry if I'm working on important things while you're crocheting and handing out blankets to snot-nosed children," I say.

"Tansae," Nasir warns.

"What?"

"I would help if you let me, you know," Mom says. I roll my eyes. *Yeah right.* I bite my tongue to avoid an argument.

"What time are you going to the children's home? I can go with you, ma," Natiq offers, breaking the awkward silence. She gives him an answer while I turn to Nasir who's still staring at me. I give him a once over, squinting slightly to ask what he's staring at. He shakes his head and sits back in his chair, but the look in his eye tells me we aren't done here.

"Well, it was nice to catch up, but I'm going to turn in for the night," I say, dismissing myself from the room.

"So soon? We haven't even had dinner yet," Natiq asks.

"Long day today, busy day tomorrow," I reply with a wave.

As I walk up the stairs, I hear a second pair of footsteps behind me. I elect to ignore them, continuing to my room and pushing the door behind me with the hope that it will close all the way. Instead of a lock click, I hear the thud of a hand stopping the door short of its frame. I sigh and turn around to face Nasir with an exasperated look. He steps into my room and closes the door behind him.

"Need something?" I ask. His expression was as usual, stoic and blank. Only those who've known him for years can really read him, which is beneficial as a guard. A scar runs from his left eyebrow, across his hooked nose, and down to the right corner of his mouth, adding to his threatening demeanor. He's a bit like a wild animal in that he won't bother you if you don't bother him. Though you could end up losing either a few limbs or your life if you do. Being the older of the two brothers by two years, he's always had a more serious outlook on the world. An ice wall of a man, except for one thing.

"What was that back there?" he asks.

"What was what?"

"With mom? Why do you give her such a hard time? She just wants to spend time with you," he says. There it is. Always defending her to his dying breath. He leans against the door, crossing his arms as he awaits my answer.

"Why do you always give *me* such a hard time about her?" I ask. "I don't have the privilege to just sit around making botched art projects. I have real shit to do here." I open my vanity drawer and pull out a pen and some notes I left behind, scanning the pages for information.

"Because, Tansae, you've been gone for almost a month and barely said hi when you walked in the door. She missed you, and it wouldn't hurt to give her a bit of your time," he says, leaning to get into my view.

"I will after I finish this mission," I say without looking up. "Why don't *you* spend some time with her? Go to the children's home with her and Natiq tomorrow. You're practically her kids anyway."

"What happened to you? You've changed since-"

"Since what?" I say, a warning tone to my voice. "Since my father died? Or since the weight of an entire empire fell onto my shoulders at eighteen years old? A weight that *she* refuses to help me carry."

"Tansae, she's offered to help you so many times," he says with a sigh.

"Please, she just spends Dad's money and sits around sipping juice out of expensive cups. Even if I did let her help, she wouldn't know what to do."

"And you do? You're twenty years old and inherited this place as a child. Her knowledge would be useful since she watched your father do it for years."

"She sat in the background," I laugh, turning to face him. "She was a trophy wife. She never tried to give me any useful advice before, so why would I trust her now?"

His jaw ticks, eyes shifting to the side. I open the drawer again and grab a brown leather journal, holding it up for him to see. "I have all the knowledge I need," I finish, slapping the journal onto the desk. "So if you're done whining."

His eyes snap back to me and a hint of pity seeps through the anger in his gaze, pissing me off. He grabs the doorknob and turns it, giving me one last glance. His lips part to speak, but he shuts them and decides to leave in silence.

I understand the soft spot for my mom, both him and Natiq. She's the reason they're alive and around to even take care of us. The reason they want to stay here. At least, that's what little they've told me. If it wasn't for my father though, they wouldn't have been here at all. My dad knew how to get things done and built an empire, while my mom reaches people's hearts and ends up with nothing but a few blankets to show for it. I refuse to follow the tattered path she's walked.

I shrug away the thought, turning my attention back to my notes. My thumb pops open the snap that holds the brown journal closed. My most prized possession. Of all the things he left behind, this is my north star. I flip it open, my lips quirking up into a smirk as I read the neat writing on the inner cover.

The Journal of Tandal Morelli

CHAPTER 21

TANSAE'S POV

The aged pages of a textbook slip between my fingers as I turn to the next, my eyes scanning for information. Nasir's question kept me up all night combing through my notes and dad's journal for hours trying to find an answer. I finally gave up around three in the morning and decided to make a trip to the library after getting some sleep. I searched through books of legend for anything I might have missed. Though, the more time that passed, the more I began to feel foolish in my attempts.

So now I'm back home sitting in the large chair at my father's desk in his office. I place the textbook against the dark brown wood and lean my chin on my palm. I sigh, rubbing my temples with the pads of my fingers. I take my last bite of the hash Nasir set aside for me as a makeshift lunch, groaning before slamming the textbook shut. I shove the bowl to the side and fold my arms on the desk to throw my head against them. This is so frustrating. I only left because I thought at I had all my ducks in a row.

"Any luck?"

I look up at the doorway across from the desk to see Natiq leaning against its frame with a curious look. "Aren't you supposed to be at the children's home?" I ask.

"We're leaving in a few minutes, Ma's getting changed," he says, making his way over to me. He flips the textbook towards him and narrows his eyes to read the title.

"This is a pretty outdated one," he says. I place my hand on top of it and snatch it towards me to hide it underneath my arms. He raises his hands in defense with a chuckle, "Touchy touchy."

"I've been searching all morning and nothing," I groan into my arms.

"Maybe you're not looking in the right place," he suggests and I lift my head. I raise an eyebrow at him and he shrugs, "I don't know much about your plan, but sometimes the answer isn't straightforward. Especially when it comes to history and legends."

"Odd advice coming from an architect."

"Well, I'm full of sage advice," he says with a wink. He goes to lean on the desk with one hand, but misses, causing him to stumble and me to laugh. I hear my mom's voice calling him from outside the room and he yells back that he's coming. He gives my head a pat and I shake his hand off, my laughter ceasing at his touch.

"Hey," I bark, smoothing my hair down.

He bids me goodbye and disappears around the corner with a smile. I lay my head on my arms again, considering his words. I don't know any other way to approach my research, but digging around hasn't gotten me anywhere so far.

I slam my fist onto the table in aggravation, pausing when I hear a light jingling sound. I sit up slightly and hit the desk, hearing the sound again. I lean my ear closer and tap repeatedly. My head moves slowly to follow the sound until I reach the left drawer of the desk. My hand grips the knob and I pull it open. The papers scatter as I rip them out of the drawer and toss them to the side. My arm pumps as I roll the drawer in and out curiously.

"What the-," I whisper to myself. I push the chair back and crouch to peer underneath the desk. My eyes land on something silver attached to the side of it. My fingers prod for the object and get a loose grip on it, using the tip of my fingers to gain leverage. I pull it out to find two identical keys hanging side-by-side on a ring. My head swivels as I scan the room for anything they could be used on. Nothing seems obvious, but the keys were hidden for a reason. I duck under the crawlspace of the desk and examine the polished wood with my hands.

Dragging my fingers up the underside of the desk, I feel a keyhole that's barely lit by the sun coming in through the window. I adjust the keys in my hand and turn them until I hear a click.

"Gotcha," I say in satisfaction. "Now what are you hiding?" I have to use both hands to slowly lower the rectangular compartment to the floor. It appears to be the inside of the false middle drawer of the desk. From the outside, it appears to be a drawer with no handle, but I guess the real compartment was underneath all this time. No wonder Dad never let me play in here as a child.

I place the compartment on the floor and push it out from under the desk, into the sunlight. My eyes widen at the contents. So many documents. I sit with the compartment between my legs, hands sorting through the many files. One had my name, the others had my mom's name, Natiq's, and Nasir's. Inside of each file were our birth documents and other personal information about us. I'm surprised at the amount of detail in each one. Even more so that, despite being orphans, Natiq and Nasir's files contained more than my mom's did. Maybe he just memorized all her important information as her spouse.

Lying at the bottom of the compartment is a black leather journal and a black and gold fountain pen which I remember seeing Dad carry around with him. His most important documents were signed with this pen. I open the journal and peek at the inner cover.

The Personal Journal of Tandal Morelli

I never knew he had a personal one. Now that I think about it, the other journal I have only covered business affairs and how he handled the company. My eyes are glued to the pages as I leave the office, taking it to my room to read. The next few hours pass by in an instant as I spend time taking in all the new information. Each section was about something different. Family, building, money, and lastly, the founding of the company. Each new entry made my chest swell with pride.

He sacrificed so much for me, for us. Growing up, all he ever talked about with me was the company and how to maintain the wealth that took care of our family. However, in this journal, he talks about how proud he is of me. He had faith that I would be an adequate successor and it gave him hope. All I've ever wanted is to make him happy, to make him proud of me. It didn't take long in my youth to figure out that following in his footsteps would get me that result. I'm glad my hard work and effort were acknowledged, though he never said it to my face.

I'm nearly done when I flip the page and see the last few are torn out. The section ends right when he gets news from the miners about finding the Water Stone. Why would he tear the pages out? I've never known him to be ashamed of anything, so that can't be it.

I return to Dad's office to try and find the missing pages. A few minutes later, the compartment is empty and its contents are strewn about, my search stopping at another dead end. Maybe they're in his old room.

I hear the front door open downstairs and loud laughter coming from who I assume to be Natiq. Footsteps bound up the staircase and I move to the office door, opening it in time to see Mom walking towards her room.

"Oh, hi honey. Sorry, were you busy?" she asks. Her hair is in a messy ponytail and she's dressed in basic villager clothing. Something about wanting to look approachable to others in the children's home since they don't have as much. An empty bag is slung across her body, hiding some of the dirt that stains her top.

"Why are you so filthy?" I ask, scrunching my nose. She looks down at her dirt-covered palms with a small laugh.

"Oh, yeah. After we made our delivery, the children asked if I could help with their gardening. They were planting new flowers today and I couldn't resist," she explains with a smile.

"Uh huh," I respond.

"Well, I need to get showered off and-" she pauses, eyes fixated on the journal in my hand. Her eyes widen, her joyful energy now depleted at the sight. She takes a step back towards her room, "A-and we can have lunch together if you haven't already eaten." I nod, watching her closely as she rushes to her room and shuts the door. *Curious.* As much as I want to ask questions now, I want to exhaust all my options first.

I push open the door to Dad's old room. Nothing has been disturbed since the funeral. His bedsheets are the same pristine white as always, tall bedframe made of polished wood placed in the center of the main wall. I take a step inside, feeling a chill run down my spine. I've only been in here twice since he passed. Once with my mom and once with Natiq and Nasir. My shoulders slump as I hesitantly approach his bed stand.

It's almost eerie. Everything is so clean it feels like he was never even here, and yet when my hand meets the knob of his bedside table drawer, I can't bring myself to open it. I remember him on this bed, the silver ring on his hand cold against my skin as he caressed my face. I remember seeing my mom hold his hand as he slept. The only time I can recall them ever holding hands, illness making him more and more pale by the day.

My attention goes back to my hand as its shaking causes a small rattling sound from a loose screw. I clench my jaw and rip open the drawer, the action allowing my previous thoughts to float away. I sort through his belongings about the room. Something in me finds comfort in the shifted items, the room coming to life with all the papers and objects that litter his desk and bed. He was always very neat and meticulous, but the slight mess makes it seem like he's still here. It gives a soul to his space and allows the tremble in my hands to dissipate.

To my dismay, I still don't find what I'm looking for. I groan in annoyance, putting away everything two inches to the left of where it was. I hold his cologne in my hand, the liquid swishing around in the brown glass bottle. The faint aroma of it leaks past the cork and into the air, mingling with the sterile scent that lingers from the last cleaning.

"Honey? What are you doing in here?" I hear behind me. The bottle clacks against the bedside table as I turn around to face my mother. She stands a few feet from the doorway clutching her baby blue robe over her matching nightgown. I don't know if she's been back in this room since I last came in here with her. Of course, she probably doesn't care enough to come in here since they always had separate rooms.

"I'm fine, just looking for something," I say simply. She eyes me curiously before shrugging and continuing to the stairs.

"If you're sure. Nasir is making dinner for us, I'd like it if you joined," she says. I hum in response and glance at the black journal on the desk.

Maybe I will.

I poke at my meal while Natiq recounts the events at the children's home from earlier that day. The joy in his voice and his ringing laughter force a smile onto my face despite the story being about him slinging dirt onto his brother. Apparently, Nasir declined the offer to help plant flowers, but Natiq convinced a few kids to join him in an ambush. They asked him to grab a few more flowers and when he returned they attacked, throwing dirt at his chest and legs.

"He chased me around for an hour, I swear," Natiq laughs, a hand on his stomach. Nasir rolls his eyes and shoves his younger brother in the shoulder, muttering *"idiot"* under his breath. "You had fun too," Natiq teases him.

A half smile cracks onto Nasir's face as he gathers more fish onto his fork, "Yeah."

"The kids even enjoyed the jagged-ass blanket you made," Natiq says, nudging his shoulder.

Nasir shoots him a glare, "Hey, at least I tried to make one."

"Please, with all those holes it's only good for keeping the kid cool in the summer," Natiq laughs. When he's on duty he's a tough one to crack, but outside of work, he's like a puppy. I miss pulling pranks on some of the workers with him. He taught me how to make various traps before Dad got caught in one. He hasn't pulled a prank since that day. For weeks I didn't see him, and when I did he wouldn't even come near me.

Seeing him be playful again and hearing his laughter brings back the joy in those memories and makes me smile every time.

"Natiq, give your brother a break. All you did was buy the materials, and you initially got the wrong ones," Mom speaks up. Natiq's laughter turns into an awkward cough causing a laugh to escape my throat. "It was a fun time though, I wish you would've come," Mom says in my direction. Getting dirt flung on me doesn't sound like my kind of party, but, although it seems like a waste of time, they always come back happy. Almost sickeningly so.

The light clinking of forks against plates and spoons against cups soothes the atmosphere as we eat. They continue to chat about random things while my mind is still on Mom's reaction from earlier. She was thrown off. I glance over at her, her fork resting against her plate as she chews her last bite. She knows something.

"Hey, mom?" I say, setting my own fork down. Everyone turns to face me, the silence allowing my words to ring clear.

"Yes, dear?"

"Did you know Dad had a personal journal?" I ask. She seems undisturbed by the question.

"I'm sure he had one. Why?" she responds, lifting her teacup to her rosy lips. She takes a sip and places it back on its saucer, the clack vibrating the waves of tension that have formed in the room. She's never been a very good liar and there is no doubt in my mind that her previous reaction was real. However, her ability to shut off her emotions in an instant is something I've yet to work my way around. If the color disappears from her eyes, I've lost.

"I was poking around in his office and found a journal. He wrote about me, about us," I tell her.

"All of us?" Nasir asks, confused by the detail.

"Yes, even you two," I answer. "There are parts in it about bringing you guys into the mines to give you a better future. How his plan to use discipline training worked to raise you guys right. He was proud of you both." Nasir looks away, his face cold as always. Natiq scoffs and presses his lips into a tight line. Their usual reaction to bringing up their past with Dad. I only got to know them as my family guards once they took on that title. Before then, I had small glimpses into their life, but never their training.

"I want to know everything, Mom," I say, turning back to her. "It makes me feel closer to him. There are pages missing, pieces of his life that I can't see. I just want the full story." Her eyes roam in thought as she searches for something to say. I can see her conflict in the way she rubs the tablecloth between her thumb and index finger.

Finally, she releases a sigh, "I'm sorry, honey. I know you want to feel close to your father, but there are just some things you can't know yet." She looks over at Nasir and Natiq with pity in her eyes. Natiq hits the table with his fist, rattling the silverware and making us jump as he stands. He swipes his plate from the table and leaves without a word. I eye Nasir in confusion as he takes off after his younger brother. Mom stands as well, calling for Natiq as she rushes out of the room.

"What's his problem," I mutter as I push back from the table. I make my way out of the dining room and halfway up the stairs when I hear Natiq from the living room. I tiptoe back down, stopping a few feet back from the doorway to evade Nasir's creepy sixth sense to know when someone's listening.

"You know very well that I can't," Mom stresses. "You know she loves him. I can't take that from her."

"It's not taking anything away. We all know who he was and made our decisions, why can't she?" Natiq replies, voice hard as stone. Even when angry he manages to keep a respectful tone with her.

"I know, and I'm sorry about what you boys went through, but she still has a chance to be better than he was. Change like that isn't fueled by hatred. She's our daughter," Mom says.

"Right," Nasir scoffs. "Your *actual* kid."

"No!" she shouts, her voice panicked. "You're both my kids too. I just mean that he was her biological father and-" She's cut off by muffled laughter, probably coming from Nasir. He whines as I hear a smack against skin, laughter escaping once again.

"Look, she's old enough to know," Natiq says. "You can't protect her forever, no matter how hard you try. How she feels about him is her decision to make and, regardless of what you decide, just know that I can't keep up this act anymore."

I duck back into the dining room as I hear footsteps approaching. Natiq's shoulders are tense as he goes down the hallway to his bedroom. I hear my mother sigh and Nasir's gentle voice as he tries to comfort her. Taking the opportunity, I sneak up the stairs and into my bedroom. I pull the journal off my bedside table as the bed creaks under my weight.

A few minutes later, I smirk as I hear a knock at my door. She could never resist a life lesson or teaching moment. I hop off my bed and open the door, dropping my smirk.

"Yes?" I ask, moving to sit back on my bed. She steps into the room, clutching her robe to her chest. "Is Natiq okay?"

"Huh? Oh, yes. He's fine," she answers. "He's just upset that I haven't been as honest with you as I can be."

"Why not?" She sits next to me and I scoot away.

"You aren't ready to bear the burden," she says simply. Something shifts in me at her words and I lose my tact.

"Bear the burden? I've been operating this entire company since it was handed to me at eighteen and *I'm* not ready to *bear the burden*?" I laugh in disbelief.

"Tansae, there are some things you're better off not knowing about your father. He's not who you thought he was," she says softly.

"Oh please, this isn't really about me. You're just too scared. You always have been," I sneer. There's a fire in her eyes as she faces me, something I haven't seen in years. If there is something Dad ingrained in me, it's the ability to get what I want, and something tells me that's just what I'm about to get.

"Tansae," she says, slowly tucking a loose hair behind her ear. "You only know what he told you because you aren't supposed to know the rest. I'm doing this to protect you, to protect your love for him." She takes a deep breath and the fire vanishes from her eyes.

"That's my decision to make," I say, repeating Natiq's words from earlier. She stares at me for a moment, considering lowering the last wall of her defense. Her eyes lower to the journal in my hands and I allow her to gently take it from me. I can't decipher the emotion that is present in her eyes as she flips through the pages. A myriad of feelings always rush to the forefront at any mention of my father. Her thumbs run over the leather as she looks back up at me and utters the word I've been waiting for.

"Okay."

CHAPTER 22

TANSAE'S POV

"Your father was a nice man once," she starts, flipping the journal open. She scans the pages to relay every detail in the right order. Her eyes are empty as she digs into her mind, pulling forward a past that I've never known. I stare at her lips as she parts them for a moment only to shut them again, this action repeating a few times before words finally flow free. "But the truth is, Tansae, your father only knew how to get what he wanted because he convinced others they wanted the same thing. As a businessman, I can respect that, but it took me years to realize he used that skill to manipulate me. I was his trophy, a doll that wasn't allowed to speak. He convinced me he wanted children when he only wanted an heir to the fortune he was building. I watched him use me to create the world he wanted, only to leave me with nothing. Nothing...but you," she says.

"So what?" I ask.

She sighs, her hands folding together in her lap, "Honey, you may see him as a rich man who never let anything stand in his way, but that's not the role he promised us. He was hollow. He used us both."

"He invested in me," I respond. She huffs and I begrudgingly make a decision to keep my mouth shut. "Continue."

She takes a deep breath and smoothes her hair down, gathering it over one shoulder, "I married your father because he said he wanted to give me the world. I do believe there was a time when he loved me, but it was short-lived. I found myself standing further and further behind him with each public appearance. He shut me out more, making each idea I had sound more idiotic than the next. I was nothing more than a factor in his equation for success."

She flips through the journal until she lands on my section, a sorrowful smile etching into her features. "I wanted children and he was thrilled to start a family, so I held onto hope that he still cared for me. He was supportive through the pregnancy, and for the first time in years, I felt like his wife again. I thought I finally had him back, but once you were born it all stopped. You were too young to remember how little he was around, but you...you were so amazing. Caring, loving, talented, and intelligent beyond words. You brought a light back into my life that I had lost long ago. I stayed for you, and only you. Your father had proven he didn't care about me the way he promised, but I could still give my love to you."

She flips a bit further, her smile fading into a blank expression, "I had seven years with you before he decided my time was up and he ripped you from me. At first, I thought nothing of it. He told me he wanted to teach you about the mines and the company, that it was a wonderful educational opportunity. He said he wanted to spend time with you and I couldn't refuse, but you soon began rejecting the things you used to love and I became concerned."

"How could you be concerned if you were never around?" I ask. Since I can remember she's always been busy and when she did come around she was too tired.

"Your father gave me some of his work. He sent me off to appearances, made me supervise the mines, and do charity work. He cut me off from our funds so that I had to work in order to live. That's how I found the children's home. I wanted to leave so many times, but I couldn't leave you behind. I wanted more children, but he insisted that one was enough. I don't know if I could've taken him taking another one from me."

Her face falls as she explains, the same pitiful look she carried in my youth. She always seemed guilty. A dark cloud has hung over her since I can remember. The day I came back from the mines injured was the only time I recall her trying to be a mother to me. The panic in her voice echoes in my mind each time I look at the scars. The way she held me in her arms. She hasn't held me that way since, but according to her, it wasn't her fault.

"So, Dad made you out to be some kind of deadbeat mother?" I ask with skepticism.

"I know it sounds strange, but essentially yes. I tried to do the best I could. Read you stories at night after he went to bed, take you with me to appearances, and even try to teach you things and bond with you. Though, each time he found out he would give me more work to do. For years I had to pay him to live with my own daughter. He used me, both of us, to get what he wanted. He got a wife and an heir from me, and he got a legacy through you," she explains.

My lips pull into a tight line as I try to take in what she's saying. "If you knew what kind of person he was, why didn't you tell me? You had moments when we were alone, and it's been two years since he died. Why hide it?" I ask.

She sighs, "He was manipulative and power-hungry, but he was also a source of inspiration to you. Even in this journal he spoke so highly of you and gave you the confidence to accomplish anything, something I couldn't give you being under his thumb. The things he taught were life skills, things to help you succeed. Telling you what he was doing to me seemed unfair to you. He had a darker side to him. The money and power he gained from finding the Water Stone only fueled his greed," she says, flipping to the next section of the journal. "He found it shortly after we got married and the company got so busy that he began to abandon me for it. Our first argument was over the new textbooks he was funding. I tried to get him to understand the value of our history, but he knew that if the city was dependent on his knowledge of the stone, the company would make more money. He didn't care for people anymore."

I stare for a moment in silence, the only sound being the clock on the wall of my room. She's serious. That look, it's like she's pleading for understanding. For pity. I feel a tightness in my chest as my body begins to shake. A hand clasps over my mouth until I can't hold it in anymore. Laughter flies from me, the force of it racking my body. Mom's eyes widen in surprise at my action, a twinge of fear resting in them.

"That's it?" I manage to say through my laughter. "That's what you were so scared to tell me? That he was a bad husband?"

"I- he- Tansae-" she stutters, trying to gather her thoughts. I raise a hand to stop her as my laughter subsides.

"No, seriously. That's all? What about the missing pages? Was that the day he hurt your feelings," I muse. Her face switches between shock and confusion as she tries to piece together my reaction.

"What...is wrong with you?" she finally says.

"You're what's wrong with me," I say plainly.

"What?"

"You heard me. I've wanted to know about my father for years. To know him outside of the company and when I finally get you to spill, you give me a sob story about how he wasn't the perfect husband. I practically grew up without a mother and you want me to hate him because of how he treated you?"

"I don't want you to hate him. I hid this from you for that very reason. When you struggled to learn things, he let you fall and wouldn't even let me pick you back up. Sure he had good advice here and there, but he didn't give you the love you needed," she pleads.

"And you did?" I laugh. "Aurora was more of a mother to me. You weren't around."

"I couldn't be, Tansae. He didn't let me."

"Let you," I snort. "You act like you had no options."

"He took everything I had," she deadpans. "Everything. My money, my confidence, and even my dignity at times. By the time I had you, I had nothing left. You gave me purpose and hope."

"And you gave me nothing in return," I fire back. "He may not have been the husband you wanted, but look at what he's done. He created an empire. He left us with power and enough wealth to do anything we desire."

"You don't know what you're talking about. You have no idea what I've gone through with your father," she snaps, voice trembling. "You don't know what I had to pretend to be for him. The things I've had to endure. He never gave me a choice, but now I'm taking my life back."

"Is that what you call prancing around in lavish robes? You act as if you're glad he's dead. You just wanted to bury your fear with him," I accuse.

"I wanted to give you a choice, Tansae," she says, taking my face in her hands. Her robe slides off her shoulder as brown eyes meet my green ones, pleading with me to listen. "He engrained this company into you, but have you ever thought about what you want out of life? You can use what he left behind to create opportunities for yourself. You can travel and be anything you want. You don't have to follow in his footsteps just because that's what he raised you to do. You can help others, be your own person, and find love."

"Like you?" I retort, pulling her hands from my face. "What I want is to keep living the life I already have. What do you have to show for your pathetic life? Some ratty blankets, old baskets, ugly pottery, and smiles from a few brats. Sounds like a dream." Silent tears fall from her eyes and roll down her wrinkled cheeks. Guilt tugs at my chest, but I brush it away as I place her hands back in her lap.

Things last, people don't. One day I'll be gone and all you'll have left is to carry my legacy. Dad's words ring clearly in my mind. I can still see him standing above me, speaking without looking me in the eye. The smell of his cologne as I cling to his suit jacket ever present in my memory. The only time he smiled at me was when I gave him a proud *'Yes, sir.'* His legacy. That's all I was. It's all I'm meant to be and I'm happy with the role I get to play. Why she can't understand that, I'll never know.

Since dad died she's always been correcting me. Always 'don't do this' or 'don't say that'. Maybe I'd listen if I knew it would please her, but she's never been proud of me. I know if Dad were still alive today, *he'd* be proud of me. That's what keeps me going.

"I'm sorry, honey," she mumbles. I look back at her, still frozen and disheveled. Many things come to mind at her expression. Disappointment, frustration, guilt. Things I'm all too familiar with coming from her. "I want to teach you what your father couldn't. I want you to value relationships and people as I do," she says softly.

"I don't care. I asked you about this journal because I want to know what's on the missing pages," I say.

"Tansae, please–"

"Do you know about them or not?" I deadpan.

She looks up at me sullenly, searching for something. I could feel her trying to peel back the layers of my mind, attempting to find a part of me she can reach, but to no avail. She had her chance. Twenty years worth to be a mother to me. If she really wanted to, nothing would have stood in her way, not even my dad. She wipes away her tears and stands from the bed, walking over to the bedroom door. Her hands clutch her robe, shifting it back in place. She pauses to look at me over her shoulder, "Well, are you coming?"

I stand and follow her as he leads me to Dad's room and slowly opens the door. Her foot taps at the floorboards as we enter and I eye her in confusion until she steps on one near the bed that clicks. She bends down, pressing it harder and the other end pops up. Her fingernails prod at the floorboard and she pulls it loose, setting it beside her and reaching inside. Her hand emerges with a few aged pages folded neatly into a small stack.

"When I saw your note about going to find the missing soulmates, I hid the journal and tore these pages out. He took things too far, but since you insist you need to know everything," she says, extending her hand toward me. I take the papers from her with a grin and she stands. "I suppose it's better that you read it. Just know that you still have a choice."

I smirk as I leaf through the few pages, scanning the words. Her face is blank, eyes empty and unchanging. I quickly shift my eyes back to the pages in my hands, ignoring the strange feeling in my stomach at her silence. She pushes past me and leaves the room. I shrug and follow after her, closing the door behind me. Her robe flows behind her as she descends the stairs and my eyes follow until she's out of sight. *Thanks, Mom. You were finally good for something.*

As I enter my room again, I see Nasir sitting on my bed flipping through Dad's journal. His shoulder-length hair is down from its usual bun, hiding parts of his face. His jaw is set as he looks up at me.

"What?" I ask defensively, sliding the pages into my back pocket. His eyes follow my movements before meeting mine again.

"So she told you?" he asks. His emotional mask is turned up to a level where I can't even read him, but based on the topic of choice I'll assume he's upset at me.

"If you mean her sob story about her failed marriage, yeah," I respond. I pull my chair from my desk to take a seat and face him as he sighs.

"So she didn't tell you," he mumbles just loud enough for me to hear.

I roll my eyes, "Look, I'm getting a bit tired of everyone's cryptic bullshit. Spill it or get out." His jaw ticks slightly, a loud clap ringing in the air as he shuts the journal. The force of the action softly blowing the hair off his cheeks. He tosses it beside him and turns so his full figure faces me. His mask falls as he takes a deep breath.

"Do you know how Natiq and I got to Iron Brimstone?" he asks.

"Wasn't it Dad's idea to take you in?"

"Kind of," he responds, a hand running up through his hair. "My brother and I were quite the troublemakers. We didn't like being stuck in the children's home here in Mysticane since the one we ran from in Eastgarde was less than satisfactory. So when your father started his correctional program for troubled teens, the owner of the children's home suggested we go. Though I'm sure the old man just wanted us out of his hair, we were happy to get away, so we went."

His gaze falls to the floor, hands clasping together as his elbows rest on his knees. "I didn't realize how awful it was for a while. Fifteen and thirteen years old, working day and night in the mines which is already no place for children. Forced to push through the pain for hours on end only to be given half a meal because, according to your father, we didn't need as much food. The men in the mines tried to help by giving us some of theirs, but once he found out he isolated us from the group. I was so happy the day the program ended. After six months of work, he deemed us corrected when in reality, he'd just beaten it out of us. We'd been trained to obey for fear of punishment, and although Natiq still had some fight in him, I learned to hold him back for his own protection. The day everything changed was the day before we were supposed to leave. When you were attacked," he explains, looking up at me again.

"Attacked? By the wildcat?" I ask.

"He saw us jump into action to save you. Natiq managed to rush you off to your mom while I fended off the animal until one of your dad's guards managed to kill it. That's how I got this nasty scar," he says, pointing to his face. My brows furrow at his statement.

"Wait, Dad was the one who killed it," I retort.

He looks equally confused at my words, "No, the head guard Nile was the one who killed it."

"But he showed me the dagger," I mumble to myself. I sit in silence, trying to remember what exactly happened that day. I saw the dagger in my dad's hands. I guess that doesn't necessarily mean *he* killed it. I shake my thoughts away as Nasir opens his mouth to continue.

"Anyway, he still planned to kick us out, but Mom begged him to let us stay. She convinced him we would make good guards for you as you got older and eventually be your right-hand men. He agreed and moved us over to be trained under Nile. The conditions were only better there because your dad wasn't directly overseeing it. We were free from his torment for a while until Natiq fucked up and your dad got caught in one of his stupid pranks."

"He was gone for weeks," I mention.

"I almost didn't come back alive," a voice says from the doorway. Our heads snap in that direction, seeing Natiq leaning against the frame with a scowl. "Those weeks I was missing, he kept me in the mines. I got food every other night and only got a full meal when Nasir managed to sneak me one," he says, moving into the room. He leans against the wall with arms crossed over his broad chest.

"When he found out, he gave me a strict curfew and told me that Natiq had to pay the price for his actions," Nasir adds. "I tried to go to your mom for help, but she was dealing with too much at the time."

"And the rest is history I suppose?" I remark with a shrug. "Mom adopted you, filling the hole in her heart and you rode off into the sunset. Everybody's happy."

"Tansae, we are both still dealing with the effects of what he did to us," Nasir says calmly. I release a small breath, bored by the length of this story yet slightly amused by their serious faces.

"What I'm hearing is that you were rowdy and received discipline. It looks to me like you both turned out alright," I say, turning back to my desk. I can't see their reaction, but I can feel their disdain for my response. Heavy footsteps sound behind me as one of them exits the room, slamming the door behind them.

"I had hope for you, Tansae," Natiq says after a moment of pained silence. "We all want you to be better than him, your mom especially."

"I will be, Natiq. You think I've been working this hard for nothing?" I aimlessly arrange my papers as an excuse to not look at him.

I hear him come up behind me before my chair is swung around, forcing me to face him.

"I'm not talking about this stupid company, I'm talking about with us. The people who've raised you, who truly care about your well-being," he seethes.

I roll my eyes. Why does everyone keep taking credit for my upbringing when they weren't a part of it? "You're paid to protect me, that doesn't exactly count."

"You think Nasir and I only care about you because we get paid to do so?" he says in disbelief. He steps back from me, running his hands over his head and down his face. "We were friends once. I enjoyed being around you until that man kept you under lock and key from everyone who held any bearing on your emotional state. We love you like a sister, but you don't even care."

"How can you hate him when he's helped you so much? You only have a home thanks to him," I point out, crossing my arms.

"That prison he called a correctional program was created for publicity. He didn't give a fuck about us or our development. He gave us a roof, sure, but a home? Mom gave us a home. She taught us kindness and showed us love beyond what we had ever known. We only grew under her care. She wants nothing more than to do the same for you," he explains, a familiar desperation in his tone.

"I can't help that we value different things. I only know what I was taught."

"But you can learn something new. You can learn to appreciate the people in your life and the relationships you have. He's not here to hurt you anymore," he pleads.

My eyes harden at his words, "He never hurt me."

"He's got you so brainwashed you don't even see it," he says. "Don't you care that he hurt us? That he hurt *our* mom?”

“He didn’t hurt you all either,” I snap, standing from my seat. The chair scrapes against the floor as I step forward to meet him. “You are just too stubborn and ungrateful to see what he did for you. He’s the reason we are all here today, why we are here together, and you guys act like you’re glad he’s dead,” I accuse.

“I *am* glad he’s dead,” he spits, the force of his statement causing my eyes to widen. The venom in his tone stings and my face drops. His chest is heaving inches away from mine. “He put me through the worse treatment of my life, Tansae. He made me feel less than human and separated me from my own brother. The one source of comfort I had in this hellhole. He wouldn’t have given a fuck if I died, so why should I care that he did?”

I eye him in disgust as he remains unmoving. It’s rare that I see him angry, but his usual playful self is gone. The intensity of his hatred rolls off in waves and forces me backward. This is the first time I’ve felt afraid of him. Something tells me that if he wasn’t a child when it all happened, my father would’ve died by his hands instead of illness.

He takes a deep breath which gives me permission to release my own. He looks towards the door, the gears in his head turning as he tries to find something to say. My mouth is clamped shut. Despite my anger, I can’t predict his reaction when he’s in a state I’ve never seen before.

“I can’t convince you of anything, but I just ask that you think about all of this. Who you are and who you want to be. He wanted you to be him, but you still have a choice,” he says, walking towards the door. My shoulders relax as he gets further away. His hand grips the handle as he steps across the threshold. He pauses and turns to look at me, the same empty look of pity and sorrow in his eyes that Mom had. The same look Nasir had before he left the room. “Be careful what you choose, Tansae. I can't speak for my brother or your mom, but if you choose to follow your father's path, you're for damn sure going to lose me." With that, he exits the room, my door closing with a soft click.

I stand frozen in place, an icy chill running through me at the interaction. My room feels lifeless. Thoughts race through my mind from all the information. *Was he really that bad?* The three of them didn't see my father like I did. They didn't see his proud smile or come to learn about all he sacrificed to give me the life I live today. The reason they can live this life is because of him, because of what he built. He used what he had to get what he wanted, even if those things were people. He wasn't perfect. He yelled at me at times and watched me struggle, but I never resented him for it. I knew he had a plan for me. He was leading me to a greater purpose. I don't choose to ignore his behavior, I choose to appreciate his methods.

I take a deep breath, my exhale releasing all the stress as I lift my head. They're too blind to see the vision he had in store for Iron Brimstone.

I free the pages from my pocket, taking a seat at my desk. If they don't understand his methods then they surely won't understand mine. My mind's been made up and my plan is already in motion. As I read the title of the final section of his journal, I am certain of my choice.

The Secret of My Success

CHAPTER 23

ENDEL'S POV

"Hey," Zyl whines while reaching for his bag of pretzels. I stand on my toes, holding it just out of reach. The blue bracelet encircling my wrist slips down a bit towards my elbow as I extend my arm. "How many times do I have to tell you to leave my snacks alone?"

"I only had one," I laugh, holding a pretzel stick between my lips.

"One you stole," Zyl points out. "At least ask first."

"Fine, fine," I say, rolling my eyes. I lower the bag so it's an inch above his fingertips, "Can I have some, please?"

"Hmm, no," he says, jumping up to snatch it from me with a playful glare.

I shrug, pushing the one pretzel I have into my mouth completely, "Worth a shot."

Heriath laughs as she finishes loading her stuff into the new wagon we got earlier that morning. We made the decision to purchase a smaller wagon for the same price as renting a large one. Plus, I will need to return home so it didn't seem like a bad investment.

The past day has been much better since our initial awkward

first date. This morning has been productive. Breakfast, a supply run, and getting our new wagon ready were made enjoyable by Zyl's early morning rambling. He's an endless book of fun facts, plus the discount on our wagon was all thanks to his negotiation skills.

I plop next to Heriath on the driver's bench, leaning back to straighten my legs while she fiddles with the engine. "So, when are you going to release me from my prison," I ask, gesturing to my stitches.

"If I tell you, you'll want me to remove them sooner," she says.

"Aww, come on. I'll be good," I grin. She sits back and looks at me with a raised eyebrow. "What? I've been good so far, haven't I?"

Her skepticism melts into an amused smile, "I suppose so."

"So?"

"They should be healed by now. I'll take them out when we arrive in Whitburn." I fist pump and she laughs, pulling the lever to start our movement. "Why don't you join Zyl in the back?"

I clutch a hand over my heart and throw my head back, "You wound me. I didn't realize you hated me so much."

"Endel," she laughs softly. "I don't hate you."

"Then why? Why cast me aside?" My melodramatic tone coaxes more giggles from her. I roll my head to the side, catching a glimpse of the hair charm I made for her. It sparkles in the mid-morning sun as it hangs from her crown of locs. It suits her. Maybe I should make her more.

"I just don't want him to be all alone back there," she says once her laughter calms.

"But you'll be all alone up here."

She waves dismissively, "I'll be fine. You go relax." I eye her for a moment as her gaze returns to the road before taking her advice.

Zyl looks up at me from the book in his lap, "Kicked off the bench, huh?”

"Not exactly," I answer. He scoots to the side and I sit next to him, leaning back against Heriath's trunk. *Relax.* All I've been doing is relaxing lately while she's been running around taking care of me. I jump as Zyl snaps next to my left ear.

"Sorry, what?"

"You alright?" he asks. "You're staring."

I wipe a hand over my face, "Sorry. Did you say something?" He glances to Heriath before looking back at me and shaking his head. I shift to grab my bag of crafting supplies and pull out my current work in progress. I grip the blue hilt of my pocket knife as I carefully work the edges of the cedar block. The jolting of the wagon makes it difficult to perfect the details, but I manage. The next few hours are filled with idle chatter as we make our way to Whitburn.

Once we arrive, we find an inn and Heriath removes my stitches before crashing. Zyl and I still have plenty of energy and I'm particularly eager to stretch my legs knowing what could be found here. I quietly set down the last of my things while Zyl is in his room changing for our walk. I take the time to freshen up, careful to not disturb Heriath's sleeping form. Her soft snoring brings a grin to my face. I pull out a quilt from my trunk and place it over her. She snuggles underneath it and my muscles finally relax when her snores continue.

I slip out of the room and bump into Zyl who is standing on the other side. He slips backward and I manage to catch him, pulling him to my chest to avoid his head knocking against the opposite wall. His weight forces me backward and my back slams against the door. I wince, hoping the noise wasn't loud enough to wake Heriath.

"Sorry, I was just about to knock," Zyl apologizes.

"It's alright," I laugh. "I just- woah!" Gravity yanks me to the floor as the door opens. Zyl lands on top of me, knocking the wind from my lungs. *Ow.*

"Whoops," Heriath says with a giggle. Her tired eyes observe us for a moment, "You boys alright?"

"I'm okay," I wheeze. Zyl stares down at me through his brown curls, our eyes locked for a moment before he pushes off of me. His freckled cheeks are bright red as he apologizes over and over. I laugh and sit up, "I guess you're rubbing off on me." He helps me up while Heriath returns to bed, tossing the quilt over her body completely as I shut the door.

The forest surrounding us sings with the breeze that blows by. Zyl and I have gone off trail and into the thicket to search for stones. A lot of the stones I wire wrap and use for other crafts are native to this area.

The grass brushes against my ankles as I scan the ground for colorful spots. There are a few flowers here and there, but nowhere near as many as back home. Downstream doesn't have as many colorful plants which would explain why everyone's attire is less bright. Zyl being an exception with his polychromatic shawls.

I clear my throat, "So, Zyl." He looks up at me with a hum. "Tell me a bit about yourself."

He chuckles, "Haven't I been doing that for the past three days?"

"No, I'm talking about the juicy stuff. Your darkest secrets. Deepest fears."

"Uh, well I'm afraid of birds," he shrugs.

I nearly choke on my laugh, "Birds?"

"They can be aggressive," he defends, bending down to pick up a pink stone.

"What's that one?" I ask.

"Rosetta Dolspinel if I'm not mistaken. Though it has a sister, Ruby Dolspinel. They vary by one or two shades on the outside."

"How can you tell which is which?"

"Ruby has a black interior and is quite fragile." He finds a larger stone and extends it to me, "Drop this on it." I take it, holding it at eye level while he places the small pink one on the ground. I drop it and the pink rock cracks in half revealing black.

I hum, "Ruby." He smiles at me as I tuck the remainder of the rock into a small pouch that hangs from my hip. We continue to walk until we reach a clearing. "Any other strange fears?" He takes a seat in the grass, leaning against a tree as I collect a few more stones around the area.

"Nope, it's your turn," he smirks. I sigh and place the last stone into my pouch before sitting beside him.

"I guess that's fair." His curls fall to frame his face as he tilts his head for me to continue. I lean my head back to stare up through the branches above us, "I am...afraid of the dark." A moment of silence. Another. Then laughter. I can't help the smile on my face when he snorts and attempts to cover it with his hand.

"Sorry," he manages through his snickers. "A six-foot-one guy such as yourself being afraid of the dark is not what I expected."

"Well, a fear of birds doesn't come out of anyone's mouth on a regular basis either," I fire back. "What's the story behind that?"

He calms down and takes a deep breath, joining me in watching the sky above us. The clouds peek through the branches as they roll by. "We had a pet bird when I was younger. His name was Archibald and he had the most beautiful green and blue feathers. I liked to take him outside when I fed him despite my mother's warnings. I spilled the bag of bird seed she'd just bought not realizing a flock of birds was sitting in a nearby tree. I was completely swarmed until my mom ran outside and swatted them away with a broom. By then I already had plenty of scrapes and what felt like a hundred feathers in my mouth and nose," he laughs.

"And what happened to Archibald?" I ask, looking over at him.

"I entrusted him to a scientist friend of mine I met in Kaelora," he answers. He turns his head with a grin, "You can laugh. It's a funny image, I know."

I shake my head, hands raised in defense, "Me? No, I take your plight seriously." He gently shoves me and we burst into laughter. The wind carries our voices between the trees as we calm down again.

"You know," he starts, his tone more serious. "This isn't as scary as I thought it would be."

My brows knit together, "Going on a walk with me?"

"No, silly. I mean this. Us. The day I found out, I hid without knowing when I'd come out. I wasn't scared of you, but more so of being important."

"What do you mean?"

He turns to face me, legs crossing in front of him, "I've always wanted to make a difference. That's why I became a historian and professor, but my talents have always put me in the background. I was so afraid I'd do something wrong, but you've made it easy. I'm used to my gifts being more important than me. Decoding information and understanding what others can't. Not falling in love." He meets my eyes, panic setting in. "Not that I don't like you. You're fun to be around and a wonderful friend. I just meant-"

I put up a hand to stop him, "I understand." His panic simmers into a shy grin. "But, Zyl, you shouldn't discount yourself. You have done something important."

He scoffs, tucking some of his curls behind his ear, "And what's that?"

I give him a reassuring smile as he meets my gaze again, "You found me. We wouldn't be here without you and your gifts aren't what make you a great friend." His cheeks turn rosy as he looks down, his curls falling to hide his face.

"I guess I did," he mumbles, standing from his spot. I take his extended hand and stand at his side. He clears his throat, "So, backtracking. What's the tale behind your fear of the dark?"

I shake my head, "That's a story for another time."

"What? No fair," he gapes.

"Life isn't fair," I joke. A green stone catches my eye and I walk forward to pick it up. "What's this one?"

He observes it, "Emerald Zinnia. Interesting thing about those, the minerals accelerate plant growth."

"That's perfect," I grin.

"For what?"

"I've been wanting to make another hair charm for Heriath. Or maybe something else."

"Are you always making things for people?"

"Why not?" I shrug. "You use your gifts to contribute knowledge and I use mine to spread joy. Besides, she's been doing so much for us lately. She deserves something nice." My thumb runs over the rough surface of the stone. It'll take some work, but it'll be worth it.

"Her healing work seems draining. She's stronger than most," he comments.

"Don't I know it."

"You know, a gift sounds nice, but what I think she needs is a chance to unwind. Maybe think about herself for once." The path to the village is easy to find and we make our way back to the village circle. I turn the small stone over in my hand as I observe the buildings around us and a small smile tugs at my lips.

"You're right," I tell him.

And I know just how to do it.

CHAPTER 24

HERIATH'S POV

The smell of wet grass surrounds me as I race to catch up with Yamala. She stops between two trees and I take a moment to catch my breath. "You're going too fast," I huff.

She giggles and pats my back, "Sorry, baby sis."

"I'm not a baby," I whine. The branches above us weave together to shade us from the sun.

Yamala points up at the tree beside us, "We can get a better look from up there." I watch as she jumps and catches a low branch. She pulls herself up and stands on it to reach the next one.

I shrink in my spot, "I don't know. It's really high." She grins down at me and hooks the back of her knees over the branch. She flips down and extends a hand to me.

"Don't worry. I'll help you."

I stare at her hand, "Are you sure?"

"It's just one branch at a time," she grins, her missing front tooth creating a gap in her smile. "I'll be right here."

I take her hand and she pulls me up onto the branch. I follow her up the tree step by step. She's careful to take it slow, matching my pace. We reach a large branch both of us can sit on and she helps me balance.

"You okay?" she asks. I nod, gripping the trunk for dear life. She stands and observes the ground below us, squinting for a better view. "Come on, help me look," she urges. I slowly turn around and hug the branch instead so I can scan the ground. "There!" she exclaims. "I think I saw something. Let's go!"

"Wait," I call as she quickly scrambles down the tree. I hold the branch tighter, my breathing picking up as the height starts to get the better of me. "Yamala!"

No answer.

I find the courage to peek down. My heart sinks at the desolate gray that spreads across the forest floor and kills everything in sight. It creeps closer to the tree with every breath.

"Yamala!" I cry louder. I desperately scan the ground, but she's nowhere to be found. "Yamala, please! Don't leave me up here! I don't know how to get down!" The gray touches the base of the tree and it shakes beneath me. Dread fills my body as the base begins to crumble into ashes. The snap of lower branches shakes the tree harder as tears run down my cheeks. I squeeze my eyes shut with one last desperate shout for my sister when suddenly everything falls still.

My eyes shoot open and the rough branch becomes a soft pillow in my arms. My head snaps to the side to find Endel perched on the side of the bed.

"There you are," he whispers. My heart pounds wildly in my chest as I try to adjust to my surroundings. "You okay, Heriath?"

I swallow and shut my eyes again, draping an arm across my face, "Yeah. I'm fine."

"You were crying. Are you sure?" he asks softly. The nightmare worms its way into my mind again and I blink back new tears that threaten to spill. "You know, if you want to talk about it, I'm right here."

I shake my head, hearing him sigh. Silence simmers between us as I collect my thoughts and emotions. I remove my arm and swipe the nearly dried tears from my face. I can feel his gaze on me as I stare up at the ceiling.

"Could I at least offer a hug?" he says. I hesitantly nod and he helps me sit up. His arms wrap around my neck, a hand cradling my head as I hug his waist. The steady beat of his heart helps calm mine's rapid pace. We remain there for a minute or two with no words uttered between us. I take a few deep breaths and we separate.

"There's that smile," he teases and I look to my lap. "Well, if you don't wanna talk then how about a distraction?" I raise an eyebrow at him as he hops up from the bed with a knowing grin. He extends a hand, "Up for a rendezvous?"

We step outside, the last rays of sunlight slipping behind the buildings to our right. The leaves crunch under our feet on the pathway, lighting it with their many hues. I glance over at Endel who hasn't stopped tugging at his bracelets since we left the inn.

"Where are we going?" I ask.

"Be patient," he smirks. I huff as he scans the buildings, eyes lighting up when he spots something. "Here we are," he says with a small hop. His hands shoot out to gesture to the wood shop in front of us. I stare at the door, the intricate carvings spelling out the name of the place. "Come on," he urges, pushing the door open.

The pillars throughout the room have swirled carvings with multicolored stones lodged into them creating a series of beautiful patterns. The light from the lanterns reflects off of the stones and gives more color to the room. He grabs my hand and brings me inside where we are greeted by one of the workers who is lighting the last lantern.

They blow out the match in their hand and discard it before waving us over to the counter. "Welcome to Sticks and Stones Wood Shop. Have you lovebirds been here before?" they ask. It takes the word *'lovebirds'* to make me realize his hand is still in mine.

"Uh, no we haven't," he stutters, letting go of my hand and tucking his into the pocket of his pants. I remain unmoving as I stand awestruck at the design of the shop.

The worker smiles brightly and begins to explain the process. Since Whitburn is between Vyelan's two major cities they get a lot of people who pass through. This wood shop became a tourist attraction over time. We can take our pick of a ring, bracelet, or necklace and a worker will guide us through the process of making our chosen piece. The charm or stone of our jewelry is made from the many natural minerals and gemstones that are native to this area.

"Here are our stone options," the worker says, leading us to a large table with small sections for each of the stones to be organized in. "Take your pick."

"Thank you, but I already have our stones," Endel says. I shoot him a curious look and he pulls his hand from his pocket. His fist opens to reveal a green stone with flecks of black.

"Is this mine?"

"That depends," he says, eyeing me cautiously. "Do you like it?"

"It's amazing. Where did you find this?" I gape, taking it from his hand.

"Let's just say that walk I took with Zyl was well worth it." He reaches into his pocket again and pulls out a yellow stone, turning to the worker to tell them we're ready.

The worker helps us polish our stones before guiding us to a new area where we choose our wood. I chose gooseberry wood, and Endel chooses pine. Working with the wood is difficult, but fun. Endel lights up during our time in the shop, happily sanding and carving the space for the stone to fit in his ring. I, however, struggle to make the circle required for my necklace. Endel freed the worker from my constant questions and took over helping me after a while. I now sit next to him at the sander and watch closely as he carefully turns my jagged rectangle into a smooth oval. He looks content and comfortable in his element.

"There you go," he says, lifting the wood to inspect the bottom in the light. I take the charm from him and run my fingers along it to admire his handiwork.

"Thank you."

"Well, we aren't done yet. You still have to carve out the space for your stone in the center," he says, standing to move to the table with carving tools.

"What?" I groan, following suit. He laughs at my reaction, assuring me that he can still help me out. I take a seat and grab a tool that matches his. I slowly carve into the wood as best I can. It's hard to focus as he sits across from me. His dark brown eyes are focused and he subconsciously bites the inside of his cheek. I've certainly gained a new respect for his crafting skills.

He swipes the flying wood chips away from his face as he etches a design into his ring band, "So, do you wanna talk about it?"

"About what?" He gives me a pointed look and I turn my eyes back to my work. "No, I wouldn't want to bore you with it."

"Do I look bored?" he asks with a soft smile.

I twist my lips," I don't want to make it your problem."

"Heriath, I'm offering. Whenever I had a nightmare it always helped me to talk about it. You know, sort things out."

I sigh and pick at my thumb, "You're sure?"

"All ears," he grins.

I take in a deep breath, "Well...my mom used to have a garden in our backyard. Some of the flowers started going missing and Yamala was convinced it was trolls."

"Trolls?" he laughs.

I roll my eyes playfully, "She was twelve."

He nods, "Continue."

I lift my carving tool and start to poke at my necklace again, "Anyways, she dragged me out into the woods to go look for them. She wanted to get a better look, so we climbed a tree together. I was terrified to come down, even when she tried to coach me from the ground. Eventually, she had to come up and guide me herself. We kept exploring and ended up getting lost. Now I was only eight, so being in a dark forest wasn't ideal. I panicked and cried for who knows how long, but she never left my side. We sat in the wet grass and she held me until I calmed down before finding our way to the Nafsi."

"Was that your dream?" he asks.

I shake my head and my smile drops, "I was back in the tree but when I looked down to her for help she was gone. I screamed and cried, but nothing...nobody came."

Endel nods, his expression softening, "I'm sorry, Heriath. I know how scary that can be."

"You do?"

He taps his carving tool on the surface of the table, his tongue in his cheek. "Have you ever seen an orange flower with dark blue spots on the inside?" he asks.

I dig through my plant journal in my mind, visualizing each one. Given where he lives it would be a northern plant. My face falls when I realize which flower he's referring to. I look up to find his eyes already on me.

"Please tell me I'm wrong," I whisper. His gaze falls and sorrow fills my chest.

"I was eleven," he says lowly. "I was exploring the fields at the far end of Pine Valley and thought it was pretty. I was going to bring it home to momma, but when I picked it this cloud of purple shot out from the center. I just remember coughing and seeing shadows dance around me. The sound of screams ringing in my ears for what felt like an eternity." He pauses to take a deep breath. His eyes have gone dark as the memory looms like a shadow over his head. "Mom was the one who found me curled into a ball on the wet grass. She said I was confused and fought for a while before I realized it was her. Those shadows still haunt me at times."

Sativa divinorum or the shrieking void is a dangerous hallucinogenic. It's usually used for dyeing clothes because of its bright colors, but the harvesting process is tricky due to the spores. "Oh, Endel. I'm so sorry," I say, placing a hand over his and he smiles softly at the gesture.

"It's alright," he says. "Are you worried about your sister?"

I bite the inside of my cheek, "She's the reason I'm even here. Why I left home in the first place. Why I came to find you. Maybe I feel guilty for leaving."

"Is she okay?"

I shake my head, "She's dying, Endel. Without the Elysir, I'm going to lose her." I pause to take a steadying breath, "She's always known who she is. What she wanted. She protected me that night in the forest. Even if she was afraid she never showed it, but you know what I saw before I left? I saw fear. Clear, unmistakable fear in her eyes. I can't bear the thought of her being alone and afraid without me, but this is my last shot."

It's now that I notice he's stopped working altogether. Both hands wrapped around my shaking one. His eyes meet mine, "You must really love her."

"She's my best friend. She helped me through countless panic attacks as a kid. Since that day I've looked up to her. I wanted to be as brave as she was. To be strong," I whisper.

He smiles, "Hey, I've been on the outside of that worrying mind of yours and I assure you that you are strong. Maybe too strong if you ask me."

"What does that mean?"

His eyes soften, "Take it from someone who was alone when it happened. Asking for help may seem scary or even selfish at times, but it's always the better alternative."

My gaze shifts to the side, "I don't really like making things about me."

"Well, sometimes things need to be." He turns my hand to open my palm and removes my carving tool. He grabs a sheet of sandpaper and places it in my hand before pushing my fingers to close around it. "Your existence is never a burden to those who care for you. I know you're used to giving your all to those in need, but your capacity for compassion needs to extend to yourself as well."

He sits back in his seat and continues his work while I consider his words. I unfurl my fist and use the sandpaper to smooth the bit of wood I was chipping at before. *Mental scars.* I glance up at him, his bottom lip tucked between his teeth in focus. He's right. I know he is. Maybe it just takes someone else to say it.

"And what about you? You're always giving to others," I point out.

His chair creaks softly as he sits back, "I'm a creative, it's my purpose. Though balance is hard to perfect. I still run myself ragged from time to time. Don't even get me started on fairly pricing my artwork." He reaches over to pick up a new tool and continues his work, "I'm a complex guy."

"Are you now?" I smirk.

"It's one of the things you love about me," he says, setting his tool down. He blows the dust off his necklace and I swat, sputtering as it slips past my lousy defenses. "Shit, sorry," he says. I blink rapidly as the grit in my eyes causes tears to form. I dig the heels of my palms into my eyes, slightly panicked as I rub at them. "Hold on. Don't rub too harshly," I hear as his hands meet my wrists.

He pulls them down with one hand while the other comes up to my cheek. His thumb gently traces over to my left eye and raises the lid so he can blow into it. He repeats this action with the other one before resting his palm against my cheek. I blink, allowing the tears to remove the grit from my eyes and run down my face.

"Sorry, I wasn't thinking," he apologizes again. He wipes the tears from my face, "Better?" I nod as my vision clears to find him staring at me. I look down, cursing myself for the way my stomach does a flip. Maybe I'm just not used to being taken care of anymore. My mom used to patch me up, but this feeling is new. I know his care comes from a place of friendship, but the feeling of his hand against my face...

"Thanks," I whisper, the warmth of his hand disappearing as he moves back to his spot. He waves dismissively and we both continue in silence for a while. Nothing but the sound of tools against wood and the occasional curses of frustration from me. Another hour passes and both of our pieces are done. I smile at my necklace with pride as we bid the worker goodbye and head toward the inn.

"So, was it worth the pain and suffering?" Endel muses.

"Yes, my hard work was worth it," I say with a grin.

"*Your* hard work?" he scoffs. "I practically did half the work for you."

"Yes, well, practically half isn't enough to take credit," I shoot back, sticking my tongue out at him.

"Real mature," he laughs.

His ring glints in the moonlight as we walk. He really is an excellent craftsman. It wouldn't have turned out half as good without his help, but that grin on his face shows he's aware of the fact, so there's no need for me to admit it. I rub my hands up and down my exposed arms as a cool breeze slips by. I pick up the pace, thinking of my warm bed that awaits in our room when his footsteps come to a halt. I turn back, brows furrowed, to see him staring into space.

"Endel?"

"Listen," he says. I focus my attention on my surroundings and hear a melody coming from up ahead.

"Music? Is that what- hey," I shout as he swiftly grabs my hand. I stumble as he practically drags me down the path. My hand slips out of his and I stop to catch my breath.

"Come on," he shouts excitedly.

"Where are we going?" I ask, jogging to catch up to him. I finally meet his side in front of Whitburn's tavern. When I finish catching my breath, I stand up straight to see him smiling brightly at the entrance.

It's twice the size of our tavern back home, which makes sense for a tourist village. Music pours out of every window and the chatter of the crowd inside is a joyful melody of its own. "I hate to point out the obvious here, but you've been to a tavern before," I state, confused by his excitement.

"The one back home is nothing like this," he says, pushing open the swinging doors. Chandeliers hang overhead and the wooden floor rumbles with the stomps from the people dancing inside. The amount of energy in such a confined space is jarring. People bump into each other as they try to find their friends while others laugh and converse with strangers on the upper deck, leaning against the railing and observing the dancers below. I can't help the smile that comes to my face at all the joy in the room.

Endel taps my shoulder, "It's a bit loud. You okay with that?" I nod, the excitement in the room overtaking the volume. "Okay, you promise you'll let me know if you need to step out?"

I smile up at him, "I promise." We both follow a barmaid to a clean spot at a long table and take a seat, looking over the menu. The band's music starts to slow and dancers take their leave from the floor to return to their tables as food is served.

"Wow, I've never even heard of some of these things," he exclaims, his voice raised so he can be heard over the noise of the crowd.

"Me neither," I say, looking over the items. He decides on trying something new while I choose something more familiar to home. He rolls his eyes, calling me boring and insisting I at least be more adventurous with dessert. I hesitantly agree after he helps me find something on the dessert menu that I might like.

Once we order, the barmaid suggests that while we wait, we look at some of the upstairs rooms which hold the history of Whitburn Village and a few artifacts from its founding. Itching to explore, Endel thanks her and we take a look around.

We go through all the rooms, marveling at the information they hold. Apparently, a man named Ardale Whitburn founded this place, settling here after finding its array of natural gemstones and rocks to be fascinating. He even identified the Crackle Stones that are used in our engines today instead of coal. They give off a natural heat and reach temperatures as hot as magma which makes our steam engines more powerful and effective.

Endel reads every sign and passage in the rooms, explaining things as if he's a tour guide. I humor him by asking questions and waiting patiently as he finds the answers. His spark bringing me joy as usual.

We return downstairs and sit at our table again to find the surface still empty. "Hmm, I guess the crowd makes for a long wait time," I remark, taking a sip of my water. The band has since changed their tune, a more fast-paced and vibrant song filling the room.

"I guess so," he responds, a mischievous grin rising onto his face. "But..."

"But what?" I ask, giving him a cautious look.

"It gives us time to dance," he says.

My eyes widen and my hands raise as I shake my head, "I don't know about that." He makes his way over to me and grabs both of my hands in his, a pleading pout on his face.

"Please?" he asks, pausing to observe my expression. "Do you not know how?"

"I do. There's just so many people," I point out, glancing around the room.

"Aw, come on. Nobody will be watching us. Besides, when will we have another chance?"

"Um," I trail off. Others laugh and twirl down by the stage, some flailing more than dancing, but nobody seems to care. My eyes meet his again and the light in them tugs at my chest. "Okay," I cave, rolling my eyes playfully.

I yelp as he yanks me up from my seat and pulls me over to the dance floor. We start by catching the beat, pulling each other in and pushing out again. I anxiously stare at the ground, trying to focus on not bumping into anyone. He hops from one foot to the other and lets go of one of my hands. He pulls me into his chest with the other before leaning down to my ear.

"It doesn't have to be perfect, it just has to be fun," he reassures. I gaze up at him for a moment and nod, releasing a breath and my tension with it. I follow his lead and speed up my steps as we both hop from one foot to the other.

I close my eyes and feel for his movements as we dance. The flute's silvery notes guide my feet as he twirls me around and around, dipping and spinning as the music carries on. The way my skirt flows makes me feel as if I can fly and my anxiousness melts away. His arms circle my waist and he lifts me. He holds me to his chest while he spins us causing a cascade of giggles to escape from me. My skirt flows around my legs as he sets me down and we continue.

My cheeks hurt from smiling as I let the music take over. The stomps of all the dancers against the wooden floor shake the chandeliers while those at tables bang the base of beer cups against them and clap to the beat of the music. The corners of Endel's eyes crease as he laughs happily, leading me through the rest of the dance. His arm lifts up and he spins me twice as the music comes to an end. One of his arms catches me at my lower back and I hook my elbow behind his neck to balance as he dips me.

My head falls back and I release a belly laugh, feeling slightly dizzy from all the spinning and jumping around. His brown eyes shine brightly as we remain in that position for a few more seconds, seconds that feel like minutes as our chests rise and fall in sync. The tips of our noses are almost touching as we try to catch our breath.

"You're a beautiful dancer," he says slowly. He lifts us to stand straight, never breaking our gaze.

"You're not bad yourself," I laugh, still drunk on the energy of the room.

A moment passes, or maybe three, before he blinks rapidly and clears his throat as the next song starts. A slower song that gives those on the dance floor a break. "We, uh," he swallows. "Our food is probably here."

"Yeah," I respond, my gaze falling to the floor. I dust off my skirt and we walk back to our table.

We made it back to the inn, tired from the night's events. As a final gesture, I offered to give Endel a retwist and he gladly accepted. The weight of his upper body leans against the base of the chair as he sits between my legs on the floor. I press the comb flat against his scalp. His hair slips between the teeth as I comb the inch of new growth to smoothen it out. I'm so glad he's not tender-headed, unlike Yamala who used to whine at the mention of a hair pick. It's the main reason she cut her hair in the first place.

He takes a sip from his mug which holds a second helping of the tea Tansae made for him, setting his small jar of honey to the side. It must be good since he's been drinking a cup a day. Zyl and I declined his offers to try it since it was a gift to him, but I do get to enjoy the pleasant aroma it fills the room with.

"Thanks again for doing this," he says with a relaxed sigh. I dip my finger into the jar of moisturizer he brought and swipe it onto the root of the loc in my hand.

"I already told you, it's nothing," I say, starting to palm roll.

"You're not gonna charge me for this, are you?"

"See I would say no, but your kitchen is a little crazy back here an-hey," I laugh as he playfully swats at me over his head. I dodge his arm and he gently smacks my knee with a laugh of his own. I finish palm rolling and pin it down with a few other locs to hold it in place. As I work, I peek over his shoulders to see him writing in his notebook. "One of your stories?" I ask.

"Yeah," he responds, the pen still scribbling across the page. "I'm nearly done with it actually."

"What's it about?"

"None-ya," he responds.

I roll my eyes at his playful tone, "Funny. Let me guess, it's one of those romance stories your mom mentioned?"

"Maybe."

The air about the room is peaceful. After we both took our showers it became warm and cozy from the steam. The crickets outside provide ambiance to what would otherwise be a silent night. The flowy sleeves of my green nightgown, a gift from my dad, are cool against my arms and make my movements appear more graceful as I work.

"Done," he sighs. The pages rustle as he flips back to the beginning of the story and I lean down, trying to get a closer look. "Hey," he says, jerking the notebook out of view.

"Aww, please?" I ask.

"No, it's private," he chuckles as I playfully reach for it.

I huff in defeat and sit back in the chair again. "But why?" I persist. His demeanor shifts as his notebook falls back to his lap. A pang of guilt hits me at his silence and I continue doing his hair, "I'm sorry. I don't mean to pry if-"

"No, it's alright. It's just that I tend to be a bit much for people," he explains simply.

"What people?" I ask hesitantly.

He takes in a deep breath and opens the notebook, flipping through a couple of the pages absent-mindedly, "People like my ex. Apparently, it was embarrassing how much I cared. It was desperate or something like that."

My nose scrunches at his words, "It seems like they were just ungrateful to me."

"Maybe a little, but it taught me that I did need to pay more attention to the way my partner receives love. It took me a year after we broke up to recover though. I really messed up the relationship after that by doing nothing out of fear of being too much for her," he rants.

"As you said, balance is tough," I respond. I gather more moisturizer on my fingers to place on a new section of hair. "So you write stories to cope?"

"Kind of. It helps me balance and play out scenarios in my head. Ones that may or may not happen," he says sheepishly. I giggle at him and he groans, telling me to shut up.

"What? I think it's sweet. My last partner was a hopeless romantic," I admit.

"Really?"

"Yeah, he was a real sweetheart. Gifts, gestures, letters, and he even got me snacks and brought them to me at work."

"But, you aren't together anymore?"

"Well, no, but for an entirely different reason," I say, lifting the comb to part another section.

"What was the reason? If you don't mind me asking," he says.

"I'll say that we weren't very compatible. Our relationship was great, but after a while, I discovered I'm not really into um...sex."

His head falls back so he can look into my eyes, his brows furrowed, "Wait, like at all or just with him?"

"At all," I say, gently tilting his head back to the position required so I can continue working. "I really liked him, but we just weren't compatible, so we split up."

"That must have been hard," he says softly.

"It's fine. I eventually realized I wasn't in love with him."

He hums in response, "How do you figure?"

"Well, to me, being in love is as much a feeling as it is a decision. You choose to love them because they're worth it."

"You make it sound so simple," he comments.

"Well, when it's the right person, it's just that simple," I smile.

After a few minutes, I finish the last loc and tie his headscarf in place so his roots can set overnight. He decides on a fishtail braid for a protective style and I offer to do it for him in the morning, but he says I've done enough. He starts to clean up and put his items away while I go to the sink to wash my hands. The warm water sends a relaxing tingle down my spine. As much as I enjoyed doing his hair for him, I can only take the feeling of oil on my hands for so long.

"Heriath?" Endel calls from his bed.

"Yeah?" I dry my hands and make my way over to him.

"I have something for you," he says. A small object is revealed from behind his back, covered in napkins as a makeshift wrapper.

"For me?" I ask, dramatically placing a hand on my chest.

"Stop being silly and open it," he says with an amused grin.

I pull the napkins from around the oddly shaped item to reveal a small wooden carving of a luna moth. Its wings are bent back slightly as it gently sits atop a flower blooming out of a wooden base. The moonflower is made of black wire wrapped around purple pieces of glass that act as petals. Tiny white dots litter the purple just as they do on the real flower.

"Endel," I gasp. "When did you-" I cut myself off as I remember him carving that morning back in Kaelora City. "So this is what you were working on. But when did you make the flower?"

"On the ride here. I also have to apologize because I snuck out the night before to get a better look at the moonflower when it was open," he says, awkwardly rubbing the back of his neck. "But I was super careful, I promise." I'm in awe at his creation, too stunned by its beauty to be mad. "I know you were disappointed that you couldn't see it so I tried to get it as close as possible. Do you like it?"

I'm speechless as I turn the sculpture to see it from all angles. I set it on the bedside table and throw my arms around his neck, unable to find the right words. He chuckles as he uses one arm to hug me back and the other to steady himself from the force. His other arm wraps around me as he squeezes tight.

"I'll take that as a yes?" he asks with a laugh. I nod rapidly against his shoulder. "I'm glad," he says as I let go. His hands meet my cheeks and my eyes widen at the sudden gesture. He freezes and quickly lets go. "Sorry, force of habit. It's how we hug in my family, so I just um," he trails off. I remember seeing it when he was saying goodbye to his parents.

"Where does it come from?"

"Well, my grandma said that you should embrace with your heart, mind, and soul," he starts. "Squeezing tight connects the heart and soul," he explains, touching the left side of his chest and center respectively. "We hold each other's faces and touch foreheads to connect the mind. I grew up with it and I only really ever hugged my family or partners so I forgot," he says with a small, anxious laugh.

I smile and move my hands up to gently hold his face, "Do you mind if I try?" He freezes, eyes widening as he stares into my own. "Please?" I ask. He hesitantly nods, a smile playing at his lips. His hands meet my cheeks again, the warmth comforting as we touch our foreheads together. I close my eyes and relax in his energy. I feel his face grow warm underneath my hands and can't help but smile knowing that the tips of his ears are most likely flushed. Though I'm sure mine are the same, I don't mind.

My eyes open to find him staring at me. Pools of dark brown that have caught my attention time and time again. His eyes quickly dart to the bedsheets and we slowly separate, sitting apart and returning our hands to our laps.

"That was nice," I remark softly. "It's a sweet family tradition."

"Thanks," he whispers.

"Thank *you* for the gift," I respond. "I'm sure Zyl will love all the trinkets you can make for them. You have quite the skill."

He looks to the side, smile slightly fading, "Right."

"What's wrong?" I ask, leaning to try and meet his eyes. "A romantic like you, I thought you'd be excited."

"I am. I just-," he pauses with a sigh. "I am," he repeats, a grin returning to his face. "We should head to bed now. It's late."

"Yeah, we still have a day's journey left tomorrow," I add.

As we both tuck into our beds for the night, I replay the night's events in my mind. Their optimism is infectious. I'm used to worrying and sometimes it gets the best of me, but they've helped me control it. They've made me laugh, made me smile, and made the world disappear when they dragged me to dance.

Something in their hushed voice stuck with me that night in Pine Valley. The way they looked at me when they whispered those two words. '*Your eyes.*' That same something fills my heart as I squeeze my pillow to my chest.

Their eyes.

Those gentle brown eyes that see a different kind of wonder in the world. Able to see the beauty in everything made with two hands and the good in people's hearts. It wasn't the color or the shape that felt familiar, it was the person within them. The safety and peace in a soft gaze. The joy and laughter in a warm presence.

I get it now. I truly understand.

And oh, how I wish I didn't.

CHAPTER 25

The Secret of My Success

I've finally found it.

Iron Brimstone has been on the rise for years and I've finally found the last piece of information I need to ensure this company stays afloat for generations to come.

Recently, I was alerted by one of the miners that a strange blue glow was emitting from the cavern of the Water Stone during our regular mine inspection. When I arrived with Nile, there were two strangers in the cavern tampering with the Water Stone. A man and his wife, hands in the water and speaking an incantation of sorts.

They refused to tell me why they were there, but had the nerve to claim the Water Stone as theirs. It was only when I had Nile hold the man's wife hostage that they began to state their business. The man claimed they were soulmates. To be more specific, the descended souls of Kofir and Elysi. I almost laughed when he said they had been called to charge the Water Stone and heal the river. They were in the middle of the ritual when we found them. I insisted they prove it, but they refused to complete the ritual in our presence.

I transferred them to headquarters and confined them to separate rooms, willing to wait. I would enter the rooms every couple of hours to see if they were ready to comply. They were more resilient than I first assumed and I had to increase incentive. It was amusing how a few carefully crafted words and something as simple as a wedding ring could force out the secret of our land's magic. The man told us the ritual in exchange for his wife's safety and freedom. It would be heartwarming if it wasn't so pathetic.

Nile convinced me to allow them to stay in the same room, which I agreed to as I saw no harm in it. However, their very existence is a threat to my bigger picture. I've already had a hand in reconstructing the history of our land in order to further benefit the success of this company. I've maintained a perfect public appearance and have a beautiful family to show for my efforts, but they could make a mess of it all.

I like to think myself above killing random villagers, but I'm not too fond of loose ends. I tried to reason with them, to explain that their sacrifice would be a greater contribution to a growing empire than any donation I could possibly receive, yet they still put up quite the fight. I will admit, the hysterical strength of a woman whose husband has just been killed is certainly a marvel to behold.

I have chosen to write this information in my personal journal as it has the power to change the course of Vyelan. The details of the ritual rest within the very pen I write this with. Followed to the letter, this company will have many generations of success to come should the owner take the responsibility of finding the soulmates. If I see the day, I will find the next ones myself. In the meantime, the true knowledge of the Water Stone and Vyelan's source of power lies solely within these walls.

My beautiful Cloveris:

If you should read this, you will surely call me a monster. It became apparent early in our marriage that our values are very different and we shall never see eye to eye. I hope you find pride in the knowledge that you have served your purpose and that this grants you peace.

To my proudest achievement, my dear Tansae:

You still have your purpose to fulfill. I have begun your teaching, yet you still have so far to go. Your knowledge may never outshine my own, but my lessons shall carry you. I leave to you the weight of the world and trust that you will be the one who makes me proud. I will be by your side as you grow and become the woman you are meant to be.

I trust that you won't disappoint.

- T. Morelli

So that's it.

"He knew them," I say to myself, staring in marvel at the pages. My eyes scan over the words as I read the note he left me in disbelief. He met the soulmates of his generation and managed to find the secret to Vyelan's power. I figured he hadn't told me everything, but he also expected to live longer than he did.

He really believed in me.

A smile tugs at my lips as I read his note to myself. I'm his proudest achievement. He trusts that I can carry his name with pride and I will, even if I stand alone.

I burst through my bedroom door and rush toward the office. I toss files to the side as I dig through the drawer and my heart beats fast in anticipation. My soft smile widens into a grin as his black and gold fountain pen comes into view. He used this pen for everything.

I unscrew the back end of the pen and eagerly shake it into the palm of my hand. A small metal compartment falls out and I pop the end off of it to reveal a rolled-up note. I unfold it to read its contents and my world finally clicks into place. It's the final piece of the puzzle, the answer to the riddle that was my life's purpose.

As I return to my room and put the pen in a safe place, I lie back on my bed and truly relax for the first time in weeks. I roll over to reach onto my desk and grab the page with the note he left for me. I carefully tear off his note and set it next to his picture.

I thought my plan was too far-fetched. That cutting off loose ends was extreme when most city folks can just be persuaded with money. Of course, knowing my own mother, I know better than that now. Some people are too kind and forgiving. They let emotions sway them to make decisions and rationale flies out the window, but they are the more easily fooled.

I move about my room, sliding off my shirt to change into my night clothes. He was right. My mom would call him a monster for what he did, but she wasn't thinking of us. My father always thought of us. He taught *me* to always think of us. It's something she still refuses to learn.

I sit at the vanity and release my hair from its ponytail, lifting my brush. I grimace at the sight of my hair draping over my shoulders as I pull through it. My mother's features shine brighter on my face as my hair mimics hers. I quickly brush it back and tie it up into a messy bun before returning to my bed.

We may be alike, my father and I, but there is one distinct difference. His plan resulted in violent bloodshed, and in that, it lacked finesse. He had his brutish ways of dealing with matters when they fell into his lap, but I arranged my pieces days ago.

I glance over to my father's note on the bedside table and read the last line with a smile before blowing out the light, thinking of the other light that dims a day's journey behind me.

CHAPTER 26

HERIATH'S POV

I groan, swatting at the hand against my shoulder as I feel a force shake my body. I attempt to pull the covers over my head, but they are ripped off and pulled to the ground. I sit up, annoyed and glare at Endel who is on his knees beside the bed. Putting aside my aggravation, I sink to my knees beside him. My eyes adjust to the dark and I notice him clutching his chest.

"Can't... breathe..." he gasps.

I place a hand on his back to steady him only to yank it away in shock at how sweaty he is. I rush over to the window and open the curtains for light. I grab my bag and return to his side, instructing him to lie down. I take a deep breath as my hands meet his chest. His hand grips my wrist but I ignore it, trying not to meet his eye for fear that his pained expression would incite my own panic. Right now he doesn't need me, he only needs my knowledge.

I push through my grogginess to check his vitals and attempt to diagnose him as quickly as possible. My heart drops when his grip loosens and his hand slides over his hip to the floor.

"Endel?" I call, my voice hoarse from sleep.

His head falls to the side and I lay my own on his chest. My breathing becomes erratic at the sound of his heartbeat growing fainter by the second on top of its inconsistent rhythm. *Think. Fucking think.*

I fumble through my bag, pulling out bundles of herbs by the bunch and holding them in the moonlight until I find the one I need. I yank out my mortar and pestle, rushing over to the sink and adding a bit of water before quickly tearing apart and tossing in what twilight nox I had left. I grind the herb and water into a thick, concentrated paste, not caring about the lumpy consistency that would usually drive me crazy. I fall back to Endel's side, his breathing more shallow than before.

Please be enough.

I scoop a good amount onto my index and middle fingers, using my other hand to pull his jaw open. I grimace as I smear the paste onto his tongue and shut his mouth. *Come on.* My sense of time blurs as I wait for a reaction. Anything at all.

"Please, Endel," I whisper, feeling tears start to form in my eyes. "Breathe for me."

My left hand tilts his head back while my right presses two fingers to the side of his neck. I've never lost a patient before. The weight of this responsibility forces a thousand emotions through my mind every second that passes, finally ceasing when his eyes shoot open. Loud coughs echo through the room as he curls up, gasping for air. His hand shoots to my shoulder as he braces himself against me. His eyes are wide as his body begins to shake from the effect of the herb in his system.

"Come on, we have to get you to the clinic," I say as I allow myself to breathe again. I quickly grab a scrap of cheesecloth from inside my bag and smear the remaining paste onto it.

"What's going on?" he wheezes as I grab his arm and use all my strength to pull him to his feet.

"Save your breath," I tell him, helping him over to the door of our room.

The walk there seems ten times as long as we hobble to the clinic that's only three buildings down. I keep tabs on Endel's condition as we go, feeling him lean on me more for support each minute that goes by. His ragged breathing in my ear makes me anxious, but I'm thankful he's breathing at all. I don't know how long this adrenaline shot will last and I'd hate to give him another one in his condition. I bang on the clinic's door with a fist and relief washes over me when an older man swings it open with a lantern in his hand.

"We need help. Fast," I huff, struggling to speak under Endel's weight. The man's expression shifts from tired to alert in an instant and he slides his free arm underneath Endel's to help me guide him to a table.

"What happened?" the man croaks as he grabs a pair of scissors to cut Endel's shirt up the center.

"I don't know," I admit. "He woke me up saying he couldn't breathe."

"Dyspnea," the man states, assessing Endel's condition. "Any other symptoms?"

The sound of his erratic breathing is like torture as I try to clear my mind of the worst possibilities, "Um, diaphoresis and heart arrhythmia."

"A fellow herbalist, I see," he says with a smile.

"Focus," I snap, my sense of urgency adding force to my words.

"Well, I see no injuries," he says. Endel's shaking is starting to let up, his muscles tensing as he lets out a pained groan. *Time's running out.* I wrack my brain to fit the pieces together. The side effects are all internal.

"Poison?" I murmur.

"What?" the man asks, no doubt fighting the effects of being awoken from his sleep.

"It's poison," I repeat louder. "Do you have any hervinia concentrate?" I ask. He nods and grabs a brown bottle from the shelf behind him, handing it to me. I rip the cork out and open Endel's mouth to pour the liquid down his throat while the older man grabs a trash can. Even in his weakened state, he manages to swallow it and time freezes again as I wait.

His body lurches and he leans over the side of the bed. The man manages to catch the mess as Endel heaves and purges the contents of his stomach. I turn away in disgust, scrunching my nose at the sound.

Once he's done, I can see his muscles relax. I set down the bottle and approach him as he flops onto his back, passing out from exhaustion. My ear meets his sweaty chest and my eyes shut as I listen for his heartbeat, refusing to move until it's returned to a steady rhythm. I breathe a sigh of relief and lift my head to see the elderly herbalist inserting a cannula into Endel's right arm.

"How's it sound?" he asks.

"Even," I reply. My elbows meet the table and my forehead rests in my hands as I try to calm my nerves. My hands shake as I take in as much oxygen as I can.

"The hervinia should have forced the brunt of it out, but we still need to flush out anything left," he says. I nod in reply, my vision blurring as my exhaustion catches up to me. I feel a strong hand clap against my back and I look up to the man who wears a proud grin. "Nice thinking on your feet there. You did well." I return his smile, though I'm sure it appeared disingenuous in my groggy state.

"Thank you, and I'm sorry for snapping at you," I apologize.

He lets out a hearty chuckle, "It's alright. We should know better than anyone not to take panic personally." I nod in agreement. He informs me that there is a spare bed in another room that I can use to sleep if needed and I thank him for the offer. He bids me goodnight and heads to the back where I'm assuming he has a bedroom like Miss Merilla does in our clinic back home.

I pull up a chair from the corner of the room and sit next to Endel, leaning my cheek against my palm. The soft glow of the lantern creates highlights on his dark skin while his muscles create shadows. I'm relieved by the peaceful look on his face as his chest raises and lowers at a steady pace. I lean forward to readjust his headwrap which must've loosened during the panic. Once it's tied snuggly, I lean against the back of the chair.

My body aches and my mind begs for sleep, but I force my eyes open, afraid that if I close them he'll be dead by sunrise. I try to think, to go through the past few days to find the source of his body's sudden reaction, but all my mental energy is put into staying awake and I give up with a sigh. I place a hand over his, my index finger resting on his wrist where I can feel his pulse. For now, every breath he takes is enough to satisfy me.

I adjust my head against my arms and release a sigh of contentment at the light pressure that rests on it. Right as my muscles start to relax, memories of the previous night flood back into my mind and my eyes fly open. I sit up in my chair, bracing myself against the table as the sudden movement causes my vision to blur. I recognize the weight atop my head as Endel's hand which is now raised in alarm.

"Woah, it's okay," he says softly.

I scan the room, which is more vibrant in the daylight. There's one large shelf of herbs and tonics by the door and another filled with books that are closer to the window. The plants that hang from the ceiling in front of the window cast a shadow over the clock that hangs on the opposite wall. My attention goes back to Endel as my brain catches up to his words.

"You're awake," I spout. "How do you feel? Are you okay?"

"He's fine," the elderly herbalist answers for him as he steps into the room. He's more professionally dressed, now in a white shirt and brown pants that match his shoes. His white beard is combed and nicely contrasts his dark skin, his mustache raising with the smile that grows on his face. "I've already checked him this morning and it seems most of the contaminant was flushed out of his system by the cannula. Though if it wasn't for the induced vomiting, he wouldn't have made it," he says, giving me a wink. Endel gives me a confused look and my gaze falls to the table. "Anyway, he just needs another hour of rest before he's free to go."

"That's good," Endel responds. "We can still make it to Mysticane today."

"Yes sir," the older man says cheerfully. "I try to get patients in and out since most are just passing through. Though I haven't had a case like yours in years." He hands me a clipboard with Endel's symptoms written on it before returning to the back room. I scan the information and stand, following after him.

"Excuse me, sir," I say, catching the man's attention.

"Call me Kelvin, young lady," he grins, sorting through a few more papers on the back table. I approach him and sit the clipboard down in an empty spot.

"Do you know which poison it is?" I ask.

"I'm afraid not," he responds. "There are only a few I can think of, but it's hard to tell without knowing the source. Do you have any ideas?"

"Well, I can rule out any food poisoning since it wouldn't have resulted in heart arrhythmia," I point out, voicing my thoughts. "I don't recall him having any allergies."

"According to the check-up this morning, his only allergy is bee stings and he has no pre-existing conditions."

My eyes roam aimlessly as my mind runs through the last few days. His diet has been steady and he's gotten plenty of fluids. We shared our food at the tavern last night, but he was the only one who got sick. *Wait.*

I dismiss myself to run back to the inn. My body freezes as I pass by the bathroom, catching my reflection in the mirror and my face starts to get hot. I look down at my green nightgown in embarrassment. I was in a rush last night, but now that I no longer have life-threatening pressure on me, I realize how indecent I am. I quickly change into a green top and black pants before grabbing what I need and returning to the clinic.

Kelvin turns at the sound of my footsteps, "What have you got there?"

"My hypothesis," I state. I lift the tea press onto the counter and place the nearly empty bag of tea leaves next to it. "He was given this tea by a friend as a gift. It's the only thing that's significantly changed about his intake in a few days." Kelvin leans down to inspect the tea press, a few shreds of leaves stuck to the bottom and a tiny amount of liquid left from last night. Part of me is glad that Endel forgot to clean it out. "That's the last thing he had last night and he's been drinking about one cup a day from this bag," I detail, lifting the bag from the countertop and setting it in his hand.

He pulls it open and peers inside, "There's only a tiny bit left, but I can test the tea while you sort through the leaves out front." I nod and return to the front room where Endel is reading a book from one of the shelves. He's loosely dressed in a large shirt I'm assuming Kelvin gave him. The size of it swallows his toned body making his face appear softer and honestly, kind of cute. I glance at the cover of the book and recognize it as one my dad used to read to me when I was younger.

"Isn't that a children's book?" I comment, setting the bag on the counter and beginning to sort through the drawers for materials.

"So?" he says, adjusting his posture. "I had a hard night, apparently."

"Apparently?" I repeat.

"Yeah, I don't really remember much. Last I recall, I was getting out of bed to wake you up cause I couldn't breathe. After that, I got nothin'," he explains. Part of me is relieved to hear that he doesn't remember the suffering he went through. I'm sure his body does, though. He may have a hard time eating today.

"I'm not judging," I shrug as I find a set of tweezers and place them on the counter. "Enjoy your book."

I roll out some gauze and lay it flat before lifting the bag and pouring out its contents. A small pile of leaf shreds forms with one red berry landing on top. Lifting the set of tweezers, I twist the arm of the swinging magnifying glass that is attached to the countertop. Once it's to my liking, I carefully comb through the pile.

"What's that?" I hear Endel ask from across the room.

"It's nothing," I respond, not wanting to let him know any details until I'm sure. "Just looking through some stuff for Kelvin."

He hums in response followed by silence and I assume he's resumed reading. My brows knit together as I lift small leaves and bring them closer to the magnifying glass. They are all shredded as tiny as possible, which shows how inexperienced Tansae really is when it comes to making tea. Most of the pile I identify as water hemlock, a simple green leaf with a bitter flavor. That must have been why Endel poured in so much honey before drinking it. The smell of the tea was severia cane, an earthy base for any good tea. The red berry is crimson shadebush which serves no real purpose other than being a natural red dye. Everything seems normal.

I hear footsteps meet my side and look up to see Kelvin with a half-hearted smile on his face. "Can I borrow you for a minute," he whispers. I nod and follow him to the back room, ignoring the feeling of Endel's gaze.

"So," Kelvin starts with a sigh. "I found traces of iverian periculum in the bit of tea you gave me. It was very highly concentrated."

"Dragonleaf?" I gape.

"Did you find any in the bag?" he asks.

"Let me check again." I approach the front counter again and use the tip of the tweezers to push things around. It isn't until I flip over one of the leaf shreds that I notice it. I squint, holding it closer to the magnifying glass and feeling my stomach drop as I see the leaf has red veins. "I- I must've missed it because of the water hemlock," I stutter. He reaches down and grabs the crimson shadebush between his thumb and index finger, humming as he holds it up to the light.

"And I assume this little beauty hid the red tint it gives off," he adds. My palms smack the countertop and my head hangs in frustration. How could I have missed it? I even brewed a cup or two for Endel during the past few days. My fingers run over the leaves, flipping them over to find more and more dragonleaf. Now that I'm aware it's so painfully obvious.

"Heriath?" I turn to look at Endel, book laying on the table's surface and his legs hanging over the side. "What's wrong?"

I grit my teeth and release a breath before my lips part to speak, "Turns out there is dragonleaf in the tea Tansae gave you."

"What's that?" he asks.

"It's a medicine that can be used for heart health, but only in small doses that we herbalists administrate," Kelvin explains.

"It's a highly regulated substance," I cut in. "Enough of that stuff can be lethal and this mixture is full of it. If this much is in the few scraps left I can't imagine how much was in the full bag. How much *you* drank," I continue, my voice raising. "I mean, how did she even manage to get a hold of that much without a prescription for it?"

"Are you sure she doesn't have a prescription for it?" Endel asks me.

"No, but if she had a heart condition I would have known or seen her take her medication. All my patients back home that come in for it have to have proof of their prescription. This just doesn't make sense," I finish. I can't decipher whether I'm more angry at her or myself for not noticing it sooner. She told me that she took notes from my journal, but I still should've checked it out.

"Didn't she consult an herbalist back in Kaelora?" Endel adds.

"She said she did," I reply.

"Any half-decent herbalist wouldn't allow something like dragonleaf to make it into a tea," Kelvin adds. "The first thing we learn is which plants are dangerous."

"If it's that dangerous, why didn't I die after the first cup?" Endel asks, confused.

"You've been having a cup a day which isn't enough to kill you due to your size. Last night you had two. You overdosed," I explain.

Endel nods as I run a hand down my face, my palm resting against my mouth as I try to process everything. The way the leaves were shredded so small, the red berries to hide the red tint from the leaves, and the large amount of water hemlock and severia cane. It almost seems intentional, but killing Endel goes directly against what we're trying to do here. It just doesn't add up. Besides, she seemed to warm up to both of us on the road.

I'm pulled from my thoughts by a hand on my shoulder. Kelvin gives me a reassuring smile, sensing my worries, "Don't stress too much, everything is okay now." My shoulders drop as I take in a breath. He turns to carefully scrape the leaves off the counter and back into their bag. "I'm going to finish up for you here. Would you mind doing your friend's final check-up?" he asks.

"Yeah, I can," I reply.

Kelvin directs me to the correct materials while he finishes cleaning the counter. I take a seat next to Endel as Kelvin disappears to the back again. I silently arrange my materials and Endel returns to his previous position, legs extended on the table and back against the wall. The wall clock ticks from across the room, filling the silence.

"Could you remove your shirt, please," I ask, removing his cannula. Endel gives me a nod and reaches back to pull it over his head. I proceed with the checkup, only speaking to ask him to adjust so I can get a good analysis of his vitals. Once that's done, I check over his scars and open a container of balsam. Endel jumps as the cold substance meets his skin and I pull my hand back, "Sorry."

"It's alright," he says with a smile. I stare at his face for a moment. How is he smiling? He just had a horrible night and he's smiling. He was poisoned. Intentional or not, isn't he mad? Isn't he scared? Am *I* overreacting? The tea being poisoned is more than just a health issue, it calls into question who we can trust. Tansae made it clear what the mission is, but everything feels just slightly out of place.

I blink as I feel the warm pad of Endel's thumb run up the bridge of my nose to my forehead. I allow my face to relax as he smoothes the wrinkle in my brow. "Hey, are you alright?" he asks softly.

"Shouldn't I be asking you that?" I joke, or try to. My voice makes it clear that I have a lot on my mind and I scold myself for not hiding it better.

"You look tired," he says. I meet his eyes before shaking my head, my vision blurring slightly in the process.

"I'm alright."

"Did you get enough sleep? I must have woken you up pretty early.".

"It doesn't matter," I respond. "What matters is that you're okay." Truthfully, I only managed to fall asleep as the sun peeked into the clinic window that morning and was in and out of it for the next few hours. Of course, he didn't need to know that. My eyes cast down to see a thick book in his hand. He must've finished the children's story. "I'm not sure you'll be able to finish that before we leave," I comment.

He raises the book with a small smile, "You underestimate me?"

"Just being realistic," I reply with a shrug. "If you're ready, we can get going in about an hour or two." Endel nods and moves back to the table as I approach the door.

"Where are you going?" he asks, adjusting himself against the wall again.

"To pack up our stuff," I say with a strained smile, my hand gripping the doorknob. "I'll come back to get you later."

I return to the inn and hear my name as I unlock the door to our room. I turn to see Zyl rushing up to me, concern twisting his normally soft features.

"There you are," he huffs. "Where have you guys been? I knocked hours ago but got no answer." I shake my head and push the door open.

"Rough night," is all I manage. I move inside and he follows.

"What does that mean?" he asks, closing the door behind him.

"Endel…He was- he-" The words get caught in my throat as the rush of exhaustion from my lack of sleep combines with my anxiousness and brings a burning sensation to my chest. It pours out in tears as I lean against the nearest wall and slide to the ground. Zyl kneels beside me as I wrap my arms around my knees to pull them to my chest. Tears create dark spots on my pants, quickly drying and fading into the black fabric. His arm falls around my shoulders as he pulls me closer.

"It's okay. Take your time," he whispers. He sits with me for a while until my sobs become soft hiccups and I manage to fill him in on what happened last night. His eyes cast downward as he takes in everything. "And Endel is okay?"

I nod, "Alive and well. He was even smiling. Can you believe that?"

"He seems to be a glass half full kind of person," Zyl says. "But what about you? It must have been scary."

"It was," I whisper, wiping my face with the back of my hand. "But what's scarier is that no matter how much he smiles, I can't help feeling like I'm failing him," I admit, that burning sensation returning to my nose as a new wave of tears threatens to spill.

Zyl shakes his head, "That's not true at all. He's alive."

"He's been in danger since we got on the road. It's taking all of my energy to keep him safe but it doesn't feel like I'm doing enough," I sniffle.

My head raises and I take in the blurred room. My gaze lands on the chair I sat in the night before. I can still smell the oil on my fingers from doing his hair. I can picture him there, his laugh ringing through the air as we talked. He's not just a patient, he's my friend, and dangerously close to being more than that.

This journey started out so simple. I didn't consider the fact that I'd get to know the people we would find, much less become close with them. Now that ugly feeling rears its head again. That same helplessness I felt the morning I found out Yamala was dying. That same feeling I had running around Mysticane to clinic after clinic on nothing but a whisper of hope and blind determination.

I bury my face in my knees again, muffling my voice.

"I'm not used to doing this alone," I whisper. Zyl sighs, rubbing my shoulder as my pants absorb freshly fallen tears.

"You know," Zyl says. "If there's anything I've learned from Endel, it's that living in the moment isn't so bad after all. We don't know what's going to happen next. Life throws things at us all the time, but we adapt. You have a gift for it. That's your job. You've done it time and time again." I slowly turn to face him and he gives me a reassuring smile. "We can't control the future, but it's never worth giving up on. While you can't protect him from everything, I'm sure he's grateful that you've been by his side every time. You aren't failing, Heriath. *Endel is alive.*"

A smile cracks through my somber expression and I lean further into him. He wraps his other arm around me to complete the hug.

"Thank you," I murmur.

"That's what friends are for."

I grunt as my trunk thunks against the wooden floor of the steam wagon trailer, my heart beating harder than usual. My hand grips my chest over my heart as I brace myself against the back wall.

"You alright?" Zyl asks.

I raise a hand to keep him from advancing toward me, "I'm good. I just need a second." He eyes me for a moment before relenting and leaving the trailer to grab more items. Footsteps come up from behind me and I turn to see Endel with both of our bags slung over his shoulders. I reach for them, but he takes a step back, shaking his head.

"I can help," he says.

I extend my hand, "No, I got it. You should rest."

"So should you," he points out, stepping around me to place the bags on our trunks.

I sigh, my arm falling to my side, "I told you, I-"

"I'm fine?" he interrupts. His eyebrow quirks upward as I awkwardly shift under his disapproving gaze. I slide my thumbs into my pockets, trying to ignore my lightheadedness. "You've been up for too many hours doing nothing but rushing around and taking care of me. You haven't even eaten yet today."

My head drops like a scolded child's, "I know but-"

"But nothing. You need rest," he interrupts again. I meet his eyes again, his look telling me he won't hear any protest. I simply nod in response and he grins. "Good. Zyl and I can go grab some food, you rest in our room until I get back. We can leave afterward, okay?"

I nod again.

We lock up the wagon trailer and I make my way back to our room in the inn. Carrying the trunk and rearranging our stuff took a lot of the strength I had left. I flop onto my bed and every muscle in my back and shoulders begins to ache. I grab a pillow and curl up around it, enjoying the cool material against my skin. I toss and turn, trying my best to relax, but the tension in my back keeps me from getting to sleep.

I'm not sure how long it's been when Endel returns with the smell of food following his footsteps. I sit up and stretch as the door closes, seeing him set down a container on my bedside table.

"That didn't take long," I comment.

"What? We were gone like an hour and a half," he chuckles. "Did you have a nice rest?"

"Not really," I admit, moving my container of food onto my lap. I open it and the wonderful aroma floods my senses. "Where's Zyl?"

"Refueling."

I nod and thank him in between bites as I continue eating. I didn't realize how hungry I was until now. He quietly eats his own meal and I glance over, noticing he removed his hair wrap and wove his locs into a fishtail braid. He must've done it when I came back to the inn.

"So," he starts. "You've been to Mysticane before, right?"

"Mhm," I hum, swallowing my mouthful of food.

"What should we do when we get there? I'm sure there are a lot of tourist attractions or historical sights to see." I pause to think. I wouldn't really know since last time I wasn't quite able to get a clear view of the city.

"I don't know, but I'm sure Tansae can guide you since it's her home. Of course, only after she apologizes," I mumble the last part.

"Apologizes?" he asks and I look at him in shock.

"You're kidding, Endel, she nearly killed you," I remind him.

"Oh, right. That," he says awkwardly. "I'm sure it was just an accident."

"No amount that large of a poisonous plant ends up in a tea by accident. Especially when she said she got help making it," I state firmly, setting my food to the side.

"She did admit it was her first time."

"Yeah, but aren't you angry?"

"Yes, I'm angry, but anger won't solve any problems right now so I'm choosing to let it go. Besides, we don't know if it was on purpose or not."

"Why are you so calm about this?" I ask, my voice now raised. "How can you smile and laugh and pretend that everything is okay when you nearly lost your life?" His eyes widen at my tone as he studies my face. I feel bad for letting my anger slip through, but it's not him I'm upset with. I open my mouth to apologize, but he speaks first.

"Of course I was scared last night. Anyone would be if they woke up not being able to breathe and with a pain in their chest, but I knew you had the knowledge to help." My anger begins to fade at his words. "I don't remember much of last night, but I knew you were there. When I woke up this morning and saw you asleep by my side, I knew I made the right choice."

"I...I was just doing my job," I manage to say after a moment, my eyes falling to my lap. His legs swing over the side of his bed as he sets his food down and makes his way over to me. He sits beside me, but I can't bring myself to look up at him.

"You did your job in what I'm sure was a terrifying situation," he says. I see his head tilt down from the corner of my eye, "Look at me." I slowly raise my head so I look him in the eye. "You saved my life, Heriath. You're the only reason I can tell you this now, and I'm lucky to have a friend like you."

Last night was full of quick decisions and educated guesses and yet he's sitting here with a smile on his face. He can afford to give Tansae the benefit of the doubt because I'm here. He trusted me, even when I wasn't sure I trusted myself.

Now, I understand what Yamala meant. I'll admit I was confused when she told me she was happy all that time ago, but the time she's had so far has been full of joy and love from every corner. She's not happy she's dying, she's happy she's lived. Happy she's had the chance to spend her life with me and share the past few years with Evreux. Her smile wasn't just a brave face, it was genuine. I've been by her side every time. Though the guilt of leaving still gnaws at me, I swear when this is all over, win or lose, I'll be by her side again.

I smile as our room door opens and Zyl walks in. "There you are. How are you feeling Heriath?" he asks.

"A little better," I admit.

"That's good, but you're not lifting a finger for the rest of this trip. I'm driving," he says firmly. His arm wraps around my shoulders and I lean into him.

I nod silently and Endel chuckles, "Oh, so you'll listen to him when he tells you to relax? I see how it is."

"I listened to you too," I defend.

"Took a while though."

"What can I say," Zyl shrugs, squeezing me tighter. "She likes me better."

Endel gasps and moves back to his bed, "Well then." I laugh as Zyl joins them and continues to poke fun.

"Let's ask her. Heriath, who do you choose?" Endel asks. I bite my lower lip and glance between the two of them.

"Well, I've known Zyl longer," I squint. Endel slaps a hand to his chest and flops back onto the bed, drawing a laugh from me. Zyl hops up in victory and rushes to hug me again. My laughter grows louder as he squeezes me tight. For the first time today, I allow myself to truly relax.

Things may have been tough, but we've made it this far. They're united and I've gained some new friends. Maybe things aren't so bad after all.

CHAPTER 27

TANSAE'S POV

I glare at myself in the mirror, gnashing my teeth as I attempt to free my hair tie from my tangled bun. *I had everything planned.* I give it a hard yank, ripping it from my head. *I had it all sorted out.* A few golden strands are still wrapped around it as I toss it onto the vanity. *How could I have made that kind of mistake?* I lift my hair brush and pull it through my hair, becoming more annoyed as it gets stuck on the knots.

I gained their trust. I planned ahead. I had been so proud last night that the fact didn't hit me until this morning. If the Water Stone can't be recharged without the ritual then I still need them alive.

I release a guttural groan and my hands slap against the top of my vanity as I stand to pace for the third time this morning. My eyes run over my father's note for the hundredth time and I grit my teeth as I reread the words I've practically memorized. A single line now stands out much more than the night before. *'Your knowledge may never outshine my own.'* Funny how just last night these words filled me with pride. Now they mock my lack of experience, hypocritical as it may be.

He made the same mistake I did. Got rid of them too soon. I thought I was better.

"Dammit," I shout, ripping my brush from my hair and hurling it forward. It slips from my fingers and thuds against the wall, just barely missing the vanity mirror before falling to the ground.

A knock sounds on my door before it cracks open and I shoot the person a withering look. Nasir peeks his head in and looks around, a wrinkle in his brow that shows concern.

"What?" I ask, not bothering to hide my annoyance.

"I heard a noise. You okay?" he asks.

"I'm fine," I grumble.

He stares at me for a moment, assessing my figure before shrugging, "If you say so. I made breakfast if you want it." I respond with a grunt and he shuts my door as he leaves.

My hand lifts to run through my hair, fingers spreading to rip apart the few tangles left from my previous efforts. As much as I hate to admit it, Heriath's obsession with Endel's return to perfect health may just work in my favor. She is skilled in her craft. I knew that when I decided how much dragonleaf to put in that tea. Now, I have to hope it either wasn't enough to kill him or that Heriath is as good as she seems.

I grab my hair tie and fold forward to gather my hair in a ponytail before standing back up to wrap it into a bun. I look over myself in the mirror before huffing out a large breath and my anger along with it. *I can't stay here moping forever.*

I exit my room and make my way downstairs. All conversation and clinking of silverware stops as I walk through the doorway. Nasir simply glances at me before returning to his meal while Natiq's and Mom's eyes linger. It has been a while since I've eaten breakfast with them voluntarily. I grab my plate from the placemat next to Mom and walk to the seat at the head of the long table. My plate clacks against the wooden surface as I push the chair back so I can sit. I look up to see Natiq shake his head and push out of his chair, to leave the room. Mom's eyes follow him with a saddened yet understanding look before falling to her lap.

I shrug and lift my fork, starting to eat the wonderful food Nasir made. It's a shame he squandered his skills in his youth or I'm sure he'd be a chef by now. A few more minutes pass and Nasir stands to leave the room. And then there were two.

"Mom," I speak, not looking up at her.

"Yes?" Her voice is light, not as cheery as usual, but a stark difference from the night before.

"I'm expecting guests today. Heriath and Endel," I inform her.

"This evening?" she asks.

"Yes, they'll need a place to stay. Have the guest rooms ready for them," I command. She says nothing in response, simply nodding as she stands from her seat. "Oh, another thing," I say and her footsteps halt beside my chair. Her robe flows gently around her ankles and she gazes down at me.

"Hmm?"

"I need you to tell them that you are the owner of the company," I say, finally looking up at her. The faint wrinkles on her forehead deepen slightly in confusion.

"Why? They are coming here, aren't they?"

"They are, but they're from smaller villages. They know I work here, but I don't want my role to be intimidating," I explain.

"That may be true, but why hide it?"

"Would you show up to the children's home in your fancy clothes?" I challenge.

She glances down at her blush pink robe, "I suppose not."

"Besides, my ownership hasn't been announced to the public," I add. Most people assume it's her anyway.

She nods, "Okay." My eyes turn back to the last few bites of food left on my plate and her footsteps fade behind me as she makes her way to the kitchen.

Things are falling back into place, and I won't mess it up this time.

"Welcome," Mom chirps as a weary-looking Heriath walks in the door. She yawns with a stretch, her breath hitching as Mom wraps her in an embrace. Heriath returns the hug, patting her back a few times before letting go. They commence with small talk while my eyes are fixed on the doorway.

When Endel's tall figure appears, I breathe a sigh of relief, unable to help the smile that spreads on my face. He sets down a few bags and looks around our home in awe.

"You made it," I remark, moving to give Endel a hug.

"Yup," he says, wrapping one arm around my shoulders as mine go around his waist.

"He almost didn't," Heriath mumbles behind me. I pull away from Endel and look over at her with a smile.

"I'm glad to see you too," I say. "Welcome to Iron Brimstone."

"It's a lot nicer than I expected," Endel says, admiring the floral wallpaper and decorative light fixtures.

"Well, our living quarters are very comfortable here," I respond. "Mom can show you around if you like."

"Wait, you're Tansae's mom?" Heriath asks, looking towards my mother.

"Yes, I'm Cloveris Morelli. The current owner of the company," Mom replies, glancing at me.

"You've got quite the business on your hands," Heriath remarks.

"Yes, it is a handful," Mom laughs. "Come in. I have your guest rooms prepared."

"Okay," Endel says, lifting the small bags again.

"Make yourselves at home," I wave.

An hour later, everyone is settled into their rooms while dinner is being prepared. Nasir has a new recipe he wanted to try and Endel is eager to help him make it. Natiq isn't any help as he stands in the corner cracking jokes, but they all take a liking to each other. I retreat to my room to relax when a knock sounds on my door.

"One second," I respond. I move to my desk, gathering the papers into a neat stack and stashing them in my drawers. I slip dad's fountain pen into his personal journal and slide it into a drawer of my nightstand. Once everything is squared away, I open my bedroom door to see Heriath standing with hands in her pockets. Her eyes are dark as storm clouds and almost force me to take a step back. Faint dark circles rest underneath them.

"Can I come in?" she asks, her voice void of emotion.

"Sure," I mumble. She drags her feet as she walks, stopping just far enough in for me to close the door behind her. She leans against the wall and crosses her arms over her chest.

"Did you need something?" I ask.

"Yes. I need an apology," she states plainly.

"What for?" I question, taking a seat on my bed.

"That tea you made for Endel? It had dragonleaf in it." So that's why she's so cold.

"So? It's for heart health, isn't it?" It's hard to keep the smirk off my face as her expression hardens. Two fingers move up to pinch the bridge of her nose.

"It's poisonous, Tansae. Where did you even learn about it?"

"I told you, I got the notes from your plant journal. It never mentioned it being dangerous," I defend. "If I'd known I never would've put it in there."

"You still could have checked with me."

"Like you would've helped. You were still pissed at me."

"Tansae-"

"I didn't know, okay?" I interrupt, trying to brush off the situation. If I'd known she'd be this confrontational about it, I would've waited to kill him myself. Her jaw sets and she releases a huff. If I continue this way, it's only going to make her suspicious of me. That is, if she isn't already. Changing my approach, I force my eyes to the floor, "I...I didn't realize. I just thought-"

"I don't care what you thought and I don't care about your intentions. You have no idea what we went through this morning," she seethes, taking a step toward me.

"It wasn't my fault," I murmur.

She lets out a laugh of disbelief, "Well it couldn't have been anyone else. I can't believe you're being so flippant about this."

"I'm not. I care about him," I say, a feigned quiver in my voice. I muster a lump in my throat and my eyes well up with forced tears. "It was an accident."

"You nearly killed him," she shouts, her body jutting forward from the force of her statement. My eyes go wide at the pain in her voice. "Do you know how terrifying it is to be woken up in the middle of the night by someone who's dying? How he must have felt? He had to fight to stay alive without enough strength to even stand because of *your* carelessness."

I bite my inner cheek as anger forms in the pit of my stomach. I haven't been scolded like this since I was a child. I feel as if I'm back in my father's office, being yelled at for interrupting him. My hands ball into fists as I keep my eyes on the floor.

"I'm sorry. I didn't know," I whisper. She takes a deep breath and I look up at her slouched figure. Her eyes shut as she runs a hand down her face.

"I'm not the one who needs to hear that," she says, standing straight. "You need to be more careful. You can't meddle with things you don't know about. If I hadn't been there," she trails off with a sigh.

"I understand. I won't do it again," I respond.

"And you'll talk to him?" I give her a curt nod. Her back turns to me as she places her hand on the doorknob. "I'm trusting you, Tansae. Just, from now on, leave the healing to me," she remarks with a glance over her shoulder.

I wipe the tears from my eyes as my bedroom door shuts behind her. I figured she would say something, but I never expected to be attacked like that. At first glance, she doesn't appear to be the type to confront anyone, but I guess for people like her it's easier to stand up for others. At this rate, she may become a problem.

Once I'm sure she's downstairs, I make my way down to find Nasir, Mom, and Endel eating in the living room. I join them, sitting on the couch next to Endel and lifting one of the plates from the coffee table.

The conversation is light, focusing mainly on Endel and his trip here from Whitburn. Apparently, he and Heriath had an eventful night there. He was showing off the ring he made and I roll my eyes when

Mom practically swoons over his craftsmanship.

"Where's Heriath?" I ask Endel, noticing the one unclaimed plate of food on the coffee table.

His attention cuts to me, "I'm not sure. She's probably resting since she wasn't able to get much sleep last night," he responds.

"Oh," I say, turning my attention back to my food.

"By the way," he says, facing Nasir. "Is there a library around here?"

"Of course. It's not far, but I suggest going in the morning," he says.

"Are you looking for something?" Mom asks.

"Well, I started a book in Whitburn, but couldn't finish it since we had to leave. I wanted to see if they had it here," Endel explains.

"I could take you tomorrow," I offer, causing everyone to give me a blank stare. The tension in the room changes in an instant and I pause mid-bite. "What?"

"Tansae, you rarely leave this place without obligation, much less offering a tour of Mysticane," Nasir points out.

I shrug, "It's just the library. No big deal."

Nasir shoots a look at my mom who simply shrugs in response. Eventually, Endel and I end up in the kitchen after a respectful tug-of-war with Mom over his offer to wash the dishes.

He releases a sigh as the warm water runs over his hands and forearms, dipping them into the suds. I stand next to him as he starts to wash. He hums an upbeat tune with a soft smile on his face.

"What song is that?" I ask.

"Oh nothing. Just something I heard at a tavern in Whitburn," he replies, clearing his throat. "You have a nice family. Your brother is a great cook," he compliments.

"Nasir? Oh no, he's our family guard. Well, one of them anyway," I correct.

"That explains why he's so big. You know, he was intimidating at first until he started ranting about his love of sweets while we made dinner," he chuckles.

"Tell me about it. I can't bring home any kind of cookie expecting it to last long," I add. He rinses a plate and sets it on the drying rack by the sink. Our light laughter fades and awkwardness replaces it, growing thicker by the second. I bite my inner cheek and take in a deep breath.

"So, Heriath told me about last night," I mention, my voice cutting through the silence. He pauses for a moment before continuing to scrub the dish in his hand.

"And?" he prompts me to continue. My jaw ticks slightly in annoyance. I hate owing things to people, especially something as meaningless as an apology.

"And, I wanted to say I'm sorry. I had no idea that plant was as dangerous as it was." He places another plate onto the drying rack and sighs. I can tell he's trying to gather his thoughts. "It really was an accident, Endel," I add. I may not want to make this apology, but I have to at least make it good. A few more seconds pass before he parts his lips.

"I'm not going to lie, Tansae. I am pissed at you," he says calmly, placing another plate on the rack. His gaze remains on the dishes in front of him, not sparing me a glance as he continues. "It was hands down the worst night of my life. I was scared, in pain, and could have sworn I wasn't going to wake up." I turn my head to the side, suddenly taking an interest in the details of the wallpaper. The slight gravel in his voice tugs at my emotions, but I force it down.

"I know. I'm really sorry, it wasn't my intention to hurt you," I lie.

"Regardless of intention, the result is the same," he states. I can feel his gaze on me as he places the last dish onto the rack and lifts a towel from the counter to dry his hands. I peer over at him, his hips resting against the counter as he runs the soft fabric over his dark skin. His eyes meet mine, "I hear your apology and I accept it, but I can't forgive you."

I fight to keep the shock off my face. Can't forgive me? "I-I'm sorry, I don't understand," I stammer as he crosses the kitchen. He's now at the opposite counter, carefully scraping Heriath's food into a container.

"There isn't much else to say," he responds, back turned to me.

"But, you said you accepted my apology," I say pointedly.

"I do. I appreciate you telling me you're sorry, but I almost lost my life because of you," he reminds me, moving to put Heriath's food in the ice chest. "That's not exactly easy to forgive, you know?"

My jaw tightens. Everyone is so emotional today and it's making things difficult. The calmness of his voice only upsets me further. He has the nerve to say he's mad at me and not even show it. I take a deep breath and nod as I feel his gaze return to me.

"I understand. I'm just glad you're okay."

"Well, you can thank Heriath for that," he says, patting my shoulder. "I'm gonna head to bed. Goodnight, Tansae."

"Goodnight," I grit, watching over my shoulder as he leaves. His footsteps fade down the hall, but I don't move until I hear the door to his room shut. He doesn't have to forgive me. I only told Heriath I'd talk to him, and that's what I did. Whether he forgives me or not is not my problem.

As I make my way up to my room, I recall the conversation from dinner. Endel spoke of the night he had with Heriath and how Whitburn had a rich history he never knew before. I remember first learning about crackle stones. As a child, it was fun to watch the tiny explosions they created when slammed together.

It's one of the few rocks we can only obtain through trade since they aren't native to this area and Whitburn has been less than friendly about sharing. That was until my father made a deal with the village. He'd provide the metals needed to produce steam engines if our company was the primary recipient of the stones.

Though, that part of his story wasn't as fascinating as the rest.

The way he spoke of her.

He talked about Heriath with wonder in his eyes. The smile on his face never dropped for a second as he described the fun they had. Even when telling us how bad she was at the wood shop, joyous laughter escaped. It was endearing at first, but with each word, I felt my tight-knit plan loosen.

I had everything planned.

I had it all sorted out.

I shut my bedroom door and flop onto my bed, my head rolls to the side and Dad's note comes into view. Those seven words mock me once again.

CHAPTER 28

TANSAE'S POV

"So how does this ritual work exactly?" Zyl asks, sitting back in his seat.

I unfurl the small page in my hand, "When the moon is at its peak, both soulmates place their hands into the river water nearest the stone, recite the spell, and acknowledge the bonding of their souls."

Heriath sits forward in her seat on the couch, "That's it? Seems pretty simple. Is that all you have recorded?"

"It's all I found," I respond.

"Strange. As far as I know, there are no known recordings of any kind of ritual for the river's magic. Who's the author of that record?" Zyl chimes in.

I tuck the note back in my pocket, "One of the previous owners of the company." He's had a lot of questions since he arrived. I'm glad I had the foresight to come up with some answers.

"If that's the case, either they were one of the previous soulmates or they knew them," he mumbles to himself.

"How do you figure?" Endel asks, picking at her green bracelet.

"Well, a ritual like this must come from the bond that the soulmates have rather than any kind of book since recorded history is often copied and shared with the masses. In my many years of teaching and studying the soulmate's tale, I've never come across any mentions of a ritual."

"You've done a lot of digging into this, huh?" Endel asks with a smile.

"It's nothing really," he responds, the red tint darkening on his tan cheeks. I know they're soulmates, but Zyl's shyness is almost sickening.

"So, how does tomorrow sound?" I ask.

"The ritual?" Zyl asks.

"You want us to perform it tomorrow?" Endel adds, eyes wide in shock. "Why?"

"Why not?" I shrug. "You both are here and able to do it aren't you?" Endel and Zyl exchange glances, each looking conflicted. "Come on. By the looks of it, it won't take very long and our mission would be complete."

"While true, it seems a bit soon, don't you think? We need to get the steps right or it could go wrong," Zyl says.

Endel nods in agreement, "Yeah, we just learned about it."

"This is all very new territory, even for me," Zyl adds.

"I know, but we have the exact steps right here," I say, tapping my right pocket. "We can try it, and if we need more time then we can always try it again, right?"

"That's a hypothesis, but are you willing to take the risk of not having multiple chances? If in the past only the soulmates knew about this ritual, then they must have gotten it at the right time and done it properly on the first try. We will be the first to have done this ritual unnaturally, so there are more factors to consider," Zyl counters.

"Like what?" Heriath asks.

"Magic is tricky. The spell can be either formally or chaotically crafted. This one seems formal since it has specific steps to follow, but the original spell to bond the souls was chaotic. It didn't dictate how or when they'd meet or that they fall in love. Plus, its container isn't an object like a wand or a staff. This spell is contained within a soul. A moving and constantly changing element that we have no control over. The only thing we know for certain is that it requires a vessel to be sustained."

"Like the sugar pine trees back home?" Endel asks. Zyl quirks an eyebrow. "When our loved ones die we choose a tree for their soul to attach to so they live on."

"Exactly," Zyl nods, squaring his shoulders.

"So what's your point?" I ask.

"Because the spell isn't tied to an object, it's more unpredictable. The ritual could be told to them by something left behind, or something within themselves. Without knowing the right moment, we could lose our one chance."

"And if we have multiple chances?" Heriath asks.

"While the chances of that are fifty-fifty, it's still a gamble on the whole of Vyelan. We don't know when the next generation of soulmates will be of age and the river magic could have faded completely by then. If that happens-"

"Vyelan will die," Heriath finishes for him. "My sister," she trails off. Endel places a hand on her shoulder, giving her a reassuring smile. Heriath returns it with an uneasy one.

"What do you suggest we do, Zyl?" Endel asks with a new sense of determination.

"Just speculating, but I'm sure we increase our chances of this ritual having the best result if a stronger bond is created between the two souls prior to performing it," he suggests.

"Why don't you guys move in together? I'm sure you could learn a lot more about each other that way," I suggest. He glances at me before his eyes fall to his lap. His head tilts forward so his curls block most of his face.

"That's pushing it, don't you think?" Heriath speaks up.

"I don't know, Heriath," Endel says. "It could help. I've spent time with Zyl, but moving in with someone pushes the getting-to-know-you process a bit more. It's not a bad idea." She turns to me, "Why don't we set a date to do the ritual and I'll stay with Zyl until then? Does that sound good, Zyl?" Zyl peeks through his lashes at her, red slowly fading from his cheeks.

"Midwinter is only ten days away," I point out. "Doesn't the Elysir grow on that day?"

"Traditionally," Heriath says.

"Then will a week do?" Zyl asks, looking to us for approval. It's taken so long to get to this point and right when I'm so close to the finish line, they move it. I push down my frustration as I wait for the others to answer. Heriath looks to Endel who nods silently, a shy smile spreading across her face.

"Alright then, you all have six days to get to know each other and we'll perform the ritual on the seventh day," Heriath states, clapping her hands together. "Now that that's settled, can we please eat? It took me forever to cut this fruit." Zyl chuckles lightly and reaches toward the coffee table to grab a napkin and a few things from the snack tower Heriath arranged with Mom earlier this afternoon.

I find myself smiling as we talk, enjoying the lighthearted banter and the warm energy in the room. It's reminiscent of years past, back when Natiq, Nasir, and I used to play around together. It's a conflicting moment to feel happy with people you're certain to lose, but in the end, I will have all I desire. Nothing, not even this moment, will have been in vain.

Eventually, Zyl has to leave for a tutoring session and Endel offers to walk him back to the library. I close the front door and find Heriath in the kitchen.

"That was nice," I comment, grabbing her attention.

"It was, wasn't it?" she smiles. "They get along so well. I'm sure this ritual will work."

"So, what do you think?"

She scrapes the napkins and extra fruit into the trash before setting the tower into the sink to begin washing it. I lean against the counter, arms crossed as she turns on the water.

"About what?" she asks.

"All of it, I suppose," I answer.

She starts to scrub the tower with a soapy dishcloth, "Honestly, they seem to get along well so far. I'm sure a week is enough time."

"Yeah, though I hope giving them more time doesn't cause any harm," I sigh.

"What do you mean?" she questions, moving to the next tier of the tower.

"I mean your clinic back home, all the shortages in supplies. The magic is fading by the day. I don't really see the point in giving them so much time when this could all be solved tomorrow."

"I'm anxious too, Tansae, but you can't rush something like this. If Zyl is right and we lose our chance, that's it until the next generation's soulmates come of age. I don't think Vyelan can survive more than five years from now at the rate the magic is fading."

"Why don't you talk to Endel about maybe shortening it to three days? She listens to you," I urge. She gives me a look of slight confusion, but I can tell she's considering it. I hold onto hope for a moment as she moves to the last tier of the tower, but it falters when she shakes her head.

"Doing it right is better than doing it now," she states simply. "You don't want all our effort to be for nothing, do you?" She's right and it irks me. I've worked so hard to get this far, it would be a shame for it all to fall apart at the end. Now I have to rely on others to finish what I started.

"No, I wouldn't," I admit.

She finishes washing the tower, placing it on the counter next to the sink. I watch the yellow towel run over the brown skin of her hands as she dries them. As she hangs the towel up, her gaze wanders to the front door. Her eyes linger for a moment and I clear my throat.

"It takes a while to walk back from the library," I mention.

Her eyes cut to me, "I wasn't looking for her."

"I never said you were," I reply with a smirk.

She rolls her eyes, "Whatever."

We leave the kitchen and make our way to our rooms. A piece of parchment is taped to my bedroom door and I pause. My brows knit together as I pull it off and unfold it:

Dear Tansae,

We've had our differences over the years, but this is one I can't ignore. I see in you what I saw in your father all those years ago. I'll be gone for a while. I've already told Mom and Nasir where I'll be staying and I do plan to visit to check up on them. I love you dearly, but I can't watch you become the monster he was.

Your Brother,

Natiq

There's a small ache in my chest, one that's been there since our argument that night. I can't deny that I miss him. His humor and foolishness that accompanies every interaction. His disappearance over the past few days hasn't gone unnoticed, but I never thought he'd leave Mom.

I fold the page and shut my bedroom door. I hover the letter above the trash, but I can't seem to let it go. I sigh and toss it onto my vanity instead before plopping on my bed. Tomorrow is the beginning of the end of this journey. Let's hope my patience lasts, and that nobody gets in my way.

CHAPTER 29

HERIATH'S POV

As promised, Tansae leads us around the city, pointing out a few historical buildings as we pass them. The cobblestone path shakes under the weight of the steam wagons rolling by. A puff of smoke wraps around us every once in a while, the warmth allowing my muscles to relax before the brisk autumn air tenses them again. Though I'm in a more stable state of mind this go around, the city itself still makes me uneasy. Endel on the other hand is enamored with every inch. Since we started walking, their attention span has shortened to that of an excited puppy, stopping repeatedly to stare into windows displaying expensive items and wandering to various food stalls. I managed to convince them to focus on our predetermined destination with a reminder that there was plenty of time left during our stay to explore.

A familiar bronze and gold revolving door comes into view and it brings a smile to my face. The golden blur of the spinning door acts as a portal to the one place in this rat maze I can breathe easily. As we enter, I pull off my earmuffs and place them in my bag. I stretch and feel my lower back pop, a sense of relief flooding through my body.

"You sure you're feeling okay?" Endel asks, tightening the golden bracelet around their wrist. "You've been tense."

"I'm alright," I respond with a smile. They beam one of their own before looking upward and their mouth falls open in awe at the inside of the library. The amazement in their eyes mirrors that of mine when I first saw it.

"Woah, look at this place," they say, cringing when someone shushes them from one of the tables. "Sorry," they whisper awkwardly and I bite back a laugh.

"At least try to keep up, would you?" Tansae whispers to us. I fight the urge to roll my eyes. She insisted on taking us but has done nothing but complain that we aren't moving fast enough for her big city walking speed. "Do you know which book you're looking for?" she asks as we reach her side.

"Yes," Endel says, digging into the pocket of their black dress.

"Remind me why you didn't get it yesterday?"

"I already told you I was preoccupied with everything we learned. The whole book thing got washed upstream." Their hand emerges with a small scrap of paper, unfolding it to reveal a series of scribbles.

"Your handwriting is awful," I joke, to which they give me a playful scowl.

"Hey, it's not mine. Kelvin wrote it for me," they defend.

"If you say so," I mumble, laughing softly when they respond with a gentle shove.

Tansae clears her throat, "So, why don't we ask a librarian where it is?" Endel nods, following her to the counter. A man with a familiar head of curls stands on the other side of it facing away from us. He grumbles to himself as he smacks a machine, trying to get it to work.

"Um, excuse me," I call, trying to get Zyl's attention.

"One second," he responds. His hand smacks the machine again and ink spurts out of the side, causing him to stumble back a few steps. He sputters a string of curses as he turns around and reaches under the counter to grab something.

"Clumsy as always," Endel teases. Zyl looks up, expression softening as he realizes it's us.

"Oh hush," he says as attempts to wipe the blue splotches from his face with a rag. "What are you all here for?"

I gesture to Endel who slides the small scrap of paper across the counter to Zyl. He lifts it and squints, trying to decipher the handwriting before nodding confidently.

"I know where that is." He lifts the neck of the apron over his head to lay it on a table behind him and walks around the counter. We follow him to an aisle as he mutters to himself, running his fingers along the spines of the books.

"I thought you were a historian," I remark, noticing the 'Romance' genre header that hangs over the aisle's entrance. Zyl's attention shifts to me with a smile.

"Just because it's my profession doesn't mean I don't dabble in a few other genres. I am an educator, and in the same vein, forever a student. There is knowledge to be found in everything. Besides, how can I have researched the soulmate's tale a hundred times and not enjoy romance?" he responds. He continues until his finger stops on a certain book, "Gotcha." He pulls a book from the shelf and holds it out to Endel.

"Thanks," they say, taking the book.

"You have good taste," he compliments. "The twist ending really shocked me."

"I've only read a third through it so far. Though the main character really gets on my nerves. I mean, it doesn't take years to confess to someone," they groan, rolling their eyes.

"I won't spoil it, but based on that, I can say she will continue to get on your nerves," Zyl says.

"Ugh, you guys are so boring," Tansae groans. "Look, I've fulfilled my promise so I'm checking out. Got a few errands to run."

"Wait, are you still-"

"Yeah, yeah," she interrupts Endel. "I'll have my guards drop your stuff at the address I got from Heriath." Endel nods and Tansae waves as she turns to leave.

I wander off to browse as Zyl and Endel continue their conversation. I pick up a few books, pulling out the cards from the inner side of the front cover to read the summaries. My reading hobby faded away once I was certified to work, with the exception of the book of legends my mom gifted me.

I glance up at Endel as they laugh at something Zyl said. A twinge of jealousy pricks at me, but I quickly swallow it down. They talk and laugh like a couple of old friends. They seem to complement each other. Endel's colorful hair and Zyl's colorful shawls. They seem to bring out the playful side of Zyl, but nobody could resist their bright energy.

"Hey, Heriath," Zyl says, turning to me. "There's something about this whole ritual situation that's bothering me."

I shut the book in my hand and slide it back in its place, "What's up?"

"I know the magic in the river is what makes the Elysir grow, but if it functions like any other plant, doesn't it require seeds?"

I hum as I bite my inner cheek, "I suppose, but there are no seeds by the banks of the river after five years of nothing growing." My eyes widen at my own words. Even if this ritual does work, there will be nothing for the flower to grow from.

"There should still be a chance, right?" Endel asks. "It is magic, after all."

"Yes, but Kofir still abided by the laws of nature out of respect for it," I explain. "He enhanced or manipulated what was already there. Combining pre-existing plants to make new ones. Infusing certain properties with others. Even the Elysir is an enhanced plant, not something new entirely."

"I thought it was a creation."

"It's a creation the same way a house is a creation. You may have stacked the rocks in a new way, but they were always there to begin with."

"Right," Endel nods and turns to Zyl. "So now what?"

"Well, I found something in the archives I'm hoping you can explain," Zyl says to me.

I extend an arm to my side, "Lead the way."

We follow Zyl as he first takes us to his office so he can grab a key. We then make our way through the lobby and shelves of books until we reach the back of the library, traveling down another winding path of hallways. Soon we are standing in front of a large set of brown double doors. The door frame is covered in golden etchings that glitter in the soft glow of the lanterns that light the path. Zyl smiles as he slips the key into the door and unlocks it with a click.

"This is my favorite part," he whispers, taking a step back.

When he slides the key out, the crack between the doors lights up gold and a beautiful shimmer spreads through the wood grain. I can hear the sound of gears turning behind the thick wood before the doors push open on their own to reveal a large circular room with a round table in the center. The walls are full of aged books, journals, and scrolls sitting on well-kept shelves. Behind the table is a small set of stairs that goes up to a second set of shelves that line the room.

Zyl enters first, "Welcome to the archives."

He takes off to find what he's looking for while Endel and I explore. I follow the walls of books, running my fingertips over the spines and taking in the smell of the aged pages. The shelves are hand carved with genre labels, the rough look a stark contrast to the newer signs that hang over the shelves of the main lobby. I pull a few books from the shelf, leafing through the pages to kill time when I hear my name. I look up to see Endel on the second level, waving for me to come up. I shelve my book and make my way over, climbing up the small staircase to meet them.

"Check this out," they whisper, tilting the book in their hands toward me. I take it from them, eyes widening as I read the title.

'Roots of Life'

It's here. It's really here.

"It seems to be a book about plants so I figured you'd like it," Endel says, leaning down to peer at the writing. The pages are a yellowish hue, reflecting the age of the wisdom on its surface. I flip through, becoming increasingly more excited by the hand drawings and paragraphs that detail each plant's properties. Some of these herbs I've never heard of or seen before and others are extinct.

"This isn't just any book about plants," I respond, a wide grin spreading on my face. "This is *the* book about plants, written by the mystic himself. Every book I've ever read about herbalism to this day has this book cited as its main reference. I've searched for years and could never find it."

"Well, there ya go," they say with a smile.

I do my best to fit the large book in one hand so I can wrap my arms around their torso. I softly squeal a thank you, careful not to be too loud. They return my hug when Zyl calls us over to the table. He lays out a thin book in front of us, the pages lined with rows and columns.

"Recognize this?" he asks.

I pull off my satchel and hang it on one of the chairs before taking a seat, "Of course."

"Nope," Endel says, sitting in a chair beside me.

"It's a collection logbook. Each herbal distributor has them. This one is specifically for Elysir," Zyl explains, pulling up his own chair.

I run my fingers over the information, "This flower grows along the length of the entire Nafsi so each city takes responsibility for its half. Upstream is Kaelora's turf and downstream is taken care of by Mysticane. To maintain knowledge of the amount of Elysir collected and distributed, they keep the numbers in logbooks so they can distribute the flower to each village as evenly as possible."

Zyl nods, "While searching for information in Kaelora, I came across their logbooks and the numbers were normal. But here-"

"The numbers are washed," I finish for him. I pull the book closer to read the handwriting. "Twenty years ago the numbers were even, give or take thirty to fifty, but ten years ago the number dropped by three hundred. The next year by five hundred. Then they go back to normal until five years ago when four hundred disappeared. Once it stopped growing, the numbers only track the amount left in storage."

"Let me see," Endel asks. I slide it over to them and they confirm my statement. "Don't crops vary in number from time to time?"

"Never by this much, unless something horrible happened," I answer.

"Do you know what could've caused this?" Zyl asks me.

I sit back to think, "Well the Nafsi was fine up until five years ago, so the fading magic wouldn't be the issue."

"So the only logical explanation is that they went missing?"

"Or someone stole them," I answer.

"Who could get away with stealing that much of a primary healing herb?" Endel chimes in.

"In Kaelora, the nature preserve is in charge of collection and distribution. Here it's done by the city right?" I ask Zyl.

"Ownership of that responsibility was handed to Iron Brimstone since they had better resources," he says, pulling the book towards him. "I'm unsure for how long. This copy should have the signatures of those in charge of collection, but they're all scribbled out."

"So the original logbooks will be at Iron Brimstone?" Endel asks.

"Yup. The signatures would confirm if they were in charge of collection the years the flower went missing as well as the person who oversaw it. If so, they'll know where the missing flowers are."

Endel nods, a grin forming as they piece together the information, "They would have the seeds we need."

"Exactly," Zyl says.

I stand, the sudden movement bringing the two of them to a halt as they stare at me wide-eyed. *Stolen.* Hundreds of that wonderful plant stolen and for what? So the herbalists at that company could have a few extras lying around? It's one thing to have that corporation risk the health of the Nafsi, but to intentionally harm the whole of Vyelan is unthinkable. My teeth gnash together as I begin to pace. Memories of the past few years flood my mind. All the times I've turned people away. Given out less than what they needed. There are even some who fell on hard times and couldn't afford what they need. We used to have enough supplies to help them out. Then we didn't.

"Heriath?" Zyl asks.

"Years of struggling and trying to make do," I grit, coming to a stop. "It's gotten worse with time. Not to mention my sister's condition wouldn't have even gotten this bad if we had the right resources." All I can see is Yamala. Her smile as I left to go to work. Our endless nights under the stars.

"I'm sure someone has to know," Endel adds. I swiftly grab my satchel from the chair I was in, throwing it over my shoulder.

"Oh, someone does."

CHAPTER 30

TANSAE'S POV

I burst through the doors of the company's medical center to find it oddly quiet. Usually, herbalists are rushing all over the place. Hopefully, Aurora is still here and not taking one of her lengthy lunch breaks. I only have so long until Heriath and Endel return from the library. I approach the counter and lift my hand to ring the bell.

"Don't bother," I hear from beside me. Aurora stands in the doorway to my right and I lower my hand.

"Punctual," I comment and she sighs, waving for me to follow her to her office. I take a seat in her office chair while she shuts the door.

"Was something wrong with your last order?" she asks.

"Nope. It was just right." *Maybe even a little too perfect.* "I'm actually here for another favor."

She leans the back of her head against the door, staring up at the ceiling, "You know, you have so much access to information and resources. Why don't you go to any regular clinic and get your own herbs?"

"Because I love you," I grin. I lean back to lift my feet onto her desk, my heels pushing aside a few papers to make room.

"I don't have the time for your twisted sarcasm," she says, stepping forward to push my feet off her desk.

I roll my eyes and stand so she can take a seat in her chair, "Then I'll make this quick. I need bloodroot."

She freezes, eyes widening slowly at my request, "What?"

"You heard me," I say. "Preferably in the next ten days."

She shakes her head, "No."

"Excuse me?"

"No," she repeats sternly. My smile falters at the intensity of her gaze. "Look, I've done your dirty work. I've gotten you what you want time and time again-"

"You've also done this same song and dance, yet you always give in," I sigh.

"I'm not playing around, Tansae. I don't know what business you had with that dragonleaf I lent ya, but this is an impossible request. Bloodroot is meant for nothing but death and you know that. You should know it better than anyone since exposure to it is what killed your father."

"Don't you speak about him," I sneer. "You don't know anything. He was poisoned."

"That what he told ya? That someone had it in for 'em?" she asks, her usual drawl sharpening to a rigid tone. "Tansae, he was into some shady business. Despite all the Elysir we had access to, it still wasn't enough."

"Well, maybe it would've been if I hadn't caught you stealing out of our family reserves," I fire back. Her eyes darken as she shoots up from the chair. The wood hits the floor with a loud crack as she steps toward me.

"You know damn well you had more than enough," she shouts. "And maybe I shouldn't have done it that way, but I had no choice."

"Oh, you had a choice. The same one you have now," I grit, stepping forward. "Get me what I want, or your husband will die. Slowly and painfully. Just like my father did." Her chest heaves. Our noses nearly brush as I stare her down, but neither of us gives in.

"You have no right to do this," she utters.

A smirk spreads slowly across my face, "But I do have the power. Over you, your husband's life, and whether he gets to see little Lindel become an adult." Her eyes sheen as they start to water, the weight of her decision becoming more clear. I take a step back and lean against the door, "Either you get me the bloodroot, or I'll take away your access to our family's reserve for four months."

Her determination weakens as she takes a moment to consider my offer. In the past when she's said no or given me less than I initially requested I could go somewhere else for what I want. This is a special case since only herbalists know where to find Bloodroot and nobody is willing to provide it. It would take forever to find someone with both knowledge and access.

Her head hangs low as she grips the edge of her desk, "I...I can't, Tansae. Not even for Mitchel. I won't."

I huff and slide my hands into my pockets, "That's disappointing. The few times I met him, I enjoyed his company." I shrug as I reach for the doorknob, "Enjoy the next six months. I wish him well."

Her head snaps to me, "You said four."

"Did I?" I blink, tilting my head. "My mistake." I pull the door open and take a step to leave.

"Wait," she cries. I slowly turn back to face her, a few tears streaming down her cheeks. "I won't get it for you, but I know where you might be able to find someone who will." I push the door shut and lean against it. I fold my arms across my chest with a grin as I nod for her to continue. She stares at the ground, "Your father kept a list of all his contacts in a red leather journal. Your mom used to use it to navigate the work she was often given."

"And someone in that book can help me get what I need?" I question.

"If you can find it," she nods. "But that's all the information I'm willing to give. If you fail that's on you." She glares at me which I return with a smirk.

"Thank you, Aurora," I say, grabbing the door handle again. "Now pack your things. I want you out of this office by sundown."

"What?" she breathes. "But you promised-"

"Saying isn't promising," I point out. My eyes narrow to slits when her hand meets my shoulder.

"You can't do this. Please-"

I quickly face her and place my right foot behind her left one before shoving her with my shoulder. She trips over my foot and lands on the ground with a loud thump, her head nearly missing the chair. She rubs her shoulder with a hiss as I crouch in front of her.

"Despite your usefulness, you have been nothing but a thorn in my side," I whisper.

She lifts her head in challenge, "I raised you. I was there when your mom couldn't be. I'd think you'd show a little more respect than this."

"Aw, are you mad?" I taunt, opening my arms. "Hit me. Come on." Despite the fury in her eyes, her gaze falls to the side and I push off my knees to stand. She's right. She was like a second mother to me, but I've grown past the need for her guidance. I am the caretaker of an empire. It comes with sacrifice. "I hope you find pride in the knowledge that you have served your purpose," I say as I step through the doorway. "And that this grants you peace."

CHAPTER 31

ENDEL'S POV

Moving in with Zyl was a challenge we both weren't fully prepared for, but we've tried our best to adjust quickly. That being said, the past two days have been a flurry of emotions. Staying at inns while on the road is one thing, but staying in someone's home is different. Without anything to latch onto, the night in Zyl's guest room was rough. Plus, the obvious differences in the way we live. From his incense in the morning to my late-night roaming about the house, we've already had a few tense conversations. Luckily, the tension was eased by a good meal and some alone time.

"Here, you want to hold the knife like this," I instruct, tilting the knife in my hand to demonstrate.

Zyl copies my movement, "Like this?"

"Yes, now," I start, picking up the small wooden block from my bedside table. "Hold your block in your other hand and place the edge of the blade against it."

He picks up his own block and adjusts his grip with a nod, "Okay."

"The trick is to go a little at a time. So add some pressure on the edge of the knife and slowly push beneath the surface of the wood," I explain, digging my knife into the block. Once I reach the end closest to me, I catch the base of the knife with my thumb and the sliver of wood falls to the floor. "Easy."

His eyes move from my hands to my face and he raises a brow, "Easy?"

"As pie," I smirk.

"Don't enjoy my confusion too much," he says pointedly.

"Stop stalling."

"I'm not stalling," he grumbles, squinting at the block of cedar. He places the knife against the wood and takes a deep breath before sliding it down the length. His movements are choppy and it isn't until he's halfway down that I notice his thumb isn't braced against the block.

"Wait," I say, halting his movements.

"Oh come on, I haven't gotten far enough to be failing yet," he huffs. I chuckle and grab his hand, guiding his thumb to rest in the proper place.

"You haven't failed," I respond. "If you don't brace your hand the knife can shoot out at you. I don't want you to hurt yourself."

"Oh," he says. "But the rest is correct?"

"Yes, keep going," I answer, turning my attention back to my own piece of wood. Time passes quickly as we whittle. I give him step-by-step instructions to create different body parts. His concentration is oddly adorable and brings a smile to my face whenever I give him a passing glance. His steady hand for painting aids him in getting the angles correct, but his clumsiness with the blade causes him to slice too far into some places. I struggle to hold back my laugh when he accidentally slices off an ear.

I make my final cut and set down the knife on the coffee table, blowing wood shavings off the small fox that I've created. Pride swells in my chest at the completion of another project. Few things feel as wonderful as finishing a piece of artwork. Art has brought something special into my life. It is a gift to be able to create things with your own two hands. My skills at woodwork helped make my home beautiful and my ability to make jewelry has helped me make friends. I love the way others' faces light up at the sight of something uniquely made for them. Every time I put my hands to work, the thought of bringing that kind of joy to others motivates me. Though looking over at him, I can tell Zyl doesn't currently share my sentiment.

He frustratedly sets down his fox and tosses the knife next to it on the table. A frown darkens his otherwise bright features. His sculpture is nearly unrecognizable. The head of the fox is tilted, one ear missing from his previous slip-up, and the body is too skinny. The sculpture teeters on its uneven base, threatening to fall over with the slightest tap of the coffee table.

I want to give him the same playful treatment he gave me during our painting excursion, but something tells me I've given him enough grief. I reach forward and lift his sculpture into the light to examine it carefully.

"Not bad for your first try."

"It's awful," he laughs, his brown eyes meeting mine. "You don't have to lie, Endel."

"I'm not. You've never done this before. It was a valiant effort," I respond. A small smile lights his face again and he brushes his messy curls behind his ears.

"I appreciate that, but you can't even tell it's a fox," he says as I place it back on the table's surface. The sculpture wobbles before falling on its side with a small clack. The sound makes me curl my lips inward in an attempt to hold my laughter. "See," he sighs.

"Aww, come on," I say, bending down to reach into my bag of craft supplies that sits next to the couch. "Cut yourself some slack. Here, you can try again." I lift another block of cedar out of my bag and extend it to him.

He pushes it away with the palm of his hand, "No thanks, I'm not going to keep wasting your wood." I grab his knife from the table, extending it with my other hand.

"There's plenty where this came from," I assure him. "One more try. I can help you."

He eyes the objects in my hands before relenting with a sigh, "Okay, one more try."

He takes the wood and knife from my hands and I stand to move around the table, stopping at the back of his chair. I lean forward and match his grip over the knife, his hand in mine. My hips rest against the back of the chair and my head lowers next to his. My height allows me to be comfortable in this position, at least for a while. He clears his throat and adjusts his grip, placing the edge of the blade against the wooden block.

"Don't forget your thumb placement," I speak softly. The muscles in his neck tense at my voice, but he simply nods in response. I help guide his hands, making sure that the pressure is correct while he easily masters the angles. Our combined effort makes a considerable difference in the final product as he blows off the wood shavings. It isn't perfect, but it brings me joy to see his smile as he holds it up to the light.

"What do you think?" I ask, folding my arms over the back of his chair.

"It's a lot better," he says proudly. "Though I did slip up here," he mentions, rubbing his thumb over a small slit on the fox's cheek.

"I think it adds character."

"You know, I think it does," he replies, turning to face me.

It isn't until now I realize how close we are, his nose brushing mine as he turns to meet my gaze. We both freeze for a moment, his warm breath cascading across my cheek. He has long eyelashes and a few darker freckles by his right eye resemble a constellation that I can't name. His lips are two-toned, the bottom only a shade or two lighter than the top. His freckled cheeks grow red and I feel my own face heat up, though the hue is not as visible.

"Endel?" he breathes.

I blink and pull my gaze from his lips to find him staring at mine. A moment passes and he looks into my eyes, his silence asking permission. I nod and he meets me halfway to close the gap as my eyes fall shut. It only lasts a few seconds. Our lips hesitantly moving in sync to match each other's pace. He's warm. The taste of jester mint from his earlier cup of tea lingers as we separate. My eyes flutter open as a shy smile stretches across my face.

His head drops and I blink, standing straight as I attempt to come to my senses. I look around, trying to occupy my mind with anything other than what just happened.

I clear my throat awkwardly, "You okay?"

"Yeah," he says softly. He looks up from his lap and over at the clock on the far wall. I follow his line of sight and realize what time it is. "Um, I'd better get ready. I have that tutoring session and I don't want to be late like last time," he laughs.

I step aside as he stands, "Right." He scurries away and disappears into his bedroom, leaving me alone in the living room. *I guess I should get ready too.* I walk slowly to the guest room to grab my book and jacket. I bump into Zyl as I walk out and he quickly mumbles an apology before attempting to run off again.

"Wait," I say, my voice stopping him in his tracks. "Are you alright?"

"Yep. Why wouldn't I be?" he asks, turning to me. One hand grips tightly onto the strap of his bag while the other runs up through his hair.

"You're running from me."

"No I-" he sighs. "I'm sorry."

"Am I that bad of a kisser?" I joke.

His eyes widen and he frantically shakes his head, "No, not at all. I got nervous and I don't know what to do when I'm nervous so I just kind of ran. It wasn't you per se. It's been a while since I've kissed anyone and it was a bit much and-"

"Felt too soon?" I cut in.

His lips press together as he nods, "It felt nice, but maybe we should wait. I mean, we're supposed to have forever, right?"

I smile softly, "Right."

He eyes my jacket, "Where you off to?"

"Oh, I thought I'd visit Heriath. Haven't seen her around since she left the library the other day."

"That sounds nice," he says, staring at his feet.

I glance at the clock, "Five forty-seven."

He curses himself and stumbles towards the front door. I beat him there and open it for him, waving goodbye as he hurries down the path. I shut the door behind me, thoughts swirling in my mind as I walk.

Something felt wrong. No, missing. That kiss wasn't like anything I've experienced before. My fingers trail over my lips as I try to remember the feeling, but I can't seem to grasp it. It's as if it was nothing but a fleeting moment. I remember how soft his lips were. Like he said, it felt nice, but that missing piece still bugs me.

Maybe it was just too soon.

"Endel? What are you doing here?" Heriath hops down from a small stool to greet me with her signature smile. The one that outshines the sun and makes a stab wound feel like a pinprick. Fate certainly led her to become a healer with that kind of energy.

"Natiq told me I could find you here," I respond, adjusting my satchel. "I didn't know Iron Brimstone had its own library."

"Apparently," she shrugs. I look up at the tall shelves that surround us. It's the size of Mysticane's archives but still packed full of information.

"What you lookin' for?" I ask.

"Nope," she says, poking my chest. "You answer my question first."

"I came to visit you. Haven't seen you around."

She dramatically places a hand over her heart with a pout, "Aww, you missed me?"

"So what if I did?" I smirk.

She playfully rolls her eyes, "Well, I'm glad you're here. I'm trying to find the original logbooks and I could use the help."

"Need help reaching the top shelf?" I tease, gesturing to the stool behind her.

"I'm only a few inches shorter than you and taller than average," she defends, stomping her way onto the stool. One of the legs is shorter than the others which causes it to wobble, but she gains her footing nonetheless.

I raise an eyebrow, "You're what? Five eight?"

"Five ten, thank you very much," she huffs. "Now, will you help me instead of teasing me all day?"

"Okay, okay," I laugh. She guides me through her thought process on where to find what we need and I help her search. We pull the books off the shelves one by one, blowing the dust off of them. A few minutes of silence later, we move on to the next aisle. "So, what happened the other day?" I ask.

"Hmm?" she questions, pulling a new book off the shelf.

"After you left the library. Did you find who you were looking for?"

She sighs and places it back while I grab a new one, "I did, but something was off. She was upset when I found her."

"Did she say what about?"

She shakes her head, "I didn't ask. I did, however, pass Tansae on the way there. She looked rather smug. It was creepy." I flip through the pages of the book in my hand before shutting it. *Nope.*

"Think she had something to do with it?" I ask.

"Maybe. She's been under my watch since she gave you that tea. Something's changed about her, but I don't know what. She has no motive."

"Motive?" I snort. "Like a mystery novel?" She shoots me a look saying my sarcasm wasn't received well.

"I'm serious, Endel," she states.

I nod, "I know I'm sorry. That night still haunts me too. I've had a few nightmares since."

Her eyes widen, "You have? Are you okay?"

"I'm fine," I smile softly. "Nothing to worry about."

She stares at me for a moment before turning back to the bookshelf, "If you say so. If you do need a calm mind, some gilliflower can help. It's good for sleep as a tea or aromatic."

"I'll keep that in mind."

She steps onto the stool to reach the top shelf and the shorter leg gets the better of her balance. Her second foot slips to the side and I drop the book from my hands to catch her. My arms wrap around her waist, pulling her away from the shelf to keep her from hitting her head. I gently place her on the ground as she takes a moment to breathe from the shock.

"I had a feeling that was going to happen at some point," she laughs. A relieved smile tugs at my lips at the sound. I release her and grab the book she was trying to reach.

"How about I handle the top shelf from now on?" I say, handing her the book.

She takes it from me with a soft giggle, "Okay, but only because you'd suck at healing me if I got hurt."

"Excuse me, I've done pretty well in the past," I defend.

"Only because you had a good teacher," she fires back. I bite the inside of my cheek as she turns away from me.

I sure did.

The next two hours fly by like seconds. I'll admit, we did get distracted at times. Well, *I* got distracted. I'd almost forgotten how much I enjoy her company. Though, I swore that concentrated knit in her brow would become permanent if we searched any longer. Her disappointment is hard to ignore as we leave the library empty-handed. She's eager to continue searching, but I convince her to take a walk with me instead.

We walk towards the southern edge of the city. The small pops of color from butterflies and other pollinators doing their work bring a smile to my face. Heriath's shoulders relax at the feeling of grass against her feet. There's this look she has around nature. No matter where she is, if she's connected to her natural surroundings it brings her home.

She stops to remove her shoes. I offer her a hand to balance herself, smiling when she takes it. She places her shoes at the bank of the Nafsi and I settle in the grass beside her as she slowly lowers her feet into it. Her eyes fall shut to take in the gentle melody of the flowing water.

The sun caresses her soft features and brings out the contrast of her birthmark. I reach into my satchel to grab my book, taking advantage of the silence to continue the story. As I open it, I notice a small yellow bloom growing beside me.

"This is pretty," I mention, gently running my fingers over the petals. "What is it?"

Heriath glances over to me, "That's a solar holly. It's a common wildflower that shows up in the warmer months."

I hum and shift my book so I don't crush the blossom. She sits up, head on a swivel before hopping up from her spot. She spends a few minutes gathering the tiny blooms and returns to our spot to arrange them at her feet. I watch as she lifts one into her hands and then another, gently weaving the stems together. Her movements are quick and steady. The furrow in her brows returns as her concentration grows. I recall the feeling of her hands on me as she cleaned my wounds. No matter what, she handles everything with care.

"You okay?"

Her voice snaps out of my thoughts. I clear my throat and nod, eyes falling to my book as heat rises on my face. A gentle breeze blows by and flaps the thin pages of the novel, the sound mixing with that of the rustling grass and flowing river. A few pages later, I feel a tap on my hand and find the flowers formed into a golden crown atop her head.

"Wow, pretty crafty. I like it," I grin.

"Thanks," she says, pushing some of the leftover flowers toward me. "Wanna try?"

I stare at them, "I've actually never made one before."

"Really? All the crafting you do?" I shrug and she takes my hand to place one of the solar holly in my palm, "Guess it's my turn to teach you."

I do my best to follow her instructions, but nothing I do can make up for my heavy-handedness. Her delicate touch is perfect at tugging the stems through each other. Meanwhile, my thicker hands snap them apart. After my fifth broken stem, I huff and toss the flower behind me which draws a laugh from her. The sound brings a smile to my face.

"I quit," I groan.

"No, you nearly had it," she smiles, completing the small ring of flowers in her hand.

I shake my head, "I'll lay this field barren before I get it."

She laughs again and extends a hand to me, "Arm please." I hold out an empty wrist. Her fingers lightly brush against my dark skin as she wraps the stems around it, pulling out a flower or two for a perfect fit before locking the ends together. I hold it up to the light, my smile growing.

"I know it's not macrame, but it's something," she murmurs.

"It's beautiful," I breathe. "Where'd you learn how to do this?"

"Miss Merilla taught me at one point. Another one of her fun activities."

"Hm, well despite your awful woodwork skills, you can actually make a decent craft," I joke.

"If you're just going to insult me, then I'll take it back." I jump back, laughing as she playfully attempts to grab for it. I grip her wrist and she falls against me. Her chest presses to mine as we laugh.

"I'm kidding, I'm kidding," I grin.

"Then what do we say?" she smirks above me.

"Thank you."

Her eyes meet mine and my heart skips a beat. Brown irises dark as night, yet shine brighter than a sky full of stars and it all falls into place. *The missing piece.* Each moment in her presence, part of me has known. Now that part is at the forefront of my mind. I know now. I know I crave nothing more than to fall deep and explore the galaxy of her mind. To cherish each new discovery until my last breath. That same familiarity I felt when I first looked into her eyes has transformed into something more. I now know the soul behind them and it calls to me in ways I never thought possible.

Something shifts in her gaze and she hastily pulls herself off me. Her eyes wander, eyebrows drawn together as she starts to pick at her fingers. I didn't mean to make her uncomfortable.

"Hey, are you alright?" I ask. She nods and I lean forward to catch her eye, but she faces away from me. "Did I do something wrong?" Another silent response as she shakes her head. She reaches for her shoes and slips them on before standing from her spot.

"I just thought of another place to look," she says softly.

"For the logbooks?" Another nod as she continues to pick and pull at her fingers. I close my book and tuck it back into my bag, "Okay, where are we headed?"

"I can handle it."

"I don't mind helping. I've got time," I shrug, standing to dust off my outfit.

"No." I freeze at the weight of her tone and she shifts in her stance. "Sorry, I mean...you've helped plenty. I can take it from here."

"Are you sure?" I ask hesitantly. She hums softly in response before giving me a small wave. I watch her walk away, her absence holding the same empty feeling that I felt in that kiss. Yet, somehow, it bothers me more that she doesn't look back.

CHAPTER 32

HERIATH POV

I drag my feet through the door as I return to headquarters and head straight for Tansae's room. I can't bear the thought of them standing alone in that field. I hate myself for pushing them away like that, but I've let myself get too close for the last time. There are still a few places I haven't looked. It occurred to me that the logbooks would be something held close to the company and the library may not have been close enough.

When I reach her room, the door is cracked open. I push it further to find nobody there.

"Need something?"

I whirl around to see Tansae standing behind me, arms crossed. I place a hand over my heart as I catch my breath.

"Geez. Walk a little louder or something," I huff. She pushes past me and I follow her into the room. I take a seat on her bed as she moves about the space to gather a few items. I take advantage to scan for anything that would resemble what I'm looking for.

"What's with the flower crown? Endel make that for you?" she asks, grabbing a bag from a corner. *I forgot I had it on.*

I lift my hand to remove it as I bite my inner cheek, "No, it's nothing."

She places her bag next to me and shoves a few things inside. She pulls open the desk drawer and my gaze follows her hands. I get a glimpse of a page inside, only managing to read the title '*The Secret of My Success*' before she shuts the drawer again and points behind me.

"Hand me that small book?" I walk around the bed to grab a small red journal and toss it to her. She thanks me and I walk around a bit, trying to search as inconspicuously as possible. I can't help noticing the empty walls. The rest of the house is heavily decorated with paintings, pictures, and other items.

"You know, your room could use some color," I comment. She pauses her packing to take in the space.

"I guess," she shrugs. "You know, I saw that sculpture Endel made you. The one of the flower and moth." I blink, staring at her. She rolls her eyes at my expression, "Calm down. I just saw it in passing since you keep it on your dresser."

"Oh," I reply, my eyes falling to the floor.

She sighs, brushing her hair behind her ears, "Heriath, the ritual is in four days."

"I know that," I groan.

"Look," she says, closing her bag. "They've made you gifts, been there for you, and it's been fun, but you can't have them."

I lean back slightly at the accusation, "I never said-"

"You didn't have to," she interrupts. "You like them. It's okay. Anybody would, but they have a job to do." I draw in a deep breath and push it out with a huff.

"You're right," I admit. "Besides, they should be able to fall in love and have their happily ever after once it's all over, right?"

"Right," she says, placing a hand on my shoulder. "You're a good person, Heriath. I'd hate for you to get in the way." She slings the bag over her shoulder before moving to slide on some shoes.

"Where are you going?"

She grabs a cloak from a corner of her bed, "Out. I'll be back in time for our dinner in a few days." *Shit.* I'd forgotten we all agreed to meet for dinner the night before the ritual. Though after what just happened, I'm unsure if I should show.

She opens her bedroom door wider, gesturing for me to leave first. I bid her a safe trip as she slides the cloak over her shoulders. She bounces down the stairs while I wander the second floor. I find myself in front of a door labeled *'Office'* that I noticed when Cloveris gave me the initial tour. I'm not one to go digging through people's homes, but this could be the best option. If not the last one.

I push the door open and close it quietly behind me. I head straight for the large bookcase that rests in the far corner of the room and begin to scan the spines. On the bottom shelf are a few unlabeled books. I pull the first one off the shelf, excitement rushing through me at the contents.

They're here.

I flip through the logbooks one by one. Annoyance twists my lip when I notice they're out of order. It's a bit hard to read the fading dates on the yellowing pages, though the more recent dates are legible. I finally find the logbook with the dates I need and disappointment quickly replaces my excitement. The signatures are all the same from twenty years ago until today.

T. Morelli

Nothing strange and nothing to report. I shut the logbook and place my head in my hands. Four days. All I can do is hope.

CHAPTER 33

ENDEL'S POV

Dinner at eight.

A simple concept or so one would think. Tansae emphasized the sophistication and grandeur of the establishment we're going to and I wasn't sure if I had anything nice enough to fit in. That is until Zyl mentioned he had something for me.

I open the guest room closet doors, eyes widening at the sight before me. Hanging in the center is a formal black trench coat with golden accents. The corset bodice has brass buttons that trail down from the lapel and meet at the base of the torso. The fabric cinches at the waist before flaring out again to drape around the lower body. I'm almost afraid to touch it.

I leave it alone for now and get the rest of myself ready. I pull on black pants and a high-neck shirt before moving to the large mirror to shape my hair into an updo. It's a lot easier to style my locs when I'm not stressed. A buzz of energy surges through me as I get ready, excited at the possibility of seeing Heriath again.

I've tried to stay focused, but the truth is, I miss her. Don't get me wrong, Zyl is great company, but late at night, my mind wanders back to her. To that afternoon in the meadow. I know I shouldn't. It feels wrong, like I'm betraying Zyl. I've spent the past three nights cursing myself for my longing when my soulmate is asleep across the hall.

I shake away the thought and finish slipping one of my handmade hair pins into my bun to secure it. My chest heaves as I release a breath, tucking in my gray loc. Once satisfied, I approach the closet once more and carefully pull the coat off the wooden hanger. I slip my arms into the smooth material and adjust it carefully. My fingers fiddle methodically with the buttons, tightening it around my torso. The golden design on the lapel and cuffs add character to the article of clothing. The only thing that stands apart is the blue bracelet that encircles my left wrist. I complete the outfit with black-heeled boots and take one last look at myself before stepping out of my room and into the hallway.

My fingers pick at my bracelet as I sit on the couch, the soft plush providing me no comfort. The clock ticks against the far wall, the repetitive sound the only stimulus I can focus on to avoid facing my own thoughts. It's been half an hour and I'm not sure how long it takes to get there.

I breathe a sigh of relief when Zyl's bedroom door opens and stand to greet him. He steps out in a beautifully decorated white outfit. The pants have their own golden designs trailing down the side that match the jacket. A link connects the sides of the jacket across his sternum and his shirt underneath has a flared golden bow that hangs slightly. His usually messy curls are neatly arranged with a side part, the other side of his hair tucked behind one ear. He looks up from his cufflinks to eye my outfit and a smile graces his features. It's odd to see him so dressed up.

"You look handsome," he compliments.

"Thank you," I respond, tugging at the base of the fabric to straighten it. "It's so nice I don't want to ruin it."

"It's only dinner, so there's no need to worry," he reassures.

"You look amazing too," I blurt, realizing I hadn't said anything nice in return.

He chuckles slightly, "Thank you." His tone is full of confidence, but I don't miss the rose color that dusts his cheeks. "You ready to go?" I nod and he smiles, linking his arm with mine before guiding us out the door.

The sun sets as we walk through the city, glittering off our detailed outfits and adding to our sense of confidence. We arrive at the restaurant right on time and enter hand-in-hand. I study the interior of the building, the walls painted green with gold accents and lantern-shaped wall sconces that provide ambient lighting. The ceiling is decorated with dozens of bright flowers that only grow upstream. They trail down the walls, mixing with an assortment of ivy.

The host guides us to a table where Tansae is already seated. She stands to greet us, showing off her red gown that hugs her form nicely.

"You all are punctual," she grins, eyes alight. She's been in an oddly chipper mood lately, though with the ritual being tomorrow, I can understand. I shrug away the thought and take my seat next to Zyl on the opposite side of the table.

My eyes land on the empty seat next to Tansae, "Where's Heriath?" She sighs heavily, crossing her wrists as she rests against the surface of the table. The red stones embedded in the golden bracelets she wears accent her dress.

"Back at Iron Brimstone. She was very indecisive about coming so I wouldn't hold my breath," she answers. A waitress approaches our table and pours water into the glasses that sit in front of each of us. She quickly introduces herself and explains the menu items before leaving to give us time to decide. Once she's out of earshot, Tansae turns to us again with an eager grin. "So, what's been going on with you guys?"

Zyl is eager to talk, enlightening her on our small adventures while I read the menu. His face always has this glow to it when he rambles. The passion in his voice is enough to excite anyone who happens to find themself on the receiving end. I've enjoyed learning random facts about history and Vyelan. His informative nature fills the quiet moments and I find the subtle way his hair bounces as his hands wave around endearing.

A while later, we place our orders and continue chatting. I speak on occasion, allowing Zyl to govern our end of the conversation. The moments I'm not engaged, I find myself staring at the empty chair across from me. My gaze lingers on the intricately carved wooden frame when the view is disrupted by a hand gently gripping the back of it. My eyes trail upwards, widening slowly at the sight.

She is elegantly draped in an off-shoulder gown. The light green hue at the top fades into a darker shade as it trails down her figure creating an ombre effect. The long bell sleeves hang by her sides, swaying softly as she pulls out her own chair. The bodice and sleeves are decorated in fake ivy. Her locs are braided into a crown with silver twine weaved throughout. Butterfly-shaped silver earrings dangle from her ears and brush the top of her shoulders. She tucks in her glossed lips, gently rubbing them together as she adjusts herself in her seat.

"Sorry, I'm so late. Cloveris took forever helping me get ready," Heriath says with a shy smile. Tansae turns to greet her, her mouth moving but no sound escapes. My mind has gone silent. The room has gone silent. I take in the smaller details of her ensemble, including the colorful luna moth brooch that rests above her heart. She takes a drink of her water, lips pursing around the glass. Her every movement is captivating. She's usually dressed well, but this is something new entirely.

She's entrancing. A vision unlike any I've ever seen.

I'm suddenly pulled from my thoughts, and obvious staring, by Zyl whose hand taps my thigh. I glance at him and he nods to Heriath who is looking at me expectedly.

"I-I'm sorry," I stammer, clearing my throat. "Did you say something?"

"I said hello," she grins.

"Oh. Hello," I reply softly. My fingers pick at my bracelet again and I choose to stare at the tablecloth, the embarrassment setting in. There I go again.

"How have you all been?" she asks. I can feel Zyl's gaze for a moment before he turns to answer her for me. Dinner continues smoothly though Heriath is awfully quiet and I can't bring myself to say much either. The soft clinking of knives and forks fills the silence at the table as we eat. I push my plate away once I'm done and relax against the back of my chair. A gentle melody is played by a string quartet near the small dance floor where a few older couples are swaying.

Desperate for relief from the tension, I stand from my seat and extend a hand to Zyl, "Care to dance?"

A bashful smile plays on his lips, "I told you on our first date, I'm a mess on a dance floor."

"It's pretty simple. I'll show you."

He hesitantly takes my hand and allows me to lead him to the dance floor. We seamlessly merge in with the small crowd and I take his hand in mine. The smile on his face spreads as he follows my instructions, starting to get the hang of the steps. I've always loved the freedom of dancing, the way it brings people together from all walks of life. From the sloppy, drunken dancing of those at taverns to the gentle swaying I'd find my mothers doing in the kitchen in my youth. An expression of joy that withstands the test of time.

I'm soon lost in the music and find myself in the memory of that night in Whitburn Tavern. The feeling of her hands in mine and the look on her face as she relaxed into the melody of the instruments. Her weight as I dipped her, our breathing heavy as her brown eyes garnered all my attention, and the way the room seemed to fall still. Her laugh...

My memory is disrupted by Zyl's groan when I accidentally step on his foot. I hiss an apology as he gains his footing again.

"I'm supposed to be the clumsy one," he chuckles. "You okay?"

"*I* stepped on *you*," I remind him.

"No, not that. You seem distracted."

I shake my head, eyes shifting to the side, "It's nothing." His gaze burns the left side of my face as he stares me down, but in the end, he says nothing. We carry on through the rest of the song, clapping once it's finished. When we return to our seats, I notice Heriath's is empty once again.

"Where'd Heriath go?" I ask Tansae.

She nods her head towards the front doors, "She mumbled she was tired and wanted to go home." Before I realize what I'm doing, I'm up and walking to the front doors. I push through them and spot her green gown a few feet away. She turns to face me when I call for her, allowing me to catch up.

"What are you doing out here?" she asks. Her gown shimmers in the moonlight, matching the sparkle in her eyes.

"I could ask you the same. You're leaving?"

She shrugs, "I figured I'd turn in."

"Oh," I murmur, shifting my stance. "I was looking forward to talking to you. I haven't seen you in a few days."

"That's true."

My hand raises to the back of my neck, "I don't want to keep you long, but I was hoping...before you go could I have a dance?" Her gaze lingers on my hand.

"I don't know," she murmurs.

I offer my hand to her, "Please?" Her bottom lip tucks between her teeth as she considers my offer. I glance down at them before quickly pulling my eyes away, forcing out the curiosity of what it'd be like to kiss her.

Her soft hand takes mine, "Just one."

A few more couples are now on the dance floor. She weaves our fingers together and I place my free hand at her lower back. After a few moments, I step back and lift my hand so she can twirl in front of me. Her smile shines as her chest meets mine again and we continue to sway.

"This is nice," she comments. "Thank you."

"Well, I wouldn't want that beautiful gown to go to waste. You look stunning." Her eyes cast to the floor as she thanks me again. "Did you ever find the logbooks?" I ask.

She nods, "Yes, but I couldn't find anything strange. Signatures were all the same."

"What about that person you tried to find? Wouldn't she help?"

"I can't find her anywhere. I even went to the clinic where her son works, but he didn't know anything. He assured me he'd let her know about the situation."

I nod silently, pulling her closer to avoid a couple who nearly runs into us. I can feel her gasp beneath my hand at the sudden action. I relax my arm so she can put a small distance between us again.

She clears her throat, "I finished that book you gave me."

"How was it?"

"It was wonderful," she sighs. "There's so much information within it. So many plants I never learned about in my studies. Most of what I learned focused on Vyelan, but this book taught me about the plants outside of it." Her eyes shine with excitement and wonder, bringing a smile to my face. She's so beautiful with passion in her eyes. "Sorry?" she says, snapping me out of my thought.

"What?"

"You said something."

Shit, did I say that out loud? I shake my head, "Nothing. Keep going."

"Well, not if you're not listening to me," she huffs, a mischievous twinkle in her eye.

"No, I was. I promise."

She shakes her head and presses her lips into a firm line. I smirk and wrap my arms around her to lift her up. Her playful indignation is broken by laughter as I spin her around. I set her back on the ground as the song ends and the people around us begin to clap for the musicians.

A moment passes. The soft light traces every gorgeous feature before me. There's that look again. The same shift in her gaze that I saw in the meadow, only now I understand why. She steps back and grips the skirt of her dress.

"We- I shouldn't have done this," she whispers. Before I can respond, she's rushing towards the front door. I follow her, dodging the other patrons until we're outside, but she keeps going.

"Heriath, please wait!" I call, picking up my pace. "Please, just tell me what's wrong."

She stops and turns to face me, gesturing to the space between us, "*This* is what's wrong." I freeze a few feet away from her as she places her face in her hands. "You are what's wrong. My feelings are what's wrong and it's going to ruin everything."

My eyes narrow at her, "Are you saying... you-" She holds up a hand to stop me and a tightness forms in my chest.

"Don't. Please, just don't," she begs, shaking her head. "I'm here because of Yamala. My sister's life is more important than anything I could ever want." Her eyes well up with tears as she looks me in the eye, "Even if it's you."

My eyes widen. A flutter of joy sparks within me, but I suppress it. It's always her. Whether I've known it or not, it's always been her. Before I met Zyl. Before I even knew her name. But why? Why her when I have someone destined for me? She's invaded my mind day and night. The ritual is tomorrow and I haven't managed to keep my thoughts of her at bay. The fate of Vyelan hangs in the balance and yet, somehow, a small selfish part of me would throw it all away for her.

Sadly, it isn't my choice to make. Nothing means more to her than her sister's health. I can't ruin the possibility of saving Yamala, even for my own selfish desires. That thought keeps me rooted in my spot as she turns to disappear into the night. I want to follow after her. I want to comfort her. I want to try, but reality washes over me like a wave.

I can't have her.

That pained look in her eyes. How she pulled away from me. It told me all I needed to know. I understand now. Why she would push me away to be with Zyl. Always thinking of others. She's beautiful. Of mind and spirit. It's impossible to not be drawn in, but she's right and I almost hate her for it.

I force my eyes away and take in a deep breath.

She's shown me the love of a true friend.

It would be greedy to ask for more.

CHAPTER 34

"You know as well as I do that is complete bullshit," I laugh, closing the guest bedroom door behind me.

"Hey, I didn't judge your taste. Even if it was a bit shallow," Zyl defends.

"Just because something has historical value, doesn't make it beautiful. Face the facts, Zyl, that bathroom was ugly."

"If you say so," he smirks. "But I found it just as charming as your portrait of me."

I gasp dramatically, pointing an accusing finger, "That's a low blow and you know it."

"At least the food was good. Stuffy places like that usually serve overpriced crumbs," Zyl remarks, now comfortable in his pajamas. His slipper-covered feet rest on the coffee table, ankles crossed. He leans forward to push down the top of the tea press that rests by his feet, separating the herbs from the water.

"Where would you like me to put this?" I ask him, gesturing to the coat in my hand while rolling my shoulders in relief. It may be beautiful, but it was a bit snug.

"I'll take it," he answers. I walk it over to him and he smiles fondly as he accepts it, "You wore it well. I'm glad it fit you." My muscles fully relax with my hands now empty and I stretch my arms in the air.

"Where did you get it from anyway? It's unlike your usual attire."

"It was a gift from my mother," he says softly, running his fingers over the details. "She said I'd grow into it, but it's still big on me." I hum in response and he drapes the garment over the back of the couch. "Tea?"

"No, thank you," I reply, sitting in the chair across from him.

"Right, I forgot," he says, pouring himself a cup. I haven't had anything but water since the incident and the smell of severia cane makes me tense. Luckily, Zyl frequents jester mint as his flavor of choice so the aroma is pleasant.

"So," he starts, taking a sip of his warm beverage. "What are your plans after tomorrow?"

I squint, brow furrowing at the sudden question, "What do you mean?"

He looks up at me from his cup with a knowing smile, "After the ritual. Do you plan to stay here?"

"Why wouldn't I?"

"Don't be coy, Endel," he says, his voice stern. His cup clacks against its saucer as he sets it down next to the tea press. My eyes follow his movements as he stands, walking toward the kitchen. "We both know what happened tonight."

My heart beats harder against my chest and I hesitantly part my lips to speak, "I...I'm not sure what you mean." He grabs a small jar from a cabinet and walks it back over to where I sit. He removes the top to reveal sugar inside and a small spoon, a deep sigh escaping as he lifts it.

"Endel, you are a nice person, but don't kid yourself. I saw how you looked at her." I look at the floor, my now free locs draping around my face to hide my shame.

"I'm sorry," I mumble.

It takes a moment to find the courage to look up at him again. His spoon clinks against the sides of his teacup as he stirs. My lips curl inward and I adjust awkwardly in my seat as my hands wring together. I wouldn't blame him if he disliked me now. Until then, I'd been hiding it well. Her absence made it easier too, but seeing her tonight... Her beauty enraptured me. The smile that I'd grown used to seeing was suddenly ten times as bright and the melody of her laughter brought butterflies to my stomach.

"I know I shouldn't, but I promi-" I'm cut off when he holds up his hand, his knowing smile fading into a soft one.

He lifts the cup to his lips again, "There is no need to apologize. I've known it for a while now."

"Really?" I grimace.

He nods, "I was so worried about getting things right that I may have been paying too close attention. There's a way you look at her, it's special. Tonight only confirmed my suspicions."

"That's why I'm apologizing," I groan in frustration, standing from my seat. "You're my soulmate. We have all of Vyelan to save and I can't get her out of my fucking head." My hands run over my face, "I have a responsibility, an obligation to you."

"Who said that?" he asks and I pause my pacing. He sets his cup down on the table again and sits forward, "Endel, what do you want? Really think about it."

I walk over to my chair, hands gripping the plush material, "This isn't about me."

"Answer the question."

"It's a selfish question."

"I'm asking you to be selfish. Now, what do you want?"

"I've never been good at decisions," I shout. His eyes widen slightly and I face the floor. My hand runs down my face as I regain composure. "I never have because I never had to be. Not about what I create, not even about who I am. And now, when the choice is so devastatingly clear, I...I can't have what I want."

I want to help Vyelan, I want to be happy, and I want to go home. Most of all, I want *her*. I'm starting to understand the burden she carries. Being forced to make the right decisions all the time. I no longer have the luxury of just allowing things to happen.

I see him stand in my peripheral vision, his slippers scrubbing the ground as he walks over to me. He places a hand against my back, "But you did decide, Endel. You chose what makes you happy. That's the most important choice anyone can make."

I squeeze my eyes shut, "But I want to complete the mission."

"There's nothing stopping you from doing that," he tries to reassure me. "Our job is to complete the ritual, nothing more."

"But we're supposed to be-"

"I know, but doesn't that mean we should want each other to be happy?" he asks.

I can't help the guilt I feel from his genuine nature. This entire situation has thrown him to the wolves and he's handled it with grace. He's been a great friend in the time I've known him and deserves what respect I can give.

"So, what are you saying?"

"I'm saying," he starts, lifting my head by the chin so I can look him in the eye. "That you're allowed to be in love with her. If Heriath is who you want, I think you should go after her. It feels...right." I process his words, studying his expression. Joy and sadness dance over his features.

"What about you?" I question.

He shrugs, a small smile growing on his face, "I'll be okay. I *did* have a life before you got here, ya know."

"I guess that's true."

"Look, I want this ritual to work as much as anyone else. Fate led us together, but there is no obligation to fall in love. Besides, if we are meant to be we'll find each other again," he states. My heartbeat slows in my chest as I stare into his eyes.

"Once again true. You *are* smart," I joke with a light laugh.

"Hey, you said it yourself. Those with extensive knowledge are nothing to sneeze at," he winks. "Plus, she's even got my mom's approval." He gives my shoulder a gentle squeeze and my smile grows.

"Thank you, Zyl."

"Ah, don't mention it," he says, moving back to the coffee table to grab his teacup. "Just get some sleep."

I nod firmly, "You as well."

As he retreats to his bedroom, I take in a deep breath and look around the home I've been welcomed into. Books and jars of herbs line the shelves while maps hang from the walls. A small heart has been drawn on one of the maps around Duskwick. The aroma of jester mint lingers even in his absence.

I relax into the relief from our conversation. We both can have what we want thanks to his understanding. It feels wrong to leave him with nothing. My eyes land on the coat that still lays over the back of the couch and I pick it up, gently cradling it in my arms.

Maybe there's one last thing I can do for him.

CHAPTER 35

HERIATH'S POV

The bright white of the half-moon shines down on the city streets. Cool air fills my lungs as I breathe in, staring up at the clouds that lazily drift across the evening sky. *Today's the day.* All the traveling and trouble will have been worth it.

I look out to the street and see two figures approaching. Squinting, I see the shorter of the two in a large wool shawl, the colorful patterns standing out in the ever-present crowd that occupies the busy city. I wave to them as they become clearer, Zyl waving back while Endel stares at their feet.

"A wonderful night to save our fair land, is it not?" Zyl jokes as they both reach my spot in front of Iron Brimstone's large doors.

I laugh softly, "Indeed it is." I glance over at Endel who is picking at their golden bracelet, still studying the ground. My smile falters, but a loud noise distracts me before I can address them.

"Oh, you're here," Tansae says as the doors slam behind her. She slides a slip of paper into her back pocket as she approaches us. She spent the day at the mines to prepare everything, just recently returning to change for the ritual. "Are we ready?"

Zyl places a gentle hand on Endel's shoulder and they glance his way before looking up at Tansae. They nod, "Ready."

The night air chills as we walk to the Trosthek Mountains. The city lights fade as we grow farther from them and soon the path is lit only by the lanterns that hang from the houses in the valley. Zyl and I chat idly, our words covering the crunch of the pebbles beneath our feet. A few minutes later, Tansae stops at the wide mouth of a cave reinforced by wooden framing.

"Here we are," she remarks, jutting her thumb in its direction. "Watch your step, there is still some equipment lying around." She leads the way with Zyl close behind.

Another frigid gust of wind whooshes by. I grip my upper arms and rub them in an attempt to shield myself from the drop in temperature. I should have known a sweater wasn't enough, but I had so much on my mind.

I pause in my stride when the weight of wool covers my shoulders. Endel reaches around to button the cape at the base of my throat before smoothing out the material.

"We should get moving so we don't get lost in there," Endel whispers.

Speechless, I nod in response and follow them as they move around me. Fluorescent blue and green stones speckle the walls as we traverse deeper into the cave, aiding the lanterns that light our way. We make a left turn, dodging a series of stalagmites before arriving at a second cave opening deeper in the mountain. As we step inside, my mouth falls agape at the beauty in front of me.

The Nafsi runs from a separate entrance into a clear blue lake that rests in the center of the space. Natural columns are spread throughout the rocky floor. Stalactites hang down from the ceiling, each with a blue or green stone at the tip. Water drips from them into the lake below, creating a unique rhythm that echos softly around us. At the head of the lake is a wide set of steps made of the same glowing minerals that line the walls. At the top is the Water Stone, a stunning blue tear drop that floats in mid-air. Above the stone, there's an opening in the cave where the moonlight has begun peeking in. Water rains down from the hole, flowing over the stone and down the center of the steps into the lake.

Zyl stands near the stairs, studying the impossible flow of water. I join him, in awe at the sight, "It's amazing."

"I assume the water gains magical properties when it touches the stone," Zyl adds. "The snowstorm has always been consistent, but I never expected to see it in person."

"Enough with the science lesson," Tansae groans. "We have work to do."

"Well, technically it's a science and history lesson since-" Zyl cuts himself off when he sees the annoyed look on her face. "Right, sorry."

"You can tell me about it later," I say, gently nudging him with my shoulder. A shy smile tugs at his lips before he walks to the base of the luminous staircase. Endel stands at the base as well, the water flowing down the steps separating them from Zyl. They both slowly ascend the stairs, turning to face each other once at the top.

"Okay, now you both need to place your hands into the stream of water nearest the stone," Tansae instructs from beside me. We both stand a good distance away from the stairs to avoid any interference.

Zyl and Endel nod, both slipping their hands into the small waterfall between them, palms facing upwards. The moonlight grows brighter as it reaches its peak in the sky, the glow illuminating the Water Stone and the stairs beneath it. The refraction of light fills the cave.

I grip the sides of the cape to pull them closer to my body. Zyl and Endel both stand perfectly straight, staring into each other's eyes through the water. Tansae digs into her back pocket and pulls out the spell. The page crinkles as she straightens it out, "Now you have to repeat after me." *This is it.*

"*By the glow of our fair moon, in the light of my love, I bask in the joy of our union,*" she reads confidently.

Zyl and Endel repeat her words and the cave atmosphere shifts. The stones embedded in the walls glow brighter and the drops from the stalactites freeze in mid-air, hovering above the lake below. With each word spoken a new memory comes to mind, our entire journey flashing by in pictures.

Joking while washing dishes together, seeing them play with Wynira in the Sugar Pine Forest, and receiving the hair charm they made me. The one I left behind tonight.

"*May the mark we bear be a sign of our devotion and the beauty of our souls entwine,*" Tansae continues. The two repeat her words and I watch closely, eyes widening as the falling water begins flowing backward over their hands and up toward the sky.

Healing them in the back of the rocking steam wagon, the way they helped me when I couldn't heal myself, and our peaceful time in the Kaelora's Nature Preserve. Each memory burned in my mind, the overwhelming emotion from them threatening to spill from my eyes.

"*For the good of our land...*"

Dancing.

The weightlessness I experienced in their arms. The feeling of the world disappearing around me. The Water Stone glows brighter, shining onto their faces.

Endel looks away from Zyl and our eyes meet as they recite the words Tansae had given them. Their figure now like a mist, the warmth of their presence torturous as I knew from this moment on I would no longer have the privilege of their hands in mine. The light of their smile a fading sunset, never to rise again in the window of my soul. But they'll be happy. The land will be healed. Yamala will live.

"Till our last breath be taken."

Zyl repeats the last few words proudly while Endel is hesitant. Their mouth opens, but nothing comes out. I push myself to smile, nodding for them to continue.

"It's okay," I mouth. I manage to pull my eyes away and stare at the ground.

Endel faces Zyl with a deep breath, "Till our last breath be taken."

With the last words spoken and the moon fully passing, the cave returns to its original form. The breath that escapes me sings a final release.

The walk is silent as we leave. Zyl and Endel walk ahead of Tansae and I down the pebbled path, stopping once we reach his house. He goes inside, bidding us goodnight and leaving Endel standing on the front porch with us. I assure Tansae I'll catch up and she continues down the path.

I carefully unbutton Endel's cape and slide it off my shoulders, "Thank you."

"No problem," they reply, staring down at the wooden slats beneath their feet.

"Goodnight," I say, turning on my heel.

"Heriath, wait."

My heart jumps in my chest at the sound of their voice, but I ignore the feeling.

"I'm happy for you, Endel," I say over my shoulder, not trusting myself to turn around. "Truly, I am." Without another word, I take a step forward to catch up to Tansae. The cold night air brings my hands to my upper arms again, the small source of warmth being all that's left to carry me away.

334

CHAPTER 36

HERIATH'S POV

This morning was peaceful. I was awoken by the sunshine and birds outside my window. I was surprisingly refreshed despite the few hours of sleep I managed to will myself into. *Was.* Until Nasir came into the kitchen after breakfast with a letter that made my heart sink to my stomach.

Dear Heriath,

I'm sorry to inform you, but Yamala's condition is worsening faster than expected. She misses you dearly and awaits your return. I know your goal is to heal her, but it means more that you're here beside her during this time.

Sincerely,
Merilla Devaris

I scan the words over and over as Cloveris takes over washing the dishes. Not now. Not when there is still much to do. The ritual has been completed, but the Elysir never showed. I still have to find those missing seeds if I want to have a chance at healing her. I knew the risk and was sure I had more time, but now...

"What's wrong?" Cloveris asks, turning off the water. I silently hand her the letter and her face falls as she reads. She hums to herself and I shoot her a questioning look. She shakes her head, "Maybe it's my age, but something about this feels familiar to me." Her eyes meet mine and her expression softens. I gently grip the page as she hands it back to me, a reassuring hand on my back. I swore I'd be by her side when it mattered most. I have to make good on that promise.

"I need to go home," I murmur.

"Of course," she smiles softly. "I'll tell Nasir to check over your wagon."

"Thank you," I reply. I exit the kitchen and bump shoulders with Tansae on her way out. She stumbles a bit, gripping tighter onto the bottle of juice in her hand.

"Watch it," she snaps. "This took me forever to make."

"Sorry, I didn't see you. What's that for?" I ask, eyeing the purple liquid.

"Just something I made for the two lovebirds to celebrate yesterday's win," she smiles. She raises the bottle to examine it, giving me a clear view of three scratches on her arm.

"What happened to your arm?" I ask.

She shakes her head, "Nothing. Just scratched myself on a bush I think."

"Let me see."

"It's really fine."

"Please," I insist.

She slides the bottle into the wicker basket in her other hand before allowing me to have a closer look. My eyebrows draw together at the red lines across her skin. They aren't scratches but rashes. Distinctly the mark of violetta thorn, a nasty invasive species Kofir banished to the outskirts of Vyelan according to *Roots of Life*. What was she doing out that far? I release her arm, eyeing her with caution.

She gives me a once-over, "What?"

"Nothing," I hum, taking a step toward my room. "Have fun."

"I will."

Her tone brings an unsettling feeling to my stomach, but I put it aside. I reach my room as the front door slams shut, sighing at the mess before me. Clothes scattered about and many trinkets misplaced from my earlier attempt to organize things. I start to pick things up, tossing clothes into my trunk which lies open near the messy bed when the door swings open.

A pink robe flows through the doorway before Cloveris peeks her head in.

"Just seeing how things are going in here," she says. "Need any help?"

"Oh, no thank you. I'm nearly done," I answer.

"If you say so, dear."

She walks to the bed with grace. Her wrinkled hands gently grip the blankets, arranging and smoothing them onto the mattress. I open my mouth to protest, but seeing the soft smile on her face I figure I've rejected her help enough and shut it again. Her hair flows gently over her shoulders. The golden strands shift slightly as she looks around the room, "I've enjoyed having you here, Heriath."

"Really?" I ask, glancing up at her as she fluffs the last pillow and places it against the headboard.

"Of course. The other day was the most fun I've had in a while," she admits.

"I see the nail stain is lasting," I nod, gesturing to her hands.

She holds them in front of her with pride, "It is! And now that you've taught me how to make it, I'll have a new hobby."

"I'm sure the kids at the children's home would love it as a craft," I suggest.

Her smile adds youthfulness to her face as she takes a seat at the edge of the bed. "Oh my, this is beautiful," she gushes, reaching out for my sculpture on the dresser. She cradles it gently as she takes in the details of the wood. "Where did you get this?"

"It was a gift," I answer. "Endel made it."

"It's amazing!"

"I know. They have quite the talent."

"The details on this butterfly are so intricate."

"It's a moth actually," I correct, folding my last shirt.

"Oh, that makes more sense."

I extend my hands and she places the sculpture into them, "How do you figure?"

"You know what they represent, don't you?" I shake my head and she hums with a knowing smile, "Nevermind then."

I shrug and bend down to slip it between the clothes in my trunk for safekeeping. The trunk thuds when I close it, my fingers clicking the latches in place.

"Where are they anyway?" she asks.

"I'm sure they're with Zyl," I shrug, moving over to the closet to grab what's left behind. My hands grip the brown leather of my thigh garter. I pull out my dagger, nausea growing in my stomach at the sight of blood against the iron blade. I guess in my rush to heal Endel in Vauxworth Canyon I neglected to clean it off.

"Do you plan to visit?" she asks as I slip into the room's attached bathroom. I turn on the water, unsheathing the blade to douse it. The blood turns the water a rusty hue as it splashes into the bowl below.

"I'm not sure," I reply, grabbing a cloth from the hook nearest the sink. My fingers fold around the blade to assist the water in removing the blood. The thought has crossed my mind, but I chase it away and press the blade harder against the cloth.

"I'm sure they'd like to say goodbye," she mentions, now standing in the bathroom doorway. "You should make time to see them before you go."

"I don't want to bother them. They should have alone time together," I grunt, flipping the blade to remove the remainder of the blood.

"They're still your friend. I'm sure they'd love to see you." I'm not sure what they'd like. I'm not avoiding them for their sake. I managed to hold back my feelings this long, I know if I see them again I'll only act selfishly. If only the ritual had replaced the piece of my heart they now carry with them. I leave the bathroom to find Nasir stepping into the room.

"Is my wagon ready?" I ask him.

"Should be another hour or so," he replies. I look over my things. I should be able to finish packing in an hour. I give him a firm nod and he returns with his own before leaving the bedroom. Cloveris leaves me to pack as well and I continue my task.

I'm coming home, sis. Just hold on a little while longer.

CHAPTER 37

My bedroom door creaks as I exit, feet dragging against the wooden floor. I hear my back pop as I stretch with a yawn, looking up at the clock to see it's a little past noon. It was a restless night. I spent hours staring up at the ceiling before giving up and occupying my mind with a task. Luckily, I was able to get a few hours of sleep in after sunrise.

I knock gently at Zyl's office door, twisting the knob to open it when he calls for me to enter. "Good morning," he greets, spinning his chair to face me. His eyes dart to the clock by the door, "Or good afternoon, I suppose."

"Oh, am I interrupting?" I ask, noticing the mess of papers and books on the desk behind him.

"Not at all," he smiles, removing his reading glasses. "Did you need something?"

"I might have a surprise for you," I mention.

His eyes light up, "Oh? What is it?"

"Follow me," I instruct and he hops from his chair. I lead him into my bedroom and tell him to stand in front of the vanity mirror with his eyes closed. Once I'm sure he isn't peeking, I quietly open the closet and remove his, now-tailored coat. I step in front of him and drape it over his shoulders. "Okay, you can open them now." His eyes open and his smile fades from one of excitement to one of confusion.

"It's...my coat?" he questions.

"Put it on," I laugh.

"Oh." He shifts to slip his arms into the sleeves. His fingers make their way up his torso, looping each button. Slowly, realization fills his features. "It fits," he breathes, taking in his appearance. "It really fits!"

"It looks good on you."

"How did you- I just- Thank you," he stammers, wrapping his arms around my waist. I laugh and steady myself as I return his hug.

"You're welcome. It's the least I can do, you letting me stay here and all."

"It's perfect," he says, releasing me. "How did you manage to get my measurements?"

"I may have raided your coat closet by the door and did some minor calculations," I admit with a shrug. "Hope you don't mind."

He waves dismissively, "Of course not. Now I have to find a place to wear it to."

"I'm glad something good came from a restless night. I can only hope my other plans work out just as well," I mutter.

"Other plans?" I give him a knowing look and his eyes widen. "When are you going to tell her?"

"I'm going to see her later."

"When?" he challenges. *When I get the courage.*

"Later," I repeat.

"Later may be too late, Endel."

I'm used to doing things scared, so why is this so hard? Everything feels so right between us, but maybe that's what I'm nervous about. Either way, that smug look growing on his face is starting to irk me. "Fine, I'll go." I groan.

"Thank you," he says, unbuttoning the coat.

"Later," I murmur, holding back my laughter when he whirls around in annoyance. "I'm kidding."

"You'd better be," he glares playfully.

I hear a loud knock on the front door and leave to answer it while Zyl hangs up his coat. A small part of me hopes it's Heriath, but instead, I find Tansae standing on the porch with a wicker basket in the crook of her arm.

"What are you doing here?" I ask, surprised.

Her head tilts to the side, "That's one way to greet someone."

"Sorry, I just wasn't expecting to see you," I correct myself. "Come in." She strides into the house, setting the basket on the coffee table. She reaches inside to reveal a bottle of juice and an array of finger foods. Zyl greets her as he enters the living room.

"That looks yummy," he grins.

"Thanks, I prepared it myself. I figured we could celebrate yesterday's success before I run off to the mines for work," she says.

"That sounds nice," I comment, glancing at Zyl. "But I have somewhere to be."

"Where are you going?" Tansae asks

"Back to company headquarters."

"Hopefully she's still there," Zyl adds.

Tansae stands straight, dusting her hands off as she turns to him, "Who?"

"Heriath," he smirks.

"She was packing when I left. She's probably gone by now," she responds, looking my way. "You won't be able to catch her." My heart sinks at the thought. She takes a seat on the couch and lifts the bottle of juice, pouring it into a few cups. "Have a seat," she says. I shake my head, pulling open the front door with a revived sense of determination.

"I'm going to find her," I tell her.

"Come on, relax. She's long gone by now," she says, standing from the couch. Her hand grips my wrist and she tries tugging me toward the couch, but I pull my arm away. Her eyes darken at my action.

"I have to try," I state firmly. Zyl flashes me a proud smile as I rush out the door. My mind is set on my destination, running only on hope that I'm not too late.

I arrive at Iron Brimstone, my chest heaving as I fight to catch my breath. I lean forward to rest my hands on my knees. *Why did I run?* Standing straight, I knock on the door while trying to slow my breathing to not embarrass myself. Nasir opens the door and I push past him, bee-lining for Heriath's room. *Empty.* My heart sinks.

"Shit," I breathe. My hands run over my head as I look around frantically.

Cloveris steps into view from the kitchen, her pink robe draped around her figure, "Oh, you're back."

"Do you know where Heriath is? I need to find her," I rush.

"She should be out back packing her wagon for her trip."

I thank her and race out the front door, following the path to the loading bay. My rapid heartbeat doesn't slow as she comes into view, but

I can no longer blame it on the running. I take a moment to breathe as I observe her. Her brown skirt dances around her ankles in the soft breeze as her eyes run over what I assume is a checklist. She's so focused she doesn't notice I've approached her.

"So, you weren't going to say goodbye?"

She jumps slightly as her head shoots up to look at me, "Endel?"

"I'm glad you're still here," I breathe.

"Yeah," she smiles softly. Her bottom lip tucks between her teeth as she stares at her feet. She folds her list and pushes her cloak to the side to slip it into her pocket. "Well, it's good to see you. I'm nearly done here so I should be on the road in less than an hour."

My eyebrows furrow, "Why the rush?"

"Well, the weather is perfect and everything is settled so, why not?" she shrugs with a reassuring smile. The same one she gave me when I was injured. It's not her. Not the smile that makes my heart race or the one that made me run all over Mysticane looking for her. This was rehearsed. Clinical. *She's lying.*

I step towards her but she steps back, causing me to freeze. Her eyes dart to the floor as her index finger picks at the side of her thumb. There's a wrinkle in her brow that begs to be soothed, but I refrain from moving closer. Her hands join together in front of her and she gently tugs her fingers.

"Don't do that."

"Do what?" she asks.

"Avoid my eyes."

"I'm not avoiding your eyes."

"Then look at me, Heriath. Or at least tell me why you didn't come say goodbye?"

She scoffs, "This is ridiculous. Why are you standing here fretting over eye contact?"

"You're right. It is ridiculous," I spout. "I've supposedly found my soulmate, we've done this ritual, beauty will return to the land, and many people will be healed. But when you leave my heart will go with *you*."

Her expression softens, "You don't know what you're saying."

"Heriath-"

"I shouldn't let the daylight fade," she says, wiping her palms against her legs. She turns to leave with hesitant steps as she moves towards the wagon trailer. I stare at the spot she was just in, unable to move. My hands clench into fists and my eyes shut as I draw in a deep breath.

"I'm a coward, Heriath," I blurt. Her steps fall silent and I look up to see her figure frozen. "That day in Kaelora City. The way the sun made your skin glow as you were drawing. Your eyes lit up being completely in your element. You were so focused and the way you explained things to me...something changed." She turns to me, eyes widening as she takes in every word, though she still refuses to meet my gaze. I take my chances and step closer, relieved when she doesn't move.

"That night in Whitburn Village. The way you smiled as we danced. You trusting me with your weight as I held you. You were so beautiful and free," I continue, taking another step towards her.

"Endel," she murmurs, looking down.

"And last night, as I stood reciting the ritual and promising my heart to Zyl, I realized it had already been stolen." I take the final step and land in front of her, lifting my hand to raise her chin. "I love you, Heriath. I love you and I couldn't let you leave without telling you how I feel."

Her eyes swirl with emotions I've yet to decipher, "But *he's* your soulmate.”

“I don’t care. I want *you*. You’ve consumed my thoughts. You’ve brought joy to my life. Your passion for your craft is immeasurable. You care for others to an extent I’d had yet to witness. Not to mention your eyes and smile. The way your nose crinkles when you laugh and your nostrils flare when you’re annoyed. I’ve cherished every moment with you and will continue to do so if you’ll allow me the pleasure.”

She blinks, averting her gaze, “Isn’t this wrong? I mean Zyl-”

“Zyl and I agreed that our job was to complete the ritual, nothing more,” I reassure her.

“I...” she trails off, conflicted. “I love you. But...” *But.* That one word squeezes around my heart.

“But?” I ask softly.

“The Elysir isn’t growing. My sister’s life isn’t guaranteed. The risk of it...it’s too much. I want you with everything in me, Endel,” she admits through misty eyes.

“You have me,” I whisper, taking her hand. “Whether you choose me or not, you have me. The ritual is over and we can find the missing flowers together. I’ll be here for you. To help you. All I want is for you to be happy and that includes saving Yamala.” I place a kiss on the back of her hand, hearing her draw in a sharp breath, “Even if I never see you again...I just thought you should know how much you mean to me.”

There’s a moment of silence as I await her response. My heartbeat in my ears once again. I wait for something, anything. I half expect her to push me away and run. To my surprise, realization washes over her features and a soft laugh escapes her lips as she meets my eyes.

“Sometimes what’s right takes a risk,” she whispers. “Maybe that’s why Zyl let you go. Maybe...I need to let go, too.”

“What do you mean?”

She grins up at me with a shrug, "It means I've fallen for you, Endel, and I can't deny it anymore. I may not know exactly how this magic works or even what I'm doing at times, but the one thing that has felt right this entire journey is you." *There's that smile.*

Relief floods my body and my chest heaves as I breathe again. How I've longed to hear those words. Her arms encircle my waist and I wrap my arms around her shoulders, gently cradling the back of her head. We've been fighting to do the right thing for so long, but whether this is right or wrong, what matters is that we'll face the end of it together. That's all I wanted and I'll embrace every last moment. As long as the Nafsi flows and she is in my arms.

"I swear I'll do whatever it takes to help you heal your sister," I whisper.

"Thank you," she says. "But did you really came back for me?"

"What else would I run around the city for?" I chuckle.

"I don't know. I thought you'd left something behind."

"I did," I reply, pulling back to see her face. Her beauty pulls me deeper with every passing moment. "I can't live without my heart, can I?" Her eyes widen slightly before she stares down, a shy grin on her face.

"Heriath?"

"Yes?"

I shift my hand to her chin again and lift it gently, my thumb slowly caressing her cheek, "Are you sure you feel the same about me? I know how sudden this is and..." I trail off as she closes her eyes and leans her cheek into my palm. She turns to place a gentle kiss against it. My thoughts fizzle away at the action.

"You know, I may not be as poetic as you, but I can't deny that there was a reason I grew distant. I didn't want to risk ruining what you and

Zyl could have. I guess that makes us both cowards.”

“I guess so,” I smile as my thumb moves down to stroke her bottom lip. Her lips part slightly and I bite my own. She lets out a content sigh. The warmth of her body against mine is pleasant, but it’s not enough. “If...if it’s not too soon I’d- can I...” Staring into her eyes is so distracting. Her lips even more so.

“Endel, I fell for you a while ago,” she admits.

“Still,” I whisper. “We can take it slow if you like.”

She laughs softly, her eyes falling to my lips, “I think I’ve kept you waiting long enough.”

Without a second thought, I lean forward and slip a hand to her lower back as I capture her lips. Our kiss is tender. It isn’t rushed or hungry, but the gentle caress of her lips against mine pushes my soul to reach for hers. It claws its way out of my chest and I can’t help but pull her closer. She’s sweet, just as I’d imagined. Soothing and comforting, like the day we sat in the meadow. The first bloom of spring after months of barren winter. One of her hands meets the back of my head, fingers weaving between my locs. I take her free hand in mine and gently entwine our fingers. Our lips move in sync as my thumb travels down to her wrist, feeling her steady pulse beneath it.

We separate and my head feels light. Too light. A strange rush flows through my body causing me to shiver. Flashing images pass through my mind. A dark-skinned woman with white hair in a neat braid, a light-skinned man with red hair, another woman with short hair, another and another. Faces I’ve never seen, yet I know, whether it’s from another place or another life. Each has a variation of features but possesses the same comforting amber eyes. When the faces disappear, I see the Water Stone with two figures standing beneath it and a sequence of familiar words scrawl across the inner walls of my mind.

By the glow of our fair moon, in the light of my love, I bask in the joy of our union. May the mark we bear be a sign of our devotion and the beauty of our souls entwine. For the good of our land, till our last breath be taken.

The words are overtaken by a blinding white light that forces my eyes shut. I blink and my vision slowly returns to normal. Heriath stands in front of me with a blank stare, our hands still locked together. I turn her head towards me and she blinks rapidly. Her eyes come into focus and a knit forms in her brow as they shift to the side.

"Did you…" she trails off, looking back to me. I nod silently as realization sets in. So many questions to ask and many more answers to sort through. The truth stares us in the face and I'm unsure how to process it.

"We need to tell-"

She cuts me off with a kiss, her arms wrapping around my neck to pull me closer. I relax into her touch before she pulls away for a second.

"Later," she mumbles against my lips.

I grin, "Later." I cup her cheek and kiss her again. She smiles into it, melting away the rest of the world for a few precious moments.

My sweet Heriath.
I'll never let you go.

CHAPTER 38

"Why did you lie?" I ask her. She shifts in her spot as we sit on the driver's bench of her wagon. I fold the letter in my hands as she hangs her head.

"I didn't want to worry you," she murmurs.

"Heriath, Yamala may not be my family, but I can tell how much she means to you. It would've hurt, but I wouldn't have stopped you from going home." I hand her the letter when someone calls her name.

Cloveris rushes toward the wagon, "Heriath wait!" Heriath stands and hops off to meet her. The older woman catches her breath before standing straight, "Don't leave yet."

"What's wrong?" I ask. She extends a hand to Heriath who hesitantly hands her the letter.

"I knew something looked familiar about this," she says, scanning the words. "This is Tansae's handwriting." Heriath steps beside her as Cloveris points to the text. "She's always double-looped her O's since she was younger."

"How did I not notice that?" Heriath whispers to herself.

"Maybe you were too distracted by the bad news," I suggest.

"But, why? Why would she do this?"

"To get you out of the way," another voice says. We all turn to face a woman standing behind us. Her hair is pulled up into a puff and she adjusts the glasses perched on her nose.

"Aurora?" Heriath gapes. "Where've you been? I tried to find you but-"

"Tansae fired me," she says. "It's a long story that I've been too much a coward to tell."

"Aurora told me about Tansae blackmailing her for extra medicine and herbs from our supply," Cloveris says.

Aurora hangs her head, "My husband fell ill just as the Elysir started becoming scarce. I learned about Mr. Morelli's secret stash and stole some in my desperation. Tansae caught me after a while and changed the lock on it. I thought that was it, but then she started making demands. I refused her most recent one and she fired me because of it." She turns to Cloveris with teary eyes, "I'm sorry. I disrespected your family and stole from you. I'll take whatever punishment you see fit."

Cloveris raises a hand with gentle eyes, "Aurora you have served this family for years. You were by my side in my husband's death and took care of my little girl when I couldn't." She reaches forward and takes one of Aurora's hands in hers. "That grants you forgiveness."

"Thank you," Aurora grins.

"Though I wasn't made aware of a stash of Elysir," Cloveris says. "It would have been good information to have."

Heriath steps forward, "Where is it? Is there any left?"

Aurora nods and waves for us to follow her, "This way." She leads us back inside the house and straight to the office on the second floor. She approaches the bookcase, pushes a book on the third shelf to the side, and lifts a latch until we hear a small click. She pulls it and the bookcase swings forward on hidden hinges to reveal a staircase.

"It was right here this whole time," Heriath murmurs as we descend. The temperature drops dramatically when we reach the bottom and Aurora points to a door. The iron entry is bolted shut with a circle in the center. In the middle of the circle is an outline of a dagger. I run my fingers over it, feeling the tiny buttons that rest in the imprint. There are too many to press all at once.

"You just need a dagger to open it," I comment.

"I tried that, but look at the shape of the outline," Aurora points out. The wavy shape of the blade portion catches my attention.

"It's a kris blade."

"We need Tansae's dagger," Heriath says, finishing my thought. "But they're behind this door?"

"All the Elysir that's left, yes," Aurora confirms.

Cloveris steps closer and slides a hand over the iron, "He kept so many secrets from me. I thought she'd be more willing to open up, but I was wrong."

"She was under the constant influence of her father," Aurora says, placing a hand on Cloveris' back. "It wasn't your fault. You did all you could." Cloveris gives her a gentle smile. Heriath's eyes narrow slightly as the gears turn in her mind.

"If you didn't know this was here, then..." She takes off up the staircase and I follow close behind. Heriath kneels in front of the bookcase and grabs a book from the bottom shelf. Once she lands on the page she needs, she rips the letter from her pocket and places it beside the book.

"It was here the whole time," she breathes. "The O's in the last couple of signatures are double-looped. Just like the letter." Her eyes meet mine, "Tansae is the owner of Iron Brimstone."

"Figured her out, huh?" Cloveris responds. Aurora closes the secret door behind them. "She asked me to tell you I was the owner to keep up appearances."

"Appearances?" I question.

Cloveris sighs, "Our company doesn't have the best reputation. She'll never admit it, but she may be insecure since she's inexperienced when it comes to running this place. She asked me to cover for her, and I agreed. I'm sorry."

"No," Heriath sighs. "Your heart was in the right place."

"That still doesn't tell us why. Why she did all of this," I mention. "Like you said, Heriath, she has no motive. She even came by with some snacks to celebrate our success with the ritual yesterday."

Her face falls and her eyes dart to the logbook before looking up at me again. She seems to look through me, searching for something in her mind.

"Success," she mutters. I jump back as she shoots up from the ground. "That could be it."

"What?"

"The papers in her drawer. The logbook the- Follow me," she stammers. She grabs my hand, nearly dragging me across the hall. We stop in Tansae's room and she heads straight for the desk, yanking open the drawer and sifting through the papers. I approach from behind and she holds up a few sheets in triumph. "Found it."

"What that?" I question. I lean over her shoulder and read the title: *The Secret of My Success.*

"I think this may tell us why she's been hoarding the flowers here," Heriath says as she begins reading. Our eyes move in sync over the words. It isn't Tansae speaking in this letter and it's certainly not about the Elysir.

"This must be where she got the information about the ritual," Heriath says softly. I gently remove the second page from her hands to continue reading. She soon joins me, peeking over my forearm. My heart sinks into my stomach as I take in the information.

"They were killed," I whisper, my hand lifting to cover my mouth. *Killed before they could complete the ritual.* Memories of that night awaken within me along with a wave of nausea. The blurry view of the inn room as I collapsed by her bedside. Desperately trying to wake her up with the little strength I had left.

I blink as a hand meets my back and look to Heriath. My breathing is harsh, faster than I remember. She rubs soothing circles between my shoulder blades and I take a deep breath. My eyes water as they continue down.

I trust that you won't disappoint.

T. Morelli

My blood runs cold as the last few words confirm what I've feared the most since that night. Every hair on my body stands on end as dread fills my body. I look back to Heriath whose eyes carry the same realization.

It wasn't a mistake.

We bolt down the stairs and push through the large front doors. Wind rushes past my ears. My feet thud against the cobblestone road. Blood rushes through my veins. My lungs burn as cold air fills them before I force it out again through my nose. *Five buildings, turn left.* I turn left down another street, frantically raking my brain for the right path to Zyl's house. *Three buildings, one right.* I make a right, nearly slipping as cobblestone turns to pebbles and sand.

Seven houses.

I can see his house before it comes into view. *Why is this path so much longer now?* My heart races. The rapid pace thuds against my chest almost painfully as I run.

Three houses.

My face burns. Goosebumps litter my arms, but the temperature is the least of my concerns. I think of his smiling face. The way he laughed at my horrible attempt at painting when we first met and the smile he gave me just before I left.

I'd give anything to be wrong.

CHAPTER 39

HERIATH'S POV

We reach his house and they jiggle the handle to find the door locked. Taking a step back, they kick it with all their strength, the wood straining beneath their boot before finally splitting near the handle and flying open.

"Zyl!" they shout, racing to the back of the house.

I take a step to follow when a sound catches my attention and I look toward the living room. The coffee table is a mess. Fruit and crackers litter the surface. The flower vase that once sat in the center is broken. Shards of porcelain swim in the pool of water that drips off the table. The source of the sound, an empty teacup, rolls away from the couch where I find Zyl slumped over. My vision blurs for a moment and my breath catches in my throat.

I pull myself out of shock and rush to his side, pushing him to sit up. His eyes are wide open. My fingers meet the side of his twitching neck as I frantically check for a pulse. It's faint. *Shit.*

"Endel!" I scream, wrapping my arms around Zyl to drag him off the couch. His limp body thumps against the floor and I cross my hands over his chest. I rhythmically press using all of my weight.

One, two, three, four...

"Come on," I grit. Endel drops to my side.

"What happened?" they spout.

"I need a first aid kit," I tell them between pumps. "Now!" They scramble to the kitchen while I focus on Zyl. His sternum bends under my hands as I press harder. Small muscle twitches throughout his body give me hope. An ache grows in my chest at the sight of his face. The color is draining. I squeeze my eyes shut.

One, two, three, four...

Endel returns to my side and rips open the first aid kit. I look inside, attempting to think past my heartbeat thudding in my ears. Luckily, due to Zyl's clumsiness, it was fully stocked. Including a concentrated vial of twilight nox.

"The yellow vial. Pour it down his throat," I instruct. They follow my order without a word. The cork pops as it leaves the vial. Their hands shake as they pull open Zyl's mouth to pour the liquid inside.

One, two, three, four...

I press my ear to his chest.

Nothing.

The twitching in his neck has ceased. I start again and push harder, wincing at the crack of his ribs beneath my hands. My vision blurs as my emotions break through the barrier I've constructed in my mind. I'm back at the inn with Endel. Their body unmoving.

One, two, three, four...

"Wake up," I plead. Another crack sounds as another rib breaks. Zyl's face is blank. His heart is still. The ache in my chest grows. I've never lost a patient. I've never lost *a friend*. I won't. *I can't.* A lump forms in my throat.

One, two, three...

My ears are ringing. Tears drip from my cheeks and onto my hands. I wipe them away before my hands return to his chest. Endel places a hand on my shoulder, but I shrug it off. I faintly hear them call my name and I shake my head. A sob escapes as I push harder.

One, two...

My technique is becoming sloppy. Tears cover my hands and I can barely keep my elbows straight. Endel places two fingers at Zyl's throat.

"He's gone," they say softly.

"No," my voice cracks. My hands slip apart and I hastily readjust. "I can save him-"

"Heriath-"

"No!" I cry. I'm supposed to be better than this. To be smarter. I'm supposed to know what to do. I'm a healer. My sole purpose is to save people and I'm failing. Endel's hands grab mine. I fight to keep going, but they force me to face them.

"Heriath!" they shout. "Stop." Their stern voice wavers. Tears threaten to spill from their eyes. I pull away and place my ear to Zyl's chest in an attempt to hear something. Anything. *Please.*

His eyes are dull, gray, and empty. Brown curls lay flat against the wooden floor. His face, the one that carries features of his mother, is barren. I grip Zyl's shirt, burying my face into the fabric. A sob rips through me as I lay over his chest. *This can't be happening.* My head is heavy as if stuffed with cotton, an ache in my chest like an empty void. Waves of grief crash over my body, the pressure making it hard to breathe.

Arms wrap around my waist, gently pulling me away from Zyl. I allow Endel to pull me to them and my face falls into their chest. I swipe at my cheeks, but each time I wipe away tears new ones fall in their place. Endel's arms circle my shoulders and their chin rests atop my head. The weight much like my father's hand brings me comfort. My rapid breathing slows the longer I sit in their arms.

My head clears enough to notice their body shaking with quiet sobs and I look up. Tears stain their cheeks, eyes squeezed shut. Their usually cheery demeanor is gone. I wrap my arms around their waist in a silent attempt to comfort them. I'm not sure how long I'm there, but Endel never complains. The quiet room consumes us as we take in our shattered reality. They shift and I look up to meet their solemn gaze. The white of their eyes is blotched with red and I'm sure mine look the same.

I look back at Zyl, the lump in my throat returning. "You should rest," I manage, releasing Endel from my hold. I blink back my tears as I push out of their arms. They don't respond, simply lifting themself from their spot to sit in the living room chair. "You can go lie down in the guest-"

"I'm not leaving you," they state plainly.

I give them a silent nod and turn to Zyl. I slowly reach up to his face, placing my index and middle fingers against his eyelids to shut them. Once closed, he almost appears peaceful. The usual pensive expression he carried now smooth as if he were asleep. A purple hue shows under the brown skin of his neck and trails downward. I take a deep breath and lift his shirt, gasping at the sight beneath. His chest is covered in deep purple lines as if lighting had struck him and left its mark. They all lead to a large splotch over his heart. I never thought I'd see it in person.

I stand and walk around the coffee table, grabbing one of the dry napkins from the surface. I cautiously wrap the napkin around the handle of the empty teacup and lift it from the ground to observe. There is a purple stain on the bottom and a ring where the lips would go.

"Find something?" Endel asks. I turn and hold the teacup so they can view the inside.

"She's consistent," I deadpan.

Their brows furrow, "Doesn't that take a few days to kill?"

"Dragonleaf does. *Bloodroot* doesn't," I state. Closing my eyes, I place the cup on the table. My index finger and thumb knead at the bridge of my nose.

"Wait, like from the legend? I thought it didn't exist anymore," they ask, eyes widening.

I look up at them through my lashes, "It doesn't grow in Vyelan, but it still grows outside of the land. Only fully certified herbalists know about this so we know what to do when we come across it."

They pause, looking down as they process, "You let everyone believe it's a legend so-"

"So the wrong people don't go looking for it, yes. She could have only gotten this information from an herbalist." So this is the request Aurora wouldn't fill. It's all been a lie. The betrayal hangs over us like a storm cloud. Endel stands from their seat and makes their way over to Zyl.

"His smile was so bright when I left earlier," they whisper. They squat next to him, sliding their arms beneath his neck and knees. I move to meet their side as they lift him off the ground.

"Endel?"

"We can't just leave him out here," they respond. I follow as we walk to the back and turn into the second room on the left. A bed rests in the back corner. The furniture is pushed up against the walls to leave plenty of walking room. The space is clean and organized except for a few papers crumpled by the wastebasket. I move to the bed, sitting on the edge with Endel who's sweeping Zyl's hair out of his face before moving down to stroke his cheek.

"Is it wrong that I just...want to pretend he's sleeping?" they murmur. I place a hand on their shoulder unsure of what to say. It shakes as they cry harder, clutching Zyl's hand in their own. "If I'd just stayed here," they say softly, voice cracking under the weight of their emotions. "If I hadn't been so selfish-"

"No," I insist. "If you stayed, you might have died too." It was selfish for us to choose each other, but not our fault he died.

They shake their head, "We shouldn't have dragged him into this shit. He didn't deserve it." The deep violet covering Zyl's chest still spreads, creeping down his arms and legs even after completing its job. Despite my experience, I can't help the nausea turning in my stomach.

It's painfully clear now how long we'd been led on by her. A spark of resentment ignites within me at the thought of her taking time to set everything up. This was her final step.

Endel stands from the bed and places their hands on Zyl's cheeks. They lean forward in a graceful bow, touching their forehead to his. They whisper a few words that I can't fully make out, but I hear a faint *'thank you'* at the end.

"We should go," they say, this time addressing me. I glance at Zyl, heart aching at the thought of leaving him behind, but there is nothing left here. I nod silently and they turn to leave the room.

Endel leads the way as we exit the house. We drag our feet aimlessly through the pebbles on the ground. After a few minutes, Lake Irridover comes into view and we approach the edge. They settle in the grass and stare blankly at the water. It's hard to know their exact thoughts, but the time they spent with Zyl seemed special. They not only have to deal with what they saw but the thought that it might have been them.

The breeze blows ripples across the water, wrinkling the reflection of the mountains behind it. There's nothing to say. I see injuries every day, but this wound draws deeper than any dagger. He's more than a patient, he's my friend. The first connection I had to the world outside of my small village. He was home to me in a strange new place. *What am I going to tell Miss Merilla?*

Endel's hand meets my shoulder as their thumb wipes away some of my tears.

"She hasn't won yet," Endel says, reading my thoughts.

"What do you mean?" I ask.

"I'm still alive," they say, standing from the ground. "And I know where she is."

The cutlass slides into the sheath that sits flush against Endel's back. They pace around the room, fiddling with the harness. I tap the cool hilt of my dagger repeatedly to steady my racing mind. My eyes follow their movements back and forth across the room. Time has slowed to a crawl since we returned to the house. Few words were said, but our decision was made. My only hesitation was the uncertainty of the outcome.

"Are you sure about this?" I ask lowly.

"What is there to think about?" they respond, continuing to strap their gear down.

"Even if she's still in the mines, we don't know what she's capable of."

"Of course we do. She's a coward," they sneer, taking a seat at the vanity across from me. "She relies on tea and poisons to do her dirty work. I doubt she'd kill us with her own hands and even if she tries, we've seen her fight before."

"She managed to gather enough bloodroot in time to kill-" I cut myself off to swallow the lump in my throat. "To *get rid* of Zyl the day after the ritual."

"I'm aware of that."

"My point is, she's obviously had this planned for a long time. We don't know what we're running into if we go after her."

"That's a chance I'm willing to take," they grit.

"Well, I'm not so sure. We-"

"*We?*" they question. I sit back at the intensity behind their gaze. The once warm brown of their eyes now dark with pain and silent anger. For the first time in their presence, I feel the need to tread carefully.

"Yes, *we*," I answer. "You expect me to stay here?"

"She wants *me*, Heriath. As far as she knows, I am the last soulmate. The last one in her way-"

"And she's already proven the lengths she will go to to get her way."

"She killed my friend, Heriath."

"*Our* friend," I deadpan. The sting of their words is unbearable. He lays in a bed across the hall and the image of his face haunts me. I swallow harshly, gripping the hilt of my dagger. "I know how you feel, but taking a life is something I don't think either of us is capable of. No matter how angry or upset we are. But *she* is." They sit forward with a sigh, elbows resting on their knees and eyes turned to the floor.

"That's why I have to go alone."

I push off the bed and walk forward until I'm standing over them, "What is this? Some kind of manic self-sacrifice?"

Their head tilts upward, the intensity of their anguish stronger in closer proximity. I push down my instinct to comfort them. It won't do much now. The determination in their eyes is unwavering. They place a hand on the vanity, pushing themself to stand without breaking eye contact. My chin lifts to account for the few inches of height they have on me.

"If you stay here, I'll know you're safe," they say.

"But you get to run head-first into danger?" I scoff. "I don't think so."

"I can handle myself."

I cross my arms, "This decision seems awfully one-sided. Not to mention selfish."

"I get to be selfish with the people I care about."

"So do *I*."

There's a pause, their jaw clenching as they take a moment to assess me. I'm not staying here. I wasn't able to be there for Zyl, but I will be here for them. It was selfish of me to choose them in the first place, but it was the right choice. I'll be damned if I lose them now. My eyebrows lift in challenge and their eyes soften with the realization that I'm not backing down.

"You're awfully stubborn," they concede, finally breaking eye contact.

"And you fell for me anyway."

They breathe a huff of light laughter, the hint of a grin quirking up a corner of their mouth, "Yeah. I did."

Satisfied, I take a step to the side and towards the door. Their hand grips mine and I turn back to face them, their gaze once again riddled with intensity.

They step forward and weave our fingers together, "I need you to promise me you won't do anything stupid." Fear, anger, sadness. All these emotions were obvious, but the warmth of their hand, the gentle caress of their thumb along the side, said what neither of us could bring ourselves to voice.

I can't lose you too.

I give their hand a squeeze and nod firmly.

"Only if my promise is yours."

CHAPTER 40

The mouth of the cave is anything but welcoming as we stand before it. Even the fading sunlight provides no comfort. I draw in a deep breath and square my shoulders, trying to calm the intensity of my heartbeat. Heriath does the same, her solemn expression now focused. The darkness creeps out and swallows us as we step inside.

I squint as my eyes adjust to the low light. The blue stones that peek out of the cave walls glow just bright enough to make out Heriath's figure a few steps ahead of me. My fingers drag along the wall to keep steady as I duck and dodge stalagmites and wooden beams. We silently travel through the first section of the mines. The wood frames groan around us as a soft wind whistles through the cave.

"Strange," I whisper as we round a corner.

Heriath's grip on her dagger tightens, "What?"

"There's no light."

"It *is* a cave," she mentions, confusion twisting her features.

"No, I mean if she was really here working, wouldn't there be lanterns lit? Other workers?" I point out. I observe the path ahead to find a view similar to the one behind us.

"Maybe she left already," she suggests, stepping forward.

This segment of the cave is wider, allowing us to walk side by side as we traverse deeper. The hairs on the back of my neck stand up and I take another deep breath. I watch my feet as we walk, the ground covered in more light than the previous portion of the cave.

"Endel," she murmurs, eyes fixated on the wall.

The echo of my footsteps dissipates and I follow her gaze to find crackle stones mounted along the side walls, stopping halfway into the tunnel. An uneasiness settles in my stomach and I pause. A moment of silence passes before a loud boom erupts. Our hands fly up to cover our ears. My head whips to the crumbling entrance of the tunnel. I can barely make out a figure shrouded in shadows. A lantern hangs from their left hand, the small light illuminating a sickening grin which is soon covered by the piling rubble.

The tunnel shakes violently as each crackle stone detonates from the force of the one before it. The explosions rapidly grow closer, but I can't will myself to run. Large holes bore themselves into the sides of the cave. Wood and debris fly in every which direction. The wooden frames lining the ceiling crack as they split, each pop sending a wave of fear through my rigid body.

"Endel!"

Two arms circle my waist, effectively pulling me out of shock. Heriath yanks me back as the ceiling caves in. She spins around and shoves me away from the crumbling front half of the cave. I trip and fall on my side, barely avoiding my head hitting the stone floor. My body curls into a ball, hands on my ears again and eyes squeezed shut as dust kicks up around us. A high-pitched ringing sounds as the last crackle stone detonates. I slowly open my eyes, swatting my hands around to clear the air. Ash seeps into my lungs with each shallow breath.

"Heriath?" I cough, crawling on my hands and knees. I tap the ground in an attempt to feel my way back to her. As the dust settles, my eyes widen at the destruction now completely covering the entrance. I scramble to my feet and lunge for the rubble, frantically tossing aside rocks and wood with newfound strength.

"Heriath!" I cry, my voice thick with fear. I stumble around, finally finding her against the wall and I rush to her side. Overall, she's in pretty good shape. A few cuts and bruises on her forearms, most likely from shielding herself. The rising and falling of her chest eases my nerves. I sigh in relief knowing she was only rendered unconscious by the force of the blasts. I clear the space around her and lift her to a sitting position. I place two fingers against her neck and the reassuring thump beneath them soothes me. My hand meets her cheek, thumb gently brushing away the dirt on her face.

My own skin is covered in ash and dust. The burning sensation in my throat makes it difficult to breathe. The light at the opposite end of the tunnel ignites hope for escape. I tear the hem of my shirt and loosely tie it around her head, adjusting it to shield her nose and mouth from the particles in the air. It should act as a decent filter until she wakes up.

"I'll be right back," I whisper, placing a small kiss on her forehead. I dust myself off and leave her to continue down the tunnel. My fingers drag against the wall as I limp along, my left ankle throbbing with each step. I must have rolled it when I fell, the adrenaline covering the pain until now. There should be multiple entrances and exits for the miners and with any luck I'll stumble across one.

I soon reach my destination, the light at the end of the tunnel revealed to be the water cave. The magical stone's pulsing glow lights the area. I take a deep breath of clean air. I hiss through my teeth as I drag myself to sit against the wall and remove my boot. My ankle is mildly swollen, but given that I can walk it should only be a sprain. Tearing more material from my shirt, I tie it tightly around my injury to make moving around easier. I slide my boot back on, the back of my head meeting the cold stone behind me. The soft hum of energy coming from the Water Stone rings in the quiet. A slight grin plays on my lips.

Who knew I'd be using her medical knowledge on myself?

Water runs down the stalactites and into the lake below. There's music in the rhythmic dripping sound. My eyes fall shut to enjoy the melody when it's soon interrupted by a louder noise. *Footsteps.* My eyelids flutter open and I push myself to stand. The makeshift wrap around my ankle alleviates some of the pain. I grip the hilt of my cutlass as the steps draw closer. The repetitive slit of a knife being sharpened sends my blood rushing through me.

Tansae emerges from behind the flight of stairs leading up to the Water Stone. Her dagger in one hand, a rock in the other. She slides the rock roughly along the length of her dagger sending a few sparks flying with each swipe. Her eyes land on me and her gaze hardens.

"You," she seethes, pointing her dagger at me. "You're supposed to be dead."

"This is senseless, Tansae," I groan.

"No. What's senseless is this infuriating cycle."

"Of what? You're lies? You're betrayal?" I spit, my voice growing louder with each word.

"Do you know how hard it is to make a death look like an accident?" she chuckles darkly. "I've spent so much time crafting the perfect excuses. Planning the perfect mistakes. Yet here you stand, refusing to die."

"I guess you'll have to try harder," I grit. I charge forward, refusing her time to think. My cutlass slices through the air and forces her backward. She staggers in her movements and I take advantage to cut a gash in her left shoulder. My other fist slams into her face, the rattling of her jaw makes the pain in my knuckles pleasurable. She loses her footing and falls to her knees, huffing as I stand over her. The pain in my leg is drowned out by the rage rushing through my veins.

I extend my cutlass, keeping my distance as she stands to regain her composure. She lunges for me and I throw my arms up to block the first punch, which nearly knocks me backward. My movements are quick, but nothing compared to hers. I duck and dodge to no avail as she slams a fist into my jaw. Her blows leave me breathless. One after another with no time in between to brace myself. The ones I manage to block are certain to leave my arms bruised. She swings again, hitting my ribs before slicing the skin of my forearm.

"Come on," she shouts, landing a swift punch to my gut. I stumble back a few steps as pain rushes through my body. My teeth gnash as I fight the pain in my ankle. I cough and sink to my knees, a bit dizzy. She stalks towards me, but I remain in place. My free hand holds my stomach as I glare up at her.

She stops a foot in front of me, leaning forward with a challenging look. "Hit me." I want to. I want to hurt her. To make her pay. She sheathes her dagger and her arms spread wide, exposing her torso. "Don't be fucking boring. Hit me!" She stares down at me with contempt before exhaling a laugh in disbelief, "You can't do it, can you?" The weight of my cutlass grows heavy as I grip it.

Her arms drop to her sides, "Even Zyl put up more of a fight."

"Don't you mention his name," I seethe. I swiftly grab a handful of dirt from the cave floor and sling it into her face. She stumbles back, rubbing at her eyes. My body seems to move on its own as I set free my anguish. My chest heaves and a surge of adrenaline rushes through me. I swipe at her with ferocity. Her eyes follow my blade and I slam my fist into her ribs. She doubles over and I slice at her face. Her eyes widen slightly as she lifts a hand to her cheek. Dark red stains her fingers and drips down to her jaw, the sight gives me a strange feeling of satisfaction.

"That's more like it," she chuckles. She attacks with twice my strength, but I'm no longer intimidated. I dodge and move behind her, gripping her ponytail and yanking her backward. She swings her arm back and cuts me at the shoulder. I hiss and kick the back of her knees. She groans as her body thuds against the ground and I sheath my cutlass to use both hands. Keeping my grip on her hair, I roughly kick her in the side before swinging my leg over to straddle her and repeatedly slamming my fists into her face. A guttural scream echoes in the space as she pushes her hips up and grabs the sides of my neck. She pulls my head down to crash into hers. I fall to the side and grip my forehead as I try to reorient myself, blood dripping from my nose.

"You bitch," she coughs with a frustrated groan. I manage to pull myself to my feet. My chest heaves as I catch my breath.

She swiftly reaches into a pocket on her belt and blows something in my face. I swat desperately and stumble backward as the cloud of purple spores swallows my senses. My hands press against my ears, but despite my pathetic attempt, I can still hear her laughter as the shrieking begins.

CHAPTER 41

HERIATH'S POV

A dull ache pounds at my temples as I slowly open my eyes. Soreness spreads through my muscles as the rest of my body wakes up. I jolt forward as the previous events flood my mind. *We were attacked. How long was I out?* Dust particles float in the air. Bits of dirt fall from the ceiling through the cracks in the wood slats that remain standing. I lift a hand to my face, feeling a cloth that covers my nose and mouth. I tug it down with a groan to see it's the same white color as Endel's shirt. *I guess they really were watching.*

A guttural scream at the end of the tunnel pulls me to my feet. I stumble forward, still dizzy from being knocked around, and brace myself against the wall. Carefully, I make my way toward the light while untying the cloth from around my neck. The second scream sinks my heart to my stomach. *Endel.* I pick up the pace and soon find myself in the Water Stone's cave.

A throaty laugh comes from Tansae as she stands over Endel. Their hands cover their ears and they fall to their knees in front of her. Their screams pull me to them, but Tansae whirls around at the sound of my footsteps.

"And then there was one," she states, her voice low.

"What did you do to them?" I sneer.

"You know, it took a lot of work to get here and you're *really* taking the fun out of this for me." For each step she takes toward me, I take a step back.

"Fun?" I spout.

"I guess a better word would be satisfaction," she says. Her fingers run over the flat side of her blade as she lifts it into the light of the Water Stone. Her lips quirk upward.

I grit my teeth, "Given what you've done, you should have plenty."

"Not quite." Her gaze returns to me, dark and foreboding. She flips the hilt of the dagger between her fingers. The way you'd fiddle with a pencil while studying. I'm fixated on the speed and ease at which she handles it as I reach for my own.

I swallow, "What do you want?"

"What do you mean?" she asks, her head tilting to the side like a curious puppy. "I want the same as you. To heal our land."

"That's bullshit and you know it," I state firmly. "Why are you doing this?"

"You always think yourself morally superior," she laughs lightly.

"The truth, Tansae."

She sighs, tapping the point of her dagger against her bottom lip. Her shoulders are relaxed as she paces back and forth, "I simply have a legacy to uphold. Something I want to protect. You know what that's like, don't you?"

"Of course I do," I reply.

"Then why do you insist on getting in my way?" she grits.

"Because your plan involves the death of two innocent people," I shoot back. My right foot slides back to set my stance as she firmly grips the hilt of her dagger.

"You got what you wanted, Heriath. The land is healed. What's two lives for the fate of Vyelan?"

"Unlike you, I'm not willing to shed the blood of those I love. I'm smarter than that."

"What you are is *weak*," she spits. "Like my mother. Like my idiot bodyguards. Like every other person whose feelings get in the way of their greatness. My father knew better. My father was great."

"Your father was a coward who relied on manipulation to get his way."

Her jaw sets, "You know nothing." I unsheathe my dagger as she adjusts her stance. "However, I do owe you since you kept Endel alive long enough to complete the ritual. So I'll give you a choice." She pulls a small glass vial from the sheath of her dagger and my eyes widen at the dark liquid it contains. "You can either have a peaceful death by drinking some of the bloodroot elixir I have leftover or you can die by my hand."

"My death wasn't in your plan," I defend.

"Plans amend," she says, dangling the bottle in front of her. "You have been a thorn in my side."

"I've done nothing but heal you."

"You got in my way," she shouts. I flinch at the volume, dread settling in my stomach when a strained smile grows on her face. "So, are you going to take this or will I have to pour it down your throat myself?" This isn't the Tansae I've come to know. Or maybe it was. She is right though. We wanted the same thing. I was the one variable she didn't plan for and now I'm the remainder. I bend my knees, bracing myself for what I'm sure would be a torrent of pain.

"If you want my life, you'll have to take it."

Her eyes light up as she returns the vial to her sheath, "Your mistake." Her dagger whizzes through the air and I manage to block her blade with my own. Her movements are sluggish compared to what I've seen before. I dodge her swings, noticing the bruises and small cuts that litter her skin.

Her fist slams into my side and I stagger. She goes for another, but I swiftly duck and step forward. My foot lands behind hers and I swing my elbow across her face before shoving her with my shoulder, forcing her to trip backward. My foot raises, slamming down onto her stomach. She lurches forward with a loud groan and I kick her in the temple, her hair streaking across her face as she lies flat against the ground. Her movements are still and I stare for a moment before another scream erupts from Endel.

I rush to where they've pushed themself up against the cave wall. They are curled into a ball, eyes squeezed shut. I try to hold their hand, but they roughly push me away.

"Endel, it's me," I plead, trying to get through to them. A faint purple hue dusts their shirt and my eyes widen. *Shrieking Void.* I grip their wrists and place my forehead against theirs, doing my best to hold them still. "It's okay, hun. It's okay. I'm right here." Their groans fade slowly into small whimpers, but their body still shakes. Their breathing starts to even out and they stop struggling against me. "That's it," I whisper.

The cold metal of a dagger sinks into my side and a scream rips from my throat, forcing me to release Endel. A strained laugh meets my ears and I turn to see Tansae, a small stream of blood running down from her temple. Blood stains the blade of her dagger as she grips it tight. Her chest heaves as her laughter subsides and she clenches her jaw. The sight sends a chill up my spine.

She stands over me covered in dirt, sweat dripping from her reddened face, "Get up. I'm not done with you yet."

I grit my teeth as I stand, blood seeping through the material of my shirt. I back away from Endel, drawing her attention away from them. "You used us. Tried to dispose of us," I hiss. "You're lucky you aren't already dead."

A crazed look sparks in her eye that sets my whole body on edge, "So are you." She raises her dagger and slams it down into its sheath. The shattering of glass meets my ears and her blade emerges, covered in the deep purple liquid.

An animalistic growl rips from her throat as she slices at my face. I block her swinging blade with my own as she begins slicing and thrusting erratically. An odd desperation in her attacks. Trying to find any exposed bit of skin to sink the poison into. I nearly dodge in time and she stumbles forward. Taking advantage of her imbalance, I force her to the ground. Her chin hits the floor as I dig a knee into her back. I release my dagger and pin her arms as she wrestles for freedom, my eyes trained on the violet blade.

She screams as she pulls an arm free. I lean to the side to avoid the poison and she wraps a leg back to roll us over. I grip her wrists as she twists herself to straddle me, kicking my dagger away from us. Pain shoots up my forearms as she presses down, inching the blade closer to my throat. My heart thrums in my ears as I become keenly aware of my weakened state. A drop of bloodroot elixir drips off the tip of the blade, landing beside me. Strands of blonde hair stick wildly to her forehead. Dark hunger glows in her eyes. All traces of humanity have vanished behind the greed that consumes her. Her teeth gnash together, primal grunts forcing their way through them as she pushes harder. My hands slip slightly against her sweaty skin and my death falls an inch closer.

My head turns to the side and Endel comes into view. Their body is slumped over and disturbingly still as they try to regain their sanity. My eyes begin to water as I strain against Tansae's hysterical strength.

We've come so far. This can't be it. The end of our journey. All we've fought for together. I suck in a deep breath and face the crazed woman above me. *Zyl's death will not be in vain. I'd rather die myself.*

I squeeze Tansae's wrists in one hand and place my other atop the hilt. With a loud groan, I swiftly push down the length of my body, angling the dagger away from me and using the weight of her own effort against her. The blade sinks into the meat of her thigh and a sharp gasp escapes her lips. Her eyes slowly trail down to her leg as realization sets in.

"No," she grits, trying to dislodge the blade. I push it deeper and she jolts against me with a pained grunt as violet lines appear through her skin. A scream rips from her and her hands fly up to my throat. My grip on the dagger is unrelenting as she presses her palms against my windpipe.

Just a little longer.

I gasp for breath. Her hands begin to shake. The bright green of her eyes fades into the misty gray of death. That hollow emptiness in Zyl's eyes that only pushes me to lodge the blade deeper into her leg.

Come on.

My head grows lighter. Spots float in my vision.

Fuck, come on.

Her fingers slowly lose their grip and she falls forward, her head landing on my shoulder. I cough beneath her as my lungs fill with air. Her body twitches before finally falling still, her full weight now resting on my chest. I place my hands on her shoulders and shove her off of me. I stare blankly at the ceiling, my chest heaving as I try to shake away what I'd done.

I grip my side and pull myself up.

The worst is over.

378

CHAPTER 42

ENDEL'S POV

Be quiet. Please be quiet.

The thought echoes in my mind over and over again. I can feel the wet grass beneath me, the cold dew drops soaking my clothes. My eyes remain shut, yet I can still see the shadows swirling above me.

Go away. Please, just go away.

They reach for me, gripping my wrists to pull my hands from my ears. "Go away!" I shout, shoving them off. I scramble back, my breathing erratic. I pull my knees to my chest as my hands fly to my ears again. Something warm meets the bridge of my nose and I pause. It slides upward and smoothes the wrinkles on my forehead, forcing my face to relax. My breathing slows slightly as I hesitantly lift my hands from my ears.

"Please, open your eyes," a voice pleads. It's barely above a whisper but still reaches the depths of my mind. I reach forward and two hands grab mine, interlocking our fingers. *Heriath.* "Please, Endel."

I shake my head frantically, "I... I can't. The shadows-"

"They aren't real," she reassures me. I try to focus on her voice. "I'm right here. Please try.”

I take a deep breath and slowly my eyelids flutter open. Specters black as night spin around me like a hurricane. They bear their teeth, singing a song of despair that clouds my senses. Their hands dart out, gripping my wrists, face, and throat. My breathing picks up and I shut my eyes again.

“I can’t see you,” I panic, trying to regain control of my own mind. I’d give anything to have her reassuring smile greet me, but my mind is not my own. The cacophony of terror blocks her out like the sun behind a patch of thunderclouds. Sobs wrack my body as I grip tighter onto her hands, “I can’t see you.” I can hear her take a deep breath and gently squeeze my hands before releasing them. I reach out for her again when I’m stopped by the feeling of her palms meeting my tear-stained cheeks.

“Then feel me,” she whispers.

Her lips meet mine and I freeze. Warm. Soft. Sweet. I place my shaky hands against her cheeks and bring her closer. All my thoughts disappear as she becomes the air I need. She pulls away and I breathe, the pace of my heaving chest becoming more steady. I wrap my arms around her and shove my head into the crook of her neck. She holds me and the wet grass returns to stone.

“You’re not alone, Endel. Not this time,” she says.

Once I find the courage, I pull my eyes open. The steady dripping of the water around us is now the only sound as my eyes meet hers, “I can see you.” She smiles weakly, pressing her forehead against mine. I breathe her in. *I’m not alone.*

Her head slides to my shoulder as more of her weight presses into me. I pull back, noticing the shakiness of her breath. My relief is cut short at the sight of blood seeping out of her side. She looks up at me through half-lidded eyes, a few of her locs loose and covering her face.

"I'm sorry," she whispers. "I...I tried-"

I shush her, pulling her closer, "Save your strength." I pull off what remains of my shirt and hastily tie it around her waist, wincing at the hiss that escapes her as I tighten it. I lift my head, frantically looking for an exit, "We just have to get out of here." I shift my gaze toward the staircase where I remember the opening I'd noticed during the ritual. My hands slide beneath her back and legs to lift her using what little strength I have left.

My body may be weak, but I will not fail her.

You're going to be okay, my angel.

I crash through the doors of Iron Brimstone. My chest heaves as sweat runs down my body. I refuse to succumb to the ache in my muscles as I clutch her limp figure. Reaching the door to the house, I slam my back into it. My voice hoarse as I scream for help. Nasir rips the door open and I collapse to my knees.

He takes Heriath from my arms, "Shit what happened?"

"She's lost a lot of blood," I huff. Cloveris emerges from behind him with Aurora at her side. She gasps at the sight of our bruised and bloodied bodies.

Nasir runs off and I will myself to follow. An arm wraps around my back, holding half my weight. I turn to see Natiq shrugging my left arm over his shoulder.

"What happened to you two?" he asks, guiding me down the hall.

"Tansae," I breathe. His eyes darken, but he doesn't pry. Something tells me he already knows.

Nasir takes Heriath into the second guest room while Natiq leads me to the first. I attempt to shrug him off, but he pulls me back.

"You need to rest," he states.

"I can't leave her."

"Endel-"

"She'll die!"

My voice wavers. I've been hopeful this whole time, but the moment Nasir took her from my arms I fell apart. I try again to pull away, but he only holds tighter, fighting me with a quarter of the strength I can muster.

"I know you're afraid, but she'll be alright," he says softly. My head pounds and my eyes fall shut. Natiq drags me into the first guest room and plops me on the bed.

I want to move. I want to get up and run to the other room. To hold her hand in mine until those beautiful brown eyes are open again, but I can't. My body sinks with the weight exhaustion as the room spins above me. My eyelids grow heavy and I've no will left to fight them. Darkness surrounds me as they fall shut with only hope to lull me to sleep.

I stare blankly through the frosted glass in front of me. A breeze blows against the trees, tugging the last of the browning leaves from their branches. My eyes cast down to her peaceful expression, the same one I saw when I first woke up.

Her chest rises and falls in a steady rhythm, shifting the blanket that covers her form. A tube extends from beneath it and connects to the cannula beside the bed. The steady dripping in time with the clock on the far wall. My thumb gently rubs over the back of her soft hand, the warmth of it reassuring.

It's been a cruel two days.

"Nasir, you don't have to keep checking on me," I sigh as footsteps approach from behind. They continue around me, stopping next to the bedside table. A hand reaches down to lift the cold plate of food that sits on the surface and replaces it with a small steaming bowl.

"Still nothing?"

My muscles tense at the gentle voice. I hesitantly look up to see Cloveris dressed in a black robe. Her blonde hair is tucked into a neat bun at the back of her head. Wrinkled hands clutch her arms as she stares somberly at Heriath. The wrinkles on her face have deepened, showing her age. Her usual youthful joy now gray and cloudy. I shake my head, pulling my eyes away. The silence of the room, once a warm blanket, is now a stuffy wool sweater.

That morning, the conversation was nearly as painful as the experience. The way she fell to her knees when I revealed the truth of that night's events in the cave. Even with the comfort of her sons, it was hours before the crying stopped. Or at least, disappeared behind the door of a bedroom. I watched her heart break in front of me. Her blonde hair shielding her expression as she wept. Guilt kept me up that night. A suffocating lump in my throat and a pounding at my chest. I hadn't seen or heard from her until now. The thickness of it creeps up my throat once again seeing the dark circles beneath her eyes.

She sits on the edge of the bed with a sigh. So much has happened in so little time I'm unsure what to make of it.

"Cloveris," I manage. She looks at me and I face the floor, fiddling with Heriath's hand for courage. "I can't begin to tell you how sorry I am." Her gaze is heavy with the weight of what I've done. A deep sigh escapes her lips before I feel a gentle hand on my shoulder.

"I held onto hope that she'd be better than her father. That she wouldn't take it too far, but I was wrong," she says softly.

"I never meant for it to go this far."

"She fooled all of us."

"Not all of us," a voice says from the doorway. Natiq enters the room and stands beside me, placing a hand on my free shoulder. "She told us who she was and had the chance to change."

Natiq squats beside me to look me in the eyes, "Tansae let greed rot her from the inside out. She was raised that way. I wish things didn't have to end like this, but it's not your fault. You did what you needed to protect those you loved. We've all done the same." He looks up at Cloveris whose eyes hold the memories of her own sacrifices. Natiq's lips quirk up into a soft smile as he gives my shoulder a squeeze.

I nod, eyes falling back to the floor. He stands and reaches out a hand, "We'll leave you be." Cloveris places her hand in his, allowing him to lead her to the door.

"Try to eat something," Cloveris says from the doorway. "You need your strength, too." I muster a half-hearted smile before they exit and shut the door behind them.

The quiet engulfs me again. The tree outside the window is barren now. The sun hangs in the center of the sky. I lower my head to meet Heriath's hand.

"I'm sorry. I'm such an idiot," I whisper. "I had so many chances and I wasted them. Each time I could've told you how I felt, but I always made excuses. I took advantage of each new day, assuming there'd be another. Now you're... You're just..."

I lift my head, my gaze tracing over the smooth contours of her face. That stunning birthmark always caught my eye. It pained me to see it smudged with dirt. Her eyes were filled with fear as I carried her back here through the cold night. She gave her all to protect me.

The combined five hours of sleep over the past two days weighs down my body as it begs for rest. Heriath was in a bad condition when I first awoke. She'd gone into shock for some time due to an infection spreading from the stab wound on her side. Luckily, Nasir and Natiq retrieved Tansae and we were able to open the vault to the Elysir with her dagger. The blue liquid in the cannula has kept Heriath's vitals steady and Aurora assured us she'd wake up, but I feel like I've been waiting years.

A light weight rests on my head and I feel myself slipping into sleep until it shifts. Warm fingertips trail down the parts of my locs and I shoot up. Her tired brown eyes meet my own, a gentle smile playing at her lips. A small part of me wonders if I'm hallucinating, but when her hand moves to cover my own I know I'm awake.

"H-hi," I stammer, realizing I had only been staring. "You're awake."

"Hi." Relief floods my body at the sound of her voice. No matter how hoarse, it was like music to my ears. She grimaces as a cough wracks her body and I clumsily reach for a small glass of water on the dresser Nasir had brought for me last night. I help her sit up to drink.

"How long has it been?" she asks.

"Two days."

"What?" she exclaims, jolting forward. She hisses and holds her side as I grab her shoulders.

"Careful, you'll open your wound again." I help her sit back against the pillow and she lifts the covers to examine her bandages. Her hands drop to her sides as she stares up at the ceiling. *She's really awake.*

"Where is everyone?"

I clear my throat, "The twins are milling about and I'm assuming Cloveris is back in her room."

"And Tansae?" she asks. "Is she really…did I…" My lack of response pulls her head to the side.

"I'm sure you had no other choice," I whisper.

Her eyes sheen with tears, "Is Cloveris okay?"

"She'll be alright," I answer softly. "She doesn't hate you if that's what you're worried about."

"But she should," she hiccups. A tear streaks down her face, "I took her life."

I shake my head, wiping the tear from her cheek, "No, angel. You saved mine." She swallows and stares up at the ceiling. Her chest rises as she inhales a deep breath.

"I suppose I did," she whispers. A hint of joy rests in her eyes that makes my heart dance. Her head turns to peer out the window, "It's Midwinter."

"It is."

She faces me with concern and I give her a reassuring grin. "We still have time," I say, holding her hand in mine. "As long as we're together."

CHAPTER 43

HERIATH'S POV

The steam wagon rolls to a stop at the far side of the Trosthek Mountains. I fiddle with the top button of my cloak, my gloves making it hard to complete the task. I grunt as it slips through my fingers for the tenth time and Endel coughs to cover their laugh.

"Is this amusing to you?" I deadpan.

They shake their head rapidly and reach forward, "Of course not."

"I can do it," I pull back. They raise an eyebrow at me and my eyes shift to the ground. They take hold of my button and loop it through with ease.

"See, not so hard to let me take care of you."

"You've been taking care of me for the past two weeks," I remind them.

"Hasn't gotten old yet," they grin, placing a kiss on my temple. I hop down from the wagon and adjust my earmuffs as Nasir pulls a second wagon next to us. Natiq emerges from the back and joins Endel and I as we marvel at the sight before us. From this angle, you can see Kofir's snowstorm hovering over the mountaintop.

"Beautiful isn't it?" Natiq says, stretching out a hand. "This portion of the cave system is actually my design."

"Really?" Endel asks.

"Yup. I didn't like how the water was being redirected before, so I pitched an idea. It was the only idea the old man ever liked from me," he chuckles. The Nafsi flows smoothly from grass to stone as it disappears inside the mouth of the cave.

"Let's get moving, people," Aurora shouts from the trailer of the first steam wagon. She pulls open the door and slides out a box. "We're wasting daylight." I give her a nod and we all get to work.

The past two weeks have been tedious, but rewarding as we gathered as many seeds as we could from the remaining Elysir. Four hundred flowers were preserved in frost in the vault, but we only managed to pull the seeds from three hundred before I was off bed rest. Though it's more than enough to start planting.

I soon grow accustomed to the cold as we work. Endel, Nasir, and Natiq focused on digging small holes near the bank of the river while Aurora and I dropped a few seeds in each and covered them up. Natiq keeps us entertained with a made-up digging song that's too catchy to ignore. It feels wonderful to be in the open air again.

A quarter of the way through, we take a break in the trailers to warm up. Apparently, Nasir packed one of the insulated boxes with a sealed kettle of tea for all of us and a special one of cider for Endel.

A knock sounds on the trailer door and Aurora pushes it open to reveal Cloveris wrapped in a warm orange coat with matching gloves. Her closet never ceases to amaze.

"Hello everyone," she greets. The past two weeks have been the hardest on her, but spending time at the children's home has brought her back to life. That warm smile and bubbly voice has gained energy again, though she still has her moments of quiet reflection.

"I thought you had an errand to run," Aurora mentions.

Cloveris nods with a light laugh, "I did." She steps to the side and gestures to a group of children behind her. "These little ones volunteered to help. They did such an amazing job planting at the home, I thought they'd like to assist us." We all exchange glances and smiles, setting down our drinks to leave the trailer.

"Alright then," I smile. "Who wants to dig?" A few of them shoot their hands in the air.

A young girl tugs on Nasir's coat, peering up at him with wide eyes, "Are you helping us this time?"

Nasir smiles and nods firmly, "Want to help me get the shovels?" She nods eagerly and he bends forward to lift her into his arms. Aurora and I get the rest of the kids organized, teaching them how many seeds to put in the ground at a time and how to properly cover them. A few remaining kids took the task of watering the planted seeds.

For the first time in forever, I felt truly at peace. Time flew by as we planted. There were a few mishaps, as expected. Some of the boys chose to toss dirt around instead of planting, but Natiq distracted them with a game while the rest of us worked diligently. Cloveris commended him on his ability to control the rascals to which he simply replied *'takes one to know one'*.

A young boy named Orion stuck by my side, meticulously counting the right number of seeds out loud. His dedication to the task was admirable. He fed me facts about the clouds and sky and I returned with my own facts about the stars.

At some point, a little girl approaches me with a Sollar Holly, telling me it's from *'the person with the colorful hair charms'*. I can't help but smile at Endel as they manage a few of the diligent diggers.

All the seeds are planted along the bank of the Nafsi just as the sun disappears behind the mountains. The children depart with smiles and waves as we thank them for their help. Cloveris takes them back to the children's home while the rest of us pack up.

"That's the last of it," Natiq says, stuffing a box into the trailer. "I need a shower."

"I think we all do," Aurora laughs, gesturing to her dirt-covered coat. Natiq attempts to wipe his hands on Nasir's coat, but he catches his hand and twists his arm backward.

"Okay, I'm sorry," Natiq begs through strained laughter. Endel laughs and I reach my hand out to wipe on their clothes when they give me a sharp look.

"Don't even think about it."

"You're no fun," I whine.

"Ready to head back?" Aurora asks us.

I give Endel a glance, "We have one more thing to take care of here. You guys go on ahead."

She gives me a curt nod, "Alright, load 'em up, boys!" Nasir and Natiq join her on the wagon, Natiq rubbing his shoulder while his brother starts up the engine.

Once they're down the path, I stand on my toes to give Endel a kiss on the cheek, discretely wiping my hand on their shoulder. They lean into the kiss, not realizing what I've done until I pull away.

They gasp, pulling at their sleeve, "Oh you little–"

I jump back as they try to grab me and take off. They chase me around and I evade their capture a few times before they finally catch up to me. Giggles spill from me as they lift me off the ground by my waist.

"I surrender," I laugh as they spin us around.

"And?" they push, smile present in their voice.

"And I'll wash it! I promise!" Satisfied, they set me down, not releasing me until I regain my balance. I peer up at the sky, the bright glow of the moon shining down on the field where we stand.

"Ready?" they ask. I nod and lace my gloved fingers with theirs. We follow the Nafsi into the cave until we reach the small lake once again.

"You know, I only have one question," I voice, removing my gloves.

"What's that?"

"Why did the magic seem to work during the ritual if you and Zyl weren't soulmates?" Endel hops over the small stream that flows down the illuminated stairs.

"Maybe it takes one to activate the magic," they suggest. They take a step up and look back, offering a hand to me, "But it takes two to complete it."

I smile softly, taking their hand and ascending the stairs. The Water Stone hangs just above our heads as we slide our palms beneath it and into the flowing water. I weave our fingers together and Endel smiles down at them, the water between us slightly distorting their expression. The moonlight shines over us and they take a deep breath to begin.

"By the glow of our fair moon, in the light of my love, I bask in the joy of our union," they recite. The minerals in the wall shine brighter and the rhythm of the cave comes to a halt. I feel a pulsing energy around me and take in my own breath.

"May the mark we bear be a sign of our devotion and the beauty of our souls entwine," I speak. My eyes widen as the water surrounding our hands flows in reverse and up toward the moon above us.

"For the good of our land..." they continue, meeting my eyes. I give their hand a squeeze as we speak in unison: *"Till our last breath be taken."*

The pulsing energy grows stronger and the water running over our hands splits in two. Each stream winds around us before connecting to each of us at the valley of our chests. My feet lift off the ground and Endel grips my hand tighter as we float. My head falls back and I suck in a sharp breath as energy is sucked from my body. The two streams pull away and reconnect at the base of the Water Stone. Its blue light brightens and the water begins to glow as our feet meet the ground again. The light travels down the steps and follows the current of the Nafsi.

Endel and I exchange glances before racing down the stairs to chase after it. I freeze when we reach the mouth of the cave and my hands reach up to cover my mouth at the sight.

One by one, the glowing blue flowers stretch up toward the sky as the light reaches them. Endel places a hand at the small of my back to urge me forward. I sink to my knees and cup the blossom in my hands, tears running down my cheeks.

"It worked," I breathe. The velvety petals feel unreal under my fingertips compared to the brittle dried petals I'm used to, but the life within these is assuring. I sniffle and wipe my nose with my sleeve while Endel gently brushes away a few of my tears.

"Happy tears?"

I nod, "Happy tears."

Endel settles in the grass beside me and I lean against their shoulder as we take in the view. The beauty of this moment exceeds that of my wildest dreams. In the still quiet of the valley the Elysir grows and with it the promise of better days ahead.

CHAPTER 44

HERIATH'S POV
(TWO YEARS LATER)

"You sure you have everything you need?"

"You've already checked a hundred times, Dad," I groan, holding the list up for him to see. "I made you a copy of the list for a reason."

"I know. It's just that last time you disappeared on us. We missed you," he says, placing a hand on my head.

I wrap my arms around him and lean into his chest with a smile, "I know, Dad. I'll write more often, I promise."

"You'd better, young lady," Mom scolds, approaching me. "I want to know every time you stop in a village, what shoes you're wearing, what shirt you have on-"

"Oh Mom, stop fussing," Yamala says, wrapping her arm around Mom's shoulders. "I'll be with her the whole way. I'll keep her out of trouble."

Mom huffs, "And you're sure you wrapped up everything at work?"

"You know I wouldn't leave if I didn't. Plus, Ardin promised to look after Miss Merilla while I'm gone," I answer.

"She seems a lot better now," Yamala says, reaching down for a bag. Evreux scoops it up before she can grab it and she gives him a look.

"I know you're not sick anymore, but I can still be a gentleman," he smirks. She playfully rolls her eyes at him as he places it in their trailer.

"Speaking of gentlemen," Yamala says slyly. "Excited to see Endel again?"

I nod, a grin spreading across my face, "Visits are never enough." I keep my response calm, but I've been itching to get on the road.

I check the list in my hand one last time as Evreux locks up the trailer and dusts his hands off, "Okay, I'm ready when you are, ladies." Yamala and I bid our parents goodbye as they bid us safe travels and we load into our wagons. Yamala hops beside me on my driver's bench and I give her a questioning look.

"I said I'd keep you out of trouble, pipsquirt," she says, nudging my shoulder with hers.

"Don't you think I've outgrown that nickname?"

"Nope, never," she grins. Her smile warms my heart. Since her treatments stopped, she's been more vibrant and energetic than ever. She's taken advantage of every step she takes. Surprising me at my house with breakfast, daily walks with me to the river, and even helping me tend to my garden. Every moment we've spent together over the past few months feels like we're kids again. What relieves me the most is the lack of fear in her eyes. I'm grateful. Grateful that the risk was worth it and that I get to spend more time with her.

"What?" she asks, noticing my staring.

I shake my head, "I love you is all."

"Ew gross," she groans, wrapping me in a hug. I laugh and return her affection. "I love you too," she says. "My brave baby sister."

She releases me and I take a dramatic breath drawing a laugh from her as I pull the lever of the steam wagon to begin our journey.

My return to Duskwick wasn't easy. I did my best to explain to my family what I went through, but trying to keep parts of the story a secret was hard. Yamala gave it to me the worst when I returned. She yelled and screamed about how I was an idiot for risking life and limb for her before sobbing in relief that I was home. I took her punches as affection and let her release her emotions without a complaint.

Returning to work was harder than I could ever imagine. Endel gave me a black coat to deliver to Miss Merilla and the truth shattered her spirit. I stayed with her for hours before making the decision to move into the clinic for a while. We spent mornings on the back porch and some evenings sipping tea together while she read Zyl's old letters to me. I did my best to pick up the slack while she recovered, even taking over the training of an eager new apprentice named Ardin. Miss Merilla went to Mysticane last year to retrieve Zyl and the service was held here. Endel even shared Pine Valley's tradition to connect Zyl's soul to a tree near the clinic, which she visits daily. With some time and company, she found peace. Though I can't say she's the same as she once was, I'm sure she'll be just fine.

I've received many letters from Aurora and Lindel. The head herbalist at Lindel's clinic was fired for negligence and Aurora took over the location and Lindel's education. Her husband is doing well and recently attended Lindel's herbalism certification ceremony. Cloveris has also sent me letters letting me know of the changes being made at the company to protect the Elysir and the Nafsi's health. She invited me to see them myself, offering Yamala and I her home to stay the night when we arrive in Mysticane. I haven't seen her since my last visit for Tansae's burial. It was a conflicting day for us all, but she's now resting with her father.

As for Endel, they decided they should return home to Pine Valley once the ritual was over. It was a tough choice, but I couldn't keep them from their family any longer. We promised each other we'd write and visit whenever possible. It took a lot for me to not leave with them after their last visit, but we had to finalize the plans for the home we wanted to move into. Luckily, Yamala is finally ready to move back to the big city and continue her career so she can make the journey with me.

It's been a long road with many bumps along the way, but we've made it this far.

Only a few more days between us.

I sit under the canopy of rainbow eucalyptus trees as a warm breeze caresses my skin. My heart thuds in my ears, but I try to keep myself calm. The colors on the trunks are brighter than ever with the river fully healed. I spent a while walking through the trails to admire them before settling at our meeting spot.

I read the letter in my hands over again, repeating the date in my mind.

Midday on the 25th

I close my eyes and lean into the pocket of sunlight that shines through the leaves above me, trying not to worry about all the possibilities. *They'll be here.*

"Angel?"

My eyes fly open to see Endel's warm smile as they stand over me.

I scramble to my feet and tackle them in a hug. They trip and fall back, laughter booming from their chest as they return my eager greeting.

"Well, hello to you too," they grin. "Hope I didn't keep you waiting long. I know how you worry."

I pull back so they can sit up, getting comfortable in their lap, "Hey, I'm getting better."

"Mhm," they smirk, quirking an eyebrow. "And what was the great disaster that befell me this time?" I twist my lip, avoiding their gaze.

"Your wagon broke down in Vauxworth Canyon," I mumble. They shake their head with a smile. "What? It could happen."

"Heriath-"

"And you'd be scared and alone."

"Angel-"

"I worry because I love you, you know. It's a privilege to be on my mind and-"

They gently grab my chin and press their lips against mine. I relax into their touch, pulling them closer. My worries melt away as I revel in the feeling of their arms around me.

The weight of the world, once on our shoulders, flows away with the waters that carry our love. We separate and they lean their forehead against mine. I place a hand at the valley of their chest where a northern star shape rests. The mark etched onto both of us the night we bonded our souls.

"I'm right here, angel," they whisper. "No more letters and visits. No more waiting anxiously for me to arrive." Their thumb caresses my cheek as they pull back to meet my eyes. That soft gaze, one that's followed me lifetime after lifetime. Forgotten in death, only to be remembered by the essence within us. I take their free hand in mine and lace our fingers together. *A love that never dies.*

"It's finally over," I breathe.

They lift our hands and place a gentle kiss to mine, "For us, angel, it's just beginning."

398

EPILOGUE

ENDEL'S POV

Another few years have come and gone and life is no less than perfect, though it's had its way of picking at us. The house we bought was full of dust and creaking door hinges that needed fixing. The back lawn was a mess that required diligent gardening, all handled with Heriath's grace and care. After a few months of work, the house was finally a home and we adjusted to our new life together.

The bite of winter pulls her to snuggle closer into my shoulder as we sit near the bank of the Nafsi. I place a gentle kiss atop her head, the rough texture of freshly twisted locs beneath my lips. A smile graces my face at her sigh of contentment as I think over our time spent under the same roof. Early mornings of warm bodies pressed together, the comfort of fingers running over skin to remind each other of our presence. Sleepy murmurs and soft kisses ghosting across each other's cheeks. Spring cleanings were always made fun by the games she would invent for us to play. I even love the way she'd scowl at me when I'd pull her in to dance after a hard day at the clinic. Her exhaustion softening into a smile as she'd lean into my arms.

It was everything I hoped for. There were many late nights laughing at nothing over the steam of freshly steeped jester mint tea. The scent of it brings back fond memories of Zyl that we often share. Not a day goes by where I'm not grateful to him and all he's done. He's the reason I can hold her in my arms each day. His kindness and understanding lives on within us. The gift of his friendship as beautiful as the colors of the painting of me he did the day we first spent time together. The same one that hangs in my crafting room in our home.

It's thanks to him that we're here at the bank of the Nafsi once again on Midwinter, waiting as the sun begins to set. I reach over and pull the blanket tighter around us and she smiles up at me. Each day in her arms is a privilege I refuse to take advantage of. I shift slightly and slip my left hand into the pocket of my thick wool skirt, running my fingers over the cold metal of the ring for what feels like the hundredth time. No matter how many times I check, it's always there, but my mind stirs endlessly with the *what ifs* I'm always quieting from Heriath's mind.

The smooth pad of her thumb runs up the bridge of my nose and over the taut skin of my forehead. Her amber eyes meet mine with worry, "What's wrong, love?"

I shake my head and remove my hand from my pocket, placing a chaste kiss on her forehead, "Nothing's wrong."

"Well, something's on your mind. You may not worry much, but I can tell when you do."

"I'm okay, angel. I promise," I assure her. Her eyes shift to the side, with a familiar sparkle that tells me she has an idea. She shrugs off her half of the blanket and stands from our spot. I stare up at her as she extends an open palm toward me.

"Dance with me?" she asks, a smile playing at her lips. The moonlight peaks through the trees around us and catches the side of her birthmark. I allow her to help me up and I adjust our hands. Our fingers weave together while her free hand rests on my shoulder and mine at her lower back. I hold her close as she begins to hum a simple melody, one I'd shared from my childhood. A passing confession made on an early morning in an attempt to calm her restless mind.

We've been rushing around lately. Me moving my shop here to Kaelora and her taking on a new apprentice while also attempting to establish her own clinic. The pressure of everything collapsed on her shoulders and spiraled into a week's worth of constant cofenia seed and nightmares. The only relief being the soft lullaby I'd shared on a whim and it stuck with her, guiding her to sleep when her mind's eye wouldn't shut.

We sway back and forth, the soft whispers of wind blowing the leaves around us. I step back and lift my arm to spin her, gifting me a light laugh that warms me in the cool night air.

"Endel?"

"Yes?"

"Why do you call me that?"

"What?"

"Angel."

I pause to consider her question, never stopping our gentle motion. The answer seems simple. I could tell her I simply like it, or how that's what she is to me. Though she'd probably wave off my flirting with a shy smile like she usually does. Or...

"It was that moment," I start. "That day in the cave when I was forced to relive the nightmare that's haunted me for years. From the moment I met you, you've always been watching over me, but that day when you broke the spell I was under you became my angel."

Her forehead meets my chest as she releases a soft laugh, her warm breath visible in the night air.

"Always the flirt," she says.

"But never a liar," I grin, lifting her chin to give her a peck on the lips. A blue light catches my eye and I place my hands on her hips to spin her around, "It's starting."

I'll never tire of it. The way the Elysir pushes its way up through the dirt and spreads its petals to catch the moonlight. The soft glow it emits lights up the whole of the Nafsi just as it did the night of the ritual. The day my life fell into place. The day I swore my heart to the most beautiful being to exist.

My left hand returns to my pocket and I pull out the small ring. A shiny silver band with a carefully polished stone of emerald zinnia to match the necklace she rarely removes. She leans her back into my chest to take in the view as the flowers sprout one after another.

"Beautiful," she whispers. I revel in this moment. Her warmth in my arms. My forever standing before me. The result of our love growing in the moonlight. It had seemed so complicated back then, choosing her. Both of us prioritizing others over our own desires. A pull to each other we couldn't ignore no matter how much we tried. But it wasn't. It was simple. Choosing her was easy. Loving her was easy. So maybe this is too.

I gently run my hands up and down her arms when a shiver racks her body. I lean forward and place a kiss on her cheek. She turns to me with a soft smile. The one I wake up to each morning and dream of during my time away from her. The one that stole my heart all those years ago.

I hold the ring in front of her chest, but she holds my gaze, relaxing into my peaceful expression. I chuckle softly, "Heriath?"

"What is it?"

I nod to my hand and she follows my line of sight. She steps away from me, a hand over her mouth as I use my free hand to grab hers. I lower myself on one knee.

"If you'll allow me the pleasure?" I ask simply. Her eyes light up and she nods frantically, allowing me to slip the ring onto her shaking hand. She falls to her knees and her arms wrap around my neck. I manage to catch her weight as her lips crash onto mine.

No story I've ever written could truly capture the feeling that consumes me in this moment. It isn't relief at her answer. Not guilt or regret. Not even joy when we separate and a thousand yeses tumble from her perfect lips.

It is peace. Peace that lulls you to sleep. Peace that brings you comfort in the darkest of times. Peace in knowing that we've found each other once again.

Our love a steady and ever-flowing stream.

ACKNOWLEDGMENTS

Hello! Firstly, I want to acknowledge you as a reader. Thank you so much for reading through my novel. This project carries my heart and soul and to know you took time out of your day to escape into a world I created means a lot to me.

To my friend Jana, thank you for being there since the first word I ever wrote. You have been a great hype person throughout this entire process. Your support kept me going through the good and bad. I'm lucky to have a friend like you.

To C.M. Lockhart and the rest of Melanin Chat, thank you so much for being a great guide and support for me. You guys have given me resources, hyped me up, and even defended me at times. It's an honor to have a village and you have provided that space for me.

To my beta readers, Kameelah, Sula, and Caitlin. Thank you so much for being the first to take a chance on my manuscript. You all gave me hope for my novel as well as some insightful feedback that improved the depth and overall quality of my story. My final product is enhanced because of your honesty.

Lastly, to my love, Daniel, thank you for everything. You have inspired me by showing me a love I never knew before. Most of the love between Heriath and Endel is inspired by our relationship over the years. Thank you for staying up with me during late nights of writing, listening to my endless rants about worldbuilding, and comforting me through my imposter syndrome. I love you, now and forever.